Black Ink

The Complete
Trilogy

Black Ink

The Complete Trilogy

N.M. CATALANO

BLACK INK, The Complete Trilogy

DEDICATION

First, I'd like to say a special thank you to Amy Mo. You, girl, have been a constant friend since we met. You help me when I didn't want to ask anyone else, you are the first to meet all of my imaginary friends, and have quieted my loud voices of uncertainty. Thank you.

Catherine and Alicia, you guys, I think, love my heroes as much as I do, thank you! Thanks for shouting it out to all of your friends and supporting me like you do. I'm forever grateful.

This incredible book is about hope, is about faith, and is about survival when faced with the most incredible odds.

I'd like to dedicate it to my daughters.

My wish is that I have given you all that you'll need when you leave my nest and go out in this big, bad world. That you will have the fortitude to persevere, even when you don't want to, (because sometimes we all feel like that), the strength to do what you need to, and the wisdom to know when you have to.

I love you both so, so much... <3 xoxo

Books

STRANGER, Book 1 Stranger Series
SWITCH, Book 2 Stranger Series
KINK, Book 3 Stranger Series
PERFECT, Book 4 Stranger Series
THE ROOSTER CLUB, The Best Cocks in Town
BLACK INK, Part I, The Black Ink Series
BLACK INK, Part II, The Black Ink Series
BLACK INK, Part III, The Black Ink Series
BLACK INK, The Complete Trilogy

CONTENTS

Title Page
Copyright
Dedication
Books
Contents
Part I
Chapter 1
Chapter 2
Chapter 3
Chapter 4
Chapter 5
Chapter 6
Chapter 7
Chapter 8
Chapter 9
Chapter 10
Chapter 11
Part II
Introduction
Chapter 12
Chapter 13
Chapter 14
Chapter 15
Chapter 16
Chapter 17
Chapter 18
Chapter 19
Chapter 20
Chapter 21
Chapter 22
Part III

Introduction
Chapter 23
Chapter 24
Chapter 25
Chapter 26
Chapter 27
Chapter 28
Chapter 29
Chapter 30
Chapter 31
Chapter 32
Chapter 33
Chapter 34
Chapter 35
Chapter 36
Epilogue
About the Author
Other Works

take

Part 1

take

CHAPTER 1

Gemma

Desperate. I was absolutely desperate. I only prayed my nervousness wasn't visible and they couldn't see me shaking. I needed this job. No one would see me, not until now. I was being punished, black balled, because of something I didn't do.

That only made me want to fight harder.

After Malcolm was arrested, the Feds took everything, seized the bank accounts, my house, the one my money mostly paid for, and took the cars. I lost everything. I was left with only my personal belongings. And a shitload of his debts.

I couldn't believe that I had to start from scratch…again. A polished, educated, professional woman, after years of building an impressive reputation, it was all destroyed by one man. My husband.

Now I have the nerve to come to the man who

had suffered the most from my husband's actions, his extortions and embezzlements, and ask for a position with his company. It was all I could do to sit across from this *kid* who'd probably just gotten out of college and kiss his ass when I *knew* I could do his job better than he could, and prove to him, not that I would be the best choice for his assistant, but that I wouldn't make him look like a fool because *he knew* he should be mine. The truth is I'm happy to have the opportunity *to* be here. There is no way I'm going to fuck this up. I would tell him whatever I had to, do whatever I need to do, to be this kids assistant.

I had to force myself to keep from looking at the imposing figure who had built this empire, Alexander Black, standing in his glass enclosed throne room watching me. I could feel the weight of his stare bearing down on me. I'd never met him personally but I knew everything about him, his ruthlessness, that he grew up bouncing from one foster home to another, had minor scrapes with the law when he was a teenager, and his broken engagement in college from that Texas oil tycoon's debutante daughter. After that, the only information about him read like a resume'. Until ten years ago when Black Inc. was born. From that point he hurled through the business world like a tornado, consuming everything in his way. If he didn't take it over, he destroyed it.

Alexander and Malcolm had begun what was called a merger, which was really a take-over, of Malcom's software development firm. It was too late by the time Malcom's Ponzi scheme was revealed and Alexander had lost three million dollars.

I wasn't involved with Malcolm's company, never had been. I worked for a prestigious law firm in mergers and acquisitions. And when the shit had hit the fan with Malcolm, I got hit right between the eyes. I was fired before Forbes magazine released the details and my house was padlocked and surrounded by yellow police tape. My office had been cleaned out and the boxes filled with the things that I'd brought in were waiting for me downstairs at security the next morning when I entered the lobby.

I was humiliated.

Now, here I sit, my spine straight, across from this snot nosed brat, determined to clear my name and prove myself once again. The only way I was going to do that was working for Alexander Black. I had to kick some serious ass to disassociate myself from Malcolm. Alexander Black was the only way I could.

And he knew it.

"Let's cut to the chase, Mrs. Stevens...," the punk was saying.

"Gemma. Gemma Trudeau. I've never used my married name," I corrected him unwaveringly.

Yes, lets, I'm tired of pussy footing around.

I didn't get my reputation by being intimidated, my poker face was securely in place.

"How can you possibly think Mr. Black is going to hire you?" he said smugly as he sat back in his chair.

"Mr. Davis, Alexander Black is a smart man. I'm good – very good - and he knows it. I would be an asset not only to you, but more so to him." I was known for being shrewd, sometimes ruthless, but always successful.

It was simple. I knew it, Alexander Black knew it, this kid was the only one who didn't.

The real question is, how is Black going to play?

I felt his eyes penetrating me through the glass wall across the room. I didn't flinch under the weight. I lifted my gaze to look directly into those eyes that I knew hadn't left me while I sat patiently during my time with this newbie who'd, I'm sure, recently finished his internship.

My breath caught in my throat.

I'd seen pictures of Alexander Black on occasion but nothing had prepared me for him. The words 'formidable and hard' would be how I would have described him, and fucking gorgeous.

Even from where I sat across the room, he hit me like a freight train and I'm sure my body showed the impact. I could feel the rush surge through me enflaming my face and igniting my every nerve endings. I hadn't had sex in so long, I thought my vagina had stopped working but it, too, roared to life.

I could tell he was tall, very tall, with wavy chocolate brown hair a little on the long side, close cut facial hair that was too long to be scruff but not long enough to be a beard and mustache, perfectly tailored black pinstriped suit with a vest, a crisp grey shirt and pink tie. He had one arm across his broad chest with the other raised as his finger and thumb stroked his jaw. Danger and power. While he studied me.

I knew the young man across from me was talking as he sat back in his chair. I saw his mouth moving out of my peripheral vision, but I didn't hear a word he said.

The world had been sucked into a vacuum of only Black and me.

He was stunning. Too beautiful for words. His features were strong and chiseled, defined cheekbones, arrogant brow and eyes, square jaw, full, deliciously full lips. His body was not lean but not bulky, well defined, even hidden inside those obviously very expensive clothes. If I had to bet I would say the suit was tailor made Brioni   I should know, I had bought enough of them for Malcolm. His shoulders and chest were broad, his waist lean, and I could tell his legs were not thin within his slacks.   I immediately envisioned thick braided, muscular thighs, the kind that a beautiful ass rested above with the cheeks dipping in at narrow hips. My mouth went dry and I had to clench my jaw to keep from licking my lips. The thing that truly took my breath away was the intense savage energy that emanated from him even with the distance separating us.

I sucked in a breath when a corner of his mouth lifted in a cocky smirk. He lowered the hand that had been at his jaw and reached for the phone at his side and broke our gaze.

I was relieved to be released from the hold he'd had on me and my eyes returned to Davis sitting across the desk as the sound of his voice was turned on in my ears again.

"...are over qualified although, from what I've seen on your information, you have an impressive history...," he was saying.

Before my mind had a chance to clear, his phone rang. The noise made me jump.

Shit, what the hell is wrong with you, get a grip.

"Miles Davis," he answered it. A pause. His eyes dart to me, his expression shocked. "Yes, Mr. Black, of course." Another pause, his eyes widen. "Yes sir." He hangs up. He blinks once. Then again. "Come in tomorrow morning at nine. Tonight you'll take your first case home with you. Familiarize yourself with the details and be prepared to present how you think we should proceed with it." He blinks again seeming stunned.

The familiar adrenaline courses through my system that fuels me each time I begin a new case, preparing me for the kill. It's always a hunt with me, and I always catch my prey. This time is going to be different as I have to do the legwork, but I find I'm looking forward to it, invigorated by it even. I was back!

"Absolutely," I almost purr.

"Ms. Trudeau."

I turn my head to the man standing behind me. From the sound of his voice, he is British, Wales probably, and wearing a bowtie, khakis and a cardigan. His clothes are perfectly pressed.

"Welcome to Black Inc. I'm Simon, Mr. Black's assistant. Please follow me, I'll show you to your desk."

"Certainly, thank you." I rise from my seat in front of Davis and glance back at him. He still has a look of surprise on his face.

"I'll bring you the file," he mutters noncommittally.

"Thank you, Mr. Davis, I look forward to working with you, I appreciate the opportunity." I know I have to kiss this guy's ass even though it hadn't been his decision to hire me. But if I want to make things pleasant it has to be done. I still can't help but wonder what Black's angle is for doing it though, the lawyer in me is sure it's not only my impressive history. A man didn't achieve what Black has before the age of forty with playing only one hand in the game.

I glance at Alexander Black's office as I follow Simon to a desk in a cubicle that is slightly separate from the others offering it some privacy. The glass has gone smoky making it impossible to see inside his office. In my mind the details beyond the glass spring to life; the modern black polished desk with the wall of windows behind it overlooking Fifth Avenue, the tufted black leather sofas with chrome legs, the matching black polished bar on the side wall with cut crystal decanters on top, a huge conference table with tufted black leather chairs surrounding it, and televisions along the top of the wall facing his desk above the glass. Black's inner sanctum, where he rules the world.

Even though I can't see inside, I know he's watching me, I can feel him. The sensation makes my heart pound and my palms sweat. A fact which completely throws me off-balance. I never get frazzled.

But there isn't anyone like Alexander Black.

Alexander
What was a woman like that doing with a scumbag weasel like Malcolm?

My fingers drum atop my desk as I watch

Simon lead her to the desk I specified she would take. I'd picked it *because* of its location, separate, and I could watch her...closer to me.

I'd felt the stirrings within me as I studied Gemma Trudeau from the moment she'd stepped inside my building.

Keep your friends close...and your enemies closer.

When her resume' arrived, I'd only smiled. I'd already known everything about her. And had been waiting for it. I'd also known she couldn't even get an interview anywhere else. She is the plague...but I'm the King of Darkness. I smirk at the fortunate misfortune.

*I knew she was brilliant, but not so...*my erection jerks. The beast inside is roaring to feast.

I am a sick fuck, I know it. I'd also thought she wasn't the type I usually played with, my taste in games a bit unconventional. The women I typically gravitated toward are more...disciplined.

Gemma is strong. The fire inside her licks at me, making me burn. I like it.

A lot.

She is also aristocratically beautiful, black hair twisted up in a reserved French twist, white creamy skin, full pink pouty lips, almond shaped hazel eyes, lush full hips, and perfect breasts that would fit in each of my hands. Her suit is impeccable, although I'm sure she'd chosen an understated one that is suitable for the position she is applying for, the one that's beneath her. I got some sick satisfaction in that as well. I wanted her groveling, warped son-of-a-bitch that I am. I want her in many positions, in many ways.

She is all woman. A woman, I'm sure, that has yet to be unleashed. Too bad I want to break her, make her scream, beg, cry, and do things to her she never imagined. And I want her to want them, love them, need them so much she can't live without them.

My cock is throbbing. The details are already forming in my mind on how this would play.

I grin.

"Welcome to Black Inc., Ms. Trudeau," I murmur staring at her through the glass. "Let the games begin."

Gemma

I unlock the door to my parent's house in Jersey City, New Jersey, the house I'd grown up in, and kick it closed behind me when I walk in with a bag full of groceries in one arm, files and a briefcase in the other. The light I always leave on in the kitchen shines from the back of the house casting a soft glow all the way up to the front foyer. I sit the bag on the table by the door along with the case file and lower my briefcase to the floor. I still hated the quiet of the house, but I'd gotten used to it. My parents had died in an accident last year.

I was an only child. My father was a detective who'd started in the police force pounding a beat in uniform. That's where I'd gotten the law bug, I am a lot like my dad. My mother was a kindergarten teacher, she loved the babies, and it had broken her heart she couldn't have a dozen of them. So she'd adopted every single one in her heart she'd taught throughout her career.

I miss them terribly.

My father was smart. A few years ago, when things had gotten really strained between Malcolm and I, my father asked me to set up an estate and put all of his and my mother's assets in it, thus protecting everything so it wouldn't go directly to me should anything happen to them. He knew his job was dangerous, always had known, but I didn't think he suspected anything would happen to the both of them. But there was something else

"Gemma, baby, I need you to set up an estate for me and your mother," he'd said to me one night at Sunday dinner. I was there alone.

"What are you talking about dad?" I was shocked. Also, talking about my parent's mortality gave me the creeps.

He took in a deep breath and let it out slowly. Setting his fork down on the table, he leaned his arms on the edge and turned his detective face on me.

I knew I wasn't going to like this.

"Malcolm is into something, I don't know what it is, but it's not good. I want to protect you, Gemma, because he's going to drag you down with him. The problem is, I'm not sure it's something you'll be able to recover from." His tone was hard but his eyes were endearing.

Foreboding coursed through me because he'd just verbalized exactly what I'd been afraid to admit to myself. I struggled with trying to convince him he was wrong, that his instincts that had always led him to solve cases was lying to him. But I knew deep down inside, even back then, he wasn't.

I looked down at my plate and cut into the roast beef. "Okay."

That was three years ago. They've been dead a year, Malcolm was arrested six months ago, and now I'm living in their house, driving their car, and working for a man my husband had robbed.

My father's friends in the precinct have not stopped investigating the circumstances surrounding my parent's deaths. They couldn't believe it was an accident. I knew they weren't telling me everything. I was more apt to get information from the guys my dad had run with in the neighborhood when he was a kid. The ones who are connected. Although they were on opposites sides of the law, they were family. Tony, my dad's best friend's son, came to me when my parents had died and told me the family was watching out for me and if there was anything I needed, come to them first.

Tony and I had history. Wild, passionate, rough, hard, hot history. He was the boy I'd given my virginity too. Often times late at night as I laid in my bed over the years, I thought about Tony and wondered how it would be with him today, thinking about how good it had been when we were kids, how much better it would be now. Would he pull my hair, leave marks on my body when he pounded into me roughly, making me cry out in pleasure? The fantasies I'd survived on during the years had kept my desire for the bad boy in check. I was a lawyer, I wasn't supposed to be this sex crazed nympho who wanted things, very dirty things, things a good girl would never want.

That's the reason I'd chosen business law and stayed away from prosecution and defense litigation. I didn't trust myself not to drop to my knees if those bad boys commanded it.

I head upstairs to kick off my Christian Louboutin's, I refused to sacrifice my shoes for the interview, to change from my modest suit into yoga pants and a thermal. My mind drifts to Malcom. Nothing, I feel absolutely nothing. Malcolm to me was a room temperature cup of tea, I drank him if I had to. Fortunately, I didn't have to stomach that anymore. The only reason we aren't divorced is because I'd never gotten around to it, I had worked too much.

I'm so happy to be rid of him, the price I had to pay was almost worth it. Almost. What I hate the most is that other people, very important people, had to be dragged into my hell. People like Alexander Black.

When I head back downstairs, my breasts bouncing braless beneath my shirt, the vision of Black makes them ache with longing.

"Shit," I mutter.

Suddenly I'm grateful to have Miles Davis as a buffer between Alexander Black and I.

That man is the baddest boy of all. The way he'd looked at me sent erotic shivers up my spine and made me catch my breath...again. He made me feel vulnerable, raw, empty, and very, very needy. The intensity of carnal longing that floods me thinking of Black immobilizes me. I let it wash over me as I stand at the kitchen counter, holding on tightly, letting myself get lost in it. If this is what a look from across the room does to me, I'm dreading, and looking forward to, the moment when his body is close to mine. I take a deep breath and pull myself from the feelings. I have work to do.

I inhale some food then grab the file. I can't wait to submerge myself in the case.

Work had been my lover, I was passionate about it, became familiar with all the minute details, giving all that I was to it. It had rewarded me very well. Malcolm had ripped it from me.

Alexander Black is going to give it back. I know he's going to make me earn it.

I settle on the couch ready to become acquainted with my latest lover. I'm determined to prove myself to the irresistibly dangerous Alexander Black.

take

CHAPTER 2

Gemma

It wasn't horrendous commuting to Manhattan from Jersey City, just a Path train and a subway or bus ride to work. I still decided to get in the city at eight wanting to avoid most of the commuter crowds. There is a coffee shop around the corner from the Black Building so I grab a Daily News and have breakfast while I wait until a quarter to nine before heading to the top floor. My new home away from home.

I feel a little foolish in the crowded elevator holding the desktop blotter with calendar, matching pen/pencil holder, post-it box, and other office accessories in matching black leather I'd stopped to buy. My desk is glass and virtually see-through, the top smoky but still transparent, and it makes me feel extremely bare. I need a barrier, the close proximity to Black's office is bad enough. The entire floor is decorated in modern minimalism in shades of grey, smoke, black, and some white. Crisp, clean and no-nonsense, and very, very chic. When I approach my desk, Davis isn't in yet, I notice a stark white envelope on it with my name penned briskly across the front and the Black Inc. logo in the corner. I set my things on the desk and place my purse on top of the black filing cabinet. I organize the office supplies on the desk before opening the envelope. I want to get settled before starting, and opening that envelope would be the beginning of my work day. As I sit in my black leather chair, I dare a glance at Alexander in his office. He's on the phone, I could see the earpiece he's wearing and he's talking while pacing the floor between the televisions and his desk. His silky dark hair is a bit ruffled, his sleeves rolled up to his elbows, and all the screens are blasting information at him. His eyes are on me. Choice of armor today is an impeccable navy suit, white shirt, and a pale blue tie. His vest is buttoned but his jacket had been placed over the arm of the couch. He's obviously been in the office for a while.

The sight of him instantly heats me and makes my breath hitch.

I jerk my direction away as he gives a slight nod of his head not breaking the stride of his conversation. The door to his office is closed and the sound of his voice only a muffle, the only thing I can make out is its very deep and very sexy.

"Get to work Gemma," I scold myself.

I square my shoulders and open the envelope.

In very strong masculine handwriting it reads:

Welcome to Black Inc. Ms. Trudeau,
The following is your log-in information for
the computer,
I have personally loaded files for you,
Review the contents of the information,
I expect to have your thoughts on the
company sent home
with you last night directly after lunch,
You should know it's a hostile take-over,
I look forward to seeing what you can do
for me,

Alexander Black

A tremor slithers up my spine as I glance back at Black. He's still on the phone but his complete attention is on me. I nod, not showing how his intense gaze affects me. It scorches me in the most intimate places and makes me sweat. I have a job to do, my life depends on its success. I have to separate myself from what my body feels. And that can only be described as a hostile take-over as well.

Black gives a slight dip to his head in acknowledgment then touches something on his desk and the glass begins to smoke, looking a lot like a magic trick. I let out a sigh of relief. On one hand I'm thankful for the removal of the distraction that is him, on the other I miss having the small gift of getting to glance at the dark beauty that he is.

Alexander

Holy fuck!

I growl. The woman is a stick of dynamite waiting to be set on fire. When I light her fuse she's going to blow. So much woman packed into that lush petite body, all curves, all sin, all wrapped up in propriety. I can't wait until I get her dirty and undone and do very bad things to her.

When I saw her on the monitor in that black pencil dress that fits her like a second skin, my dick swelled to throbbing. I waited until she exited the elevator and saw her in the flesh to squeeze myself. Her jet black hair pulled back in a sleek ponytail made my palm itch to wrap around it and pull, yanking her head back and watching her lips part, hearing her moan. I envisioned it loose and cascading down her bare back, leading me to her pale round ass. I want to bend her over, spank it and see my handprints all over her white skin, spread her wide and fuck her. Hard.

International business is just wrapping up, the final call to London ending. I talked to Hong Kong, Japan, India, and Switzerland already this morning.

It's time.

A knock on the door draws my attention back. I know its Simon. He always checks in with me when he arrives. I appreciate his thoroughness and professionalism but mostly how he understands the importance of discretion.

"Good morning Mr. Black. As you requested, your schedule is clear until noon. Do you need a car this morning?"

"No, thank you Simon. I'll take care of it." I remove the earpiece and set it on the desk before unrolling my shirt sleeves and shrugging on my jacket.

Simon would be a terrible gambler, he can't hide anything from his face. I know he's shocked.

I don't acknowledge it as I continue. "Send a message to Davis and tell him Trudeau is to submit her proposal directly to me today. She knows I want it right after lunch. Give her fifteen minutes." I pick up my cell phone and walk to the door.

"Yes sir. Anything else sir?" he asks trying to keep up with my long strides.

"Let PR know I've already assigned Ms. Trudeau's system information and she has them."

Another surprised rise of Simon's eyebrows. "Yes sir. And would you like lunch waiting for you when you get back?"

"No, I think I'll make a pit-stop." I pull my office door open and walk to the elevator as my assistant follows.

"Very well Mr. Black."

The elevator dings its arrival as I stand with my hands in my pockets. I've been waiting for this morning ever since Gemma's interview was scheduled. Time to put things in motion. The doors slide open and I step in, our eyes colliding as they close.

I walk the block to the public parking garage around the corner. They don't know me here. I slip them a bill, enough for them to leave me alone, as I walk to the elevator. I know where the van is parked, I don't want any help. A perk of wanting to own the world is when you have enough money you have everything you might need at your disposal. I did whatever I had to do to make sure of that. Today I need a maintenance van and a uniform, and one of the companies I own has supplied both. The small commercial van is perfect with no windows in the back, allowing me privacy to change into the company uniform they also left waiting for me. An hour later as I pull onto Gemma's street in Jersey City, its nondescript appearance gives me the casual professional anonymity I need to get into her house.

The row house sits on a block in a typical neighborhood, all of them almost identical. As I walk around to the back yard, the neatness and outdoor furniture along with an old tree swing make me slow my steps. This is a home not a house and I wonder what Gemma was like as a little girl.

Don't turn into a pussy now, Black.

With a ladder under one arm and a toolbox in the other, I spy the basement door. Just as I suspected, the only thing between me and the inside of her house is a padlock. I pause and glance up, looking for motion detector lights. There are none but there is a spotlight directed at the yard and another light just above the door. The spotlight has to go. I lean the ladder against the side of the house and climb to loosen the bulb. I run my fingers along the wires so I appear to be looking for a short, just in case a nosy neighbor is watching. After I climb down, I rest the ladder on its side against the house and turn my attention to picking the padlock on the cellar doors. I've done so many of them in my youth, it pops open under a minute, it's like riding a bike. I open one door and step into the musty darkness. Quietly easing the door shut above me, I turn on the flashlight and look around the large room. It's set up like a family room with an old couch, a throw rug on the floor and posters on the wall with the washer and dryer on the far wall below the steps that lead upstairs. I glance up at the exposed rafters and a sadistic smile curves my lips.

"I know what we could do with those," I murmur.

I walk across the room and ascend the stairs and try the door, not surprised it's locked. I pull out the small tool kit again and insert the thin instrument into the hole. The knob clicks and the door swings open into the kitchen. Looking around I see what I want. Above the counter there are several hooks screwed in underneath the cabinet, one of them holds an extra set of keys. I slide it off and toss it in the air a couple of times before pocketing it. Following the hallway that leads to the front of the house, I enter the living room and move to a wall full of family photos.

Gemma's life is displayed in black and white and color. The family looks so happy, a scene that is foreign to me. As she gets older from the point of her college graduation, I notice there are some empty slots.

"Did you take yours and Malcolm's pictures down? Does that mean you weren't a part of his schemes? I didn't think he was smart enough to get so far on his own, but it's an interesting thought…highly unlikely but interesting none the less, little Gemma."

The contempt I feel is evident in my voice. It's really not the money. It's the fact I was made a fool of. It enrages me every time I think how that little piece of shit took me, *me,* and I didn't see it coming.

"Well, I will find out just how much you were involved, and I have a feeling you're going to enjoy every minute of it but not nearly as much as me. The fact you are so stunning is a bonus I hadn't anticipated."

I study the pictures and sense a sadness in Gemma's face in the more recent photos.

"That little weasel was definitely not enough man for you, but there's more to it than that, isn't there Gemma?"

"Meow."

The sound of a cat surprises me.

"You agree with me don't you little pussy. What other secrets do you know?"

"Meow."

The cat saunters over and weaves itself through my legs as if it were perfectly normal for me to be in this house.

"So Gemma doesn't have the only pussy that needs attention, is that right?" I ask the attention hungry animal.

"Meow."

"Hah. Come on, take me upstairs."

I head to the second level and look for Gemma's bedroom.

"Not like that shithole I was at when that little prick made me who I am," I growl, my voice cold and hard.

All these houses are set up the same way. I spent the early part of my life in a lot of different ones but the one in particular I remember the most, the one I refuse to forget because it still fuels me, is the one

I was raped in when I was thirteen. The foster family's sixteen-year-old son fucked me while his friends held me down. Some of his friends tried to stick their dicks in my mouth. They're lucky I didn't let them pry my mouth open or else I would have bit their scrawny little peckers off. Not long after that he found himself flying down the stairs and was partially paralyzed. I think he finally killed himself. All the friends experienced similar fates.

"Good because I was going to do it for him." The hate I feel for him is as powerful as it was that day.

Gemma's childhood bedroom is soft and feminine with pink floral wallpaper and a coverlet with English roses in the same color, and lots of white embroidered accent pillows. I'm filled with her scent. It stirs me with primal hunger wanting more. I walk to her dresser and study her things, then I pick up the bottle of Chanel 5 and inhale deeply.

"A classic. So appropriate."

Placing the bottle down, I open the top drawer and smile lasciviously when I see it filled with her panties and bras in shades of black with lace trim, pink, blue, red, and white. Sliding a finger over the soft fabric I pick up the black thong with the cream embroidery. I hold it to my face and inhale again, the hint of her musky scent makes my mouth water. An image of her bald mound between her spread legs, pink wet lips, the same pink of her mouth, and swollen clit flash in my mind. The desire to suck that nub and lick those folds overwhelms me and fills my shaft almost to the point of pain. I place the underwear back in the drawer and shut it, resisting the temptation to put one in my pocket. I move to the nightstand next to the bed and open the top drawer. There are books and socks and a large Prada cashmere pouch, the kind the pocket books are shipped in. It appears old and worn and the contents are wrapped up tightly. Grabbing it, I immediately know what naughty little Gemma has at her side. Inside are two vibrators, lube, and clothespins.

"Mmmm, I knew that little shit was no man for you." My cock is aching now with visions of sliding in to her velvet pussy as I have one of these in her luscious ass.

Putting the toys back, I turn my attention to what needs to be done. I place the tool box on the floor and look around trying to find the best place for the surveillance device. The vent on the wall across from the bed is perfect. The cat stays with me and makes sure I do the job right. I have to look for evidence linking her to Malcolm's schemes, camera's throughout her house is going to help me.

By the time I'm done there's a camera in her bedroom, the bathroom, (I have no conscience), kitchen, and living room. I glance at my watch and see I have just enough time to get back to the city on time. I didn't find anything that links her to her douchebag husband but I know I'll be back and I feel content I can search the house again if I need to. That fact sends a thrill through me.

Gemma

The morning has flown by. I've been so absorbed in the case and presentation I didn't notice anything else. Although, when Davis arrived I went to greet him in his office because I knew the drill.

"Good morning," I couldn't bring myself to call him Mr. Davis and he hadn't told me to call him Miles.

"Good morning Gemma. What did you think of the case?" he asked and his pleasantness took me a little by surprise.

"The fact it's a hostile take-over is a bit…invigorating," I smiled.

He leaned his head back and laughed. Actually laughed. "I know, that shit gets us off."

I smiled again and felt my cheeks heat but I didn't agree, not wanting to admit I felt the same thing. I had to remind myself I'm only an assistant.

"Mr. Black wants you to present directly to him today. I'm not surprised really. He wants to see what you've got."

My eyes widened a little remembering the intensity of his presence. "Is that so?"

"Yes, right after lunch. But if you have any questions, want to bounce anything off me, don't hesitate. We're a team, all of us here."

His offer touched me and surprised me. This didn't seem to be the same guy from yesterday.

"Thanks, I appreciate it. But I think I need to do this on my own so Mr. Black can see what I do, and I can get a more honest idea of how he likes to play things."

"Smart, but I knew that already," Miles grinned.

"Is there anything you'd like me to do, Mr. Davis?" I asked, happy at the newly relaxed vibe between us.

"Miles, Gemma. And no, you've got your hands full, this is your initiation. I think it's safe to say we're all watching to see how it goes. I for one, am stoked," *stoked,* I had to stop myself from quirking a brow at him, "to see how you'll handle it. I gotta tell you, you have one hell of a reputation, aside from the Malcolm shit that got dumped on you. I would be a fool not to admit I'm going to learn from you too."

His honest declaration humbled me and made my cheeks burn with embarrassment.

"Thanks Miles, you don't know how much I appreciate that."

"Alright, get the hell out of here and get to work. You've got a big presentation and not much time." He booted up his computer as he shooed me out.

This time I laughed. "Yes sir."

That was three hours ago. Simon told me I would be meeting with Mr. Black at one fifteen and that I have a quarter hour to present, the realization sends a nervous tremor through me. *Don't act like professional virgin, you've been doing this for years and you are one of the best in your field. Obviously Black knows that or he wouldn't have hired you.*

All day my attention had been focused only on the arguments in front of me and in my head. I was thankful Black had been out all morning saving me from distraction. I instantly became aware of him when he returned, I could feel him. His eyes were on me as he moved through the office. The erotic heat that pulses from him is intimidating and breathtaking. The man is a walking sex god. I know he would fuck hard, rough, and mind-blowingly incredible with a focus that made my toes curl. His gaze felt like a dark caress. His lips curled in a wicked smirk like he knew me intimately, knew all my secrets, that I was laid bare in front of him. He stripped me with that simple glance and I felt raw and naked right to my soul.

My stomach is instantly in knots and thoughts of eating disappear.

Simon is by his side talking as they walk past everyone and into his private world and shut the door. I can see inside and watch as he sits behind his desk. There is something different about him from this morning. I squint my eyes trying to figure it out. *He left his jacket on.* I'm sure that's it as I remember him pacing earlier with his sleeves rolled up and his hair ruffled.

I look back at my monitor and start to read from the top of the page, my head going back and forth from the notes on the pad next to me and the screen. A little chime makes me jump as an instant message pops up on the right side of my computer screen.

Are you ready for me Ms. Trudeau? Alexander Black

I blink, my fingers hovering over the keys.
Alexander Black is IM'ing me!

Yes Mr. Black, I believe I'll show you exactly what you want to see. Gemma Trudeau

Do you now, Ms. Trudeau? Never assume, it's a sign of weakness. Alexander Black

I'm not assuming, I'm confident. Gemma Trudeau

I'm sweating and my breathing is heavy as I fight to hold on to certainty and calm.

Then I look forward to seeing how you'll perform in front of me, Ms. Trudeau. Alexander Black

On my back, on all fours, kneeling in front of you, tied and bound... the words and images flash in my mind before I can stop them, bringing a fresh wave of heat coursing through me.

"Fuck!" I mutter.

Don't curse Ms. Trudeau, it doesn't become you. Alexander Black

I jerk a stunned gaze at him. He's sitting back in his chair at his desk staring directly at me, his hand at his chin, fingers stroking it again. I blink. He smiles, but it isn't a friendly or warm grin, but cold and hard, leering and intimidating, and it tells me this man should *never* be underestimated.

He swivels his chair back to his desk and begins typing. The ping of the message alert draws my attention.

One hour Ms. Trudeau, you'll have only fifteen minutes in front of me, don't waste it. Alexander Black

I swallow hard and almost choke on my dry mouth. Why do I suddenly feel aroused and scared at the same time?

The phone startles a short time later. "Miles Davis' office, Gemma Trudeau speaking."

"Gemma, it's Simon, five minutes until your appointment with Mr. Black."

"Thank you Simon, I appreciate the heads up."

"You're welcome, I saw how engrossed you were. This being your first appointment, I thought it would be helpful if I gave you a five minute warning," he chuckles.

"You're the best," I smile.

"Yeah, I know, and you'll be fine, you're a

confident, intelligent, strong woman. Remember that."

For some reason I have a feeling I'll need to hold on to that little reminder when I face Black.

"Thanks Simon, I'll be right over."

I click *print* as I hang up and turn to watch the pages spit out of the machine.

Five minutes later Simon is pulling the door closed to Alexander Black's office behind me. The glass is smoked to give us privacy. He's on the phone and doesn't acknowledge my presence when I walk in. Deciding the best tactic would be to play offensive, I walk to his desk, place the arguments I'd prepared down and sit in a chair across from him. And wait.

"He's rebutting the offer? Is he out of his mind? The company hasn't operated beyond the red in years, it's barely able to pay for itself. What could he possibly think it has that would be attractive in a market it has no place in? It's outdated." A pause lapses as he listens to the caller and picks up my prospectus. "You want to know what I think? I think he believes that Black Inc.'s interest has to do in that company as it is, that we find it attractive. Lower the offer, resubmit, and let me know. Every time he refuses we'll lower it again until he understands. I don't give a shit about that company. Make him understand." Another pause. "Are there any other negotiations on his table?" He listens again. "Get me answers. And if there are, make them go away. The next time you call me will be to tell me he accepted or the company ceases to exist. Understand?" He slams the phone down and continues to read my presentation.

Ruthless. Powerful. Commanding. Slightly criminal even.

I sit perfectly still and force myself not to squirm in front of him.

...look forward to seeing how you'll perform in front of me... his words resonate in my mind. Now I have the voice to place with it. It floats through me like thick brandy, heating and seeping into every part of me.

It seems like hours pass as the minutes tick by while I watch Black skim through my argument. Finally, he places the papers back on his desk and turns his chair so his back is to me and he's looking out the window.

"Tell me Ms. Trudeau, do the thoughts of predator, domination, taken illicit feelings of fear in you?"

I'm stunned...again. It's a moment before I can squeak out, "Excuse me?"

"The first thing you feel, the first thing that comes to mind, tell me." His words are so commanding I can't help but blurt out.

"Yes."

"Good...does it excite you?"

I lick my lips and am so happy he can't see me.

"Yes." I take a slow deep breath and can feel my now hardened nipples scrape against the fabric.

He turns slowly back to face me. I can see the color of his eyes now, a crystal clear blue, so light they look like ice and their piercing force sends a shiver through me. His gaze drops to my breasts, the pebbled points clearly visible through the thin layers of fabric.

He slowly stands as he unbuttons his jacket, then his vest, his eyes never leaving mine pinning me down. He comes to stand behind me and my heart beat accelerates. He smells divine, fresh, crisp, male, and a hint of muskiness. He lowers his body so his face is so close to mine I can feel his warm breath and the soft scruff of his facial hair on my skin. He raises his hands to grip the edge of his desk in front of me, his arms touching mine. I'm captured.

"There is a process of possession, Ms. Trudeau. One doesn't just claim and control, it must be given. It must be seduced, earned, the submissive must feel with every fiber of their being that they must be owned, must be taken thoroughly and completely," he says evenly, his mouth close to my ear. "They must need to be claimed, knowing that only then they will find the ecstasy of freedom." His tone drops. "Sweet release, Ms. Trudeau."

I squirm unconsciously in my seat, my heavy

breathing pushing my breasts against the fabric, each scrape on my tight nipples pure torture. The hem of my dress rises to show the top of the stocking and the clip of a garter. I catch Black's sharp intake of breath telling me he sees it too.

"Write it over. Show me what it's like to be seduced, Gemma," he says deeply, his voice rough.

He moves to the windows and looks out at his city before him. The absence of his body leaves me feeling empty and wanting. He's such overwhelming contained strength, power and control. It's scary and sensual.

"Is seduction your usual tactic Mr. Black?"

I hear a rumble from deep in his chest, almost like a chuckle.

"Always, Ms. Trudeau. The secret is knowing how to seduce, what your prey thinks it wants, but knowing what they need. They will give you anything when you can give them that."

I sit staring at his back feeling completely unraveled and totally needing to be fucked.

I bet that man would know exactly *what I need* and *how to give it to me.*

Simon's voice cuts through the erotic mood in Black's office.

"Excuse Mr. Black, Mr. Wilcott is here."

"Thank you Simon, Ms. Trudeau and I are finished."

That's my cue to leave, Black is finished with

me. I'm so far from finished it hurts.

"Thank you for your time and your information, I will have the revised arguments on your desk by the end of business today."

"I have no doubt you will give me exactly what I want Gemma."

"Yes sir," shit!

"Simon has lunch waiting for you. You have to take care of yourself Ms. Trudeau."

How the hell did he know I didn't have lunch?!

"What did I tell you about cursing Gemma?" his voice warning.

"Yes sir, I'll leave you to your appointment."

I leave his office quickly, afraid I'll say something else stupid.

What the hell happened to the intimidating lawyer I've been for the past decade and a half? One sexy man and it all goes down the crapper. And how the hell did he know I cursed again?

As I pass Simon, "Thanks for lunch," the words come out a little choked.

"It's on your desk Gemma. Go take a break, you look flushed."

And totally wet.

Alexander

Fucking stockings and *garters?!*

I saw the look of need slip over her eyes, the

slight parting of her lips asking to be kissed, her hard little nipples aching to be sucked. I almost shoved her chair around, spread her legs and buried my face in that sweet cunt I have no doubt is wet. Then I would have fucked her until she screamed. I wanted to punish her with my cock, make her beg.

I had to get away. My dick is so hard, I couldn't face her.

I can't wait to feel her seduction in her own words, feel the passion simmering inside begging to be set free.

I wonder which one of me you'll want more, Ms. Trudeau.

take

CHAPTER 3

Gemma

As I put the finishing touches on the revised proposal, I let out a ragged breath. The sexual frustration fed my direction, spurred me toward a course I'd never visited before in a legal argument. I set myself up as the company, and Alexander Black the deliverer of the takeover. By the time I was done, I would have begged him to take me, the company, to only be owned by him.

It was brilliant.

The only problem is I'm so damn horny I could scream. Flashes of Black doing dirty things, very bad things to me was my inspiration, each one more vivid, more kinky than the next. By the time my mind had my hands bound over my head from the ceiling with Black flicking a riding crop over my bare flesh begging him for more, I was so close to coming I was almost delirious. My body is vibrating from the carnal hunger clawing at me.

Giving it a last once over, I click print and rush to the bathroom to splash cold water on my face. My expression makes me laugh.

"You look like an animal in heat Gemma."

On the way back to my desk I see the office is virtually empty. I'm shocked when I glance at my Rolex and realize it's almost six.

"Shit."

Alexander Black is still here and on the phone again.

The revisions are complete. Gemma Trudeau

I know, it looks good...brilliant even Ms. Trudeau. Alexander Black

It doesn't surprise he knows what the revised edition looks like even before I've presented it to him.

Thank you. Gemma Trudeau

Bring me the hardcopy. Alexander Black

Be right there. Gemma Trudeau

I take a cleansing breath to try and shake the desire still licking my insides and gather the paperwork. Straightening my spine, I walk into the lion's den.

I stay standing and wait for him to finish his phone call, not really wanting to put myself in the same position as before. I don't want to be more vulnerable than I already feel.

Black raises an eyebrow at me then lowers his

ice blue eyes to the chair, directing me to sit. My body moves of its own accord and takes a seat and I place the document in front of him.

"Fine, that's good news. Let me know when the negotiations are complete." He hits a button on the phone and disengages the call.

Sheez, ever hear of social etiquette?

"Ms. Trudeau, I'm very pleased with you. Your passion resonated in the pages and achieved the desired results."

His smirk leads me to believe he's not only talking about the take-over.

"Thank you Mr. Black."

He studies me.

"Tell me Gemma, do you understand why it works so beautifully?"

His fingers stroke his jaw again. I want to push them away and follow the hard line with my tongue.

Then it finally seems so clear, why the seduction seemed so perfect for the take-over approach.

"Because it is a hostile take-over."

The corner of his gorgeous mouth lifts and his eyes narrow to slits.

"Go on."

"The approach removed the hostility allowing for pliability and acquiescence. They will want to submit…"

"Exactly, Gemma," his voice is like silk caressing me.

"It's brilliant." I smile.

"It's need and desire, fulfillment and vanquishment. It's sex, Gemma, knowing what you need and giving it to you, making you want it."

I swallow, holding back the desire rising in me again.

"Natural human instinct Mr. Black."

"No, Ms. Trudeau it's primal and primitive, it's the essence of what we are, animals with a desire to consume and devour. And...," he shrugs, "some need to be taken, bitten, marked, erotic welts on their skin, fucked in the ass hard and rough. They need pain with their pleasure to go over the edge."

My eyes fly open with his filthy graphic description as heat envelopes me, inside and out.

His grin makes me want to writhe. "Your first day was pleasurable."

"It was interesting, yes." I breathe out.

He dips his head back and laughs. The sound of it makes me smile.

"Good. Let's see what tomorrow brings, Ms. Trudeau."

I rise to leave, looking forward to getting out of the close proximity of this insanely sexual beast and wanting to throw myself in it.

"Goodnight Mr. Black. Let me take this moment to thank you for the opportunity. I have a feeling it's going to be quite a learning adventure."

His eyes glint with a hint of mischief. "Yes it is. Goodnight Ms. Trudeau, get home safe."

Alexander

"Jesús, I'm coming down now. Ms. Trudeau has just gotten into the elevator on her way home." I listen to his update. "Good, let me know when she arrives there and if she stopped to talk to anyone."

Keep your friends close and your enemies closer.

The flat black armored Hummer is waiting for me outside. Obnoxious vehicle? Maybe. But with its bullet proof glass and reinforced walls, it serves its purpose: it keeps me safe. A lot of people hate me, for good reason, and my boys, Jesús Ramirez and his brother Carlos, always have my back.

Fate had thrown us all together during the time I'd been raped by that piece of shit and his friends. Carlos was a member of a Latin gang and his little brother Jesús was following in his path. It was too late for Carlos, once a member always a member, but he didn't want that life for Jesús. Carlos helped me take care of those friends, so I took Jesús under my wing. I was no better than the gang members, but I wasn't a member. I taught the kid what he needed to know to survive on the streets. When I went away to college, the gang sent Carlos to the Army to get battle trained and Jesús had followed.

The streets are their own enterprise. Gone are the days of simple mob racketeering and prostitution. It's a business, a very big business, encompassing corporations that would boggle the mind. I should know. I basically bought Carlos when my company earned its place with the heavy hitters. Jesús was waiting for me when I'd finished college, picking up right where we'd left off. It was only a different ball game at that time. New players and playing field, but survival at its fittest with heavier stakes.

Carlos is waiting outside the black wrought iron gates when we pull up to my Louis XVI style mansion on East Ninety Sixth Street off Fifth Avenue. It's the only private residence on the island of Manhattan with a driveway and its own garage, the only reason I'd bought it.

"You're late," Carlos states flatly.

"Yeah, I know. Trudeau." I don't have to say anything else, they know the story.

"Mama's going to be pissed dinner got cold."

Jesús and Carlos' mother is the cook and overseer of my house. Various other family members are staff as well, some of the males are gang members too. At least to the outside world that's what it looks like. They are my family, the only family I've ever known. They live with me in the house. I take care of what's mine.

"She'll understand when I explain it to her."

I can't help having a soft place in my heart for that woman, the only woman I've ever trusted. She coddled me when I was a kid, feeling the rage that had filled me threatening to destroy me completely. Her love, caring, and compassion eased some of my fury, and I love her for it.

"Yeah, after she beats your ass," Carlos laughs.

"You're just jealous because she loves me more than you," I tell him, giving him a shove.

"You flirt with her, man!"

"A woman is always a woman, no matter who she is."

And right now there is only one woman I can't wait to see when she gets home.

Gemma

The commute home was a complete blur, my mind in a hazy fog of horniness. If the Latin guy hadn't asked me on the subway if he could catch the Path train from one of the stops, I would have probably kept going to some place in Brooklyn. By the time I walk into the house sometime after seven, Kitty is screaming at me.

"I know, I'm sorry I'm late. You got spoiled with me being home, didn't you baby?" I coo at her.

"Meow."

"Alright, I'll feed you before my shower, you

pushy little thing you."

"Meow."

After a nice long hot shower and a sandwich, I curl up on the couch with my laptop.

"First things first, this has waited way too long."

Because I don't have access to legal documents, I pull up LegalZoom.com and click on divorce. Even though I'm not a civil lawyer and haven't worked with divorces, I breeze through the information and get the divorce paperwork filled out pretty quickly.

"If I'd done this years ago, I wouldn't be in this mess."

I click print and immediately hear the machine kick on from across the room. Retrieving the document, I then stack the pages on the coffee table in front of me and grab my phone. I take a deep breath and make the call.

"Girl, it's about damn time you returned my calls. If Tony hadn't told me you were okay, I was going to drag your ass out of that house and tie you up in little Sal's room so I could take care of you."

I laugh. It's so good to hear Gina's voice. She's my only friend from the neighborhood. And she happens to be Tony's sister, the youngest of the Salvatore children, number one guy in the Jersey mob family under the Capo de Tutt'i Capi, the boss of bosses. She's a lawyer as well, (ironic), but she has a private practice here in Jersey City.

"I know, I'm sorry. I had to get my shit together and it took all my concentration. I'm really sorry, I didn't mean to blow you off."

"Gemma, are you okay?" she asks concerned, all joking aside.

"Yeah, actually really good. I started working today. You'll *never* guess where." I grin, remembering Black.

"Yeah? That's great. Back at your old firm?" I can hear the baby and I'm sure she's got him on her hip, she's got three boys. A pang of longing stabs at my heart.

I take a deep breath. She knows everything that I know.

"Black Inc."

"You are fucking kidding, right?!"

I hear in the background, "Mommy said a bad word!" and it makes me laugh. If her kids only knew what a truck driver their mother was as a kid, they'd be shocked. We both had hung out with the mafia boys and pulled no punches, we had to hold our own.

"Nope."

She yells to her husband, "Frankie, take the baby, I've got to talk to Gemma!" Then to me, "Hold on right there, don't you go anywhere!" A little shuffling and huffing as I'm sure she's going to find a quiet spot where she can speak freely.

"Okay, go."

"What? There isn't much to tell, there was a listing for a position with his firm in mergers and acquisitions with a professional headhunter so I applied. I'm one of the best in what I do. Black is a shrewd and successful business man. He put the fact my ex screwed him for three million dollars aside and hired me." The absurdity of the situation rings clearly in my ears, I can only imagine what Gina thinks.

"You did just hear what you said, right?"

"Yeah. But professionally, hiring me was a smart decision on his part."

"Maybe not just professionally, Gem. You know the kind of people we grew up with. They go to any lengths to know what their enemy is doing. What better way would Black be able to keep an eye on you if he didn't have you all to himself eight hours a day, five days a week? He'd be able to monitor your communications, your comings and goings, without any extra effort at all. You're handing it to him on a silver platter."

The cold truth hits me like a blast of ice water jolting me awake.

"Oh my God…"

"But the bonus is…," Gina continues, "you can use him as well to re-establish your career. You have absolutely nothing to hide, *you* didn't do anything wrong. Work the fuck out of that situation, go balls blazing wild. Then after Malcolm's trial and no implications are made to you, move on to greener pastures."

"I knew when I applied Black was the only way I'd be able to get my life back professionally. I knew I had to get a job there, the sucky thing is I'm a legal assistant. But I don't care, I had to get my foot in the door, no matter how."

"Yeah, it sucks but you were right."

"I hadn't thought about him wanting to keep an eye on me assuming I was involved in Malcolm's scheme."

"Gemma, you said it yourself, he's shrewd *and* extremely successful. Is he as hot as he looks?" she asks, shifting directions.

"Fucking hotter G," I almost pant.

"You need to fuck him."

"I am *not* going to fuck him!"

"Why not? Does he seem like he'd be a bad lay?"

"Quite the opposite. He looks like he'd devour me and I'd shamelessly beg him for more."

"Oh girl, you are in so much trouble. You are extremely sexy, beautiful, and smart as hell. I bet he's already imagined all the ways he'd like to screw your brains out, he's a man."

"He's a hell of a lot more than just a man, he's a beast, a primitive animal, and so damn good looking I can't even look at him."

"You are so going to fuck him, just make sure

you tell me all the details when you do. Grabbing quickies when I can now that kids are all over the place is not much fun."

I laugh. It's been so long since I really laughed from down deep in my belly, it almost makes me cry.

"Listen," I begin when I catch my breath. "I've filled out divorce papers. Do you think you could get them filed in the clerk of courts office when you send someone down there? I hate to ask but now that I'm working, I don't want to ask for the time off."

"Shut up, of course I will, I almost filled some out for you myself but I didn't want to push you. Shove them in my mailbox on your way to the Path in the morning and I'll take care of it."

"I love you G, see you soon."

"Oh no, girl, you don't get off that easy. Sunday dinner, four o'clock, gravy, meatballs, sausages, braciole's."

"Deal, I'll bring the cannoli's."

"You are such a Godfather nerd," Gina laughs.

"I can't help it, you know I've always loved the bad boys."

"Yeah I know, too bad their not good for our health."

"Considering how things turned out with a straight boy, I'm beginning to think otherwise."

Alexander

On the fifth floor of the nineteen thirteen house I live in, dressed in only sweat pants, my gaze is riveted to the large computer monitor on the desk in my home office. This is my private sanctuary, with my bedroom, office, workout room, and playroom. The basement and lower levels are occupied by the Ramirez family and the rest of the staff. But this area is my retreat where I do whatever the fuck I want. Often times it's to a female in the dark boudoir where I satisfy my twisted tastes.

My intention for watching Gemma is to see her in her own environment, hoping she'd expose her affiliation with Malcolm in his schemes and incriminate herself. I want revenge and I'll get it any way I can.

After I watched Gemma get out of the shower, her creamy white skin glistening and moist, I had to beat out some of my sexual need with a workout. Tonight I have no doubt there will be more right here in front of the monitor watching her.

She wasn't the only one who'd been affected by the intense sexual energy that had charged between us, albeit fueled by the direction I'd pushed the business agenda today.

If I was going to break her, one way or another, she needed a harsh shove out of her comfort zone. She's wrapped up so tight, careful with her words, her movements, even her glances, a reserved persona she'd perfected over her career.

I'd seen the casual, relaxed Gemma when she was talking to her friend Gina, (I made a mental note to find out who this Gina is), and she'd looked beautiful. With me she was guarded, reserved, calculating even. *Smart girl.* Now I know why. It's funny the things one finds out when it's thought no one is listening.

She'd planned on using her position with my company to further her own career, or to re-establish it. Which was precisely what I thought she'd do when I had it dangled in front of her, the perfect opportunity for her to clear her name and prove herself as the masterful lawyer she is. Or to tighten the noose around her neck. Although I couldn't hear what Gina had said, she'd obviously made Gemma realize I'd hired her to keep an eye on her in order to determine her involvement, if any, with that slime ball husband of hers, (which is partially true). Apparently soon to be ex-husband.

"Good, it's about damn time you're going to unload the piece of shit," I murmur to her image on the screen.

Remembering her words...*more than just a man, he's a beast, a primitive animal, and so damn good looking I can't even look at him.*

"You have no idea how primitive, my pet."

Her eyes had widened with lust and her face

had flushed, and those needy little nipples hardened when I mentioned how I would take her hard and rough, fuck her in that tight little ass of hers and mark that flawless pale skin with my teeth and hands.

She's getting ready for bed. My dick has been rock hard with anticipation. She already stripped off her clothes and left them at the end of the bed.

"You have to stay out for a little while Kitty, I have to take care of myself first before I explode," she tells her cat.

"Fuck," I moan.

I knew this was coming, had no doubt, but now that its time, I'm sweating and my balls are pulled so tight under my throbbing shaft, I'm almost ready to come.

After putting the cat out, her luscious little body walks to the nightstand and pulls out her Prada pouch of toys. I resist the urge to pull my dick out and pound out the waiting eruption barely held back.

I watch her remove all of her supplies then place them in an orderly fashion on the table top. Her OCD makes me smirk.

The only precision when you're with me will be from me.

Then uncapping the lube, she parts her legs and smooths the slick gel over her folds and her ass.

"Fuck," I grit out again.

Next she palms one vibrator and covers it

with gel, then the other.

"Yes," the head of my cock is oozing pre-cum, imagining what she's going to do with both of them.

When she picks up the clothes pins, my head falls back against the chair. "*Shit,* you're going to put those clips on your perfect nipples."

"Better not," she murmurs, "I'll come as soon as I touch my clit if I do."

"Thank God," I groan gutturally.

After all her supplies are ready, Gemma crawls to the center of her flower garden bed and lays on her back, baring her succulent body completely. She slides her hands up her sides to cup her breasts. Her fingers clasp her nipples and she begins to play.

"Oh, I cannot wait to suck those beautiful tits into my mouth and pull those nipples with my teeth," I grit out. "Twist them, baby, pull them, feel it all the way down to your pussy."

Her fingers are working the peaks, pulling, twisting, flicking them. I hear her breathing get heavier and raspier as her back arches and her hips begin to squirm. She bends her knees and lets them fall to the sides, opening her up to my view.

"Look at that hungry cunt, pet, she's so needy. Touch it Gemma, make it beg to be filled."

Her hand slides down her stomach, over her bald mound to circle a finger around her clit. With her other hand she reaches over and grabs the flesh colored vibrator. Inserting only the head, her hips begin to move into it.

"I would smack your clit for you, pet, it would make you scream with need."

"Oh, Gooood," she moans.

"Not yet, Gemma, you can't come yet. You need more."

My fingers ache dying to slip inside her. My hands clench needing to see their marks on her flesh. My mouth waters yearning to taste her.

"Show me, Gemma, show me some of your darkness. I know it's there pet, waiting to be set free."

She sets the vibrator aside and reaches for the other, the bright pink one. This one is not as long and thick as the other.

"Yes, pet, take what you need."

I feel the darkness seeping through me, the need to claim, control…punish. It flows through me in hot, thick, burning waves. It has been my salvation, my destroyer, my conqueror.

She turns and gets up on her knees and faces the wall. She grips the brass headrails with one hand as she slips the vibrator beneath her with the other…at the entrance of her ass.

"You're such a good girl. Slow, let me see it slip in that tight ass inch by inch."

She lowers her body down to the bed with her ass in the air.

It's such a beautiful sight, Gemma naked and spread open, preparing to get fucked in the ass.

Her free hand reaches beneath her to work her clit. I can almost feel that swollen little nub on my tongue. My teeth clench from the emptiness.

"Mmmm…"

I can see her tight hole opening above the head of the vibrator. Its slips past the crown then the shaft slides in.

I'm riveted, consumed by the vision in front of me, lost in nothing but the pleasure this woman is giving herself. She slips it in and out, her body still, taking the fake phallus, but wanting a man. Me. I know her mind is filled with me, wondering how my cock would feel slipping into her tightness, how my mouth would feel branding her skin with my tongue. I'd made sure I left my mark on her psyche, burning her with it.

"Soon, pet, very soon."

Gemma pulls the vibrator from her ass and switches it for the other. I know she hasn't come yet. She shifts to her back and opens her legs. Then she starts to fuck herself with deep rhythmic thrusts with one hand as the other rubs her clit.

I can see frustration flash across her face.

"You need more, pet, I know. But come."

With determination on her lust hungry face, she works herself. I can almost feel her tight pussy clamp down on my cock, ready to explode.

A long moan escapes her as she continues to thrust the plastic dick in and out, her fingers working her clit, her back arching off the bed. She's coming. What delicious sounds.

"So good, pet, I'll make you come again and again."

I slip the waistband down and palm my swollen shaft and grip it tightly to the point of pain. In my mind Gemma's arms are bound behind her back and her hot little mouth is sliding up and down my cock, sucking the cum from me. The image makes me explode with one, two, three pumps.

"She has made me want to come all day. That was just a warm-up."

As I watch her laying there, not entirely satisfied but at least having a release, I begin to rub my cock again nice and slow. I suddenly realize she didn't turn on the vibrators.

She wants to be fucked, needs to be fucked. I wonder how long it's been.

Compassion for the woman ebbs into me. A part of me wants to hold her, make her realize what an amazing, captivating woman she is. The other part, the sadistic animal inside me wants to punish her until she breaks.

But what she needs, what she desperately craves, is to step into her darkness, embrace her carnal fantasies, indulge in the forbidden she's kept locked up tight. I can see it, the need obvious when she shoved that dildo up her ass. Some pain with her pleasure. The thought makes my darkness surge.

With my hand sliding up and down my cock, I'm enjoying the thoughts of all the things I'm going to do to Gemma Trudeau.

take

CHAPTER 4

Gemma

Taking the chance that Black would be in early again, I got my coffee and croissant to go at the coffee shop this morning. The elevator doors slide open a little after eight. I approach the outer doors of Black Inc. to see if they're locked and as soon as my hand hits the knob the buzzer sounds to give me access. When I walk in I spy Alexander in his throne room in much the same situation and state he was yesterday. His intense savage beauty stuns me again as heat radiates throughout my body.

Here we go again.

I drop my things off at my desk and use the restroom to freshen up. When one faces battle, their war face must be properly in place. Mine is red lipstick, black liner and a fresh application of powder to my face. A slight ripple seeps through me. The garters and stockings weren't a bad idea either.

Taking my seat, I turn on my computer and open the coffee and breakfast while it's powering up. I open my emails, one from PR asking if everything is fine and should I have any questions don't hesitate contacting them, and the other from Alexander Black. It was written at ten forty last night. Right when I'd climbed into bed to finally release the sexual tension that had built all day.

Ms. Trudeau,

Again, you did a nice job on the case yesterday.

We'll be submitting it today and should hear back from them by weeks end.

They'll let us know if you succeeded in your seduction.

Today, I've given Davis a possible copyright infringement situation, a copy is attached.

Discuss it with him.

I know, not as exciting as seduction.

It could excite you as much none the less.

Alexander Black

CEO

BLACK INC.

"Yes, Your Highness," I mumble as my cheeks flame crimson in embarrassment.

No...there's no possible way...he couldn't

know…what I was doing…when he wrote this.

I can hear his murmured rumblings from my close proximity to his office as he talks on the phone. The now familiar ding sounds as the IM pops up on my screen.

Did you have a good night? Alexander Black

Yeah, it was great after I finally got my divorce paperwork done and let my freak out to play, no thanks to you.

I did, thank you. And you? Gemma Trudeau

I did. I watched the most amazing woman perform. Alexander Black

"What the fuck?" I spit my coffee out.

I jerk my head to glare at the man.

Tsk, tsk, Ms. Trudeau, not only did you make a mess, but cursing too? Alexander Black

"What an insufferable, narcissistic, ego maniac," I say, stunned.

I choose not to reply. It doesn't warrant one. And what do I say to that? Besides, I have a mess to clean up. Stupid glass desk.

I literally hate that man!

Alexander

"Go ahead," I bark, answering my cell phone.

"Nothing out of the ordinary, Mr. Black. Actually, she hasn't had much activity at all. The only communication she's sent since her resume' was submitted to Black Inc. was to Legal Zoom last night."

My IT guy, Rashad, had gained access into Gemma's email and files since we received her IP address when she forwarded her information for the position. It was giving us the keys to her front door and saying, 'Come on in.'

"How far back have you gone so far?" I ask looking at the woman who now seemed to have become an enigma.

"About two years."

"Anything suspicious?"

"Only some information she received about her parent's death."

"Who did it come from?"

"The officer who filed the police report."

Is this another piece to the puzzle that is you, Ms. Trudeau?

"What about the husband?"

"That is a bit harder to access. The Feds have got all his stuff locked up tight for evidence, I'm having to work around blocks and walls. I'll get in, it's just going to take a little more time."

Rashad is a boy wonder at technology. He loves computers more than he does women, I have no doubt he'll succeed at whatever challenges he faces.

"Alright, thanks Rashad. Keep me up to date with whatever you find."

"Will do boss."

Gemma

I avoided Alexander Black all week, only talking to him when absolutely necessary. Fortunately, my immediate boss is Miles Davis, and that was turning out to be a pleasant surprise. On Wednesday, he'd asked me to lunch and the invitation had made me feel like the new kid at school and this was the confrontation by the popular kid to see if I fit in.

"Sure, that would be nice," I'd accepted the invitation with trepidation and a smile.

"Great, I made a reservation at Sergimmo Salumeria, it's in Hell's Kitchen. Great little place, just out of the madness. You'll love it. I'm guessing you like Italian, right? Who doesn't?"

His friendly forwardness continued to surprise me. My natural instincts led me to follow his lead and see what he had planned. As a lawyer, I knew motives always presented themselves eventually.

Apparently Miles was a regular at the little Italian restaurant because everyone knew him by name. After we ordered, I let him order for me since it seemed this was like a second home to him, he made the first direct hit.

"So Gemma, what's your deal?"

I quirked an eyebrow at him. "Could you elaborate on the question?" It was so loaded, I wasn't touching it without further clarification.

"You are obviously too smart to be have been involved with your husband's…"

"Soon to be ex," I interjected.

"Bravo.   Your ex-husband's bullshit.   So what the fuck, did you not have any clue?" he laid it out.

I took a deep breath deciding on how I was going to answer that.

"To be honest, yes I did, so did my dad, but I didn't *want* to know I guess. So I pretended for a long time that I wasn't suspicious, that my feelings were because of other things, not his business dealings." I wanted to be honest, but I didn't know Miles and wasn't going to pour out my shitty life in front of him.

"Sucks to be you."

I snorted my agreement and stopped myself from flipping him off.

"Well," he continued, sitting back in his chair and clasping his fingers behind his head, regarding me. "I must say, it's brilliant you being at Black Inc. and all. What better place for you to crush this whole situation other than working for the man Malcolm stole three million dollars from? You couldn't have negotiated a better deal if you tried."

I winced under Miles' words.

"I know, call it luck or fate, it doesn't matter. I am just extremely grateful."

"You had nothing to do with it?" he asked, his analytical eyes studying me.

"No." I replied flatly, knowing he meant Malcolm's scheme.

After a moment, he lowered his hands to the table and began to drum them nodding his head to the tune his fingers were playing.

"I believe you," he said simply. The topic officially finished.

Holy shit, this guy switches gears so fast, he's got to have ADHD.

"Thanks, I just hope Black does," I muttered.

"Hah, you never know what's going on inside that brilliant diabolical mind."

"You're not shitting," I agreed.

"So tell me," his tone dropped, "now that you're a single woman, are you dating anyone?" he asked, moving closer.

You are not hitting on me!

"No, nor do I want to, I've got enough complications in my life."

"Having a lover isn't a complication," he said quietly, his finger lightly stroking my arm, "but a distraction. I love older women."

"Dude, we are not doing this. Thank you for the compliment, but it's not happening. With no one. Period."

He laughed and the mood returned to normal.

"Let me know if you change your mind, you

are hot!"

This never would happen if he worked for me. What do men think, just because you work for them, sexual favors come with it? But it's been so long since I've heard that, it felt good.

"Thanks Miles," I meant it.

"Do you think the company is going to budge on the take-over proposal you presented?"

Falling back into the topic of work, we got a lot more comfortable with each other, going back and forth with opinions and arguments. It turned out to be a really good lunch.

When we returned to the office I didn't think anything of it when Miles led me through with his hand on my back, the both of us relaxed and joking.

Alexander

I'd known Miles and Gemma had had lunch together, I was the one responsible for suggesting it in order to feel her out in a different environment. But when I saw his hand on her, I wanted to cut it off. Then rip his fucking head off his body and watch the blood gush from him.

It's late Friday afternoon, and I'm well aware that everyone's worked very hard this week and are ready to blow off some steam, but Miles asking Gemma if she "wants her world rocked" nearly made me blow a fucking gasket! It took me an hour to calm down so I wouldn't grab him by his puny little neck and slam his head into the wall until it was crushed.

"Ms. Trudeau speaking," she answers her phone.

"Dinner at six at Harry Cipriani's," I snap, the anger still lingering.

A very surprised, "Excuse me?"

"We are having dinner tonight at six o'clock at Harry Cipriani's," I state, clarifying my words.

I could hear her breathe in as she gathers her patience. "What if I have plans?"

"You don't. Besides, it's not a request." I'm an arrogant prick, and something other than coherent thought pushed me to make the demand.

"Do we have business to discuss that I'm not aware of?" she asks icily.

"Ms. Trudeau, you do realize you work for me as a legal assistant…"

"I'm completely aware of that, Mr. Black, I'm not an idiot. I'm only trying to ascertain whether there is something I didn't realize was critically pending."

Good for you not taking my shit, but you're still going to pay for it.

"Everything is critical. The sooner you realize that, the easier things will be. You'll ride with me." And with that I hang up.

Gemma

How the hell am I supposed to sit through

75

dinner with him…*looking like* that?

Today Alexander Black was true to his name, dressed completely in black. He appeared sinister, dangerous, deadly even. It made my heart pound and loins quiver. Instead of the suit and tie, he's wearing black slightly fitted jeans that hint at his perfect ass and muscular legs, a black suit jacket, and a black silk jersey t-shirt (with nothing underneath). The fabric of the shirt shows every ripple and contour of every muscle from his shoulders all the way down his abdomen and beyond. His long feet in shiny Italian black leather shoes had my mind wondering if the myth was real.

He can't *be so damn perfect, maybe he suffers from erectile dysfunction.*

I giggle to myself at the thought of Alexander Black not being able to get it up. An obvious very sad and extremely improbable situation. Anyone who radiates sexual dominance like he does has no problems in the lower regions.

Five o'clock came and went and still I sit at my desk, refusing to glance at the beautiful bullying ogre in the glass throne room, pretending whatever I was working was en masse critical importance. At five forty-five he messages, and startles me.

We will be going down in five minutes.
Alexander Black

I growl low in my throat. I feel as if I'm being railroaded into something I know nothing about, something that leaves me almost breathless, but deep down I know I would take the path either way. The discomfort is more for myself and my own inhibitions, my lifelong habit of following the safer road, staying in my self-imposed comfort zone.

When I exit the restroom after freshening up, Black is waiting for me.

"Shall we?" he asks tightly.

"I just need to grab my things," I clip with a lift to my chin.

We descend to the lobby in silence, the energy almost crackling between us. I was determined not to say anything until I knew what this was all about. This was his party, I was only along for the ride.

I'm shocked to see a black Hummer waiting for us at the curb, obviously for us because Alexander directs me to it with his hand on my lower back, not slowing his steps until I'm in it with him immediately behind me. The driver is a Spanish man, probably around thirty. Regardless of his expensive clothes, he is total street. I can feel it in him, thrumming through his veins and the way his eyes saw everything without looking. He had 'thug' written all over him.

"Jesús, Cipriani's," Black barks out.

"You got it," he replies with relaxed familiarity.

My mouth falls open at the level of comfort

and casualness they apparently share. These two are more than driver and employer.

Harry Cipriani's restaurant on the street level of the Sherry-Netherland Hotel is in a class by itself. Elegance blends seamlessly with Old World ambiance. It's evident Alexander Black is a regular when we're escorted immediately to "his" table. I've never eaten here and my first impression is this is the private hide-away for the elite echelon of New York. Fashion designers, dignitaries, celebrities are all casually enjoying themselves without the risk of paparazzi or intrusion. Cipriani's is the patriarch of restaurants, and this is a sacred domain.

Alexander Black not only is a part of this world, he has a front row and center seat.

As we pass by tables, some faces I immediately recognize, others I don't know the names but had seen on the news or in Forbes, we come to a table of Oriental men, all distinguished. All the men bow their heads in the traditional Chinese salutation at the imposing man at my side.

"Mr. Black what a pleasure it is to see you. Thank you for coordinating the transactions we discussed, everything went exceptionally well."

Black bows in return. "It was my pleasure Mr. Jieyi. We shall meet in a few weeks to examine further developments. Enjoy your meal."

As we continue to our table I give Black an

inquisitive sideways glance.

"UN Chinese Ambassador LIU Jieyi."

He works with UN ambassadors?!

He is a lot more powerful and complicated than I'd ever imagined.

Black dominated the evening, ordering for both us without glancing at a menu. Artichoke appetizers, Tortellini and Prosciutto for us to share, Veal Piccata al limone for me, Filet Mignon with green peppercorn sauce for him. Two Bellini's were placed in front of us as soon as we were seated.

The entire meal he dominated *me* with his massive presence.

I was a throbbing mess of hot need when I got home.

take

CHAPTER 5

Alexander

I took the van to Jersey City. I'd already changed into black sweats and a black zippered hooded sweatshirt and sneakers in the parking garage where I'd picked up the van. Jesús was on his way back from taking Gemma home after dinner and he'd confirmed that the same cars were on her street that were always there and it appeared her house was empty. After making my appearance to everyone in my house, I had a shower and replied to all important messages. Everything pending had been addressed and, if I should need one, my alibi had been established.

I had a feeling I wasn't going to need one.

I parked in a spot a few spaces down from Gemma's house, a place I could watch the monitors without being disturbed. I noticed the cars in front of the houses, a gold minivan, a white Volkswagen

Rabbit, a black four door Chrysler sedan, all belonging to the Gen X group, a house in the suburbs and two point five kids.

I didn't notice anyone in any of them.

I let out a soft sadistic chuckle as I make my way to Gemma's house, my face hidden by the hood pulled low over my face.

She was so pissed at me at dinner.

She had a right to be. I had acted like a barbaric controlling lunatic, telling her she was going to dinner with me. Then I enveloped her with my overbearing presence, a part of my body constantly touching hers, my thigh pressed to hers, a finger stroking her lip to wipe a dot of cream, my hand touching the exposed flesh of her neck brushing her hair away. Combined with the consistent sexual overtones of the conversation, everything was designed to seduce her. I could see by the glaze in her eyes she needed to be fucked right then. She wasn't the only one.

If things had been different, I would have told her to go to the bathroom and remove her panties, then come back and give them to me. Then I would have stroked her velvety slick slit, fondled her clit, and slipped my finger in her tight, wet heat until she spasmed with her climax right there in the restaurant.

First objective, break her down...

She's just getting in the shower.

Perfect timing, I sneer.

Shutting down the laptop, I look around to make sure no one is around before I get out of the van. I make my way to the back of her house and up the back the steps to let myself in the backdoor with her keys. The cat greets me with a meow and rubs herself against my leg. I enter the living room and turn off the lamps and the light in the stairwell, leaving only the light on in the kitchen I noticed she had on when I was here the other day. Then I silently climb the stairs. Slipping into her bedroom, I extinguish the lights. I step up to the bed and pull up the sash I'd already wrapped around the bottom rail of the head board, then the others at the foot of the bed. I can hear she's mumbling to herself in the shower, probably complaining about me, and it makes me grin.

Good. It's time for her to get out.

I slip my hand through the slightly open door and turn off the light in the bathroom.

"Shit!" She exclaims.

I hear the jerk of the shower curtain then the *thump, thump, thump* of her hand against the wall as she gropes for the towel.

"The power must have gone out," I hear her mutter from my dark corner by the door in her bedroom.

Her footsteps approach. My body is charged, I feel the blood thrumming through my veins, I'm mainlining on the thrill of excitement.

"Ouch!" she says just outside the doorway. My grin is hidden beneath the cloak of my hood.

Then she's there, two steps inside the bedroom, the towel held tightly with one hand in front of her, clutched to her chest.

I step quietly behind her and clamp one hand on her mouth, then wrap my arm around her waist, pinning her arms down in an iron clad hold.

"Gemma," I whisper against her ear, her skin moist and her hair dripping.

She screams against my hand as her body goes rigid.

"Sssshhhhh, I'm not going to hurt you," I whisper gently.

Her chest is heaving, I can see her eyes are wide in terror, and her body begins to shake.

I press my front firmly to her back, knowing she can feel my erection pressed against her round cheeks. She jumps in my grip but I hold her tight.

I press my cheek against hers and tell her again quietly, "I'm not going to hurt you."

I hold her tightly, both of us very still, giving her a minute to settle down, neither of us moving or saying a word.

"You know me..." She thrashes in my tight grip. "I've seen you watching me, Gemma. I've seen the hunger in your eyes, your need." She freezes. "I want to take my hand from your mouth...if you promise not to scream." She feverishly nods her head. "Good girl." My hand loosens on her mouth but doesn't leave it. She makes no sound, my hold turns to a capture of her jaw. I feel her hard intake of breath. I shift my face slightly and slide my tongue slowly up her cheek.

"Who are you?" she pants out, her heart pounding against my arm.

"Who do you think I am?" I whisper against her ear.

She doesn't answer.

"I've come to give you want you need."

Gemma

My first screeching thought was someone Malcolm had robbed was coming to kill me.

The next mind-numbing thought was it's some maniac coming to rape me.

My wish is that it's Alexander Black.

He said I knew him, said I wanted him.

"Let me see you," the words come out choked.

"No," he whispers firmly.

His grip loosens around me to free his hand to rest on my stomach, fingers splayed out. The intimate touch sends a ripple through every part of me.

"Are you going to kill me?" I rasp out, barely hearing the words over the pounding of my heart.

"I told you I'm not going to hurt you," his

hushed words lick across my neck.

I can't think, my thoughts are swirling around my mind in a chaotic mess.

"Ssshhh, Gemma, just relax…and let go," he whispers again roughly, his breath brushing the flushed, damp skin where his tongue stroked me. Another heated tremor.

His fingers begin to float against the flesh of my rigid body causing goosebumps to erupt over my nakedness and my nipples to harden. I can't stop my body's reaction to his touch.

"You have such beautiful tits, Gemma, absolutely perfect," his whisper is rougher as he begins to draw slow circles over my breasts with his fingertip. Jolts of electricity surge from the point of his touch straight to my loins. His mouth and tongue move over my skin slowly and hypnotically, licking, nipping, sucking, overloading me with sensation.

The tidal wave of emotions pounding down on me makes my knees buckle: lust, fear, need, confusion.

"Stop," the word comes out in a gasp.

I know I must fight him but I can't. The sweetest drug of desire is melting me, caress by torturously delicious caress.

"No." He flicks my nipple gently with the tip of his finger as his teeth softly capture my jaw. His tongue glides a long lick up my shoulder and neck to move over my ear and I swallow the moan that almost escapes me. Molten heat morphs with the fear coursing through me and ignites the nerve endings in my skin where he touches it. His fingertips capture the point and he begins to tug and twist it, pinch and flick it, sending a rush of pulsing shockwaves straight to my core.

The desire from Black that had begun on Monday, the one that had never quite seemed to dissipate, the fiery liquid that had burned hot all through dinner, was now escalating into the beginnings of a raging inferno. He is seducing me, breaking me down, consuming me in the darkness.

This man I can't see licks then nibbles, sucks then bites, blazing a trail down my neck with his mouth, (my neck instinctively bends freely under his assault), then down the front of my throat to dip in the hollow beneath it. I could sense he is tall, tall enough to curve over my body, and hard, his body pressing against my back. And very aroused. I know this because my body wants to grind onto his erection pressed against my ass. I hadn't comprehended he'd tugged the towel gently from my grip, but it's gone because my hands are empty, clenching at my sides. As his mouth explores me and one hand teases and tantalizes my breasts, his other begins to mimic the circular strokes down the flesh on my front, going round my belly button, over my hip bones, then to outline my highly sensitive mound. I must have parted my legs because they're open, allowing his fingers to brush along the creases on each side of my sex. A soft hungry moan slips past my lips.

He's expertly stripping me of my defenses bit by bit, with each touch of his finger and every stroke of his tongue. I have no control. His take-over of my body is happening so fast I have no time to think, only feel and surrender. My mind is frenzied, crashing in a sea of erotic oblivion as the darkness envelopes us in a thick cocoon of danger and passion. The only thing I'm aware of is his touch, his breath, his mouth, and the places he touches me with them.

"So wet...," he whispers huskily.

I knew I was wet, very wet, I'd already been aroused when I'd gotten home. This ravagement had grabbed that lingering need and was running with it.

A single finger traces my folds, circles my entrance, then dips inside me.

Oh God...

"No...," I moan.

"Yes..." His lips flutter against my ear, the soft moist tip of his tongue outlines the shell.

My walls instinctively grip it, needing more, wanting him to fill me. My traitorous body yields to him as my head falls back against his chest. I hated that I loved how he smelled like a man, a hint of sweat, male muskiness, and soap. It made my mouth water wanting to taste him. His teeth bite down on my collar bone, just shy of too painful, but just enough. My back arches pressing my ass into him and my breast into his hand.

"I'm going to touch your clit, Gemma, and you're going to come."

I can't fight his domination of my body, I have no control.

Predator, domination, captive...Black's words echo somewhere in my mind.

A moan comes from a deep carnal place inside me, the place I'd always kept hidden. This man had found that door and thrown it open, letting everything out.

With his mouth on my shoulder, a nipple between two fingers, his finger flicks my clit, and my body shakes. The climax starts from low in my belly and seeps downward causing a ripple of pulsing and throbbing as my breasts hang heavy and hungry.

"Oh God, please…," I groan deeply.

I needed more.

He gave it to me.

He bites down on my shoulder, pinches my nipple hard, and presses his finger on my clit and rubs.

"Yessss!" I hiss out and wantonly ride his finger as the jolts of pain from his bite and his hard grip on my nipple shoot through me, coming as he'd commanded. Mindless with erotic need. It is so good.

His animalistic growl vibrates against my flesh as he palms my sex and grinds it into me. I want him to fuck me so hard, I could scream.

"Such a hungry little pussy, Gemma," he whispers hoarsely against my ear.

Yes, please give me more! I beg silently, grinding into his hand.

His touch turns softer as I begin to come back down.

He states quietly into my ear, "I'm going to blindfold you now. Then you're going to lay on the bed. I'm going to restrain your wrists and feet. Then I'm going to suck your cunt. I've been dying to taste you, Gemma, smell you, have the memory of it make me hard for days."

His words make my insides throb hungrily, aching to be filled.

"Let me see you."

"No, you can't see me or touch me."

What he described, being taken in darkness, bound and captive by a predator is so darkly thrilling, it sends a shiver up my spine.

"You like it, Gemma."

I didn't reply, I couldn't, but he knew. I was so ashamed, so embarrassed because I didn't fight. I wanted him to do so much more.

"There are so many things you're going to like, things you've been afraid to admit even to yourself alone in the dark," his whispers caress my soul as the soft fabric of the blindfold falls gently against my skin. I tremble again, fear still making my heart pound as its voice tells me to run, but hunger makes my body ache, wanting all that he promises.

Securing the blindfold over my eyes, he says, "I'm going to lead you to the bed," as he strokes my arms.

The caress helps to stop the hint of hysteria flashing inside me.

"I'm not going to hurt you. Trust me Gemma."

He doesn't move just strokes and pets me, waiting for my tenseness to soften under his touch.

I believe him.

My body slowly relaxes as I breathe out heavily, his hands weaving a spell over me. His tongue glides up my throat again as he clasps my arms before moving me to the bed.

"Bend over and touch the bed in front of you." His whisper is firm.

I do.

He strokes my exposed sex with a single digit. The light touch makes my body quiver willing it to slip inside me.

"Get on the bed and lay on your back."

My heart is pounding in my ears. I'm so scared and so turned on, I can't think. But I do what he tells me to.

"Good girl," I hear him whisper.

Shockingly the praise makes my heart skip.

"Raise your arms over your head, Gemma, together. I'm going to tie your wrists."

My breathing is fast and my mouth is dry. I do as he asks and slowly raise my arms over my head. Everything is magnified because of the darkness I'm in. The touch of his fingers on my skin, moving so softly with a feather light touch, sends shivers through me. He glides them up one side, then over my breasts, my mouth, the blindfold, down my neck, shoulder, side, the curve of my hip, then up the inside of my thigh. Both his hands travel down my legs until he's at my ankles, his grip wrapping lightly around them.

"I'm going to pull you down a little to where I need you."

"Okay," I breathe out heavily.

"Such a good girl, Gemma."

He places open mouth kisses on the tops of my feet then the arch, one foot then the other, as I feel the slip of fabric encircling my ankles,

There's nothing but blackness and his voice, the bed underneath me, the feel of the ties around my ankles, and the tingling in my skin where he touched me. Then the sound of his clothes rustling. I know he's getting naked. My eyes fly open behind the blindfold but there's nothing. The sound of his zipper ignites a trail of nerves straight down my body stopping right between my thighs. The bed dips and creaks and I know it's from the weight of his body.

My breathing is ragged meeting the pounding of my heart. The image my mind's eye sees is Black, confident, intimidating, coming in for the kill. It's all erotically overwhelming and scary as hell.

The faceless man grips my ankles firmly but doesn't move. His hold begins to unbelievably calm and ground me with the surety of his touch.

"Trust me Gemma," I hear through the whooshing noise of my blood pumping through my body inside my head.

He might have broken in my house, subdued me and is tying me up. Something tells me he's not going to hurt me. I know in my heart in some sick way I *can* trust him. What I can't admit it is that I want to.

I close my eyes. My focus is drawn to where our bodies are joined with his hands on my body, the spot throbbing, wanting more. I take a deep breath and tip my head back.

Alexander

That was the moment she submitted. When she exhaled, freeing her body with the simple tip of her head, she let go.

She is mine to do what I want.

I realize I have to go slow and gain her trust. It's a lot for a strong and intelligent woman to find a strange man in her house taking her sexually. It's a hell of a lot more to make her want it.

She's just handed me that trust. It's up to me to show her she made the right choice. I have no doubt that I will.

My grip tightens around her ankles, "I'm going to slide up your body now, Gemma, and bind your wrists."

"No," she responds automatically.

"Yes, pet," I say as I begin the slow ascent up her body, beginning with my hands moving up the insides of her thighs.

Her hands jerk down to stop me. I stop her from shooting up from the mattress with a hand at the center of her chest.

"Ssssshhh, Gemma. Don't touch me or I'll stop."

The statement freezes her as I thought it would.

"Grab the headboard and hold on tight. Don't let go."

I see her small hands move slowly back to where they were over her head and her fingers curl around the brass.

Returning both my hands to her thighs, I squeeze the meaty flesh.

"First, I have to have a small taste. Keep your hands there Gemma," I warn her.

My tone barely goes above a whisper. I can't risk her recognizing my voice, or feeling my face and seeing my features with the touch of her hands.

My mouth is already watering when I dip my head between her legs and take a long slow swipe over her glistening pink lips. I've been waiting for this since I whiffed a small hint of her essence on her panties.

"So fucking delicious," I growl against her.

"Oh Gooooood," her moan is long and guttural.

"Be patient, you're almost ready," I whisper, stealing one more lick.

I roll a condom on then make my way up her body, sliding the length of my body against hers, with licks, bites, nibbles, and wet open kisses over her flesh. I want to mark her, leave behind proof of where I've been. All over her, inside and out. There won't be one inch of her body she can't think of and not remember my touch.

When my body is sprawled on top of hers, I resist the strong urge to kiss her, wanting to embed my taste on her tongue. My cock will have to do. I'll leave that for later. Sliding my legs over each of her sides, I sit on her pelvis, my balls dangling against her slickness. I reach above her head and wrap the silk ties around her wrists. My movements rub my tight sacks against her, teasing her and her swollen clit.

"Please…," I hear the quiet moan.

"Please what Gemma?" I ask quietly at her ear, capturing both her nipples between my fingers.

Her hips jerk up with the teasing friction of my testicles sliding against her, searching for fulfillment.

I can feel her pelvis clenching beneath me, frantically trying to find satisfaction.

She hesitates, searching for the courage to tell me what she needs.

"Tell me Gemma. It's just you. You can't see me, tell me your darkest desires. Let go…"

The silence is filled with her breathing, her scent, and the intense sexual energy between us waiting to explode.

take

CHAPTER 6

Gemma

It's so freeing, the darkness, the anonymity, the restraints. I can't do anything except feel. It's the most incredibly erotic experience, a high that's consuming me and setting me free.

But my tongue is tide, bound by my insecurities.

My need is skyrocketing with the friction of his heavy testicles against me, taking me over, pushing me higher and higher.

"I'll tell you what I'm going to do to you now, Gemma," he whispers pulling my earlobe between his teeth. "I'm going fuck your sweet cunt with my mouth, suck that hungry little clit between my lips, until your juices are spilling out all over my tongue when you come."

"Oh God...," I suck in a deep breath.

"He can't stop me, baby girl."

"I don't want Him to stop you."

Did I just say that out loud?!

He chuckles deep and low in his chest. "Good, because I'm far from finished with you."

My body pushes against his pleading for him to touch me.

"Now beg me, Gemma."

"Please," I whisper, *"please...,"* trying to convince myself I'm only doing it out of fear I'll make him angry and he'll hurt me.

I need to beg, I have to let the hunger demand it, freeing itself from its confinement.

He slides his hard muscular frame down my length until he's settled between my open legs. Resting his hands on my inner thighs, he spreads my legs wider, his fingers digging into my flesh, and begins his ravishment on me.

His mouth begins to lick my sensitive sex with complete abandon, feasting on me with a single minded focus. Consume. I'm forced to take it bound and blindfolded, every suck, every nibble, every plunge of his tongue inside me.

I feel a finger slip inside my heat, sliding in and out slow and deep, twisting and turning, bending and rubbing, his tongue circling my clit tortuously teasing me. His seductive assault on me is powerfully consuming. Nerve endings are exploding without and within me. Nothing else exists but this man between my legs.

Black....his image reverberates in my mind, his sexual presence still lingering all over me.

Sucking my clit in his skilled mouth, plucking at it with his lips, he slips his finger from my sheath, slides it down until it's pressed against my tight back hole.

I reflexively spread my legs wider. I'm panting, all coherent thought has left me, I am only lust, need, and a raging desire to be fucked.

"What a beautiful pussy Gemma, so sweet, so hungry," he rasps out, pushing the tip of his finger into my ass as his tongue rims my achingly empty hole.

"Please…," I moan again.

"Suck it in, pet, pull my finger all the way inside you. Let me feel your cunt clenching for it in your tight ass."

His words are pushing me over. I rock into his hand shamefully, stripped of all propriety. He's reduced me to banefulness, possessed by him and his domination.

"Fuck it Gemma, give that beautiful tight ass what it wants."

More, please give me more!

"Please…," I'm almost sobbing, a vortex of conflicting contradictions: fear, desire, humiliation, lust, greed.

With his finger sliding slowly in and out of my ass, he blazes a trail up my inner thigh with his teeth biting just past the point of soft as his thumb circles my clit.

"OH GOOOOOOOD!" My back lifts off the bed on the brink of diving head first into a climax I can't wait to ride.

"You need to come."

"Yes!"

"Not yet."

"Please!"

His thumb slips into my pussy and he begins to move both digits so slowly in and out of me, inch by inch, so good but not enough. Not enough at all.

"Do you want me to fuck you?"

"YES, YES, YES." My head is thrashing from side to side, I'm beyond reason, beyond denying I'm enjoying this, accepting this, *wanting* and *needing* this....wanting him. Just. Like. This.

Taken, forced, bound, blindfolded.

Exactly like this.

"Tell me."

His tongue flicks my clit.

The first tremor of my orgasm cries out.

"Fuck me, please fuck me."

The first tear seeps from the corner of my eye.

"I'm going to fuck you. But not yet."

"No, please, now..." I'm such a whore. I can't help it. He is exactly what I need. I allow myself to admit it, the silent declaration materializes in my mind, freeing me and humiliating me.

"Not yet Gemma. Trust me."

His lips pull my throbbing clit between them. Removing his thumb and leaving his finger in my ass, he begins to circle it in my tightness. When his tongue hits that vibrating nub sucked between his lips, I dive into the waves of the sweet orgasm pulsating out from my core to every part of me.

I lay rigid and motionless in the ecstasy he's giving me with only a finger and his mouth.

"Yessssssssss…oh God yes."

Sucking me, tantalizing me, it feels so good.

"*Now* I'm going to fuck you, Gemma."

In my lust drugged fog, he turns me to my stomach and pulls my hips up. The feel of his cock sliding over me makes me moan. Resting on my forearms with my wrists still tied, I lay my cheek on the bed, lips parted, eagerly waiting for him to fill me.

"Kitten, you need to be stroked." His whisper is so deliciously husky.

I don't care anymore, I passed the point of fighting long ago.

"Yes," I murmur.

"Then feel me pet, feel my cock."

Slipping inside with just the head, he pulls back out.

"So good," I whisper, letting go.

"So tight pet, so hot, so wet. Perfect. I could fuck you all night."

He pushes all the way in as he pulls my hips tightly against him. He's so hard, so wonderfully thick, filling me completely, his length presses heavily against my uterus.

"Yes, yes, yes," I whisper.

His strokes are slow and languid at first, petting me inside, the tremors of my orgasm still vibrating inside me. I grasp him tightly with my walls, hugging his thickness.

"Mmmmmmmmm."

I begin to meet his thrusts unhurriedly, keeping his pace, relishing every stroke, every inch of him building it slowly.

His fingers dig roughly into my hips. He thrusts deeper and more demanding.

"Ooooooooooh," my longing comes out in a heavy breath.

"Your cunt is so tight, so greedy pet. It loves to be fucked."

Yes, it does. Fuck it, Black, fuck it hard, fuck it deep. Fuck me, make me scream.

It's Alexander Black I'm envisioning, his power, his intensity, his body controlling me.

My fingers grab handfuls of the bedding, I dig my elbows into the mattress, bracing myself as I slam my ass into the faceless man setting me on fire, matching his demand.

"Say it pet," he commands roughly.

Why? Why do you have to break me down

completely?

"Say," smack! His hips pound into me. "It."
Smack.

"Fuck me," I growl, the last thread of my
control snapping.

Our hips pound ferociously against each
other. The sounds of our flesh slapping, the feel of
his balls hitting me, the smell of our sex filling the
air, our grunts and moans piercing the silence,
everything is fueling the hurricane about to hit. I feel
his thickness swell inside me.

"Yes, yes, yes." I still and arch my back,
taking everything he's giving me, letting it push me
over.

He leans over my back and places one hand
on the bed, bracing himself, as he slides the other
down to where our bodies meet.

"Feel that pet?" He scissors his fingers
around his cock slipping in and out of me, the heel of
his palm on my clit.

"Yes," I rasp out.

He slips his fingers back to my clit and rubs.

"Come, kitten, milk my cock with your
pussy. I want to feel you sucking me dry," his
whisper is a rough command.

I shatter. Explode. Crumble to a million
pieces. And sob with the intensity of it, the tears
pouring from my eyes.

He pounds his release into me, not letting up

on his carnal assault of my clit, the orgasmic oblivion going on and on.

He bites down on my back holding back his roar of pleasure. As the last spasms of his orgasm rocks him, he licks the love mark on me, and kisses my back tenderly. My arms and legs quiver, I am so spent, every drop of earth shattering pleasure wrung from me. Bringing us down to the bed, he strokes my skin as the last waves of desire pulse through us.

Alexander

"Tell me how long it's been Gemma," I whisper in her ear.

I feel her stiffen in my arms.

"Please stop." Her anguish is clear.

I grasp her chin firmly and kiss her cheek. "Tell me."

"Five years," she chokes out.

That worthless scumbag!

I give her a moment. She's on the verge of sobbing, humiliated and defeated. Of all the things I want to do to her, that is no longer tops on my list. My thumb strokes along the line of her jaw, caressing her until I feel her relax.

"Gemma," my tone is gentle, as gentle as I can be. "You were too much woman for him. He knew he couldn't handle you, so he tried to destroy you. He didn't succeed."

"How do you know so much about me?" her

voice is tight.

"Ah, pet, I've been waiting for you. So have you."

I feel her body tremble before I hear her holding back the sobs. I don't tell her not to cry, that everything will be okay. Instead, this time I make love to her crying in my arms. The rush of emotions pouring from her is intense and overwhelming. Everything she's kept locked up tight is coming out in torrents as some of her demons are finally released. I take her gently, adoring her body, showing her how much she's also wanted tenderly and with devotion. I'm embracing the pain inside her, caressing it, letting her know that too is beautiful.

She falls asleep content, but broken. And she is beautiful.

Gemma

When I'd awoken from the deepest sleep I've had in months, I felt I didn't wake up alone. There wasn't a body there but the faceless man's presence was all over me. First I felt the ghosts of his touch, his teeth, lips, and tongue. I could smell the heat of our passion hanging heavy in the air. Then my loins clenched searching for his thickness wanting to be filled by him again. The blindfold had slipped from my eyes. I draped an arm over them in its place. I laid there listening for him, reaching out with my senses. He wasn't there. My mind relived the night, the total erotic abandon, his captivity of me. A shiver traveled through my body.

That's when I saw them, the handprints in black ink drawn on my breasts, big man's hands like they were being filled with me. I pulled the blanket down and saw the note he left me…written on my abdomen. It read, "I'll be back," in big letters covering me from breasts to pelvis. Below that, a handprint captured my mound, gripping me, possessing me. And on each thigh two hand prints, as if holding my legs spread open for him, with bruises at each fingertip. My stomach did a somersault of delight, a twisted sense of glee filled me, hand in hand with guilt. This was undoubtedly the most warped, wonderful thing any man has ever given me. I traced each line over and over again, then closed my eyes reliving every moment while I cried, raw and vulnerable.

On Sunday when I walked into Gina's for dinner, cannoli's in tow, I was still fighting with myself, berating myself for longing for more of him, my Faceless Man. Refusing to accept I loved he was still on my body.

I handed the dessert to my best friend and hugged her tightly, unable to hide the fact I'd been fucked into oblivion.

"Did you screw Alexander Black already?"

"What? No, can't I just be happy to see you?"

I asked knowing full well my face was beet red.

I felt like I'd gotten caught reading my dad's Playboy magazines.

"I know 'seeing my friend happy' and I know 'a good lay happy'. That is definitely not the first one."

Gina was a good friend, and a damn good lawyer. I was busted.

"I'm just feeling good. I'm working again and I actually like it. I'm getting out, here with you. Hopefully life is going to be better for me."

Her facial features softened and her expression looked slightly pained.

"I know, I'm sorry. I should have been there for you more."

Now I felt guilty for lying. She'd read me like a book and I turned it around on her.

"Stop. You tried. I kept the door locked and wouldn't let anyone in. I'm at a better place now." I shrugged sheepishly. "Better late than never."

She put her arm around me and pulled me close, leading me to the kitchen. "Come on, everyone's waiting for you."

"What do you mean *everyone?*" I asked a little nervous.

"You know what I mean, it's family day."

In the dining room, Gina's husband Frankie was feeding the baby in the high chair, her other two boys were playing with their Matchbox cars on the floor, and Tony was there on the phone.

I suddenly felt a little uneasy.

Tony jerked his head to the side, motioning for me to go to him and patted the empty chair at his side. I followed Gina into the kitchen instead.

I'd found myself going out of my way to be anywhere else but near Tony. After dinner, he cornered me upstairs when I went up to get some diapers for Gina.

"What is wrong with you, Gem?"

"Nothing." My heart was pounding and I was feeling really uncomfortable, but I couldn't put my finger on exactly why.

He came up behind me and put his hands on my hips as I bent over to take the diapers out of the baby's dressing table.

"What are you doing, Tony?" I asked jumping.

"Nothing babe. It's good to see you."

"It's good to see you too," I backed away. I was tense and wanted to get back downstairs.

"Show me." He got me in a corner and closed me in with his body, lowering his face to kiss me.

"Where's your wife Tony?" If that wasn't a cock blocker, nothing was.

"She's at home where she belongs."

What an asshole.

He wrapped his hands around my arms and squeezed them tightly, bringing his mouth to mine again. I jerked my face to the side and his lips landed on my cheek.

"Come on, babe, I know you've got to be lonely. I'll fix that. It used to be good between us."

"Stop Tony. I'm not lonely. And you're a married man."

"Who are you fucking Gemma? Is it that slimeball Black?"

You've got a lot of nerve, your hands are so filthy I don't know how you can touch your kids!

He was making me feel dirty and cheap and it was pissing me off.

"*IF* I was fucking anyone, it wouldn't be any of your business. Now let me go."

"Everything about you is my business now. Remember the family is taking care of you."

Something about the way he'd said it made me feel extremely uneasy.

"I appreciate it. But Malcolm is in jail and there's nothing else he can do to me so you don't have to worry about me. I don't need any help."

"Too late Gemma. It's already done."

With the mob, that could mean so many things. But my mind couldn't apply that to me. I didn't ask for any help from them, so I felt I wasn't indebted to them.

The salvation of Gina's voice came from downstairs. "Hurry up, Gem! The baby's getting fidgety."

"Gotta go Tony."

"It's not finished Gemma. It hasn't even started."

Warning bells went off inside my head.

take

CHAPTER 7

Gemma

I'd bought the biggest, blackest pair of sunglasses I could find to hide behind so I could study everyone I passed in obscurity. All the men on the trains, on the platforms, the street, even at the coffee shop. I was certain I'd know the Faceless Man if I saw him, how could I not after being so intimate? There wasn't a single man I could recall I've looked at with even the slightest interest, forget about attraction. None but one. I walk into the office behind my protection and look at that man, Alexander Black, very intently.

*Oh God...*he is too beautiful for words. Today he is sleek in a light grey Armani double breasted suit, matching tie, and pink shirt. His dark hair and skin color are stunning against the light colors, his ice blue eyes glowing with intensity

My body reacts to him of its own accord, heating and pulsing. It's even worse now since Friday night and the Faceless Man than before. The power of the sexual energy between us hits me with such unexpected force my breath catches in my lungs, my breasts actually seem to quiver, and my loins tighten. My body tingles with the memory of his touch, the places where he'd marked me with black ink seem strongest, like a branding. My eyelids dip behind their protection recalling the intense arousal. I walk to my desk trying my damnedest to look nonchalant and unaffected.

It is these times early in the morning when Alexander and I are here alone before the world dumps on us and contaminates the electricity that surges between us that it's the strongest. It shines brightly with jolts of energy, sparks crackling threatening to burn us with its strength. The air pulses with it.

Doing the same thing I've done every morning since I started with Black, I unload my things first, but today I slip my regular glasses on as well. I need to hind behind these barriers between me and the world. I admit it. I still feel raw and vulnerable. I want nothing more than to be as bland as possible. I head to the bathroom to make sure my reserved mask is believable. When I return to my desk, I glance at Black in his office, worrying my lip between my teeth.

I have no reason to be nervous. No one knows and no one can see. It's your secret.

I'd fought with myself nonstop all weekend because I *didn't want* to call the police and report the intrusion. I'm still badgering myself about it.

What is wrong with me? Am I so pathetic to have a man's attention? I didn't fight him, I let him take me...I wanted *him to take me. Oh God, I wanted him to touch me, bite me, suck me, fuck me like he wanted to punish me.*

I rationalized it was because he said I knew him, but that was a convenient excuse I'd latched onto, a perfect alibi.

And those black handprints he left on me should have horrified me. But it was so...possessive, marking me, branding me. And I loved it. I'm so horrible!

The message scrawled across my abdomen in that same blank ink that said he'd be back should have had me running to change my locks and bar the windows. Instead, my mind screamed in heated anticipation, "WHEN?"

I relished the knowledge I had his marks still on my flesh beneath my clothes. I didn't want them to disappear, I'd lain in my bed tracing the outlines reliving that dark erotic night, the feel of his touch still haunting my skin. Sometimes I cried, sometimes I climaxed, but every time my body ached for his touch, needing him, wanting him, begging him silently to please return. With fear lacing that lust.

I don't know how long I've been sitting dazed, staring at my computer, coffee and croissant untouched when the IM pings a message.

Are you ill Ms. Trudeau? Alexander Black

The sound jolted me from my memories battling with my feelings.

No Mr. Black, why? Gemma Trudeau

Because you've been sitting there for fifteen minutes deep in thought. Was your weekend so memorable, you can't leave it? Alexander Black

I feel my face flush with the rush of embarrassment overcoming me.

You are a professional, Gemma, get a grip and compose yourself.

I don't bring my personal life to work, Mr. Black. Gemma Trudeau

When you're here, you belong to me. I don't want anything or anyone interfering. Understood Ms. Trudeau? Alexander Black

Gemma the lawyer would have argued that he had nothing to do with me other than being my employer. The still sex drugged me is in psychological and emotional turmoil. The man I'd envisioned being The Faceless Man *was* Alexander Black. Every swipe of his tongue, every pinch, bite, caress, thrust, everything was him. It had been Black's face I saw in the blackness. To me those are his hands etched on my flesh. The naked woman was bending to the voice in the dark, saying, "Yes, I belong to you. My body is yours to do what you wish."

Fortunately, there is still some clarity in my sex drugged brain.

Mr. Black, I assure you I am a professional. When I am here Black Inc. is my only concern. Gemma Trudeau.

I am Black Inc., therefore, the only thing in that brilliant beautiful mind of yours is me. Alexander Black

Narcissist or not, Black has no idea how completely right he is.

Alexander

I'd watched her struggle all weekend, torn between doing what she thought she should do and call the police, and reliving the dark night with her faceless man ravishing her.

Me.

She'd even picked up the phone and dialed it a few times, only to not connect the call. Then other times she would touch herself, fuck herself, place her hands within the black handprint outlines I'd drawn, then scream out her release as tears slipped from her eyes.

It was evident she was having an internal battle. On one side she wanted to follow her conscience and do what was supposedly morally correct, then put the incident away like a car accident: horrible but something to overcome. On the other hand, she allowed herself to admit the night and the man was almost everything she secretly desired, the taboo and the erotically forbidden.

Almost.

She knew she wanted more, more darkness, more forbidden...more.

I knew it too.

I saw it all over her. How her body had yielded to me, wet and hungry, begging to be taken, forced, fucked, used and submerged in ecstasy.

She's trying to hide that sexual animal inside her, barricading herself in those demure clothes. That plain tan dress does nothing to hide her passion, it oozes from her. She'd even toned down her make-up opting for nude lipstick instead of the I-Want-To-Suck-Your-Cock red. The only thing she allowed herself to indulge the sex goddess inside her are the six inch Please-Fuck-Me heels. Her glasses? They only make me want to have her on her knees in front of me while wearing them.

I have no doubt if I stroked her succulent pussy lips, they'd be slick with need.

First goal, make her want.

As she'd sat staring lost in thought, I knew she wanted. More.

Second goal, make her need.

An individual would do practically anything when their need is powerful enough.

I'm going to make Gemma Trudeau need so badly, it will make her insane if she doesn't get it.

Gemma

The copyright infringement case is pretty cut and dry. Mostly time consuming research, mindless work swimming through miles and miles of information to confirm registrations.

Exactly what I need.

I didn't need anything that would tip me over to one side of the precarious perch I'd established for myself on a ledge of 'even keel'.

"Gemma Trudeau, Miles Davis' office," I answer the phone.

"Mrs. Stevens," a man's voice replies.

Caution makes the hair stand up at the back of my neck.

"It's Ms. Trudeau, how can I help you?" I answer flatly.

"You're working for Black, how interesting," he states lazily.

"Are you a client?" I force professionalism into my tone.

"You could say something like that," he responds, sarcastic amusement dripping from his voice.

"What *exactly* would you say then?" I ask,

holding back my impatience.

"More of an interested party, my dear," he coos.

"Interested for whom?" I ask, completely wary of this stranger.

"In due time, my lovely Gemma."

The line goes dead.

I'm thoroughly perplexed by the strange phone call.

I know I'm not exactly non-existent to the public because of the publicity Malcom's received, and all of it was bad. But this call seemed to be something more than a curious individual.

The phone jars me again.

"Ms. Trudeau."

"Yes." It's Natasha, the stunning young receptionist that looks like a Nubian princess.

"You have a delivery here. Shall I send someone back with them?" she asks excitedly.

Them?

"No thank you, Natasha. No need to bother anyone. I'll be right up."

"You don't have to hurry. I wish someone would send me something so beautiful," she coos almost breathlessly.

Oh shit, now what?

"I'll be right up," I say hurriedly and rush to reception.

When I exit through the frosted main glass

doors of Black Inc. into the reception area, I halt mid-stride. I know Natasha is somewhere behind that huge black lacquered desk but I can't see her behind the mountain of long stemmed red roses.

"No…," I whisper shaking my head.

"Yes!" Natasha squeals. "You are soooooooooo lucky. Someone must really have it bad for you. There must be four or five dozen here," she adds giddily practically clapping her hands and jumping up and down like a little kid with a surprise.

Some of the girls I wasn't acquainted with yet in the office come scurrying out. Natasha must have called them, filling them in on the latest office gossip.

"Oh my God, Gemma, who are they from?"

"They're beautiful!"

"Where can I get me a man that would send me those?"

I stand frozen in place, so many things running through my mind. None of them good.

"There's a card, Gemma. Open it!" Natasha squeals again, waving the little white envelope at me.

I'm so happy that there's no one waiting in reception as I approach the falsely innocent looking little piece of paper that has the capacity to be deadly. I tentatively take it from Natasha's clutches with just the tips of my fingers as if it would combust on contact. This innocuous two by three piece of paper has the ability to throw a bomb into the one thing in my life that could be good right now.

I cautiously slip a fingernail inside the tiny opening.

"Hurry up!" the girls say in unison.

I take a deep breath and tear it open.

Who are they from? Tony or Malcolm?

The thought of either one of them makes my blood boil.

I pull the card from its enclosure. It is a bright white heavy card stock, embossed and printed with the logo of the finest florist in Manhattan, La Vie en Rose.

I'm shocked.

I will see you again soon. Very soon. XOXO

The Faceless Man.

He knows where I work.

"Who are they from?" Natasha asks impatiently.

"No one...," I mumble.

"It's obviously *someone* or they wouldn't be sitting here. Tell us Gemma, we're dying!"

"Someone I...um...," what Gemma? "Someone I just met."

"You *just* met him? Like this weekend?"

"Yes, Friday..."

"How romantic, I am SO jealous."

"Me too," the others chime in.

Romance had absolutely nothing to do with it, I laugh.

A warm feeling seeps through me followed by flashes of desire pulsing in my veins, igniting me all over again.

He sent me flowers.

I'm stunned.

"Okay, back to work ladies. It's no big deal," I try to get some control over the Hallmark moment.

"*THOSE* are mostly certainly a big deal!"

I grab the massive arrangement from Natasha's desk and go back to the door. Unfortunately, I can't open it. The flowers are too big and too heavy.

"I got it," one of the girls rush over to get it for me.

I walk stiffly back to my desk refusing to make eye contact with anyone. Especially not with Alexander Black.

The strong perfume of the roses fills my senses and my space, followed by the scent of a man, a hint of sweat, a hint of soap, and his erotic muskiness in the throes of passion. I breathe in deeply and close my eyes allowing myself a moment of weakness, and I moan softly.

Alexander

She liked the roses. She accepted them.

I grin.

All morning I'd watched how tense and distracted she'd been. The roses seem to have given her a sense of comfort. Maybe she feels relieved that she'd made the right decision not reporting the incident to the police.

Excellent.

"Mr. Black?" Simon's voice asks over the intercom.

"Yes."

"There's a Mr. Tony Salvatore on the phone for you. He said you'd take his call, in quite a colorful way."

"He did, did he?"

Tony Salvatore, Gina Salvatore Franco's brother, Gemma's friend. And Gemma's childhood boyfriend. The son of the first in command to the Capo di Tutti Capi, head of one of New Jersey's major crime families.

"He said it was about Ms. Trudeau," Simon adds.

"Put him through."

I grab the receiver as soon as the line blinks.

"What do you want?"

"Black, long time no see. How you been, Gumba?" the arrogant asshole asks in his heavy Jersey mob accent.

"Cut the shit, Salvatore."

The last time I saw Tony Salvatore was at a sit-down with his father, a meeting of the minds between business associates. That was ten years ago. Things have been going well since then.

The first time I saw Tony Salvatore was on the street, my fist was pounding his head in the pavement while my boys were busy with his crew. That was twenty years ago.

"Gemma. She's ours, she belongs to the family. Which means she belongs to me. Don't forget it, Black."

"Oh? Last I heard she was married to Malcolm Stevens."

"We're protecting her."

My jaw clenches and I grip the receiver tightly.

"Does she know this?"

"Yes, Black, she knows."

I could hear the satisfied sadistic smile in his voice.

"Did she *ask* for it Salvatore?"

"It doesn't matter. She's mine, Black. Stay the fuck away from her," the cold hatred poured from him.

"Now that I allowed you to spill the sewage from that cesspool you call a mouth, you will listen to me. In case you have forgotten, I own you and your family. If you touch her in anyway, I'm going to kill you. Then all the business dealings your family is involved in will be immediately terminated. You will be responsible for starting a war because torturing two women isn't enough for you. I will not let you do that Gemma." My voice is barely above a threatening whisper.

"You filthy little homeless boy. You think you can tell me what to do?"

The boy those comments used to hurt no longer exists. They only make me smile.

"Salvatore, you will not get another warning."

Slamming down the phone, I throw open the door to my office and go directly to Gemma.

I grab her by the arm and drag her to my office before she realizes it.

"Sit down," I tell her.

I'm dangerously close to losing my temper. My tone is quiet and icy, restraining the rage engulfing me.

"What is it?"

Locking the door, I walk to my desk and press the button that frosts the glass. No one needs to hear or see what's going on in here.

"Would you like to tell me what your involvement is with the Salvatore family?"

She blinks at me trying to comprehend the question.

"They're friends of my family. That's it."

I take a deep breath before I begin.

"Apparently not according to Tony Salvatore."

"What did that asshole say?" The ruthless lawyer is back, her fire flaring in Gemma's eyes.

"He just called me…"

"*He* called *you?!*"

"Yes."

"And you took his call?"

"The family and my company do business together."

She might as well know some of the truth if she's going to be an attorney in my firm.

"The Salvatore family and Black Inc. do business together. And with UN Ambassadors."

As long as young girls are beheaded because they were raped by an old man, and pregnant sixteen year olds run away after being tortured and raped for years by their stepfather, I will do business with anyone I have to.

"The D'Angelo family. Vinny D'Angelo."

"You're shitting me, right?"

"Ms. Trudeau…and no, I'm not shitting you. Back to the question, what is *your* involvement with them?"

"Nothing. I swear. My dad was friends with Tony's dad, John, when they were kids. The daughter Gina was and is my best friend. That's it."

"Then why does Tony Salvatore think that you belong to him?"

"*WHAT?!*"

"Tony Salvatore said you are under their protection. Therefore, he thinks you belong to him." I raise my hand to stop her outburst. "*If* you entered into an agreement with them asking for their protection, then yes, you in fact are indebted to them. Did you offer yourself to that scumbag in return for protection? Tell me the truth."

I need to know everything before I can proceed in dealing with this situation. Which has turned into a major cluster fuck. Not only am I trying to find out if she helped her ex steal three million dollars from me, I might have to protect her from the psychopath Tony Salvatore.

"I did *NOT* do any such thing. When I moved back into my parent's house after mine was confiscated by the feds, Tony came to me and told me that the family would take care of me if I needed anything, to come to them first. He said that they're watching out for me. I never went to them and asked for anything, nor did I ask for their protection. That's everything."

I study her face. I know she's not telling me something.

"There's more."

That beautiful ass of hers squirms in the seat, and my dick starts to get hard remembering pounding into her.

She lets out a heavy breath. "I was at Gina's yesterday for dinner. Tony was there, he tried to kiss me, and reminded me again about the family taking care of me."

"What *exactly* did he say?"

"He said, 'Everything about you is my business now. Remember the family is taking care of you.' I told him Malcolm is in jail and I don't need it. He said it was too late, it was already done." She's twisting her hands nervously in her lap.

"Did he send you the flowers?"

"Of course not!"

"Who did?" I narrow my eyes at her.

She glares at me and clamps her mouth shut, her nostrils flaring.

"Did you fuck Salvatore?"

"WHAT!? NO, I didn't fuck him, I didn't even let him kiss me. He makes me sick."

"You fucked him before."

That knocks her off guard.

"You know quite a bit about me, Mr. Black, don't you?"

"Your husband stole three million dollars from me, and you work for *me*. I told you, when you're here, you belong to me. I need to know everything about everyone that belongs to me. But you, you're special." I smile crookedly at her, a dangerous grin letting her know I mean a lot more.

"I understand that," she replies curtly, quickly pulling her guard back up. "I assure you, I have no dealings with them other than what I've told you. I did not ask for help nor did I offer myself in return."

I approach her slowly. When I reach her

she's pressed against the back of the chair, hands holding the arm rests tightly. I place my hands on the chair back, bending down so my face is an inch from hers.

I say dangerously quiet, "Listen to me carefully Gemma. Tony Salvatore is a psychopath. Do *NOT* trust him. Don't be alone with him. If I find out you have fucked him or *are* fucking him, I'm going to tie you over this desk, strip your ass, and spank you so hard, you will beg for mercy. Then I'm going to lock you in a room in my house so you wouldn't be stupid enough to do it again. I. Am. Not. Kidding." I stare into her eyes, daring her to say one word. "Understand?"

"You wouldn't dare." Her eyes are glazed, her breathing is heavy.

She's aroused by the image.

"I would without hesitation. Tell me Gemma, how many more men do you want to destroy you and ruin your life? Malcolm wasn't enough, you want Tony Salvatore to do it too? Because that's exactly what would happen. Except with him, you would probably end up dead."

The words hang heavy in the air like the ticking of a bomb.

Her eyes widen with fear. Those lips I want to suck open. I place my hand on her chest between her breasts and feel her heart pounding against it. The simple touch claiming her. My mouth comes down hard on hers, crushing her lips, I shove my tongue into her mouth, consuming her, taking her.

Fuck, she tastes so sweet, I growl.

She grabs the lapels of my jacket and grinds her mouth into mine, fighting me with her tongue. The kiss is savage and ferocious. I lean in and push her body back, forcing her to take it, take everything I'm giving her. Her arms wrap around me, her hands sift into my hair, holding me close.

I want to punish her for being so damn naïve, so damn beautiful…and making me want her so much.

take

CHAPTER 8

Alexander

Watching Gemma dress has become part of my every day. As I'm on the phone at dawn with my international associates, she's there with me. Unfortunately, it's on the computer monitors. I should feel guilty about this invasion. But I don't. I *am* sick and twisted, life made me this way and I don't apologize for it. I don't know when it happened, but I *need* to see her like this, unguarded and free.

Entering her bedroom, the soft early morning sun is filtering in through the window and gives a golden glow to her pale skin. I'm mesmerized when she slides on her lingerie, some with little bows, others with ruching between her ass cheeks. Then she places her foot on the bed to slowly pull up her stockings, clipping the tops just beneath the bare flesh. My mouth waters wanting to run my tongue along the edge, then slightly sink my teeth into the meaty flesh just before I graze my nose against the heat between her spread thighs and smell her arousal. And at night alone I watch her and listen as she talks to that stupid cat that doesn't shut up. She loves that cat, spoils it and coddles it. I hate to admit it, but I'm jealous of the mangy thing. When she climbs into bed I can almost feel the softness of her skin beneath my hands, her lush little body pressed against mine. I have to remind myself that she might also have been involved with Malcolm in his scheme.

But each day it's getting harder and harder to believe it.

I ordered a single black long stemmed rose to arrive at precisely eleven this morning. On time, I watch the elevator door open with the delivery man carrying the long white box tied with a sheer black ribbon. Natasha's face lights up. She couldn't be more excited if it was her own.

I make a note to have flowers delivered to all the females who work for me. Women should get flowers sometimes for no reason at all. I take care of what's mine.

A minute later Gemma walks through the doors eyes wide, prepared for the worst.

A pang runs through me.

She shouldn't have had to go through this shit with Malcolm, she doesn't deserve it.

Another sneering voice retorts, *Well, what about you? What are you doing to her? Playing mind trips, lying, that's what,*

"I'm giving her pleasure, making her realize the woman she is."

Bullshit, you're trying to break her down so she'll collapse under pressure.

The painful honesty makes me wince.

But not enough to stop me.

She's followed by a group of girls, most of them from accounting, all of them smiling and giggling.

I watch as she reads the card, her hand going to her chest to stroke a fingertip along the bare skin at her neckline. I see the flush creep up from beneath it, up her neck then to her face. Her lips open slightly and a ghost of a smile plays at a corner of her lips.

Natasha's demanding Gemma tell her what the card says. Not looking at her, she tells her.

Tonight. XOXO

"Oh my God, that is soooooooooo romantic. I want to know all the deets on Monday morning," Natasha squeals.

"Yes!"

"Definitely!"

Gemma blushes.

"There won't be anything to tell," she replies smiling shyly.

"Oh please. The only thing I need to know is

if that secret man can out-do my book boyfriends," Natasha comments and rolls her eyes.

Gemma turns a bright crimson and laughs, bowing her head to hide it.

"You bet your ass I will," I murmur.

At nine o'clock I park the van on Gemma's street. I'm fuming. Jesús phoned me at seven stating Ramon called and that Tony Salvatore had just pulled up at Gemma's house. I was working out so I hadn't been watching the monitors. It took every ounce of control not to order Ramon to go into the house and throw his ass out. That would have given up our surveillance, something I couldn't risk. The monitor hadn't left my side since then, I'd even taken it with me when I showered so I would know what was happening at all times. If that greasy scumbag so much as brushed a hair from her face, I was sending Ramon in balls to the wall.

Salvatore was gone fifteen minutes later. That was enough time for him show what he was after.

Gemma

"Tony, if you come barging into my home one more time, I'm calling the cops. Knock like a normal human being."

I am so furious at Tony Salvatore's arrogance, thinking he can do whatever he likes, coming into my home like he owns me and it.

"Gem, stop acting like a self-righteous bitch. You came from the same neighborhood I did, I was the first one to fuck you, and I know what a little slut you can be. You belong to us," he says with finality, plopping his tacky ass down on my couch.

"Get the fuck out of my house, Tony, and don't come back." I am so enraged, I can barely speak. "I would never belong to you, and I definitely don't belong to the family. I didn't ask for anything from them. And if you *ever* say anything like that to me again, I won't hesitate letting your father know you're trying to scare me. He won't tolerate it."

"Nobody tells me what to do, Gemma," he sneers at me.

"Get out." I hiss back.

"Is it Black? Are you fucking that wannabe already? What, has it been a week and you're already sucking his cock?" he spits out at me, moving so fast he's so close, his chest is pressed to mine.

"Get out Tony!" I step back and walk quickly to the door.

He's reaching out to grab me but his phone chimes with a message and stops him.

"Shit! I've got to go, but I'll be back."

I hold the door open and slam it when he's barely outside.

Just what I need, another man to make my life hell. Black was right.

After storming around the house for two hours, I get in the shower and let the hot water pulsate over my body, trying to wash Tony from my system. As the water streams down me in rivulets, the force of Black's kiss comes back with a vengeance again.

That kiss...

It wasn't gentle or romantic. Nothing about Alexander Black is gentle. Or romantic. He captures, he owns, he conquers. He did exactly that with his kiss. It was rough and punishing, angry and threatening, and something inside me rose up to meet his assault. I wanted to possess him, punish him like he was doing to me.

The kiss blurs into tongues licking, teeth biting, nails scratching.

...I'm going to suck your cunt... he whispered in my ear.

No, it wasn't him...

My sex aches with need, remembering how good he filled me, fucked me...The Faceless Man.

It wasn't Black.

I rest one hand one the wall to brace myself as the other slips between my legs over the slickness. The passionate force of that night with The Faceless Man surges through me and every part of me comes alive.

He's coming back tonight.

A thrill makes me tremble with both fear and

anticipation.

Christ, what's wrong with me? I loved the flowers, the handprints, the bruises from his hands and teeth. All of it. How he took me, forced me, tied me, and controlled me.

I want to hate that the mere memory of everything is enough to bring me to the brink of orgasm.

I can't. Because I want more.

"God...," I moan.

The lights go out. My head shoots up as my heart pounds and sweat instantly pores from my body.

He's here!

I'm immobilized, riveted, the scene from before playing over and over again in my mind, pounding in my brain and over my body. Finally, I slide the shower curtain open. Being careful not to make a sound, I search for the towel. Moving on autopilot, I dry myself and step softly from the tub, the cotton securely tightened around my body. When I walk out onto the landing of the stairs, the soft glow from the kitchen illuminates the downstairs foyer. My ears are silently screaming to pick up any noises. Nothing, just the pounding of my heart. I move slowly towards the bedroom and tentatively push the door all the way open while scanning the room before I step in. My heart's beating so hard and I'm trembling as I cautiously enter.

I feel him before I hear him, sensing his nearness.

"Gemma," his whisper's strong as his hand clamps over my mouth and his arm traps me.

I can't stop the scream.

"Sssssshhhh," he whispers, his lips butterflying over the thin skin of my ear, his breath stroking me.

I freeze in his grip.

"Don't scream…," he whispers again.

I shake my head frantically.

"Good girl," his lips are still at my ear.

"Did he touch you Gemma?" he whispers hoarsely.

He knows Tony was here.

That shocks me.

I move my head from side to side telling him no.

"Good, if he had I'd have to kill him," the words slip easily from him, sending a chill up my spine. "I wanted to, just knowing he was here. He's dangerous."

His declaration perversely excites me. No man has ever been protective of me. Ironic that the one man who is, is the one who broke into my house and took me sexually. It wasn't rape. Not at all, I wanted it. I want it now. I know I've been waiting for him.

"I need to fuck you Gemma."

I make no move, neither refusing nor inviting him as he waits for a sign from me.

Apparently satisfied by my reply of no reply, his hand leaves me mouth. My breathing is deep and quick, fueled by fear and rising lust. Sliding his hands to open my towel, he lets it drop to the floor then fills his palms greedily with my breasts, squeezing them tightly.

He takes, he possesses, he claims unabashedly, and God help me, it turns me on.

His voice is strained.

"It's going to be rough and it's going to be hard, Gemma. This is for me. I need to fuck the image of that scumbag here with you out of my mind."

Everything tightens within me, my walls clench and my nipples harden in his hands. Shoving a hand in my hair, he fists it at the roots and pulls my head to the side, leaving my neck open for his mouth, tongue and teeth to assault. He slides the other hand between my thighs and grasps my clit tightly between his fingers. Jolts shoot through my body from the erotic pain and it makes me tremble.

The room is black except for the filtered light of the street lamps through the window as he leads me to the wall, my hair held tightly at the roots and my clit gripped in his fingers. The fear thrills me, his need consumes me, and my body reacts feverishly.

"Don't look at me."

I scrunch my eyes shut and mutter, "No."

"If you do I'll spank you."

My heart jumps and my loins quiver.

"Mmmmm, like that little pet? Maybe I will."

He pushes me hard against the wall pressing my front against it.

"Spread your legs," he commands quietly, shoving my feet apart with one of his.

He lifts his back from mine and I hear the rustling of clothes. Then flesh against flesh as he leans into me again, the soft hair from his chest titillating my skin. I hear the tearing of paper and a spitting sound. The condom. The presence of his body is gone, replaced by a firm hand between my shoulders blades that keeps me against the wall.

"Get ready Gemma, I'm about to fuck the shit out of you."

Oh God, yes, I quietly moan.

Wrapping my hair around his hand, he begins to slide the head of his cock over my slickness and rubs my clit with it. Then he presses it into the entrance of my ready sex.

"Rough and hard, pet, hold on," he whispers gruffly at my ear before pulling the lobe between his teeth.

He grips my shoulder with his free hand, turns my head to the side with the handful of my hair to rest my cheek against the wall, then slams into me with one thrust, pulling me onto him by my shoulder.

"What a greedy, tight little pussy you have Gemma. She's so beautiful."

My nails are digging into wall, and his into my shoulder, as he pounds into me. Murmuring filthy endearments in my ear, he fucks me like an animal, primitive and wild, ravenous and completely.

He grabs me by my hips and pulls me back, bending me at the waist. I brace myself, hands against the wall, arms straight. Preparing.

"Whose cock is it when I fuck you, Gemma?"

Slam! He pounds into me, his balls banging against me.

Black... I don't answer.

He lowers his mouth to my ear. "Black." His hands clasp my nipples as his tongue licks and his teeth capture the tendon at the crook of my neck.

I grip him tightly inside as I suck in a breath.

"He wants you. But it's me who's fucking you, me who knows what you need."

A low growl comes from somewhere deep inside him.

Slam! My ass to his pelvis.

Slam! His thrusts pound my uterus.

Slam! Deep and hard.

Slam! Slam! Slam! Slam! He fucks me continuously, nonstop, slamming my ass into him with each of his thrusts, until he grinds his hips into me holding my hips tightly against him. I can't catch my orgasm, staying just beyond my grasp and slipping from my hands.

"Fuck!" he grits out tightly coming so hard, I feel his shaft thicken as it jerks inside me.

Releasing his Vulcan grip from my hipbones, he licks my spine from the base to my neck.

*Oh...*my back arches and a push into him, tilting my head back, my body reverberating from the stroke of his tongue.

"I'd love to watch my cum drip from your cunt, then dip my finger inside just to have you lick it off. Are you clean pet? I know it's been a long time since that pussy of yours has been adored."

I nod my head slowly, unable to speak because my mouth is dry from the image of his thick white cream seeping from me, him slipping his finger in coating it with our juices then giving it to me.

"Good Gemma. I am too."

He stands not pulling out from me, I can feel he's still semi-hard.

"I don't have your blindfold, you do. We'll use your panties instead."

The idea of tying my panties around my face strikes me as a touch dirty and taboo.

"It's in the...," I begin.

"It's okay, I like the thought of those sexy little things that hug your pussy on your face. You can smell what I'm smelling knowing what it does to me."

This man is so fantastically filthy.

"Don't move," he whispers in my ear, pinching my nipples.

As he moves to my dresser I listen as he opens the drawer and rifles around my lingerie.

"You must look so good in these. It's almost a shame I only see you naked."

Coming back to me, he directs me to stand to tie my underwear over my face. The faint scent of my sex wafts to my nose.

"Smell yourself Gemma? It's so much more pungent when you're aroused, thick with lust," his words stroke me like his lips at my ear.

"Get on the bed, I'm going to tie you. It's time for a little fun."

Why don't I think it's going to make me laugh?

I take the same position I had last week, hands above my head and legs spread, almost appearing eager for what he has in store for me. The Faceless Man doesn't straddle me to restrain me this time, but stands at the side and foot of the bed. His fingertips caress the length of my body, trace my contours, and outline all of my intimate ridges as he binds me tightly. Then he opens the nightstand drawer. My eyes fly open behind the strip of fabric as I turn my head toward him.

"What are you doing?" I ask almost panicking.

"Shhhhhh, I'm getting your toys," he whispers as he licks the outline of my ear and jaw.

"Why?" my voice is almost a shrill, I'm so embarrassed.

"We're going to play. The game is called 'Forced Orgasm'. Don't be embarrassed, Gemma, every woman should have toys, and they should be played with."

Oh God, no... I moan silently.

"Please don't," I whisper.

The Faceless Man gently caresses my cheek under the blindfold with his knuckle.

"I know how ludicrous this sounds, Gemma, but trust me. I would never do anything you wouldn't enjoy. I won't give you anything that won't take you out of that place you've locked yourself up in. Everything that I do is for you to free yourself. Know this. And," I can almost hear him shrug, "I love it." There's a definite hint of warped satisfaction to his tone.

I let out a heavy breath. I know everything he's just told me is the truth, I know it in my heart. Although I wasn't aware of it before, this is why I wanted more.

He is giving me myself.

The thump of my cashmere Prada bag on the tabletop makes me jump. And wince.

Here it comes, shoot me now!

Seconds tick by and the anticipation is killing

me.

"Gemma…"

"Yes?" I answer apprehensively.

"I'm going to put the clips on your nipples," he whispers. Although it's quiet, his voice is husky with arousal.

I swallow and try to make the saliva come back to my dry mouth.

"Okay."

"This is going to be intense, pet," his whisper now even quieter.

I swallow again, my heart beating wildly.

"Okay."

He begins to slowly circle each nipple getting closer and closer to the tip. With each pass my chest rises trying to push him to the needy points. Finally, he takes each one between fingers and pulls them taut. I feel the brush of the wooden clothespins along my bare areolas until they capture them just below the tips. The sweet familiar ache begins to seep from that point throughout my body. He brushes his fingertip over the captured nipple and the sensations are incredible. My lips must have opened because The Faceless Man is gliding a fingertip across my parted lips, beckoning my tongue to taste it. His flavor explodes in my mouth from that tiny contact, satisfying some unknown need in me. The decadent drug of arousal begins to wash over me and I let it begin to take me away.

The tip of the hard vibrator startles me when it makes contact with my clit. It was a light touch, soft and gentle. My walls clench recognizing its inanimate lover, welcoming it with hunger. He slides the head along my folds but doesn't enter me with it. The whirring sound of the motor startles me along with its vibration. He's got it pressed firmly against my clit. This time, he's got my arms and legs bound so tightly, there's no give for even the slightest movement. The wave of an orgasm rapidly rises and takes me with it, higher and higher, and the crash follows quickly behind it.

"Please," I moan, my breathing coming rapidly.

"You're going to come, and you're going to keep on coming pet."

The wave crashes quickly, slamming me down with the force of the orgasm.

"Oh God, oh God, oh God!" the chant spills from my mouth.

"You're far from finished Gemma."

He's right.

On the tail of that climax comes another wave blending with the first one. It throws me up and slams me down. The orgasm that evaded me when he fucked me is claiming me with a vengeance.

"Let it take you pet," he whispers holding the vibrator against my pulsating engorged clit.

My back arches pulling against the restraints,

the merciless captivity is sweet torture.

"OOOOOH GOOOOOOOD!"

My body is vibrating on such high frequency, I can't think. There's nothing except the rapid relentless pounding of climax after climax.

"I want more Gemma," I hear him whisper through the lust engulfing me.

"NOOOOOOOO!" I scream as another orgasmic wave crests.

"Yes, pet, this one is going to be special."

The pleasure is so intense it almost hurts. It's ripping me apart and squeezing me back together, throwing me around and pulling me tighter. I throw my head back and scream from the intensity. Suddenly, wetness begins to saturate me, I feel it splattering my naked thighs.

"I'm peeing!" I yell, lifting my head.

"No you're not, your squirting Gemma. It's beautiful."

He lifts the vibrator and replaces it with his hand, rubbing my sex as I shoot all over him.

The spasms of the tidal waves from my climaxes begin to recede and I slump into the bed, disoriented and panting. He removes the clips from my nipples and palms the breasts, trying to ease the discomfort. He kisses my collar bone and shoulder and whispers, "I'm going to get a towel."

When he returns, he gently wipes me then unties the restraints, rubbing my ankles and wrists tenderly as he does.

"Roll to your side, Gemma, let me take off the blanket. I'll get another."

I don't argue, I'm too spent.

"Other side pet."

He works the blanket from beneath me and replaces it with a clean, dry one. Then he lays down next to me and pulls me close. I press myself against his warmth and let his familiar scent fill me.

"You were so perfect. How do you feel?" The Faceless Man asks against my neck as he cups my breasts, my ass resting snugly in his naked groin.

"It *was* intense," I answer quietly, smiling.

He chuckles, "Yes it was. But how do you *feel*?"

His erection is growing pressed against my bare ass. An emptiness begins to grow in my loins, snaking through me, heating and pulsating inside me.

"I feel…," I try to say the words.

His hardness is now between the cheeks of my ass. My hips grind into him longingly.

"Do you feel empty?" He nibbles my shoulder. "Needy?" Pulls and twists my nipples. "Aching?" He slides a hand down my inner thigh and wraps my leg over his.

"Yes," I whisper, tilting my head back against him.

"You need, pet."

He slides into my wetness. His rhythm is

slow, taking his time, as his hands explore my body, touching, scratching, biting, nipping, marking me inside and out.

take

CHAPTER 9

Alexander

Gemma is different. I saw she's been different all weekend as I watched her. She's calmer, more relaxed and unguarded. She seems freer.

I didn't want to leave her Friday night. I wanted to wake her as I pushed into her, watching her orgasm in that in-between sleep and awake state, raw and completely bare.

I run a hand roughly through my hair frustrated.

Snap out of it Black! What the hell is wrong with you?

I wasn't supposed to want *her.* The plan was to get her close, get her in a position to be exposed, then get her vulnerable. Use whatever I had to in order to accomplish the task. A man of my means, and unscrupulousness, has a wide array of arsenals at his disposal, and very little risk, no matter the method.

Find guilt.

That was the plan.

So far, nothing has come up on her computer and communications. Outwardly, she appears to be completely innocent of any involvement with Malcolm. Intimately, she's far from innocent but apparently void of any attachment to him that way as well. It's evident that weasel hasn't been a husband to her. He'd probably only been married to her as a façade to hide his illegal dealings.

It infuriates me.

What I hadn't factored in, because it had never been a problem in the past, was getting involved. Right from the very beginning living out on the streets it has been, 'Get in and get out quickly and efficiently.'

I have no idea when it happened but it was a very sobering realization when I noticed I craved Gemma Trudeau. The thought of her made my mouth water and the blood pound through my veins. As I'd watched her dress this morning on the monitor, picking out a black lace bra and panty set with bows and velvet trim, possessiveness raged inside me. My mind screamed *MINE!* Every instinct was pushing me to claim her in the most barbaric and primitive way. I wanted to climb the stairs to her bedroom and throw her over my shoulder in her fucking lingerie and stockings, then tie her to a chair directly in front of me and keep her there. All. The. Time.

She's radiant.

I watch her as she walks from the elevator toward her desk, no hiding behind sunglasses this Monday morning, and she's glowing from within. Her outfit matches her mood, a little daring with a slit up the back of her tight red skirt, and her sleeveless metallic grey silk sweater molds her breasts perfectly. She's got on my favorite shoes, the black six inch 'I'm-Ready-To-Be-Fucked' stilettos that make her ass swish just right.

I stop pacing and halt whatever I was saying mid-sentence.

She waved at me! Wiggled those little fingers at me and smirked!

The grin spreading across my face is automatic as I nod my head at her in response. So is the tightening in my pants. She has never even acknowledged me before unless I made her in this quiet time of the morning when it's just she and I in the office. It has always been me in her face. It had all been part of the plan.

Apparently things are different and the game is changing.

I'm glad your weekend was so enjoyable Ms. Trudeau, the fact does indeed give me great pleasure.

Gemma

There was only a single hand print drawn on my stomach the next day. The note he wrote next to it said simply, 'Need'.

I wanted him so bad, I had needed him. So much I ached.

Embracing that, accepting it, made me feel alive...and strong. It seemed the world was made new and was opening itself up to me saying, 'Here, indulge, you deserve it. Live a glorious life, it's yours for the taking!'

Monday morning when I walk into Alexander Black's empire, I feel like a new woman. I want to do just that: indulge, partake, and live for me. Truly free, as if the chains I'd been carrying around with me for so long were finally broken and cast aside.

I was no longer held down by my hurtful ex-husband anymore. I knew I was going to get through this mess he threw me smack in the middle of, trying to destroy my life, and me in the process. The Faceless Man had been right, Malcolm did try to destroy me every opportunity he'd gotten in very subtle calculated ways, and was still attempting to even behind bars. He is going to see how strong I am, and the best part is he'd have a very long time to think about it.

I'd had half a lifetime to learn how to deal with Malcolm.

Tony Salvatore is a different story entirely

As I sit at my computer waiting for it to boot up, the one in my head begins its analytical process of putting pieces together, gathering data to assimilate a conclusion, and the best possible means to achieve it.

What's Tony's angle? Could it be as simple as he only wants to get in my pants?

For a man like Tony Salvatore, it could be quite plausible that he would react so forcefully when faced with rejection. He's the epitome of a spoiled brat.

But why now? There's something else besides the fact I'm virtually single. Tony Salvatore has no morals where women are concerned, no mobster does except with their mothers. If he'd wanted to sleep with me, he would have made it known way before now. Our lives have always been intertwined.

As my homepage icons load, I drum my nails on the glass desktop thinking. Glancing at Black, I sit back in my chair and cross my arms across my chest.

That man. No one has the right to look that good. It truly does hurt *gazing at him, he's so stunning. Sleek, powerful, incredibly chiseled face with an air of danger. He is the devil incarnate, luring you with sweet dark seduction. His eyes dare you to take him, and all it will cost is your soul.*

I hadn't realized how strongly I'd been ogling him until the IM pings with a message.

Is this going to be a regular Monday thing, Ms. Trudeau? You still hung over from your fuckfest weekend? Alexander Black

The gall of that man!

I shoot him the middle finger, I'm so appalled, the reaction is immediate an automatic.

By the expression on your face when you were staring at me, that is precisely what you want. Please come in, my call to China is almost finished, then it will be your turn. Alexander Black

"How dare you!" Pushing myself from my chair, it slides across the cubicle and crashes into the bookshelves behind me. I march into his office and slam the door behind me.

He's watching me in that casual arrogant way of his, jacketless and leaning back in his chair like he owns the world, and he loves it.

"Who the hell do you think you're talking to me like that?!" I glare at him, hands on my hips, anger boiling inside me.

"Mr. Yu Lee, everything is going according to plan. My associate will be arriving in China in two days to finalize the agreement. I look forward to a very successful future with you," Alexander Black ends the call. Swiveling his chair to face me, with a very smug look on his face.

He doesn't say anything right away, only

considers me, studies me, and examines me inch by inch. The intensity of his glare chips away at my attack bit by bit.

He slowly raises an eyebrow at me. "Tell me, Ms. Trudeau, do you think you *really* know who I am?"

The question throws me so off-guard, I very unquestioningly admit the bare minimum cold, hard fact...I don't. But I won't be intimidated or undermined by him.

"Mr. Black, I have no doubt the depth of all that you are is so complex, no one could truly understand it. However, it is evident that you are a narcissist and a megalomaniac." I take a step closer. "You think you own everything and everyone and, therefore, feel it is your right to use them when and how you see fit." Another step. "Here's a secret, Mr. Black, I am *not* one of your possessions." I close the space between us and bend down to peer directly into his face, (He smells so incredibly good). "Get that through your thick fucking head. You cannot speak to me in any way you choose." Jabbing my finger into his (very firm) chest, "Got that?" I glare into his icy blue eyes.

There's amusement in them, sinful mirth lifting the corners of his lips, those lips that rocked my world last week. All the intense passion from the very arrogant Faceless Man washes over me, the same cockiness, same I-Know-You-Want-Me-To-

Fuck-You. I want to kiss the smugness off his face, then slap it. Because he's right.

My body reacts to him as if he has *already* had me intimately, knows my deep dark secrets, is completely familiar with how I melt under control, and submit to all his demands willingly.

It's not him! I vehemently remind myself.

"Ms. Trudeau," his voice is like warm cognac gliding over me, thick and burning, seeping into me completely.   He stands, his massive presence unaffected by how my body was towering over him, and the simple act pushes me easily out of the way. "The moment you accepted the position, you belonged to me. I have not even begun to use you in all the ways I intend to," his body looms over mine. "There's only one thing standing in the way," he says dangerously quiet. "I've yet to make a conclusion on that matter yet." He hits the button on his desk to smoke the glass walls of his office, never breaking his penetrating look. "Such an interesting word, possession, don't you agree? Control," he grabs me by my hips and sits me on the edge of his desk. "Force," then yanks my skirt up so my panties peek out above my stockings and garter clips. "Taken," he spreads my legs wide and stands between them. "The thing I hadn't considered before is that the thought of someone else fucking you, especially that scumbag Tony Salvatore touching you with his filthy hands, makes me insane." He cups my ass cheeks firmly and shoves me against his bulging crotch. "If he touches you, I'll kill him."

"...*if he had I'd have to kill him,*" the Faceless Man's words echo in my memory.

My heart is pounding against my ribcage, my arousal is skyrocketing, I can feel the slickness already coating me.

"Tony Salvatore makes me sick," I mutter.

"Good Gemma. I knew you had better taste than that." He presses my sex against his erection, and the pressure makes my loins quiver. "You didn't have anything to do with Malcolm's scheme." It's a statement.

"How could you even think that I did?"

"You're his wife, he's stupid, you're brilliant."

He pulls my skirt up leaving the lower half of my body exposed in my underwear.

"You are the most incredibly sensuous woman I have ever seen, Gemma," his voice is rough and deep. He strokes a finger over my now damp panties, then brings it under his nose and inhales deeply. "Delicious Gemma, your scent is an aphrodisiac. Pull your panties to the side, let me see you."

I gawk at him, shocked at his pornographic request. It makes my heart skip a beat.

"No," I whisper, my fingers curling around the edge of the desk to keep them from doing anything he asks.

"Yes."

Placing his hand over mine, he lifts it and places it between my legs. Then pushes my thighs wider, gripping the meaty flesh firmly.

"Now, Gemma."

I have no control, he's stripped me of everything, and my hand does his bidding. I slowly move the thin black fabric to the side and bare my hungry mound to his penetrating gaze. I close my eyes tightly, I can't look.

"Open your eyes Gemma. I want to watch them when you're coming."

I open them cautiously, my body trembling with need.

"Your pussy is exquisite. Don't close your eyes or I'll stop."

"...I'll stop...," the familiar words repeat in my memory.

Alex uses a single finger to trace my folds, then circles my pulsing clit, and dips just the tip inside me. My hips flex into him wanting more. He holds my legs as wide as they'll go with a hand gripped tightly on one and his body pressed against the other. I feel so naked, so exposed, so open to him. His strokes over my pussy are slow and leisurely, bringing me just to the point of coming and no further.

I'm biting my lip, wanting to beg for release.

Fuck me, just fuck me and make me come! my mind begs.

"I want to fuck you Gemma, sink into you, your sweet delicious pussy hugging my cock, but not today. Do you want to come?"

Why are you making me admit it?

I nod my head 'yes'.

He lifts his finger to his mouth and licks it, then brings his mouth to mine.

"Taste how sweet you are Gemma."

He traces my lips with his tongue then. My desire is at a fevered pitch, I suck it into my mouth, staring into his eyes as he watches me. Our mouths fuck each other in a slow heated frenzy as he pushes two fingers inside me and fucks me with them. I thrust into his hand over and over again chasing the wave that won't crash as we glare into each other's eyes. When his thumb hits my clit and rubs, his two fingers bend inside me and rub my walls on that sensitive place that blows my mind. I scream in his mouth with the force of my orgasm. He's mercilessly keeping me coming on his hand.

When my body slumps against him, he pulls his mouth from mine and lowers to lap up my juices hungrily.

"Oh God, Alex," I moan.

He kisses me again, hard and possessively.

"Whoever your fucking Gemma, stop."

His words are direct as he puts my panties

right and pulls down my skirt.

"I'm not..."

"Just stop."

I can't lie to this man, it's as if he knows everything about me, straight down to my soul.

"Okay," I mumble.

"Good, I have to return five phone calls I missed for you. Lunch at one o'clock. Simon will arrange it."

"Sure." Another mumble.

He lifts me from his desk and places me on my feet.

"It's killing me not to fuck you right now, Gemma. I've wanted to since the first time I laid eyes on you."

"Me too, Alex."

"I know," he smirks.

"Ass," I grin at him.

"Yours is nicer," he says lightly, a full blown grin exploding across his gorgeous face.

Holy shit! What the hell just happened?

Lost in the project I'm working on, I answer the phone.

"Gemma Trudeau, Miles Davis office," I say absently.

"Mrs. Stevens, you've been busy," that same strange man says.

"Who are you?" I ask, instantly alert.

"Someone who has an interest in you."

"What kind of an interest?"

My mind is racing trying to recognize his voice to put a face to it.

"A very large interest…"

"What do you mean, *busy?*"

I have to get information from him to figure out who he is and what his link is to me.

"Your newest associates, and those lovely flowers, Gemma. I see you're enjoying your freedom."

"You've been watching me?!"

Alarm rings loudly through my brain.

"If Tony is behind this, please tell him he will be very sorry, I guarantee it."

He laughs mockingly at me. Then the line goes dead.

And I thought things couldn't get any worse.

take

CHAPTER 10

Gemma

He's killing me. Slowly but surely killing me. The kiss last week, how he touched me and made me come Monday morning. Then telling me to stop fucking The Faceless Man, (how he knew I was having sex with someone is something I'll never figure out). The worst part of all these is he hasn't touched me since. On the contrary, he's been distant, aloof even. The longing that's been clawing at me since I orgasmed spread eagle on his desk has been eating me alive. I needed more. I needed him. Inside me. Now.

Screw him!

I'm in such a shit ass mood by Friday, I could throat punch the first person who even looks at me wrong.

The strange phone calls, the irrepressible heat

between Black and me, his hot and cold behavior, all of it was wearing me down.

Hence, the huge blackest black sunglasses are securely back in place. I walk stiffly to my desk, coffee in one hand, bag with croissant in the other, not giving that asshole Black even the slightest glance.

If he thinks he can tell me what to do when I'm not here, he is severely mistaken. How dare he touch me like that, make me feel vulnerable, then ignore me? God, I exposed myself to him, and he's acting like a cold son-of-a-bitch!

I'm too worked up to sit still just yet so I bend over my desk to turn it on. After dropping my purse down on the file cabinet, I march to the bathroom to wash up after the commute and to make sure my makeup is right in order to take on the world. Alexander Black in particular. Furthermore, to say I'm a little disappointed that I haven't heard from The Faceless Man this week is putting it mildly.

If it's possible to be angrier than I was, then I am. I thought I hated Black before, that was nothing compared to how I feel now.

This day is going to royally suck!

Alexander

She is so pissed off. She's even got the sunglasses back on but that doesn't hide the scowl or the flaring nostrils.

I almost chuckle to myself but that would be cold, even for me. This week hasn't been easy for me either, but it had to be done. It was excruciating not being able to touch her, taste her, take her.

I can't resist.

I see the glasses are back. What are you hiding from? Alexander Black

I see her spine stiffen and her jaw clench from here.

Bravo to you, Ms. Trudeau, for your stoic determination.

Did you need something Mr. Black? Gemma Trudeau

There are so many things that I want, but I'll start with you bent over with your pussy open wide for me, I smirk.

You. Now. Alexander Black

She's shocked.

Excuse Me? Gemma Trudeau

My office. Alexander Black

Her eyes narrow to angry slits as her mouth tightens into a thin line as she glares at the screen. She won't even look at me.

Is there some business we need to discuss? Gemma Trudeau

If you're not in here in five seconds, I'm coming out. Is that what you'd like others to walk in on? Alexander Black

I can see she's muttering something and I can only imagine what it is.

Five seconds later, no more, no more less, she's standing in my office doorway looking stunning in a grey silk body fitting wrap dress, sheer black hose, with patent leather heels the same color. What's underneath is what I really want to see in the flesh.

"I'm here, what do you want?" She's tapping her foot impatiently with her hands on her hips.

After removing my earpiece, I walk to the door. I can see she's breathing heavily by the rapid rising and falling of her chest. Anger, anticipation? It's probably both. I take one of her hands and lead her in the rest of the way then close the door behind her, and lock it. The glass is already smoked.

I've been waiting for today.

"Please come in, Ms. Trudeau."

"I'm in. What do you want?" Her words are clipped and tight.

"I want to fuck you."

Clutching her firmly under her jaw and holding it still, I capture her mouth with all the pent-up aching that's kept my dick throbbing and hard all week. I wrap my other arm around her to press her against me.

It was hell not touching her all week.

She reaches up and grabs handfuls of my vest and grinds her mouth just as feverishly into mine.

"You," she bites my lip. "Are," licks it. "Such," sucks it. "A prick," plunges her tongue into my mouth.

"Don't think I didn't want to touch you, Gemma," I say roughly against her lips.

With her body pressed against the glass door, I feast on her delicious mouth as I untie the sash of her dress. It parts softly against her flesh revealing the black lace bra and panties and the very sheer black thigh highs I watched her dress in this morning.

"Alex…what are you doing?" she moans.

"Taking."

"You can't," she pants as I lead her to the desk.

"I can, and I am."

With her ass against the desk's edge, I push the dress down her shoulders and let it fall to the floor to pool around her feet.

"It's a tragedy you can't walk around like this all day, Gemma. Such beauty shouldn't be hidden," my voice is husky and my cock is throbbing.

Her cheeks flash pink as she lowers her eyes.

I touch a finger under her chin to raise her face to look at me.

"You are the kind of woman that every man wants Gemma, never think otherwise."

Her gaze softens.

I lower my face to run my tongue along the edge of her bra as I stroke the hardened tips with my thumb over the see-through fabric. Her head dips back in a heavy exhale. Tucking my thumbs into the cups, I pull them down to free her beautiful breasts. I take each in one in my hands firmly, squeezing them so the tips poke out, pointing at my mouth.

"Such perfect tits, so greedy and ready," I murmur, sucking each of them, pulling them into my mouth, flicking them with the tip of my tongue and catching them with my teeth.

"Alex…," she breathes.

"Patience pet. I've waited all week, I'm going to get my fill."

"Oh God," she whispers.

Feasting on her succulent breasts, I pull my shirt over my head and throw it to the couch to land on my jacket.

"Alex, let me look at you." Her words are hungry from weeks of visual deprivation.

"Look at me, Gemma, touch me, burn my image into your mind so all you see is me when you close your eyes."

Her hands begin to outline my chest and arms, stroke down the center and around my waist, then up to trace the contours of my abdomen, her gaze following the trail. Her fingertips lightly outline the words tattooed peeking out beneath my bicep. Lifting my arm, she runs her finger adoringly along each letter, Veni, Vidi, Vici, *I came, I saw, I conquered.* She brings her face closer and licks the skin of my shoulder to get a taste of me. She's so hungry to fill all her senses, it's beautiful.

I slide her panties down her shapely legs and tuck them into my pocket, giving her a smirk. Then I unfasten her bra and throw it to the couch with my clothes. Next, I lift her and sit her on the edge of the desk.

"Give me that pussy, she's waited long enough."

Getting down on one knee, I grip her thighs firmly and spread her legs wide.

Running my nose up her slit, I murmur, "I love how you smell."

"Alex...," she whispers hoarsely, grabbing my hair.

"I'm going to fuck you Gemma. Are you on birth control? I want my cum inside you. My dick will be hard all day thinking how it's dripping out bit by bit."

I've already asked her if she's clean.

A flash of anguish mars her face.

"I can't have babies," it's barely audible.

"Ah, pet," her pain tears at my heart.

I kiss her tenderly then, pulling her face to mine, wanting to blot it out. I want the strokes of my tongue against her lips, her tongue, everywhere to heal her.

"Lay back, Gemma."

Gemma

He is ecstasy and anguish, control and chaos, madness and seduction. He is a vortex of oblivion that I want to consume me.

Who is this man? What happened to the ruthless, callous, megalomaniac Alexander Black?

My body is humming as he grabs my ass and pulls me so it's hanging just a little over the edge, then he leads me to lay back against the cool surface of his desk. He spreads my legs wide and begins to tease me with a single digit over my lips, clit, dipping inside me only to remove it to trace over me again and again. My breasts are heavy, aching to be touched, my walls are clenching hungry to be filled. Finally, he slips a finger inside me, pulling it back and pushing it in again, twisting and turning it, so slowly it's torture. He adds another keeping up the torment.

"She's greedy, she wants to be filled," he murmurs huskily.

"Yes," I whisper, arching my back.

He laughs a sadistic little chuckle.

"Put your feet on my shoulders Gemma."

A tremor ripples through me.

With his fingers still taunting me, I'm clad in my heels and hose, I slowly bring my feet to his shoulders. He lowers his face to my sex and begins to follow the path of his finger with his tongue as his two fingers move inside me. His lips close over my clit and start to pluck it. He slides his fingers from me and traces a line down to my puckered back hole.

"I'm going to fuck you here, Gemma...soon," he mumbles against me, his lips fluttering over my pulsing nub.

Yes, please, Alex... another shiver seeps through me.

His finger circles the entrance then presses against it, demanding it open to let him in. As his tongue circles and flicks my clit, he reaches up with his free hand and fills it with my breast, squeezing it possessively. Taking my nipple between two fingers, he sucks my pulsing nub into his mouth and tantalizes it mercilessly with his tongue as his finger slips completely into my ass.

The thick, sweet, decadent drug of desire is melting me, taking me higher and higher, burning throughout my body. I feel wantonly exposed on his desk with the world behind me through the wall of windows, about to be plunged into a raging fire. He's thrusting me into the flames and I can't wait to be burned.

"Oh, Gooooooooood," the orgasm begins so slowly, like the rhythm of his finger and his tongue, the molten heat seeping through me thick and thoroughly, leaving no part of me unsinged in its wake. I melt into him, merging and melding, it's so good. I'm intoxicated riding that wave as he lifts his mouth from me but not his finger.

"So fucking sweet, Gemma, spread out like that," he growls.

Then he's there, the head of his shaft gliding over my slickness.

"I'm clean, Gemma. I never go unprotected. But you…I have to feel you completely, have to have you feel me. It's an obsession."

"Yes, Alex, please, I need you now…"

"Fuck, pet," he growls as he removes his finger and thrusts completely inside me.

Yes! Yes, that's it!

My back lifts off the flat surface welcoming him in, finally getting what I crave.

"You feel so good, so tight, so perfect," he moans.

His thrusts are deep and slow, deliriously leisurely, stroking me back into that vortex of oblivion.

"Wrap your legs around me, Gemma," he says roughly as grasps my hips and digs his fingers into my flesh.

His hips move harder and more demanding into me, taking me higher and higher. Then he grinds, circles, and plunges into me, rubbing every nerve ending inside me. The wave is cresting higher, taking me with it. Then he's on top of me, skin against skin, body against body, one arm wrapped tightly around me with his hand under my bottom, the other by my head, leaning my face to his.

"Grab my cock, Gemma, squeeze it." My walls bear down on him, gripping him tightly. "Yes, just like that, baby...fuck!" His mouth devours mine, consuming it.

He pushes my ass up into his thrusts, my clit feeling every incredible move of his body. He's got me pinned beneath him, I can't move, taking everything he's inflicting on me.

"I can feel you're ready, pet, that hungry pussy getting tighter and tighter, squeezing my dick."

His mouth latches onto mine as he grinds his hips into me and pushes me over the edge.

I scream my release into his mouth, and he growls into mine.

He lifts his body from me, grabs my hips with both hands and pounds into me hard and deep. I feel his shaft swell and twitch as he thrusts in and arches his back, dipping back his head.

"God Gemma...!!!"

I can feel his hot spurts inside me. I love it.

"God woman," he says roughly, lowering back to me, nibbling, kissing, and licking along my face, my shoulders, my breasts, leaving a trail across my flesh. "I'll get a towel, stay here."

A soft moan of protest slips past my lips when he pulls out, still hard.

"I know, I could stay there all day, Gemma."

He enters the private bath in his office and returns with two towels, one clasped in his hand, the other wiping his shaft.

"Here, Gemma, let me clean you," he says positioning himself between my legs.

"I can do it," I protest shyly.

"Sssshhh, I want to, let me adore this pussy a little longer," he smirks wickedly at me.

I blush profusely.

He smiles. "You do that a lot."

"What?"

"Blush. It's adorable."

My blush deepens. "You have consistently shocked me since I started here."

"Oh, baby, you haven't seen anything yet," he winks mischievously at me.

I roll my eyes. "That's what I'm afraid of."

He laughs loud and freely, the first time I've heard him so carefree. He pulls my panties from his pocket and feeds them up my legs.

"I was going to keep these but I think you're going to need them today." Another wicked wink.

"You, Alexander Black, are a very wicked man," I say, taking his hands to stand.

"The wickedest," his smile is naughty and boyish. And absolutely charming.

He walks to the couch to retrieve my dress as I put on my bra. Feeding it up my arms and arranging it, he ties the sash. Then he pulls his shirt back over his head and closes his pants, putting himself in order.

He pulls me tightly to him and peers deeply into my eyes.

"What?"

"You are going to stop fucking him, Gemma."

"I'm not…"

"Don't start lying to me now," he says simply.

I clamp my mouth shut.

Three hours later the delivery man arrives with a bundle of orchids and a card.

I'm coming...xoxo

Butterflies take flight in my stomach. I'm elated The Faceless Man didn't forget about me, but I'm torn.

I want Black. I can't deny that I've wanted him since the first day I stepped foot in Black Inc. I can still smell our sex on me and feel him seeping from me slowly with each step, and it sends a jolt of heat through me.

I worry my lip as I steal a glance toward his office. The glass is clear and I feel like I'm taking a walk of shame.

Stop it! You didn't do anything wrong.

He's staring right at me, glaring at me, I can feel it like daggers piercing me.

When I get back to my desk, there's already an IM.

If you fuck him this weekend, I'll know.

Alexander Black

I'm insulted.

I'm offended you'd think me so cheap, Alex. Gemma Trudeau

I saw your face the past two Mondays Gemma. You were so fuck hung-over, you could barely function. Alexander Black

I cringe at some of the truth to his words, but that wasn't the only reason. I was in shock and an emotional mess the first time. The second time, well he's pretty much right about that.

I'm not a whore, Alex – yes I am, but only for one man – Gemma Trudeau

Yes, you are, but you're mine. You're going to be my whore when I touch you and do dirty things to you, make you scream my name, MY NAME, every time you come. Mine to pleasure and worship. And you'll beg for it. Alexander Black

Heat explodes across my chest and face with both arousal and embarrassment.

What the hell do I say to that?

Know, Gemma, that is one of the things I adore about you. Alexander Black

I'm a quivering wanton mess of need.

Alexander

When I silently step into her bedroom I hesitate. She's waiting for me.

"What happened?" I ask, although I already know.

I'm such a shit. The flowers today, me coming back tonight, is almost a test. I wanted to see her sense of loyalty, test her ability for faithfulness. I hadn't given her any words of promises or affection. On the contrary, I was my typical prick self. And I actually felt bad about it.

She inhales deeply and the rise and fall of those succulent breasts makes my mouth water.

"I want to see you." Her voice is tight.

"You can't."

"Tell me your name." There's a tinge of anguish.

"Gemma…"

"I need more." It's almost strangled.

"I've given you everything you need. I know your pussy is clenching hungry for my cock, your nerves are tingling beneath that beautiful white skin waiting to come alive. Tell me what happened."

She takes another deep breath as her fists clench and her thighs squeeze trying to relieve her need.

"Black…" it's a pained whisper.

My dick twitches.

"Black."

"Yes."

"And you liked it." She can't see the satisfied smile spreading across my face.

She doesn't answer, she doesn't have to. I felt how her body reacted in my arms, the same way it's reacting now.

"Do you want him?"

"I don't know who you are…" I hear pain in her words and it makes my heart constrict.

"Do you want him, Gemma? Don't lie to me, I'll know."

"…yes…," the declaration comes out choked.

The euphoria I feel is almost impossible for me to contain. I want to go to her and kiss her until she's breathless and drunk. I want to tell her how much I ache for her as she screams coming over and over again.

"Then I've done what you needed. Remember, make sure he deserves the gift that you are. Goodbye, Gemma."

As I head down the stairs her pain wrenched sobs breaks my heart.

take

CHAPTER 11

Alexander

I am such an asshole.

In my office at home I pace the floor waiting for Gemma to get home. When she'd left work, she'd been furious, confused, aroused? I'm not sure.

I don't blame her. I called her a whore.

"Yeah," I snatch my cell phone and bark at Jesús.

"Mira, Ramon just called. Se parece que ese hijo de gran puta is waiting for Trudeau at her house, Tony Salvatore.

Fucking Latins and their Spanglish.

"Explain." My tone is dangerously low.

"Ramon said he pulled up a little while ago and tried the door. She's not home yet, it must have been locked, so it looks he's waiting in his car in front of her house. Ramon said he looks real comfortable."

My blood is boiling.

The little pussy didn't seem to take no for answer. I'm going to make sure he does.

"Tell Ramon to not take his eyes off him. Have somebody look for her and if they find her, follow her home. I want eyes on her constantly. That WAP slime ball is a fucking lunatic and he is NOT to get his hands on her. I'm on my way. Have the Hummer out front."

Shoving the phone in my pocket, I'm already on the third floor, taking the steps two at a time.

Twenty minutes later I'm screeching to halt in front of Gemma's house. Salvatore's car is there in front of a black sedan. It's empty. I already know she's been home five minutes as Ramon approaches me.

"Wait here," I growl, bounding up the steps and throwing open the front door.

What I see unleashes the savage in me.

Gemma

"Tony, what are you doing?" I'm panicking, the words raspy and I can barely breathe with the agonizing pain.

"Who the fuck do you think you are telling me to get out? We're taking care of you now, you belong to us. You know what that means, it comes with a price. I can collect any time."

He's choking me, his hand pressing so hard

on my throat I'm sure he's going to crush it. I'm clawing at his arms trying to break free. My vision is going black as my head feels like it's going to explode. Survival instinct brings my knee up to connect with his groin.

"BITCH!"

CRACK! His hand smashes the side of my face but his grip loosens around my throat and sweet air fills my lungs. Then he's gone.

CRASH!

"What the fuck!" Tony shouts.

Black has Tony by the throat smashing his head against the wall.

Tony pulls a gun from somewhere inside his jacket.

"Alex, he's got a gun!" I scream, horrified.

The pounding Tony's taking prevents him from levelling the pistol at Black. Alex rips it from his hand and proceeds to pound his skull with the butt of it.

"STOP, you're going to kill him!" I shriek as I rush to them and grab Alex's arm to stop the brutal assault.

"Fuck!" Black growls with such violence, it makes my blood run cold.

He throws Tony's body to the side like a ragdoll.

"Consider this even Salvatore. You don't want a war, but know, you touch her one more time, so much as look at her, I *will* kill you. I don't give a shit about a fucking war." Alex turns to the man I hadn't noticed standing in the foyer. "Get him the fuck out of here. Call his father, tell him to get the piece of shit to the hospital before he dies. Tell him I'll call him later."

The whole scene is so surreal, I'm fighting to comprehend the reality of it.

Black turns to me, his piercing blue eyes hard and cold. "Are you okay, Gemma?" He's panting, his body is rigid, ready to attack again.

"Yes," I croak out.

His gaze rakes my body up and down, searching for blood I guess. His focus narrows in on my face. I realize it's throbbing from the blow I took. I resist the urge to touch it.

Alex takes a deep steadying breath. "Get in the car. Now!"

"What?" I ask still stunned.

"You. Are. Coming. With me. Right now. You have thirty seconds."

"I'm not going anywhere."

I'm getting really tired of all this bullshit in my life.

"Yes you are."

"No I'm not. He won't bother me again," I retort defiantly.

"Oh, he won't? Why don't you ask the two women he beats on a regular basis, each of them rotating a hospital bed so often, they've probably got one reserved."

"That's not true," I choke out.

"You don't think so? Why don't you ask your almost crushed trachea and that crack on the side of your face?"

The truth of his words hit me hard. Alex's eyes soften fractionally as he sees the torrent of emotions storm across my face.

"Let's go Gemma."

I can see he's calming down as he steps toward me.

My body begins to shake. I feel I'm on the verge of an emotional meltdown, one that's been building since my parents died.

Black's arms envelope me, instantly comforting and soothing me. I press into him, needing the safety and security I can't believe I feel there.

"Sssshhhh, let's get out of here Gemma."

"Okay." I'm holding on to my last strands of sanity.

I see Kitty peek out from the around the doorway, eyes wide, scared to death.

"It's okkkay Kkkkitty," I try to comfort her but my teeth have started to chatter.

He tightens his arms around me, holding my trembling body closer, and rubs my back whispering in my ear.

"It's okay, Gemma, ssshhhh, it's over. He's not going to touch you again…EVER."

"Thank you for being here," I choke out.

Then I realize.

"What *are* doing here anyway?" I ask, pulling back to look into his face.

"I felt a little bad for what I'd said, I wanted to apologize."

He refuses to let me go.

An apology coming from the ruthless Alexander Black?

"You did act like an ass."

"I know, I said I'm sorry, Gemma. Let's get out of here before Salvatore's people show, I don't feel like dealing with that with you here. Get some things together, we can come back for more another time."

"Alright, neither do I. One Salvatore is enough for one day."

Alex turns to look behind him over my head.

"Don't forget the damn cat," he mumbles.

Kitty hasn't stopped meowing, her fear of being in a car matching my own emotions. When Alex pulls up in front of a gorgeous stately home, I peer out the window, my eyes taking in everything across the front, the black wrought iron gates at the entrance of the driveway, the French design balconies on each level, then all the way up the four stories.

"Which floor do you live on?" I ask nervously.

"All of them," he answers flatly.

I look at him disbelievingly. "This is your house? I mean mansion?"

"Yes." Nothing else.

Alex's eyes are studying me, waiting for me to be ready to exit the car before he opens his door.

I narrow my eyes on him, thinking again that he'd just shown up at my house for no reason.

"Why were you there?"

A flicker of something flashes in his eyes, then it's gone so fast I'm not even sure I saw it.

"I told you, I acted like a dick. I wanted to apologize."

"So you came all the way to Jersey City? You just *happened* to arrive just when I did? Even for you that's a bit much to be coincidental."

He takes a deep breath. "I felt bad when you left. I couldn't leave it like that and I needed to do it in person. Can we go inside now Gemma? Please?"

"Fine, Black, but this isn't over. Pop the back so I can get my bags."

"Jesús will get it," he states, opening his door to the same Latin man who drove us to Cipriani's.

Alex throws him the keys when he unfolds his tall, muscular body from the car. He's in expensive perfectly fitting jeans and a white silk t-shirt. The man could wear a burlap sack and still look perfectly put-together.

"Jesús, two bags in the back, and we're going to need cat food, a box and litter."

"You got it. Mama's going to love having the cat around," Jesús grins broadly, showing off a gold tooth.

"Your mother is here?" I asked surprised when he opens my door.

"The closest thing to one I've ever had," Alex murmurs tightly. "Come on, I'm sure she's waiting," helping me out of the car.

He places his hand on my back and leads me to the very tall, modest, double front doors. When he opens them, the opulence only hinted at outside explodes in black and white, marble, crystal chandeliers, and a double curved staircase with intricate black wrought iron railings. There are alcoves to the left and right in the foyer with the most beautiful carved statues, and paintings on the walls that are ten feet tall. My gawking at the surroundings is interrupted by a short matronly dark skinned woman with an apron wrapped around her round midsection as she shuffles in.

"Alex, hijo, is she okay?" Her face is etched with worry.

"Yes, Hilda, she's not hurt...not *too* badly," he answers, the simmering rage threatening to flare again.

"Dar me, give me the cat, amor, then you'll come to eat," she holds her arms out with a tender smile. "Dios mio, look at what he did to you," she gently caresses my still throbbing cheek.

I'm flooded with an ache of loneliness and sadness, for a family I don't have, for having to pay for the crimes my husband did, for trusting people I shouldn't have.

"No te preocupes, don't worry, Alex will take care of you," Hilda smiles affectionately at the man I've mostly thought of as hard, cold, and maybe dangerous.

What I feel for him now is affection, gratitude, and a longing to be close to him, for him to want to take care of me.

Some of that danger reared its ugly head tonight as he bashed the handle of the gun into Tony's head, clearly wanting to kill him.

"I'm taking Gemma upstairs, Hilda, Jesús went to get cat food and a box with litter for her. I don't want to be disturbed."

"Pssssssst, no me diga eso. Do not keep this woman locked up in your dungeon all night sin comida," Hilda reprimands Alex gruffly. "Alex! You have blood on your shirt and jacket!"

A look of reproach clouds Alex's usually stern features.

"It's nothing Hilda, I'm fine," he replies curtly.

The infamous Alexander Black does *have a heart and this woman definitely has a huge place in it.*

A slither of jealousy ripples through me. I want a small corner in that well guarded place.

"No one is to answer the door except Carlos, please make sure everyone knows. Let the service pick up my calls," he begins to rattle off instructions as he leads me to the elevator.

"Si claro," she clucks at him, turning back to go where she came from with Kitty in her arms. I can hear her cooing to him as she strokes her fur.

Alex is tense beside me, his hand on my back firm. The elevator makes its slow ascent to the fifth floor with neither of us saying a thing. The doors part on the top floor to a luxurious penthouse suite paneled in heavy dark woods and rich furnishings.

"This way," he directs me past closed doors toward the back of the suite.

We come upon the last door which is a massive mahogany work of art in and of itself. When he turns the gold handle and pushes it open, we could have walked into another world smack dab in the Middle Ages. The enormous king size four poster bed is draped in red velvet and sheer linen hanging from the canopy, there's a full size suit of armor standing guard in the corner, and a life size painting of him swathed in a gilded gold frame.

"Hilda had that made for me. I find it rather

ostentatious but I could never tell her that, and you can't either," he mutters in explanation.

"You're embarrassed," I smile at him.

"It's a little much, even for me," he smiles.

"She loves you...like a son," I say softly.

"I'm very lucky, she kicks my ass like one too," his smile is unguarded.

"Who is she to you?"

The mask instantly shutters over his features again. "She's Jesús and Carlos' mother, along with other members of my staff." He Continues to lead me through the bedroom. "The bathroom is here."

"How many others?"

"Enough of that, you'll find out things soon enough. We have other things to discuss." His reply is curt and to the point.

I stop and he almost bumps into me.

"Mr. Black, I appreciate how you stopped Tony from choking me to death, and bringing me here so I would not have to deal with Tony's father and the inquisition that was sure to follow. But if you're going to continue to be a dick, I can MOST certainly go someplace else," I tell him coldly, my eyes daring him to push me further.

His jaw clenches as he scoops me up and throws me on the bed.

"First, Ms. Trudeau, no woman has ever been in my bedroom. Second, you are not going anywhere. Period. Third, I am a prick. But this thing...with you...is like an obsession. It claws at me, to have you, take you, devour you, to punish you even. I'm dark, Gemma, and I want to take you to my darkest places, to consume you in the blackness. I want to hear the echoes of you begging for more in its depths. Tell me you don't want that, tell me to let you go. Now. Before it's too late." His face and body are hard and controlled, assessing every one of my nuances that would give him an indication of what I'm thinking and feeling.

Erotic heat oozes through me with Black's dark declaration. Fear and lust entwine together, embracing and seducing, taking me with them. I should run, tell him no, he's too dark, too black, too dangerous.

I lick my suddenly dry lips and whisper, "Okay..."

Outside the man in the black sedan makes a call.

"She's staying with Black."

Own

Part II

*"But the bravest man among us is afraid of himself.
The mutilation of the savage has its tragic survival
in the self-denial that mars our lives. We are
punished for our refusals. Every impulse that we
strive to strangle broods in the mind, and poisons
us. The body sins once, and has done with its sin,
for action is a mode of purification. Nothing
remains then but the recollection of a pleasure, or
the luxury of a regret. The only way to get rid of a
temptation is to yield to it. Resist it, and your soul
grows sick with longing for the things it has
forbidden to itself, with desire for what its
monstrous laws have made monstrous and unlawful.
It has been said that the great events of the world
take place in the brain. It is in the brain, and the
brain only, that the great sins of the world take
place also. You...have had passions that have made
you afraid, thoughts that have filled you with terror,
day-dreams and sleeping dreams whose mere
memory might stain your cheeks with shame...."*

An excerpt from
"The Picture of Dorian Gray"
By Oscar Wilde
Written 1890

CHAPTER 12

Gemma

What happened to my life? What the hell did I do to warrant getting stuck married to a man that destroyed my life, and almost choked to death by another? At what point did I take a drastic turn to make everything spin wildly out of control? Then what did I do to have unseen forces come in to intervene and make the King of Darkness rescue me from it all?

But did he?

My throat is still sore from Tony Salvatore's death grip, and my face is still tender from the whack he gave me.

Sometimes life has a strange, complicated, completely unexpected way of putting you right where you want to be, exactly where you need to be, and precisely when you need to be there.

In the midst of the turmoil surrounding me, I've landed in the middle of Alexander Black's bed, quite literally. The impeccable and intense force of the man himself is looming over me with his eyes searing into me. I'm frightened, the possibility of terror still peering just around the corner. Alexander Black is imposing and tremendously intimidating. He is undeniably dangerous, and yet he makes me feel safe. He is a juxtaposition of contradictions. A lethal force within a polished gentleman.

Apprehension and anticipation are warring inside me.

He just told me he wants to do very wicked things to me, wants to take me to the darkness inside him. He said he'd give me only one opportunity to escape.

This is it.

My emotions are rolling turbulently within me. I want to forget the mess my life is and dive into his darkness, let him consume me with it until I'm lost in him. My own deepest darkest places are awakening with that promise, stretching and reaching for his to find fulfillment, to intertwine in a dance so forbidden I have always refused to imagine it.

But I'm afraid of what would happen to me when he's done with me, when he's sated his appetite and was finally bored with me. Can I walk away the same person unmarred after having tasted from the well of temptation, satisfied and content? Am I strong enough to face another rejection, used and cast aside when I no longer serve his purposes? Can I add this to the troubles plaguing me?

Use him.

The whispered thought comes to fruition.

Use him. Let that woman free that you've ignored all these wasted years. Denying it has done you no good. Indulge…

"Tell me now, Gemma, if you want to leave, because there's no turning back after this."

His perfect and stunning self is standing poised and erect, waiting for my answer. He frightens and seduces me all in the same breath. Control and power resonate within him, so strong it lures like a magnet, like the serpent to Eve. "Come, taste all that you crave, it's all here waiting for you, all you have to do is say yes…"

The promise is loud and unyielding.

Here in his Louis XVI style mansion, his lair, I'm a lamb who's come to slaughter, and I cannot wait.

I unconsciously bend to him without question.

"Yes, Alex," the whisper is barely audible.

I can see a glimmer of satisfaction and a hint of relief in the depths of his ice blue eyes swirling around his need.

Alex takes a slow, predatory step toward me as a smirk lifts his lips.

"The things I'm going to do to you, pet, all

the ways I'm going to have you."

My heart races and my breathing becomes ragged.

"What I want, when I want, how I want, where I want."

Those promises, the things I've always known but didn't, things my soul longed for but I refused to admit. Things my mind doesn't know but my body yearns for. Things I've been waiting for but have denied, they're all there.

"We have to have a certain level of trust between us, Gemma. There can be no secrets, no inhibitions, nothing. I have to know everything. Is there something you haven't told me? Anything else lurking in your shadows besides Malcolm and Salvatore?"

My heart races and my mouth hungers to taste him as I anticipate the places he'd mentioned.

Reality forces me to stay focused on his question.

Malcolm, my soon to be ex-husband who stole three million dollars from Alexander, and Salvatore, member of the New Jersey mafia family. Who says I belong to him. Who Alex just stopped from choking me to death. Then almost beat him to death with his own gun.

When did my life become such a mess?

"No, Alex, there's nothing…," I was going to confirm there's nothing else, then I remembered the two strange phone calls I received since I started working for him.

Alex's posture goes rigid with apprehension.

"What is it?"

"There were phone calls…"

His jaw clenches and the violent look returns to his eyes, the one he'd had when he found Tony with his hands around my throat.

"When?"

"The first came the week I started working for you, the second this week."

The same feelings of caution I'd had during the conversations return and I see them reflected in Alex's eyes.

"Where?"

"At the office."

"How many?"

His hands ball into fists and his nostrils flare with suppressed rage. His look is frightening and at the same time sexy as hell.

"Just the two," I reply.

"A man?" he asks, but he already knows.

"Yes."

"Do you know who it was?"

"I didn't recognize the voice and he didn't say."

"What *did* he say?"

I take a deep breath.

"Both calls were very brief. The first one he

told me it was interesting I was working for you and he said he had an *interest* in me. The second time he said I have interesting associates, and he mentioned the flowers. He made me feel like he's been watching me."

Recalling the conversations and putting the contents out for inspection was making me very nervous, along with Alex's very deadly reaction. I hadn't considered all the aspects and danger that were possibly associated with them until he started to dissect them.

"Any other phone calls or visitors, run-ins with people?"

The Faceless Man.

I'm struggling with telling Alex about the man who'd entered my house and took me blindfolded on two of the most illicit and passionate nights of my life.

He doesn't have anything to do with the calls.

I am certain of this.

"No, that's it."

I'm not ready to tell him about The Faceless Man, I only hope I never have to.

Alex studies me, examining me to see if I'm keeping anything from him. He knows there was someone I was sleeping with. I'd received flowers at the office on three different occasions.

"If there are any other calls, mails, emails, deliveries, anything at all Gemma, tell me immediately."

He seems satisfied that I've told him everything he needs to know. For now.

"I will, I promise."

"You are apparently a target for someone and I have no idea how many people want you other than Salvatore and this anonymous caller. Malcolm's schemes haven't fully come out yet, and I'm sure we haven't seen the end of Salvatore. Things haven't even begun."

His words of foreboding send a cold tremor through me.

"Son of a bitch!" Suddenly, with a look of realization, he runs a frustrated hand through his hair. "I should have known, dammit!"

"What are you talking about?" I ask, now a little confused.

"It's obvious Gemma, but I was focused on you, I didn't even allow myself to consider it."

I fold my arms across my chest starting to feel very annoyed. I wish he'd fill me in on his enlightenment.

"Would you mind telling me *what* exactly is obvious?"

"I've told you this before," he stops pacing to look intently at me. "Malcolm is too stupid to have put together such an elaborate scheme that even had me unaware. He wasn't working with you, but he was involved with someone. Someone powerful, someone who has very solid connections, someone who was using Malcolm."

"What does that have to do with me?"

A thought begins to push from the back of my mind, a very disconcerting thought. A thought that is literally scaring the hell out of me.

He closes the distance between us and extends his hand to me. I tentatively place my cold hand in his large warm one. He pulls me to him and embraces me tightly, looking into my eyes.

"Gemma," he begins softly. "There are circles of people who play for very high stakes. There is an intricate business world that exists and thrives behind the scenes, the Salvatore's and DiAngelo's know it, even UN Ambassadors are well aware of it. But other heavy hitters have their places within this world, people and companies you would never believe but would recognize. Powerful people…people who don't like losing."

"The Black Market is something I'm aware of, Alex," I reply, trying very hard to sound unconcerned.

"Gemma, the Black Market is this world's infant. It's nothing compared to the elaborate and very profitable enterprise that spans the entire globe. The woven intricacies that link things together is an empire no one wants to get involved with…unless you can win."

"So what does that have to do with me?" I ask

again nervously.

He hesitates. I can see he's struggling with the answer; an answer he does not seem to like.

"Malcolm lost."

Those two words, as simple as they are, hit me with such force, my breath is pushed from my lungs and my vision begins to swim.

"But I had nothing to do with it," I gasp out.

He pulls me closer and cradles my head against the firmness of his chest.

"I know that. Nothing is going to happen to you Gemma. I'll find out what's going on and who's involved. People may not like me but they respect me, and wouldn't fuck with me. It'll be well known that you're with me now, and no one is going to dare jeopardize the delicate balance of things. Not unless they want a war." His tone drops and becomes ominous, the weight of his threat quite clear.

Holding me so he can look into my eyes, he says, "You need release, pet, you need to let go and forget about all this for a while. I want to show you something."

His eyes flicker back and forth on mine, gauging my reaction and reading me.

He's right, thoughts are crashing around in my head and my heart is beating wildly. There's been too much today, Tony Salvatore's attack, then ending up in Alexander Black's house, and his proposal, this newest revelation is pushing me to my limit. My insides begin to heat up with his suggestion that hints at a glimpse of his previous dark promises.

"What did you have in mind?" I ask quietly.

A slow lascivious grin lifts the corners of his mouth.

"Come with me."

He takes my hand and leads me from the bedroom to a closed door two doors down the hallway. Pausing, he cups my chin gently and says, "I want you to look at everything in here; touch, feel, smell, hold. I'm going to leave you alone in this room while I make some calls. I want you to choose three things you'd like me to use on you tonight. Three things, Gemma. If you don't choose, I will."

His tone holds no sign of uncertainty. He's confident and direct, and he makes me believe this is where I need to be. My heart is pounding. My mind is racing, and I'm on an overload of emotions, up then down, then back up again. I'm conjuring visions of what's behind that door.

He turns the knob of the heavily polished wooden door and slowly pushes it open. There is a soft glow from the recessed lighting in the tray wooden ceiling. His hand is on my lower back gently coaxing me in as his eyes never leave mine.

The room is fashioned in the same taste as the bedroom with the exact bed, deep reds, rich dark woods, and gold embellishments. The walls and ceiling are richly polished dark carved wood. The renaissance art hanging on the walls in gilded gold frames all have different scenes of erotic pleasures. The whole thing is really quite beautiful. As I step in further, other things begin to catch my eye. There is a large tufted padded X attached to one of the walls that spans floor to ceiling. I glimpse metal hooks fed into beams that run across the ceiling and walls, the hooks placed in very deliberate locations, places perfect for an outstretched arm and spread legs. Next to the table is what looks like a tall cushioned vaulters horse. I take another step in and turn my head. My eyes settle on a rack on the wall at my back that holds leather tailed floggers, crops, canes, paddles, restraints, and a wide array of other things all meant for the same purpose.

To give pain with your pleasure.

...locked up in your dungeon...

Hilda's words come back to me.

My body is quivering, whether from fear or incredible anticipation, I'm not sure. What I do know is I am hypnotized, spell bound, and a part inside me longs to explore the secrets hidden within these four walls.

I step once to turn and I catch my reflection in a mirror. I look intoxicated, I can see my desire in the flush of my skin, with my parted lips, and my half hooded eyes. Alex is looking intently at me in the mirror, his gaze is riveted to my face, his eyes are piercing into mine. He steps closer, his front almost touching my back, and slides a hand from behind me to rest on my stomach, his eyes never leave mine in the mirror's reflection. Slowly he moves his hand up to stroke my parted lips.

My body craves his touch all over it.

"Welcome to my darkness, pet. Here there are no secrets, nothing is hidden." He slips a finger past my lips. It's so delicious, I suck it deeply into my mouth and let out a long exhale. "And you will be free."

His voice is deep and sultry, hot and thick, and slides over me, wrapping him around me.

Removing his finger slowly from my mouth, he turns me to face him, clasps my chin, and holds my gaze to look at him. "This, Gemma, is where your darkness will be born. She's so hungry, I can feel her. You can hear her, I can see it in your eyes, hear it in your breaths, feel it when you come. You need more, you always have. I'm going to give you all that you think you want, then I'm going to take you to that place where your soul can soar."

Yes...

I've always been drawn to the darkness, the macabre, the forbidden, and taboo. Fear and lust walk hand in hand through the dark corridors of my mind, leaving a whisper of longing in their wake. I tried desperately to resist the lure of the darkness that called me for years, I tried so hard to be normal for so long. I've lived empty and hungry, resigned to the fact that this is what life would be for me, no relief, just endless aching for something I should not want.

Now the King of Darkness is standing before me offering me everything I've yearned for. And so much more.

I'm scared shitless and on the verge of euphoria.

"Take off your clothes and explore your desires, see everything that awaits you, Gemma. I want you only in your bra and panties when you fondle the secrets you've kept buried. Then after you've chosen the three things that you'll start your journey with tonight, go take a shower, it's just through that door," he directs my gaze to a door at the other side of the room, "and then we'll begin." He smirks wickedly at me and it sends a shiver up my spine. "I'm interested to see your choices, pet, wondering if you'll be true to your hunger."

I have no reply, I don't know what to say to that. I'm finding it difficult to look into his penetrating gaze.

He lets go of my face and steps back.

"Take off your clothes, Gemma."

My heart is pounding and I'm so aroused, I can't think straight.

"Now, pet," he's voice is quietly firm.

I tentatively toe off my shoes then slowly pull down my yoga pants. The sway of my hips back and forth make my loins clench with need. After placing my pants to the side with my shoes, I pull off my t-shirt. The cool air on my skin makes the hair rise-up over my bare flesh.

"Fucking beautiful," he whispers huskily while tracing the point of his finger along the edge of my underwear. "Tonight is only the beginning, pet. You're going to show me what you want, then I'll give you what you need. I'm going to push you, take you to places you've been afraid to admit you've wanted to go. There you will find yourself, Gemma. It's going to be incredible."

"Alex…," I whisper breathily.

"Are you afraid, pet?" his eyes glint devilishly, the whisper of his savage lust in their depths.

I've always been a little afraid of him, from the first moment a saw him. I felt his intensity bearing down on me with only his gaze from the other room, penetrating me. He possessed me right from the beginning, he seduced me with his words, with his eyes, he stripped me straight to my soul.

"Yes," the word is so quiet I almost didn't hear it myself.

"Good, that means you're embracing your darkness, letting it come to the surface. She will come, you can't stop her, not anymore. This is her home."

"Oh God…"

He smirks wickedly at me.

"He can't stop me, pet."

...He can't stop me..., the echo of a memory with The Faceless Man comes from the recesses of my mind.

"I don't want him to," I repeat the answer I'd given to him.

"I know."

He lowers his mouth and ravages mine with it, kissing me hungrily, the act a demand of surrender. I melt into him as his hand tangles in my hair and pulls it gently as he grinds his mouth into mine. I'm breathless when he pulls away from me.

"I can't wait very long, pet. Explore, search, find your three things, and I'll be back soon."

He bends to retrieve my clothes and looks back at me. "Remember, I'll be back very soon."

Alex pulls out his phone as he walks to the door.

He turns before he leaves and takes a last glance at me. I'm trembling with anticipation, like a kid left in a toy store at Christmas, but not sure what to choose.

"If you can't decide, I will, Gemma."

"I'll choose, Alex."

"Good, because this will be the only time you will."

My heart does a flip as he opens the door and steps out. I hear him talking as he pulls it closed behind him.

"Jesús, call Rashad. We need ID's on all the cars on Gemma's street, trace all the calls her phone's received since she started at Black Inc., and tell him to put a code red on Malcolm's activity." He listens for a minute. "Someone's been stalking her in the office, and I want to know immediately who it is. And why."

Own

CHAPTER 13

Alexander

If Gemma had tried to walk out, I would have stopped her. The faint outline of Tony Salvatore's handprint was still on her face and there's no way I'm letting her out of my sight and give that scumbag another chance to finish what he started.

I try to deny it, but I can't.

I feel more than responsible for her. I feel possession.

This bothers me. What started as a ploy to use her has turned into more. *She* has become more. With more comes feelings, feelings I long ago thought didn't exist in me. I can't have that. Feelings make you vulnerable, and vulnerability makes you weak. I am a prick, a cold, heartless prick. I'm incapable of emotions. What I feel for Gemma must be lust, insatiable, intense, ball busting lust.

I'm going to blot that whole incident out of her mind as she comes over and over again. There's no way I'm going to forget it though.

I remind myself the Salvatore's are business.

I have no doubt he would have raped her after he beat her. Which leads me to her lowlife husband, Malcolm. The man's a fucking coward, dragging her into his mess. Now someone's stalking her.

It's business.

I have to find out who it is.

Who was Malcolm Stevens involved with?

This is the million-dollar question.

No one else has come forward with extortion allegations. Why?

I sit at my home office desk trying to find a path, any sign to indicate where Malcolm's source of strength came from.

Dammit!

I slam my fist down on the desk and everything jumps.

With all Gemma has just told me, a new player in the game has come to light.

"He made me think he's been watching me..."

Someone has been watching her.

In my office.

There's a plant. Of that I have no doubt. I also know I have to contact the only person I trust to help me find out who it is.

But why? And how long have they been there? And who are they watching, me or her?

Things have just gotten a lot more complicated. And dangerous. For Gemma.

By bringing her here and thinking I was protecting her, I've created an even bigger problem.

Malcolm's people have been watching her, just like I've been, maybe for the same reasons; to find out what she knows about his dealings, which now I'm sure is absolutely nothing. Even if she does know something, it's obvious she doesn't know she knows. Which could be fatal for her.

This was her original problem.

No one else has reported embezzlement. The simplest reason for that would be there is no one else. Just me. Just me...someone had Malcolm target me.

The glaring truth floods me and makes my blood boil.

How far would it have gone if things hadn't come out when they had? And slipped a spy in my company.

Why?

My thoughts shift to Gemma gasping for breath as the life was being choked out of her with a huge red handprint on her face. Rage engulfs me knowing I had allowed Tony Salvatore time to get his filthy hands on her and hurt her.

She should have let me beat him to death.

Every fiber of my being roars, 'No one touches what's mine!'

It's business.

I have long far surpassed wanting to merely taste and savor the delectable Gemma Trudeau. My only desire had been to break her and make her need so badly, it hurt. I had wanted revenge and vengeance. How trivial that is to what the truth is now.

I can't deny it.

Possession. I need to own her completely, make her give herself to me heart, body, mind, and soul. I ache for her so deeply, there is a hunger in me that only she can satisfy. My darkness needs her, there is no denying it.

My selfishness has put her in more danger. I've made her more appealing, more valuable to whomever is behind this by setting her up to take the job with me. I handed her the keys to her destruction with a big fucking red ribbon.

This is the problem now.

I rake a hand through my hair agonizing with the thought of letting her go, sending her home, before it's too late.

Maybe it's already too late. What if I put her in the car and send her back to Jersey City tonight, then tomorrow she's dead. I could never live with myself.

It's my responsibility to keep her safe and protected. I'll do whatever it takes.

These new emotions take me to a place from a long time ago. The crypt inside me I'd long since left creaks open with the corpse of my very young mother laying lifeless within. I had only been six years old when she died on the filthy single bed we'd shared. Tilting my head back, I welcome the memories, the residual feelings of terror, rage, isolation, everything from that horrible storm I'd been lost in for so many years. As far back as I can remember my normal life was chaos and misery. Then after her overdose, it was enveloped in blood-red rage and fury. The little boy had wanted to grow up and save his mother. The young man had wanted to kill her all over again. The man wants to prevent any other child from living in such hell.

When I was thirteen, the demon inside me was born in a house in the suburbs of New Jersey, a place that assuredly led straight to hell. The demon wanted blood, craved it, wouldn't rest until I fed it. I finally learned how to use it, control it, and make it do my bidding instead of me its slave. It has served me very well, but every day I feel its hunger.

My mother had been a child, only sixteen years old, when she gave birth to me. After years of being raped and beaten by her step-father, she ran away pregnant for the third time. She'd told me one night when I was too young to remember, but I never forgot anything she'd told me, that she'd be damned if she'd let that scumbag beat this baby out of her like the others. She'd said I was the only good thing she'd had in this hell she lived in every day. She'd run away and lived on the streets and did what she needed to in order to survive. The only thing she knew was fucking and sucking cock, she'd been doing it since she was ten, and so that's what she did. Sometimes social services had come and taken me away when the cops found me sleeping in a car. My child mother, with gaudy makeup and track lines, would get a single room in a shit-hole and I'd be returned to her custody.

I loved my mother, she was so beautiful, even with all her pain. As a small child I'd wanted to save her. God, how she needed to be saved. Then she left me, saving herself from this fucked up world, and I was left alone. I hated her for a long time. Then finally, after so many years and so much blood on my hands, I understood and was able to forgive her. I vowed to do something to stop young girls from being used and destroyed like she had.

Eventually, the way for me to do that presented itself in a strip club one night. I'd been dealing drugs for the gang my boys ran with, but the shit I had was clean. It didn't have all that under the sink poison in it that killed everyone. The club manager liked that, and respected me for it. That got me in permanently. I took my connections with me to college, and expanded on the business. Then I fell in love with Amanda. She was the most perfect thing I'd ever seen, so pure and angelic, the complete opposite of the ugliness I was. She made me feel I could be something, anything other than what I thought I was. She didn't know about my 'profession', the moon lighting I did to make money, or my dark past. Surprisingly, I'd gotten a scholarship but that wasn't enough to eat.

The girls on campus needed money too. Some danced, others were desperate but didn't want to be in public. I coordinated an upscale escort service, I screened out the john's and made sure every call was accompanied by either me or another guy I trusted. The services weren't cheap but they were the best, and they were safe, that's what was most important.

My enterprising had begun.

Life was good. Until the night Amanda's father called for three girls to come and service him and two of his business associates in an orgy, all of them Texan oil tycoons. I had no idea who the john's were, I hadn't taken the call or done the screening. Not until I drove the girls there and walked in to check out the place. I laughed at him when he threatened to call the cops, and asked if he'd like to get his face on the eleven o'clock news for solicitation, the caption, "Oil Tycoons New Venture, College Orgies." They kept the girls but that had been the end of my engagement with the only person that was good in my life.

It was the beginning of something else. Amanda's father was the first person in my deck of cards of people I would use later on my climb up.

Losing Amanda had been for the best. We would have made each other miserable, I wanted her because she was everything I wasn't. She wanted garden parties and PTA's. I needed twisted and dark, my demon still needed to be sated.

I've found it.

Gemma has a beautiful darkness inside her and she's mine. I caressed it in her room as The Faceless Man, reached inside her and pulled it from its captivity. Tonight I'm asking her to let it lead her on its release. To give her what she needs and has always yearned for. But there's a light inside Gemma that makes me feel alive again.

I need that more.

It's time to begin.

Gemma

Swathed in the opulence of this decadent cocoon of the taboo, my body hums with need. As my hand traced the dildos and vibrators, ran along the lengths of leather hanging on the wall, and held the coolness of the metal plugs, I felt every whisper of sensation each and every thing promised.

My rational and proper mind reprimanded me as my body clenched and quivered.

I had to decide what I wanted Alex to use.

But that wasn't the question.

The question was what would I allow myself?

He knew it. That is why he asked me to choose. He wanted to gauge my comfort level, he knows I want to indulge, he knows I yearn to, but he wants *me* to tell *him* where *I thought* I want to begin. How safe was I going to play it?

I already knew I loved how I melted with him, consumed by his intensity knowing he would take me where I needed to go, he'd already done it in his office. I loved the depth of hunger his eyes bore into me with, his need so intense when he looked at me made me tremble each and every time. From that first moment, I'd wanted to lay myself at his feet and say, "Take me, use me, fill yourself with me and leave nothing left."

For my first night, I decided on restraints that had two Velcro wraps on each side, I assumed they were for both wrists and ankles. That was the first item. The second item, I chose a butt plug. He'd told me he was going to take me there, this would show him my desire for it. The third, and most difficult item, were nipple clamps. I struggled with the thought of choosing something else, like a crop, or a flogger. Because this was my first night with Alex in his room of decadent indulgence, I decided to play it safe so to speak.

I couldn't help feeling that I was settling because these were all things I was familiar with. I'd never indulged using things like this with anyone except The Faceless Man, all but the plug. Opening myself and becoming vulnerable with my secret desires, handing them to Alex, was like saying, 'This is what I like. Please take me with you with these.'

It's scary.

I laid my choices out on the table at the end of the bed and made my way to the bathroom. I was struck by the beauty of its design, rich like a Roman bath house, and just as impressive as the rest of the house. As the water washes over me, I focus on it, trying to drown out the pounding of my nervous heart.

Dear God, can I do this?

The lights go out; the large room is now illuminated by a single flickering candle. The familiar tremors slither through my body from my nights with The Faceless Man. Those nights, the lights all went out, then he captured me in my room as I entered. The first night initially I was terrorized, I thought he was going to rape me or kill me. But then it turned into a fantasy I didn't know I had, being forced, bound, and taken. Tonight the man I had seen in my mind those nights while The Faceless Man used my body is walking toward me. Alex's large and imposing frame blocks the glow as he silently approaches the shower. His naked body glides toward me, he's powerful and dark, and it makes my breath hitch.

He is too beautiful. But there's something wonderfully dangerous about him.

He steps in and envelopes me, his massive presence wraps around me as he captures me in a kiss that makes my head swim. His erection is pressed tightly between us, thick, tall, and ready. I've been ready since he threw me on the bed.

He doesn't say a word as he turns me and begins to wash my body, rubbing and kneading my muscles from my shoulders, down my arms, my ass cheeks, and both legs. Alex's very touch consumes me and holds me captive. His hand slips between my legs but doesn't stay there, the slight touch only makes me want more.

When he's finished with me, he places my hands on his chest with his on top. Then he starts to guide me over his tautness, washing himself with my hands. I try to move my hands freely, but he stops me. My desire to touch him, feel him, taste him, explore him completely, spikes higher and higher as I travel over every inch of his incredible frame. My inhibitions have melted away and left only intense need.

"Come pet, it's time," his voice is husky with the first words he's spoken since he entered the shower.

I tremble as he dries me then leads me into the room. The only lighting is two candelabra's, one on each side of the room. It lends a sacred hint to the macabre and taboo, perfect for my initiation into his world of darkness.

My King of Darkness.

"Your choices for your first night are quite appealing, Gemma. I hint of pain while making you want, let's begin with the nipple clamps. Then I have a surprise for you."

Fear mingled with heated anticipation grips me.

Am I in over my head?

His fingers trace the curves of my breasts as my nipples harden and my chest rises and falls with heavy breaths. He teases and taunts them, flicking the pebbled points with his fingertip, twisting and pulling them, shooting molten heat through my body. He captures one pebbled point, then the other, securing the clamps on them, as the sweet bite ebbs deliciously to my loins. He crooks his finger and slowly pulls the chain, my nipples stretch with it. I suck in a slow hiss between clenched teeth as erotic pain deliciously courses through me.

"I'm going to blindfold you now, pet. I want you to get lost in your feelings, everything you're experiencing. You are nothing but sensation, want, and need."

"Alex…"

Hunger and fear swirl with each other inside me. The erotic ache from my breasts seeps through me stoking the fire building inside me and makes my pulse quicken. I feel the heat radiating from Alex's body, my heart beat resounds in my ears as his warm breath caresses my bare flesh. Nothing can stop me from giving this powerful man my body. I only hope I can keep my soul.

You're getting in too deep… a voice whispers.
I know…

Alexander

Gemma is here in my room naked and ready to be fucked. But is she ready to truly submit?

I know she's afraid, she feels vulnerable and raw, I can see it quivering in her eyes as it dances with her desire. She's ready for my cock, I felt it with her slick cunt and greedy hands in the shower. I can also tell she's guarded by her clenched fists and rigid posture. The twisted fuck inside me loves it.

Teasing a nipple held in the silver clamps, I say, "I know you're afraid, Gemma."

She takes a long slow breath.

I lower my face and flick the other one with my tongue. "The things I want to do to you." I nibble a long line over her shoulder and up her neck. "I want to tie your hands behind your back, fuck you with my fingers in your cunt and your ass, and feel you come all over them. Then I want your tight pussy wrapped around my cock," I whisper roughly as I move my mouth to bite gently into the soft flesh of her breast only to graze my tongue over the mark.

A soft little moan escapes her kiss swollen lips.

"Do you know how much I love to see my marks on your pale skin?"

Like the handprints I drew on you.

I move my mouth to the other breast and do the same thing. I can feel her shiver against my lips, and it makes dick swell.

"No," she whispers.

I step softly behind her, our bodies barely touching, my hands at my sides, the distance separating our flesh so small, it feels like a whisper between us. I breathe deeply and take in her luscious scent, feminine and musky, it stirs something primal within me. I watch her from behind and over her shoulder, still not touching her. As I listen to her deep breathing, I see the matching rise and fall of her breasts. She's waiting for me to do something, anything, but she's not sure what. As The Faceless Man, I captured her, bound her first with my arms, then with a restraint.

Again, she's not sure what's coming.

"Do you like it, pet, do you like to see me on you?" I say quietly at her ear, my lips barely touching the soft shell.

She gasps lightly through slightly parted lips. "Yes."

I know you do. I watched you trace those handprints on your flesh over and over again with that delicate little finger of yours.

"It's like a branding, just like my cock is going to leave inside you." I flick her nipple with my fingertip, my face at her neck, as I speak softly against her skin.

I glide my hand between her thighs and cup her warm mound. She tenses and leans her head back against my chest and sucks in a breath.

"Mine, Gemma, your hunger, your release, is all mine. I plan to use it all in every way."

Her eyelids dip with longing, the sweet release that's waiting for her is whispering in her ear.

"Tell me Gemma, tell me to take her, that woman inside you, tell me to use her, and I will set her free."

She turns her face to mine and arches her back. She has just stepped over the line of giving up her control to me.

"Take her Alex, use her."

My cock jumps.

"Oh, pet, I plan on using her in many different ways."

I wrap my hand softly around her throat, careful not to add to Salvatore's pain, then clasp her

220

chin, and kiss her. I want to consume her, I need to penetrate her very soul. I flick a captured nipple again and elicit a deep moan from her.

Releasing her, I secure the blindfold on her lust glazed eyes. She presses her nails into the bare flesh of my thighs.

"I want you to bend over the horse and give me that sweet ass of yours. It's time for your surprise."

She bends forward and lowers herself while I guide her down, her glistening pussy and tight ass open and inviting me in.

"You are so fucking exquisite, Gemma. I am going to love every minute of your awakening."

Her body tightens, I know she's quivering inside with anticipation. My demon is clawing, aching to be set free, wanting to devour and ravage Gemma's perfection. I keep it tightly leashed. I'm going to push Gemma past her boundaries, but not tonight. Tonight, I'm going to open the door to her darkness and let it taste sweet fulfillment.

For some women, the rougher the better, and sometimes that is exactly what I need. They want whips, they want blood, they want real pain. Not with Gemma. She wants danger, she wants sensation, she wants to feel. I want her to feel me consuming her, penetrating her completely, body, mind, and soul.

Walking to the dresser, I bring back a candle. I trace my fingers down her spine, the soft touch causes goose bumps to erupt all over her skin. I continue down the crack of her ass, past the puckering hole, and slide my finger through her slickness.

"Such a perfect pussy, Gemma, you're practically dripping. I'm going to fuck you with the plug in your tight ass tonight."

Another heavy breath tells me she likes the sound of that. I slide one finger into her hot sheath, then twist it around, pull it back and forth, slipping it in and out, before bending it to rub my knuckle against her sensitive little g-spot. Her walls clench around it and grip me tightly. I lift the candle above her ass and turn it to the side to watch the hot wax drip and land on her soft skin.

A squeal of protest fills the room as she jumps.

"Ssshhh, stay still. Just feel, pet." My voice is a husky whisper.

Her only movement now is the rapid rising and falling of her back from her breathing, her body is tense. I continue to drip the wax beautifully over the curve of her derriere, so round, so soft, so lush, so inviting. My fingers begin to dance within her as I leave a trail of melted wax molded to her curves. She grips me with every drip of wax, trying to pull me deeper, squeezing me tighter, fucking my fingers with her walls.

Perfect.

I turn the candle upright.

"Do you want to come, pet?" I ask roughly as my dick throbs with my finger still buried in her wetness.

"Yes," she whispers.

I continue to rub her inside, feeling her muscles clench tighter, pushing her closer to the edge. I remove my finger to slide in two, penetrating her, then pulling back, in then out, twisting and turning, bending them to fill her more.

"Do you want me to fuck you, Gemma?"

Moving slowly in and out of her now soaking pussy, I rub her sensitive spot again.

"Yes," she almost whimpers.

"I'm going to fuck you, but first you're going to suck me with your plug in."

"Yes," she gasps.

I thrust in and out of her wetness slowly and deliberately as her walls clench and grip, fucking my fingers. I bend my fingers and rub my knuckles against that spot, and push her over the edge.

"Come on my hand, come all over me, make me drip with your juices, pet."

Her body tightens as she grips me tightly and her pussy spasms around me. The sweet sound of her moans is music to my ears.

"That's it, come, pet, I love how you take what you need so selfishly."

Her erotic whimpers make my balls tighten, and the sight of her clear white skin bathed in dripped candle wax makes me long to leave marks all over her. It's my turn to groan as I sink my teeth tenderly into the meaty flesh of her thigh.

"Oh God," she moans deeply as she arches her back while still coming around my fingers.

When her orgasm slows, I tell her, "I need to get your ass ready for your present," as I bend to nibble on her other thigh, biting and licking it, unable to resist the urge to mark her flesh more.

I return the candle to the stand then squirt some lube on my hand, warm it in my palms, then spread the gel on the plug and over her, rimming her hole, enjoying how she squirms under my touch. Pushing against it, I love how it opens slowly to let me in. I watch her ass pull me in greedily as my finger disappears in her tightness. I slide my finger slowly out then press the tip of the plug against the entrance of her ass. Fondling her clit with the other hand, I watch the plug sink in. Just before it dips in, I begin to fuck her gently with it as I work her sensitive nub. Her soft whimpers of pleasure float toward me as my engorged cock pulses, hungry to fuck her.

"I can't wait to sink into you with this filling you up, feeling it rub against my cock inside you."

"Oh God, Alex," she moans louder.

"I need you to suck me now, Gemma"

"I want to taste you Alex."

"I know pet, you're hungry…for everything."

I know she's almost ready to come again, but I'm going to make her wait.

After inserting the plug carefully in her ass, I wrap her hair around my hand and lift her body from the horse, then turn her.

"On your knees, Gemma."

Lowering to her knees, she finds my legs with her hands and lifts her face to me, her lips parted. I slip my pinky under the chain of her nipple clamps and pull slowly. Her nipples stretching with the clamps is such a beautiful sight as her shoulders roll forward. She sucks in a breath and my hard-on jerks again.

"Give me your hands."

I place my hands on hers and guide them to my groin. She leans forward and rubs her cheek against my hardness, the tender gesture makes me tremble, but that twisted dark part of me wants to cram her throat full of my cock. She turns her face and begins to lick the length of me, from the root to the head as she clasps my balls tightly in one hand and the other grips my shaft. That sweet tongue of hers covers every inch of me, but when she runs it along the underside of the rim, my head falls back as my balls tighten.

"God Gemma, so good, so fucking good."

She begins to suck me feverishly, pulling me all the way to the back of her throat. I resist the temptation to force it deeper.

"That's it baby, swallow, let me push all the way down your throat."

She swallows and clamps down on my head over and over again at the back of her throat, feasting on me. She grips my balls tightly again as she pumps my cock with her other hand.

"I'm going to come pet," I growl.

She sucks harder, grips tighter, and fucks my dick with her mouth and hand like an animal, pulling my cum from me. I explode into her mouth, fucking her face with the force of my climax, bringing her face into me with my grip on her hair. She keeps on sucking me with that same fevered pace, getting me hard and ready to fuck her like I want. Like she needs.

Pulling my cock from her mouth, "Gemma, you're going to make me come again," I grit through my teeth.

"I love how you taste, Alex."

The drips slipping from her mouth are one of the sexiest things I've seen. I want to cover her with my cum.

"I want that pussy now, baby," I growl, my shaft aching to sink deeply into her.

Guiding her up by her arms, I turn her to the horse to bend over.

She bends forward, ass in the air still covered with the residual wax, ready and open, the blue stone at the end of her plug twinkling at me.

Running a finger along the curves and creases waiting for me, I ask, "I know you chose a certain restraint, but I'd like to use another, do you mind?" I rub my hands over her cheeks, dusting the remaining wax off and caressing her curves.

Her back is rising and falling with her breaths, anticipating what I'm going to do, and eagerly waiting for that orgasm she was ready for.

"No," she answers quietly.

"Ah, pet, you are perfect."

I move to the armoire that holds the restraints to find the spreader bar and Velcro cuffs. After turning on a cello concerto, I return to her as the haunting symphony fills the air. I stroke her flawless skin and watch as she begins to float on each note. She barely notices when I separate her legs to attach the bar on her ankles then restrain her arms to the legs of the horse.

In my mind, now I would glide the flogger or the crop over her flesh before using it to make her skin sing.

Soon...

Stepping behind her, I slide myself between her thighs, and my erection against her slick mound. Her back arches as her hips reach back to me. I begin to stroke her from her shoulders, down her arms, up the sides of her back, then I press firmly as I glide down her spine, scratching slightly, my cock thrusting against her with each of my movements. The dance becomes faster, harder, my shaft rubbing her mound and clit, until I press my fingers into the flesh at her hips and my length into her heat. Pushing so deep into her, I hold her hips against me and relish the feel of her wrapped tightly around my cock. I want to reach inside her, fill her completely, I don't want a single space within her not filled with me. I need to consume her entirely, possess her, own, make her mine.

"Yes," she moans.

The light red lines glowing on her back drives me, the need to mark her more, make her feel me inside and out, have every inch of her know I've been there.

The music sets the pace of my thrusts, and hers as her body arches with it, her ass reaches back to me, calling me in. The wave rises to a fevered pitch, my hips drive into her harder, deeper, demanding her to meet me. The tightness inside her from the plug rubbing my cock fuels me and pushes me faster. The crescendo crashes, pulling us into its frenzy as I bury myself inside her and reach to rub her clit again, and we both explode. She cries out as she comes, her body rigid and her pussy pulsing around my cock, pulling every drop of my climax from me.

"Gemma," I growl deeply as I slide in and out of her, the burning rush going on and on, thrusting us together, spiraling out of control.

"Alex, yes, more…"

Her walls are still grabbing, still gripping me tightly, clenching and unclenching, the heel of my palm not letting up on her climax swollen clit. Her back arches and she moans loudly again as another wave takes her. I reach down and open her wrist restraints then pull her body up to press against mine, one arm around her waist, the other holding her by her chin, needing her close.

"Ah, pet, the things I'm going to do to you," I murmur breathlessly at her ear.

"I can't wait, Mr. Black," she pants.

"I know."

I take a long slow swipe on her cheek with my tongue and relish her taste as the last tremors ripple through our bodies. Turning her face to me, I kiss her hungrily, our tongues clashing and twirling together, tangling and feasting on each other.

"Hold onto the horse, Gemma, I'm going to release your ankles."

When the bar is off, I pull her against me again and stroke her sex, smearing our cum all over her.

"Taste us together," my voice is husky, the desire to see her do this has been a long time coming.

She opens her mouth and I slip two fingers in covered in our cum and watch as she sucks it clean.

"So fucking sweet, pet. Let's have a bath, then I'm taking you to bed."

"Mmmmmm, your wish is my command," she mumbles.

I remove the blindfold and kiss each of her eyes, then her nose, and finally her mouth.

"Any place, anytime, anywhere, pet."

And anyway, my demon whispers from the shadows.

It's starving. Her body was not enough.

CHAPTER 14

Alexander

I pick up the phone to call a man I haven't spoken with in almost ten years. I don't hesitate, we're brothers, born from the same shitty streets and circumstances, fought side by side against our enemies. There are things we did for each other that we will never speak of, those demons are best left in hell. Although we went down different paths, I know I can call him, just like he can call me, and we'll be there for each other without question.

I listen to the line ring as I sit in my still empty office. Seven in the morning, it's even too early for Gemma to come strolling in.

Will she have the sunglasses on this morning?

My cock jerks remembering how I whispered to her to spread her legs at four thirty this morning. She was deliciously still hazy from sleep but her instincts obeyed immediately. I needed to make her come, had to feel her quivering and hear her moans. Her orgasms are my addiction, they're my fix, and I'll shoot-up any fucking time I want.

God, I can't get enough of that woman.

"Black, long time no hear, how've you been?"

My old friend. It's so good to hear his voice.

"I've been good, bro, but this is a business call."

"I figured, tell me what you need."

This man is the one person I can trust to get me exactly what I need, and the only one with the resources at his disposal to get it, legitimate or by less desirable means.

I take a deep breath and sit back in my chair.

"I've got a spy in my company."

There is no sound as he contemplates what I've just said.

"Interesting."

"Very."

"The source must be quite impressive to have bypassed all your security checks."

"That's why I called you."

"Send me all the employee files as hardcopies. I'll text you my address."

"I will. There's one more thing."

"Nothing is ever simple with you, is it, Black."

The humor in his tone makes me smile.

"What fun is simple?"

"None, boring as fuck. What's the other thing?"

"A woman, new employee, Gemma Trudeau. Soon to be ex-wife of a man who stole three million dollars from me, Malcolm Stevens."

"That's different…but not for you."

I can hear his grin; he knows me very well.

"That's not the most unusual part of it…she's living with me."

I hear rustling on the other end of the line and can picture him bolting upright in his chair.

"Tell me I heard that wrong?"

"No, you heard me right."

"You're shitting, bro, right? Like intimately living?"

"Very, and don't even think of her like that, I'll kick your fucking ass."

He slowly whistles.

I continue.

"There's more. She's been contacted by someone, a stalker, since she started working for me. He referred to her acquaintances, her affiliation here, and some of her activities inside the office. That's what alerted me to the plant."

"Stop. Have you had the place checked for bugs?"

"Yes, over the weekend and again this morning. Several were found Saturday but not today."

When I find out who it is, I'm going to enjoy tearing him apart bit by slow, bloody bit. He saw me with Gemma...in here...exposed and raw. If I could kill him a hundred times, it wouldn't be enough.

"Shit's getting real, bro. For someone to fuck with the business world's biggest prick, Alexander Black, they've got to have a huge set of balls." He pauses. "This Malcolm Stevens thing is more than just a deal gone bad. A whole lot more."

I smirk. No one else would get away with calling me that except him, even though it is true.

"I knew you'd catch on fast."

"I'll find out what I can on Stevens and Trudeau while I'm waiting for your package."

"Thanks." I hesitate. "Listen, Hilda misses you."

I take this opportunity to go where I know he doesn't want me to go.

"Don't, Black."

"We've all got our crosses. I just wanted you to know."

"Thanks, I'll be in touch."

The line goes dead.

Sitting back at my desk, images from the past flash through my mind. There is so much pain and wasted lives, heartache and anger. There'll be time to cross that bridge when I finally see him, you can only avoid the ghosts for so long.

I feel content now things are in motion, and when the work day begins, I'm sure the floodgates are going to blow.

I'm NOT going to let anything happen to Gemma. I couldn't bear it if she were hurt because of me.

There's a crack in my thick veneer and she's penetrated it, and slowly seeping inside.

It's too late to turn back now.

Gemma

An erotic tremor ripples through me as flashes of last night play in my mind and on my body. I can still feel the strength of Alex's kiss on my lips, the memory alone has the power to consume me. I could not have asked for anything more perfect for an initiation into the dark side. But I have a nagging suspicion Alex was holding back. Another heated ripple slips through me as I imagine him really letting go.

Take it easy, you're supposed to be using him, it's only supposed to be sex.

I remind myself this is only physical between Alex and me, and yet I can't help feeling safe and protected with Alex. When he touches me, he owns me, I can't deny it. It's hypnotic and natural, in that moment I belong to him completely, yet my mind doesn't want that. It warns me I'm only going to get hurt. So, I'll put up my guards along with my clothes.

I know this is going to be a very weird day!

It's certainly starting out that way. For God's sake, I'm dressing for work in Alexander Black's bedroom in the penthouse suite of his five story mansion. This is something I NEVER anticipated doing. I feel like Cinderella and the clock is stuck on one minute to midnight.

The phone next to the bed rings and pulls me from my daydreams and thoughts, but I'm confused because I'm not sure if I should answer it.

"Everybody in the house knows he's not here." I mumble. I walk to the nightstand and answer it. "Hello?"

"Señorita, you come for breakfast before you leave, sí?"

It's Hilda, Alex's house manager, the woman who is like a mother to him.

"I, uh," I was going to decline but I change my mind. "I'll be down in just a minute, Hilda, thank you very much."

"Bueno."

This would be a perfect opportunity to find out what Mr. Black is really like by someone who truly knows him the best. Filled with a new sense of purpose, I rush to finish dressing and head downstairs.

When I enter the spotless black and white kitchen, the design is monochromatic just like the rest of the common areas on the lower levels, I smell fresh brewing coffee and bacon. My stomach rumbles as I take a seat at the breakfast bar.

"Sentarse, I told that boy if he kept you locked up all the time, I was going to spank him with a switch."

I almost spit out the sip of rich coffee she's just given me. I can't stop the chuckle after I swallow it, envisioning this five-foot matronly middle-aged woman spanking the very intimidating Alexander Black.

That is something I'd like to see.

"You laugh, he knows I would do it," she smiles genuinely, sporting a gold tooth just like her son Jesús. She continues as she places an overflowing plate of scrambled eggs, bacon, hash browns, and English muffins in front of me. "The part of New Jersey we all came from, Alex too, everybody needed to be able to protect themselves, even me. I have kicked many asses in my day, including Alex's."

My respect for this surrogate mother has just shot way up.

"You're from New Jersey? I am too, Jersey City," I make small talk, attempting to create a bond with her as I begin to inhale the delicious breakfast.

"I know who you are Gemma Trudeau," she smirks cheekily at me. "There isn't anything that goes on in this house, or with my boy Alex, that I don't know."

Okay, I'm officially in love with this woman.

"I think you're the one with all the control in this house," I smile at her, giving her the admiration she deserves. "Maybe you can tell me really why Alex brought me here," I say, taking another sip of coffee.

She raises her eyebrows at me and gives me a sideways glance. "A lot of reasons Gemma, it wasn't just to get his dick wet."

This time I do choke on the coffee still in my mouth.

Hilda throws her head back and laughs as she returns to the stove. "Niños, get in here and eat," she yells over her shoulder.

"We were waiting for you to finish giving her the once over before we came in," a young man I don't recognize comes in followed by Jesús.

They take two seats at the other end of the breakfast bar, as far away from me as possible.

They either can't stand me, or they're following orders.

Hilda places their breakfast in front of them.

"These two are my sons, you know Jesús, and this is Carlos, his older brother."

"Mama, why do you still have to call him the older brother? I'm a man, it doesn't matter," Jesús comments as he digs into his breakfast.

"It always matters, and don't talk back to me."

Hilda comes around to stand behind the men eating heartily and gives them both a big kiss and a hug.

"You will all always be my little boys, no matter how old you get." Hilda turns her gaze to me as she places her hands on her hips. "Now, I know you have some questions and I'm not really going to answer. BUT," she cuts me off seeing the surprise on my face, "I will tell you some things. You do need some information because you are in this house now, and Alex is protecting you." She raises her hand, cutting all three of us off. "Shush, boys, she needs to know." Wiping her hands on her apron, she begins. "You know Jesús, and I'm sure you're not stupid so I'm assuming you also know he's more than just a driver." I nod my head once. "Carlos watches Alex's businesses on the street, and in the house. Alex has a lot of enemies; they've been lining up since he was a boy. Apparently," she grabs the coffee pot to refill her son's cups, "your husband was working for one of them." She turns to wash the dishes indicating she's given me all the information she's going to.

Alex's enemies.

The words hit me like a punch in the stomach. These kind of people don't use words and slander as their weapons, the game to them is lethal.

When I arrive at Black Inc. at eight, I don't bother going to my desk, but straight to Alex's throne room. Even though he'd made me come while it was still pitch black outside, my lust crazed body still yearns for him

"Good morning, Mr. Black. I had quite the dream earlier. I was almost late for work," I grin at him slyly as I lean against the doorway.

This man takes my breath away. He's perfectly polished, undoubtedly the envy of every man, and the wet dreams of every woman. But he has a hint of something sinister in him. There is always a touch of fear in the rush of my desire when I merely look at him.

"Ms. Trudeau," he walks toward me with erotic arrogance, "had you been late for work, there would have been certain 'repercussions' you would have had to face. I do not tolerate misbehavior."

He slides an arm around my waist and pulls me in, then closes the door behind me.

"Oh? I was not aware of repercussions when I took the position. I would have to argue that would make that clause null and void due to lack of disclosure," I respond, pressing my body into his as I slide a hand up his chest.

"That is where you are incorrect. I listed the details quite thoroughly. Let me remind you: I will bend you over my desk, bare your ass, and spank you so hard, you will beg for mercy. Then I will tie you up in nothing but your sexy bra and panties, and keep you there. All. Day." His smirk is delightfully wicked.

"Oh yes, I do recall the conversation. You neglected to mention that would be the result from any infraction. Lack of disclosure. I object." I slide my hand around his neck and lift my face to his.

"Overruled, Ms. Trudeau. Anything, anytime, anywhere," he replies deeply before his mouth covers mine in a slow, hungry kiss.

"You," I breathe out heavily, "are," swipe his lips with my tongue, "quite," suck his bottom lip in my mouth, "demanding."

He silences me with his tongue plunged deep in my mouth.

"I am. You're going to find out how demanding."

He turns me and pushes me roughly against the glass door. He yanks my skirt up and kicks my legs apart with his foot before he pulls my shirt from me, then palms my sex forcefully. It makes me moan.

"This is mine, Ms. Trudeau."

"Alex," I whisper.

God, I love how he takes me.

"I'm going to fuck you Gemma. Right now. It's going to be rough and it's going to be hard."

...It's going to be rough and it's going to be hard...

The flicker of a memory with The Faceless Man floats like a feather in the back of my mind. My pulse quickens and my loins clench.

"On your knees pet, take my cock out." With my hair wrapped around his hand, he pulls my head back gently.

Without hesitation, I lower to my knees in front of him, my mouth watering, hungry to have him sucked deep inside it. I open his pants and pull out his very large erection, getting harder, longer, and thicker by the second. I flick my tongue and take the drop of clear precum before sliding my lips over the swollen head and licking his long, thick shaft.

"Bend over the desk. Now." His command is tight and urgent, just like my need.

He guides me by my hair to stand, the sensation sends tingles all down my body. I push whatever's in my way on his desk to the side and bend, instantly ready for him to fill me. He pulls my panties down and off my feet before spreading my legs and sliding his cock over my wetness.

"God Gemma, so wet, so ready."

"I'm in a constant state of readiness with you," I pant.

"Good baby, because I want to make you come," he pushes inside me, "all," he pulls back, "the," pushes back in, "time," pulls almost all the way out only to slam into me hard and deep.

My nails dig into his desk as his steady, deep thrusts take me away.

Hours later after being thoroughly and deliciously serviced, my cell phone rings.

"Don't think this is finished, Gemma."

Tony Salvatore!

"I'm not mad at you, Tony," *Bullshit! I'm so fucking angry at you, I could scream!* I struggle to keep my voice calm, it's obvious he's unstable. "But please leave me alone."

"Do you think I give a fuck if you're mad at me or not?!" he shouts at me. "Where the fuck are you? With the piece of shit, Black?"

"Tony," I say as calmly and as firmly as I can. "Don't call me again."

I hang up.

My body is shaking. The fear from that night he attacked me floods me again as rage consumes me.

"That is one sick man."

Alexander

"Mr. Black," Simon's voice cuts through my concentration as I'm examining the information on my computer screen.

"Yes."

"There is a John Salvatore on the phone. He said you'd know what it's about."

Damn straight I know what it's about. I'm only surprised he didn't send his guys here in person. Maybe he knows his son better than I thought he did.

"I'll take it Simon."

I pick up the receiver and swivel my chair to look out the windows overlooking Fifth Avenue behind me.

"John. I've been expecting your call."

"Black. You know why I'm calling. Business has been very good between us. We don't need things that would cause any problems."

"You should keep your son on a tighter leash then, John. I tried to kill him but Gemma stopped me. He deserved it."

"Alex, you shouldn't talk about my son that way, he is blood."

"This is business John. I don't have anything to do with the two women he keeps in the hospital on rotating shifts, but I'll be damned if he thinks your family owns Gemma and he can do that to her too. THAT is bad business. And very, very personal."

"Is that what she told you?" the older man's voice is very hard.

"That's what I heard. Tony's recorded saying that, amongst other things."

"Gemma's father was a good friend of mine. I offered my protection from that pussy husband of hers, and anything she might need because of the friendship out of the kindness of my heart. Nothing else."

"I'm sure of that John, its Tony who seems to think otherwise."

"I'll take care of it."

"Thank you. We need to have a sit-down with the heads of all the families. And it needs to be immediately."

"I'll arrange it. How soon do you want it?"

"Tonight."

He takes in a deep breath.

"It'll be hard, but in light of the circumstances, and I'm sure you have your reasons, they'll all make it. Same place?"

"No," *I don't trust anyone.* "I'll let you know an hour before it's to take place and the location."

"I trust you Black, and things have only been good between the families and you. I'm sure no one will have a problem with that."

It's me who doesn't trust you.

"You'll hear from me soon," I say before I hang up.

Because of that lack of trust, even in my own employees, I send Gemma a text.

I need you to come to my office. I have to talk to you about something.

Her reply is instant.

I'll be right in.

"Simon," I call him. "I'm expecting Ms. Trudeau, let her right in."

"Certainly, Mr. Black."

A minute later she's walking through the door. My raging need to fuck her again slams into me.

"Close it behind you," I instruct her, my voice rough with that need.

"Ready so soon, Mr. Black? I could get fired," she teases as she closes the door quietly and takes a seat across from me.

I have to force myself to keep focused on business, and not on her body and what I want to do to it.

"There isn't a minute I'm not ready to fuck you, Gemma. If I could have you tied and open for me all the time, I would. Unfortunately, life has thrown us into a situation."

"You are insatiable, Mr. Black, but yes, reality does have a way of demanding attention." She shifts nervously in her chair.

There's something she needs to tell me.

"Speaking of life, Tony Salvatore called me today."

Cold, hard rage, and a need to destroy him, that's what I immediately feel.

"What did he say?"

She's afraid of him, I can see it in her eyes.

"He said this isn't finished…and he asked if I was with you."

I sit back in my chair.

He wants to fuck with me? Let him try.

"Did he now? And what did you tell him?"

She tilts her head at me with the fire back in her eyes.

That's my girl!

"The only things I said were 'Don't call me again,' and, 'Leave me alone.' What do you think I would have said? 'Let's have lunch?'

"With you? I would have thought more along the lines of, 'Go fuck yourself,' which is about what you told him but in a nice way."

The fact she's being so honest and open with me is almost surprising.

"I'm glad you told me, Gemma."

"No secrets you said, Alex."

"I know. I just want you to know that I appreciate it."

Do I deserve you, Gemma?

Time to get back to business.

"I'll take care of Salvatore. Now, what I wanted to speak to you about. You know what's going on. It's because of the strange phone calls you received that alerted me to the fact there's a mole in my company."

"I'm so sorry Alex, I feel responsible. I'll leave…," she responds with a pained expression.

"No, I really doubt it's because of you. What I do believe is whoever it is thinks you being here is an added bonus." I pause. "You are the only one here I can trust, how ironic, don't you agree?"

"Yeah, a total blast," she rolls her eyes.

"I know this isn't easy for you, but I promised, nothing is going to happen to you. I swear."

"It's not that, Alex, I can't help feeling responsible."

"You did nothing wrong, you're a victim in this. But we have work to do."

"Tell me what you need."

"First, you are no longer working for Miles. As far as anyone is concerned, you are a legal representative of Black Inc., which from today you are. You answer to no one except me. The first thing I need you to do is prepare a hardcopy that lists every one of my employees. I'm sending it to a friend of mine who is going to check everyone out. No one can know what you're doing. This," I slide a piece of paper across the desk to her, "is the information you'll need to gain access. It is my personal information. Every minute detail of my business will be at your fingertips, Gemma."

I can tell she's uncomfortable.

I add, "Using that is the only way you'll have access to everything. I trust you, Gemma."

Pulling herself up straighter, she squares her shoulders. She's ready to fight.

"Thank you, Alex. That means a lot to me."

"Good girl, pet. We're going to get this son-of-a-bitch. And we're going to make a lot of heads roll on the way."

"Yes we are, Mr. Black."

Her satisfied grin tells me everything I need to know.

Own

CHAPTER 15

Alexander

Carlos and I enter the private meeting room I reserved in the Plaza Hotel for the sit-down with the five families of the Cosa Nostra. This is my meeting; it will be done on my terms on my turf. I sit down and make the call to notify John Salvatore of the location.

I wasn't going to take any chances. I wanted to be here when I notified them of the place and time. The bad guys are like cockroaches, they're everywhere and you never see them coming.

Carlos is restless, he's primed for something to go down. Some soldiers are so deeply programmed; they need situations to blow off steam in order to have a sense of calm. Carlos is one of them. He was a street soldier before he enlisted in the Army, but the military turned him into an animal of war. Conflict is his sustenance. A lot of gang members are soldiers. To keep the peace, I set up a private boot-camp where these guys can go and get their fix and blow off that raging steam. If they didn't have it, there would be a hell of a lot of unnecessary bloodshed all over the streets.

Carlos has arranged for several of his military gang brothers to be strategically placed in and around the hotel. These men's strongest loyalty is to each other, and the gang. That is their motto, fuck everyone else. I proved my loyalty to them a long time ago, that's the only reason they're here. I am one of them.

I'm not taking any chances.

"I'm gonna go do a quick sweep around," Carlos throws me a glance over his shoulder before leaving the room.

"Thanks," I mutter in response.

Good, he'd probably shoot someone if they opened the door.

With Carlos here with me, I can't help worry about Gemma. I know she's with Jesús, but if I don't see her with my own eyes, have her close, I'm worried.

It's only because I feel responsible for her, the attempt to justify my actions comes quickly.

"Gemma." Her voice on the phone strangely soothes me.

"Black, are you okay?" She sounds concerned.

"Yes, are you at the house?"

I know she is, Jesús already checked in with me when they'd arrived. I only use it as an excuse for my call.

"Alex, I'm not stupid, I know you're aware of that. What's going on?"

Her tone becomes tender and comforting.

God, I miss you.

That thought out of nowhere shocks the shit out of me.

"Nothing. I'm meeting with the five families in an hour. I wanted to check on you while I'm waiting."

She chuckles, not surprised in the least that I'm meeting with the Italian mob, and the sound is a melody to my ears.

I'm turning into a soft little pussy.

"Well, Mr. Black, I'm working. You have a lot of employees but I'm about half way finished getting all their necessary information listed. Your office at home is a lot cozier than your lion's den, sir. Do you suffer from multiple personalities?"

I grin remembering the first time I watched her on the computer screen fucking herself right where she's sitting.

"No, Ms. Trudeau, I am very aware of all my different facets, each one serves me well. When I get home, I want you laid out on that desk in nothing but one of my shirts. As a matter of fact, I want you to strip right now."

"You're joking," her tone has dropped and is instantly laced with desire.

"Is this going to be you're first infraction? I do hope so. I'm dying to see that ass of yours bright red with my handprints all over it."

"The clothes are coming off, Mr. Black." She's almost breathless.

"Good pet. Now, go to my closet and pick out one of my shirts. That will be the only thing you'll have on until I get home."

"You, sir, are a brute."

"Fair warning, Gemma," my tone is now almost menacing. "Tonight I'm going to be."

I hear her breathe deeply.

"Gemma?"

"Yes?" she whispers.

"You want it." Of this I'm certain.

"...Yes...," she whispers again.

"I know, pet. See you soon."

"Bye Alex."

I can hear she's aroused, and it makes my dick throb.

"Till later then, baby."

I hit end and focus on the upcoming meeting, wondering if I'll be looking into the face of my enemy.

A short while later Carlos slips back in.

"News?" I ask.

All my senses are peaked, reaching out for anything to alert me to an upcoming conflict.

"I got a report from the rear of the hotel that a delivery van just pulled up."

"At seven o'clock on a week night?"

"Exactly," Carlos spits out, pacing the room like a caged animal.

"What do you think?" I ask him.

I trust his instincts implicitly. He can sense a threat from ten miles away. Carlos saved so many lives in his unit, and on the streets, he knows when something bad is waiting.

"Bro, nothing's gonna go down here. I'm sure those guys are soldiers just like you've got. But I've got a real bad feeling, hombre. Shit's going to get bad, real bad, like nothing we've ever seen before. I can feel it."

"I know."

I sit quietly contemplating Carlos' words, the very same things I haven't wanted to admit.

He checks in with all security points systematically, keeping his visual going from the confines of this room.

Finally, we get word that the guests have started to arrive.

I take my place at the head of the table. Carlos has called in two other men to stand-by as extra guards in here with us, both of them his cousins. I won't ask for anyone to leave their weapons, or sweep them for bugs. This is a business meeting, and an opportunity for me to look at each of the bosses in the eye.

As they trickle in, I greet each man with a tight smile and a handshake. The table has already been set with refreshments and food to avoid any unnecessary interruptions. Business is business and I cannot risk jeopardizing their trust.

John Salvatore walks in. I study his face to search for anything that will tell me he's going to betray everything we've built with the families.

"It's good you called this meeting Alex," John greets me with his usual condescending attitude.

I eat more powerful men than you for breakfast.

"Everyone's here, let's get started."

I take my place again.

"Gentlemen, thank you all for coming on such short notice. We'll try to get through this quickly so you can get back to your families."

Each man nods his acknowledgement and waits for me to continue.

"Let's start with telling me what you know about Frank Trudeau, Gemma Trudeau's father."

The tense atmosphere gets even more strained. I can see the surprise in all their faces, they weren't expecting this.

John Salvatore is the first one to speak, which is what *I* expected.

"He was a good friend of mine. He was never a threat to any of our businesses or people, he knew we are a family, and he was a family man."

The others nod their agreement.

"Then why was he and his wife killed?"

I steeple my fingers in front of me and wait.

They look to each other cautiously to see who will be the one to answer. Giancarlo stands and begins to slowly pace.

"They were killed, but for some reason their death, as you know, was classified as an accident. We found out differently. The hit didn't come from us, this I can promise you. A handful of cops refused to accept it, they were quickly silenced, but we don't know by whom. It wasn't our business so we didn't keep probing. However," he stops and turns to me, "the man thought to have caused the accident is dead. Out of respect for Frank and his wife. Frank was our friend."

I nod. They had the guy killed. Good. Unfortunately, he's gone and I can't interrogate him. Then kill him myself.

"What was his name?"

Giancarlo opens his hands, palms up. "Alexander, he's been taken care of."

"What. Was. His. Name?"

All these men hesitate, staring at me cold and hard.

"His name," Salvatore speaks up, "was Anatoly Bykov."

"Russian."

This news does not sit well with me. My gut is screaming this is not a coincidence.

"Yes," Salvatore confirms it.

"Was he part of the Odessa group out of Brighton Beach?" I press.

The Odessa group is the most prominent and dominant criminal Russian group in the United States.

"Our sources told us he was not a made man, only a hired hand."

"What did you give them in return for him?"

I'm boiling now. There wasn't any retribution done. Gemma's parents were killed by a Russian gangster and this Anatoly Bykov was given as a peacekeeping for these men to save face.

"Nothing, Black." Salvatore's tone is almost threatening.

"Don't give me that shit. No one loses a man without demanding justice," I snarl at him.

"I won't take offense to your insinuation. The hit on the Trudeau's didn't come from the Odessa group. Bykov was disposable."

"Where the fuck did it come from then?"

I can barely contain my rage at his flippant attitude, at all of their lack of concern. The Russian's killed a cop, one of their friends, and they don't give a shit. Something is definitely not right.

"We don't know," he states with finality.

We glare at each other. Salvatore knows I'm far from finished with this. But it's clear I'm not getting anything else from him. It could be any reason. One, because he made a deal with the Russian mob. Two, the Cosa Nostra doesn't have the means to get to the top of this. Three, it has nothing to do with them.

I believe it's all three of these reasons. I have to find out where the order came from.

The coincidences are too extreme. Gemma's parents got killed by a Russian gangster, her husband, Malcom Stevens, lures me into a Ponzi scheme and steals three million dollars from me, there's a spy in company, and I do business in Russia, very dangerous business.

I know I won't get the answers I need so I move on.

"What about Gemma?"

"As I told you, it was a gesture of friendship that I extended our help, nothing more, no strings. We take care of family and she lost hers. That piece of shit husband was nothing but trouble for her."

"Did he have something to do with the deaths?"

A collective eyebrow raise goes around the table.

Fucking WOPs.

Giancarlo continues, "Like I said, it wasn't our business."

"I don't give a fuck. Answer me, did he have something to do with it?" My voice is menacingly low.

Luciano from Staten Island speaks up.

"It's safe to say that Gemma would not be in the situation she's in if it wasn't for him."

"Malcolm was involved with the Russians."

A cold chill seeps up my spine.

The fucking weasel's puppet master was the Russians, could that be possible?

Luciano's back straightens and a mask slips over his features.

"That we don't know. We wanted to find out who was responsible for the Trudeau's deaths, and we did. That was the job, and we took care of it."

That is the final piece of confirmation I need. I take a deep cleansing breath attempting to keep my rage in check. These men are street people and everything they're insinuating goes way beyond their realm.

"All of you know what happened with Tony," I begin the original topic that brought us together.

Salvatore raises his hand. "That was a misunderstanding, it will not happen again. My apologies for the…indiscretion. My family does not wish to do anything to disturb all that we've gained, much thanks to you, Black."

"That's wise. Gemma is my responsibility. Make sure he leaves her alone." My meaning, and the promise of revenge, is resoundingly clear. "You should know someone is stalking her. If someone even threatens to hurt her, there will be retribution. No matter who it is."

My warning is obvious, if anyone fucks with Gemma its war. I say nothing about my part in it, I want them to tell me about it with their looks and actions. Unfortunately, they all appear to be surprised. I glance to Carlos knowing he's observing as well. We lock eyes and I see he hasn't noticed anything to cause alarm when I brought up Gemma.

"If we can be of any assistance, do not hesitate to ask," Luciano makes the obligatory offer.

I know the strong arm of the mob is outdated. Their expertise, with my help, has been shifted to other avenues. They can't help me. But they could be an annoyance if their delicate balance is upset.

My work here is finished. For now.

"Gentlemen, if there isn't anything further to discuss, I will bid you goodnight."

They all stand and say their farewells and shake my hand on the way out. As John Salvatore turns, there is a very hard look of hatred in his eyes.

That's the real man I've been waiting to see. What are you capable of, Salvatore? What would you be willing to do to satisfy the sick fuck you really are?

When the room has been cleared and Carlos and I are alone, we take a seat at the table.

"What do you think about that?" I ask him.

"The fucking Russians, bro, that is some serious shit."

"I know. The question is what did Frank Trudeau know that got him killed?" I sit back in my chair. "I doubt it was only that Malcolm was involved with false business schemes."

"It's too close to home, homey."

"Exactly. Everything is too close to home."

"Funny how that's looking." Carlos' chuckle is a sneer.

I look him in the eyes.

"Do you think the mob is in with the Russians?"

He gives me a sarcastic laugh. I am well aware of what he thinks of the mafia.

"They know you're their golden boy, but I wouldn't be surprised. Those fucking guys are all has beens, the entire institution of the mafia. It's outdated and they're only riding your coattails to keep them profitable. They don't give a shit about you, you're just a meal ticket for them. If it weren't for you," he looks at me, "they'd all still be only picking up garbage and taking bets. If they are, they're playing both of you."

I agree with him. But it's better to have them in my pocket because of my bigger projects. That way I can control their business, rather than try to destroy it.

"Do you think any of them are involved with the mole?"

He takes a moment to really consider it.

"Honestly, I don't think they've got the initiative, or the power to attempt something that extreme. They're all greedy as fuck to do it though, if someone approached them. No fucking loyalty, not one of them. But whoever is behind it, it's not one of them."

"Do you think that person is using one of them though?"

"That," he answers slowly, "I'm not sure of."

Neither am I.

"Get some men, we need the best Information Technology people in their field, and counter intelligence professionals. I want the elite, the most decorated, I want the men the Pentagon wished it had. There are no coincidences, and there are too many lives at stake not to see this is a lot bigger than what went on in this room."

There's a deal going down in China in a few days, transactions that took me years to quietly set-up. So far, they've been transpiring perfectly. Russia has already been established, linking other European countries. There's too much at risk.

But why Malcolm? Why did they choose him?

My mind is racing trying to figure that out.
What about Gemma? Was she next?
Never.

CHAPTER 16

Gemma

It's been a struggle trying to stay focused on the extremely boring task of compiling the list of more employees than I can even count. Especially because I'm naked under one of Alex's shirts. And I can't stop remembering what he told me...what he warned me.

...Tonight I'm going to be...

I've been envisioning things, things he might do to me, with all those delectably wonderful toys he's got in that, what did Hilda call it?, dungeon. An excited tremor ripples through my body and makes me giggle.

I've been torn about freeloading on Alex, fighting with myself every day that I should leave and go stay with Gina, Tony Salvatore's sister. I would be safe there. Even though Tony is her brother, she wouldn't let him anywhere near me, and would kick his ass if he tried. But each time Alex gazes at me with that penetrating look of hunger, that insatiable need, when he strokes a fingertip over the smallest bare flesh, I crumble. My body rages with a yearning so deep, it shakes my soul.

I try to convince myself that I'm only using him for sex. I'm only here to fulfill all those unknown fantasies I've had. Too bad my heart's not listening. There were no promises for more spoken between us, only sexual release. Pleasure that would make me burn.

Which is exactly how I've felt since he called me, his words had the same intoxicating effect.

I'm waiting for you.

His text sends a fresh wave of anticipation through me.

Where?

Come into the room. There will be a blindfold for you at the foot of the St. Andrews Cross, that must be the big cross attached to the wall. *Slip off my shirt and let it fall to the floor. Put on the blindfold, turn your back to the wall. Raise your arms to rest on the cross and spread your legs as far as you are comfortable. Then I will come to you.*

OH. MY. GOD!

My heart is racing, I'm trembling, and a thin sheen of sweat has just erupted all over my body.

I feel like I'm moving in slow motion as I close all the open windows on the computer and straighten the documents I've printed. It's as if I've become disembodied and I'm observing myself from the outside. Although I showered after dinner, I can almost smell the scent of sex all over me.

He's created an animal, a ravenous lust hungry beast. I need more...I need it all.

Walking slowly toward the dungeon, the beautiful room of every erotic desire I could ever imagine, I know I'm about to cross that line into the unknown I've always wanted to submerge in. When I turn the knob and quietly open the door, the soft strains of classical music float out. The room is completely black except for a soft white light illuminating the St. Andrews Cross, the glow highlighting the chains and cuffs hanging from it. Another heated tremor passes through me.

Where is he?

Closing the door behind me, I walk softly to the cross. I let his shirt slip down my arms and fall to the floor at my feet. The cross looks unforgiving, but inviting, and tempts me to run my hand along its length. I'm quivering inside as I press my nakedness against it, I need to feel it beneath me before I give myself over to it. I tentatively clasp a cuff and chain in my hand, the weight pulling a response from deep within me. I spy the blindfold folded neatly at the foot of the cross so I bend to pick it up and carefully tie it over my eyes. A rush washes over me as the darkness and the music engulf me, it's so strong I have to ground myself by holding onto the cross. My entire being is thrumming as I turn to rest my back against the padded wooden X. I spread my legs, raise my open arms above my head, then I take a deep breath.

Alexander

My body shook with possessive rage imagining Gemma in danger.

NO ONE IS TOUCHING HER. Except me. She's mine!

It wasn't even a conscious thought. From somewhere deep inside me I KNEW there isn't anything I won't do to protect her. The possession I feel for her is natural and immense, strange and unfamiliar, it takes me off-guard, but it's right.

From my chair in the darkened corner, I watch her. I love to watch her. She has no idea what an incredible sensually stunning woman she is. And she's giving herself to me.

I am one lucky son-of-a-bitch.

I have to stifle a groan when she runs her hands up the length of the padded plank and caresses it like a lover.

Ah, pet, that isn't the only thing you're going to be introduced to tonight.

I watch the rise and fall of her breasts with each intake of breath, how her fingers close and open in her palms, and the slow lick of her lips with her pink tongue.

Lifting myself from the chair, the carpet muffles my steps to her. I have to get close to her, feel the heat of her body penetrate mine. She can feel my closeness, I can tell by the hardening of her nipples and how her head dips back ever so slightly.

That's right, pet, let go.

Very gently, I touch a pebbled nipple with the tip of my finger. The slight touch sends a ripple of electricity coursing through me. Her body goes rigid, arcing to it as she gasps loudly. I follow the line of her body up her arm to clasp her wrist to enclose it in the padded cuff. I do not touch her as I fasten the other wrist and her ankles. When she's restrained, I step back and fill my eyes with her.

Fuck!

I grit my teeth and growl silently.

Placing my hands on the wall at the sides of her head, I lean forward and take a soft swipe of her lips with my tongue to taste her. Her mouth drops open. I pull her lower lip between my teeth and bite. She gasps. I close my teeth on the outer curve of her breast needing to see my mark on her. She pushes it into my mouth. I brand her all over her body with my teeth, lips and tongue, licking a long line up her arms and nibbling a trail up and down her thighs. She writhes beneath me. Still, I don't touch her except with what I'm imprinting her with.

She's here, she's safe. She's going to stay that way.

The music rises and falls, dips and bends, carrying us into the darkness.

I step back and watch her breathe. I can see her loins pulse with each roll of her stomach. Picking up the crop, I place it on her cheek. She turns her face to it and lifts her shoulder, her expression that of a woman welcoming her seducer. I know she can smell the leather, recognize the shape, and she's imagining how it's going to feel when it kisses her skin. I slide it down her neck, over one breast, leg, then up the inside of her thigh, over her pussy, (she moans deeply), down the inside of the other thigh, up her leg and over her abdomen to slip over her other nipple, until it comes to rest below her chin, lifting it up. I hold her face like that as I lower my mouth to hers and trace her lips again with my hungry tongue. I can feel her trembling, the longing consuming her.

I pull myself and the crop from her.

I've been waiting for this, Gemma.

I bring the crop down on one of her breasts with the flick of my wrist.

"Oh God!" she moans.

"Feel it, pet, feel it kiss you, burn you. Feel me…"

The other breast.

"Yes!"

I leave a trail of love bites with the crop down one side of her body, then up the other.

Her moans, wails, and cries come out in a continuous chorus, an incoherent song of letting go.

The first contact of the crop on her clit makes her scream. The second one begins a succession of pleas for more.

"YES! YES! YES!"

My cock is screaming at me to fuck her, my demon is appreciating the taste of her body and the marks on her flesh.

When the chant turns to another scream, I know Gemma is coming, her greedy clit pushed to the extreme with the crop. I drop it on the floor, remove her blindfold, and kiss her, swallowing her pleasure, sucking her inside me. She feasts on my mouth, devouring it in her rapture.

Still I don't touch her.

Her body begins to slump against mine, crashing from the ride.

"Alex," she whispers hoarsely.

"Pet, I'm going to fuck you now."

I have to be inside her.

"Oh God," she moans as her body presses into mine.

I reach up to release her wrists, and bring each one to my mouth to kiss and rub.

"Hold on to my shoulders while I get your ankles."

When she's free, I lift her in my arms and carry her to the bed. My cock is so hard, it hurts the most exquisite pain. I could do that all night if she wanted and still not come. But Gemma needs more. I do too. I need to feel her wrapped around me

"Lay back, pet, give me your sweet cunt, I want your cum."

"Alex, please…"

"Please what, Gemma?"

I'm straddling her body, my face hovering over hers. I know she can see my raging need in my expression.

"I...," she hesitates.

I clasp her chin firmly.

"Tell me, or I'll stop."

"I need more...," she whispers.

"Say it, pet."

I take her nipple between two fingers and pinch.

"I ache. Fuck me now, Alex."

"That's not enough."

My gaze bores into her.

"Alex..."

Her eyes are pleading.

"I need you," she whispers.

She's completely vulnerable and open beneath me.

An all-consuming heat of possession floods me.

I kiss her. It's raw, it's claiming, it's a turning point neither of us will ever come back from.

"First I'm going to suck every drop of your cum from that hungry cunt, then I'll fuck you."

Her eyes close and her head dips back.

Gemma

He is my destruction and my salvation, my death and my resurrection, my oblivion and my fulfillment. All that I want in all that I need.

I am not here but I feel every wisp of his breath on my skin, my every nerve scorches where he touches me. I am no longer me but an extension of him.

The first swipe of his tongue over my still pulsating sex plunges me back into the throes of ecstasy.

I am lost.

I am home.

He is not separate from me but a continuation. I do not end...we do not end but go on and on.

Alex's mouth on me, licking, sucking, flicking, and nibbling, his hands gripping, stroking pressing, pushing, pulling. He's thrusting me into another abyss, and the fall is spectacular.

Then he turns me on my stomach, pulls my hips up and spreads my cheeks with his hands. My loins ache to feel him inside me, the thought of that sweet first push of his thickness has my heart pounding.

"So sweet, Gemma, so perfect, I don't want to fuck you because I don't want to come. The lust drugged look on your face, your dripping cunt, the soft little moans you make when you whimper for more, THAT is my drug, that is what fuels me, I need it so bad it hurts."

"Please Alex." The groan is a plea for a release I so desperately need.

"I will let you come just a little, I want more, pet."

OhGod, OhGod, OhGod, OhGoooooooood....

Sliding a single finger inside me, he begins to thrust it in and out so slowly, it's wonderfully torturous.

"What a greedy pussy you have, pet, she's grabbing my finger begging me to fuck her."

I moan, "Yes, I need you to."

My hips begin to gyrate, circling and dipping round and round, trying to take my release.

Smack!

His hand lands on my ass cheek and the sting shoots straight to my sex and makes my walls pulse and my hips buck.

Oh God, yes...

"Keep still, pet, your orgasms are mine. *You* are mine," he growls.

Yours completely...

I bite my lip, I'm this close to coming again, I could scream.

He continues his soft stroking, building my need with every thrust of his finger. I grip him tightly inside me, squeezing him, hungry for more.

"So ready, you're dripping."

"Yes...," I breathe.

He slips in two fingers keeping up his hypnotic rhythm, in then out, twist and turn. Finally, he buries them deep inside me and bends them, rubbing his knuckles against my front wall.

"Come for me pet, squeeze down on me and come," he whispers roughly at my ear.

I bear down on him pulling my orgasm from him, pulling everything from him into me that he'll give me, and it shoots through every part of me. The hungry pulsing seeps the warm release through me and I moan a long cry of relief. The slow drug rushes through me, seeping into my limbs and mind, creating a hypnotic kaleidoscope of colors dancing behind my eyes.

But I want more.

Alexander

Make her scream.

The demon inside me howls for satisfaction, demanding pain and punishment, trying to push me.

No!

The struggle to force him back, the struggle for control is constant.

Fighting the desire to ram my cock into her ass, its puckering tightness taunting me, I dig my fingers into her hips and slam into her velvet heat.

CHAPTER 17

Alexander

"Rashad, give me something."

Frustration is fucked up.

"Mr. Black," he breathes out, he's got frustration all over his voice.

"Just spit out," I bark.

"The phone that was used to make the calls to Gemma's desk line was a burn phone," he says apprehensively. "A piece of shit pre-paid he picked up at some drugstore. We've got nothing on that."

"Fuck!" I growl. "What have you got on Malcolm Stevens?"

"Not much more."

"Explain."

"I was able to break through some of the walls the Feds put up. The only things I found were nondescript communications listing places and times followed by very vague confirmations. Nothing gave away any information."

"What about the other parties, do you have an IP address, anything that would give identities?"

He lets out a heavy sigh. "All the messages on both sides were opened at public computers, libraries, internet cafés, not one private, aside from his personal one. Then they were routed through an intricate system through European and Eastern countries, making the trace a tangled mess. I'm still working on following it. Whoever set up the communications knew exactly what they were doing."

I pause as I digest this information.

"Or...,"

"...That was the location...," he finishes for me.

"Yes. What countries?" I ask, closing my eyes, hoping he's not going to tell me what I think he's going to.

"So far, I've got Russia and China."

"Son-of-a-bitch!"

That's what I was afraid of.

First, I find out the man who killed Gemma's parents was Russian and affiliated with the Odessa group, not officially but he was still connected. Second, I have an envoy heading to China in a few days under the guise of a business transaction that will be dealing with a more private and dangerous ongoing project.

I grit my teeth.

This is not a fucking coincidence!

Accepting the information, I ask, "Is there anything that would identify what the communications were about?"

"I haven't been able to make any sense of it, but they use the words pretty, ripe, and pure."

Oh God, no...!

"Send me copies of all that you've been able to get so far, and don't forward anything electronically. Don't talk to anyone about this, don't let anyone see any documentation. I'm sending over a private system that's not on our servers you are to use for this from now on. I'm setting up a new location that I'm moving you to soon. NOTHING is to be done through Black, Inc., do I make myself perfectly clear, Rashad?"

"Yes, Mr. Black, of course," he replies nervously.

Checking my anger, I continue, "We have a mole in the company. If these people find out you have information on them, although you have no idea what you've got, you could be in danger. I'm sending over Carlos to pick up your system. Clean out what you've got before he gets there."

I only hope it's not too late.

"I'll get started on it right away."

"Get whatever you need for the new system, and route it however you need to. But hide what you're doing, Rashad, I can't stress that enough."

"I understand, Mr. Black."

The guy's shitting his pants, I can tell. He should be.

"Good, and don't worry. Call me when the system arrives and I'll talk you through how I want you to set up your access. You're not using your current information."

"Good idea," there is obvious relief in his voice now.

"Excellent, and thanks, I sincerely appreciate everything you're doing. I mean that."

"Of course, Mr. Black. We'll get them, I promise."

"I know we will. Talk soon."

I disengage the call and contemplate this newest light on the mess that's unfolding.

I am so enraged. I have no doubt now what's happening. Someone is trying to destroy my empire, take down everything I've built. I don't give a shit about myself. What I really do has nothing to do with me. It's for those innocent victims that live in hell every day.

This is huge. And it's only just beginning.

I glance at Gemma, completely lost in thought, through the glass wall.

This was supposed to be a game. All I wanted was to find out what she knows. I am now absolutely certain it's nothing.

Her intention was to use me too.

Get her close, break her down, use her, and make her need.

That was the plan. When the fuck did she crawl under my skin?

She has no clue what's going on, no idea of the power at play here. She's in danger. I'm not going to let anything happen to her.

Malcolm's three million dollar embezzlement was a game of cards compared to what I think is the bigger prize.

What the fuck have I dragged her into?

I remind myself I didn't start this shit, her scumbag ex-husband did. Also, if it hadn't been for Gemma being here, the spy wouldn't have been exposed and I wouldn't have found out about the Russian connection. Hopefully it's early enough for me to stop it before it goes any further.

They want a war, bring it, it's on motherfuckers!

This persona I wear for the world in the expensive three piece suits only serves to allow me entrance into the global world. I sneer behind the mask of civility I've perfected. I'm a killer, an animal that hungers for blood, the song I love the most is the cries of my victims begging for mercy. It's been so long since I've heard them. I've had a lifetime of training in every war preparing me for this. The battles have changed over the years, but its fucking war, no matter where it is.

They've just unlocked the cage and dangled fresh meat in front of my demons face.

I dial Carlos' number.

"Yeah, boss," he picks up on the first ring.

"How soon can your guy meet me?"

"We can be to you in an hour."

"Have Jesús pick you up, then come and get me. We've got things to discuss."

"Okay, I'll be there in an hour."

"Call your boys, it's time to start preparing," I say ominously.

"Fuck yeah! It's about time."

I glance at Gemma again, forcing myself to harden to her. I can't let even the slightest bit of weakness distract me. There are too many people at risk.

Yes, it is. The key is finding out where the battle is going to start.

Gemma

"Ms. Trudeau, do I need to call you that now?"

I didn't hear Miles Davis walk up to my desk, nor did I see him standing in the doorway leaning casually against the frame like he's got nothing better to do.

"Jesus, Miles, you scared me, I didn't hear you."

I minimize what I was working on the computer screen.

Miles Davis, the man I was hired to be his assistant, the man who asked me if I wanted a boy toy, the man who I'm sure probably recently finished his internship.

He saunters in to my little private space, pushes my purse out of the way on the top of the file cabinet, and makes himself comfortable.

"I hear the boss-man made you a legal representative. I'm not surprised, and I figured it was going to happen, but damn, that was fast," he laughs.

I try to sound indifferent and laugh. Unfortunately, I sound like a strangled duck. I don't know if Miles is joking or is there distaste disguised in his offhanded comments.

"Yeah, I know, it surprised me too."

You and I both know it's you who should have been my assistant. I'll let you play, but don't push me.

"So, do I have to call you *Ms. Trudeau* now? Make appointments to talk to you and shit?"

You had to push.

"Only when I'm Vice President. Gemma will do for now." My tone is humorous, but the words ring loudly with sincere possibility.

"Touché, touché. I knew you were a badass when I interviewed you, haha! Truce, okay?"

"Come on, Miles, you know I'm only playing."

My attempt to lighten my ball-busting teeters on bullshit and the truth. It all depends on what he thinks of me.

"You might be joking, but I know it's highly feasible." He lowers his head, shaking it, still chuckling. "Damn, wait until the business world finds out that Malcolm Stevens' wife…"

The atmosphere shifts from tight to playful. I can't keep up with this guy.

"Soon to be ex-wife, Miles, watch it," I shove his shoulder, keeping up the now light mood.

"Yeah, yeah, ex-wife, is one of the infamous Alexander Black's legal representatives. They are going to SHIT! This is so fucking great."

He's like a kid getting ready to toilet paper a house on Halloween, the mischief and mayhem is pouring from him.

"I am *so* happy you think this is hilarious, Miles. Let me know when I'm supposed to laugh."

I've got my arms folded across my chest trying to glare at him, but I can't stop the smirk from exploding on my face.

His eyes are dancing with mirth.

"You've got to admit, Gemma, the whole situation is incredible. No one would believe it looking in from the outside."

"I know, I know. But seriously, Miles, in all sincerity, do you think my being here is going to hurt Black Inc.?"

I pull my lip between my teeth, worrying it. This has been a concern of mine since the whole mole thing came up. I feel responsible for it, even if Alex said it had nothing to do with me. My affiliation with Malcolm alone makes me guilty by association.

"Come on, Gemma, you must surely know Black by now. Do you honestly think he gives a flying fuck what anybody thinks? He's got so much damn money, controls so many companies, he could wipe his ass with thousand dollar bills and it wouldn't make the slightest difference."

I consider the weight of what he's just told me, rolling the words around in my mind, each one adding a brush stroke to the masterpiece that is Alexander Black.

"He's that powerful?" I ask hoping to get a more vivid idea of who the man really is.

Miles leans in closer, his eyes wide. "He's so powerful, Gemma, he could pull the strings on the President of the United fucking States," his voice is a hushed declaration brimming with awe.

Good God, that can't be possible! What have I gotten myself into?

"You're exaggerating, but I agree, Black is pretty intimidating, that I will admit," I brush off his comment.

"I shit you not, Gemma. He's got his hands in so many companies around the world, I haven't been able to figure out the rhyme or reason of it all. Some of them are so diverse, there's no correlation with any others. But there is a reason for every little thing he does. That right there is the magic key. Black is the only one who knows what that key unlocks."

I've seen the avenues he takes to get there. UN diplomats, mob bosses, complete opposite ends of the spectrum. The man is a complex enigma.

"So what does Black have you working on?" he asks, peering over my shoulder. "Some top secret case?"

I'm instantly on guard.

Why do you want to know? Are you the spy? Are you so desperate now you've got to come in and ask for the information, thinking I'm just going to hand it over to you so you can destroy Alex? You must think I'm completely stupid.

"Oh yes, international secrets. They're so important, the entire free world would be destroyed if they ever got out."

I play along, looking like the proverbial clueless female perfectly.

"Really?"

"Yes, these copyright infringement situations would take down dynasties."

"Of course, we wouldn't want our Eastern associate's worlds to fall into ruin." He smiles. "More boring shit, huh?"

"Very," I laugh.

He stands and heads to the doorway.

"We should do lunch again soon, I enjoyed it. My offer still stands, Gemma." His smile turns into a smirk. "I've thought about you. Like I said before, a lover isn't a problem, but a wonderful distraction."

"Miles, if I didn't like you, I would show you exactly what my father, the cop, taught me about dealing with boys who needed to learn their place. Do you want me to show you?" I quirk an eyebrow at him, daring him.

He throws his hands up and laughs.

"Okay, I get it."

"Good. One more comment, and I'm going to beat your ass so fast, you're not going to know what hit you."

"Damn girl! Still, let's have lunch soon. I had fun."

"Me too. We will, now get out of here, I've got work to do."

"Yeah, right, the exciting copyright stuff. Wouldn't want to keep you from that," he replies with light sarcasm.

"It's so boring, I have to fight to stay awake."

I do have to fight to stay awake because Alex had me coming before the birds woke up this morning.

"I've got something that will wake you up," he grins lasciviously at me.

"GO MILES."

I shove him out the door and hear him laughing all the way to his desk.

Before Miles is seated, my phone vibrates with a message. I roll my eyes.

Here we go.

First I'm going to cut his dick off, then I'll fire him.

I smile.

Why, Mr. Black, could it be you're jealous?

Jealousy is for those who want something someone else has. Possessive, Ms. Trudeau.

My heart is beating faster as a wave of desire pulses through me.

Remember what I told you about your possessions, Mr. Black? I am not a thing.

I wait as my heart pounds. I know I'm pushing him, and it's exciting the hell out of me.

No, Ms. Trudeau, you are flesh and sin, yearning and hunger, and you are mine to take. Only.

The things you do to me, Black, scare me. I should run fast and far. This game we're playing is dangerous, very dangerous. I'm going to lose, I know it. I'm going to give you everything, body, mind, heart and soul, hand it all over to you. Is it worth it? Be careful, Gemma, don't show him you're weak.

Yes, Mr. Black, quite a delicious little game we're playing.

A minute ticks by and there is no reply so I begin to worry if I've gone too far.

"A game, Ms. Trudeau?"

My pulse quickens and my body heat instantly rises.

He's standing directly behind me looming over me with his hands on my shoulders squeezing me tightly.

"Mr. Black," I feign casual indifference. "So nice of you to visit me…out here…in the middle of the day."

"You're fucking with me, Gemma," his mouth is at my ear and his voice is deceptively low. "I don't enjoy getting fucked with." He stands to his full height, all powerful six foot plus, radiating savage authority. "Come with me."

He grabs my hand and pulls me up, practically dragging me behind him.

"Mr. Black," I'm making every effort to maintain aloof professionalism as he leads me through the crowded office. "I would be happy to, but slow down."

"It's apparent I have to prove a point to you."

All eyes are on us, especially Miles'. Every mouth is hanging open dumbstruck, except his. He's grinning from ear to ear.

Asshole!

I glare at him.

Alex pulls me into the conference room and locks the door. I've never been in here. It's huge but completely silent, with extra thick carpeting on the floor, sofas and loveseats along the walls, and sound absorbers on the ceiling, designed so that nothing that is said in here can be heard outside.

Alex pushes me back against the table until my ass slams into it. His face is a hard mask.

"So you say this is a game we're playing, is that right Ms. Trudeau?"

"Yes," I lie.

"Let's see if that's the truth, shall we? Let's play a game."

…let's play a game… The Faceless Man said that just before he made me come over and over again with my vibrator, he called it forced orgasms. My eyes go wide.

No...

He steps closer to me, his eyes cold, his lips smiling tightly.

My mind is racing, my heart is pounding, and my body is pulsing.

This is the ruthless man I knew was inside him, calculating and dangerous, the deadly man who stopped Tony Salvatore from choking me then beat him with a gun with rage in his eyes. He is a predator, lethal and fierce. My blood heats up as I tremble. I'm afraid but so aroused, the slickness is already pooling in my sex.

He yanks my skirt up roughly, grabs my thong with both hands and shreds it from my body, then shoves it in his pocket.

"Alex..."

"Quiet," he whispers hoarsely. "Don't say a word," he states with his finger against my lips, "until you're screaming to come."

I clench my teeth fighting the urge to moan.

He picks me up and sets me roughly on the table then pushes me to lie down.

"A game, Ms. Trudeau," the words are menacing. "Not mine?" He shoves my legs apart. "Is that what you think?"

"Alex," I pant.

"I said quiet," his hand smacks my mound and hits my already throbbing clit.

I scream out loud as erotic spasms rock my body.

"You're not coming, pet, let me make myself perfectly clear."

He thrusts two fingers into my wetness. I squeeze them tightly, hungry for more.

"You lied to me. Look at how wet you already are. I don't like being lied to. That is an infraction, remember what I said about that?"

He's going to spank me!

My body tenses with longing.

"Yes, you do. You're going to beg for more. That will be your punishment."

His fingers begin to move so slowly, so deliciously, but so torturously unfulfillingly, making me yearn for more. He can feel my walls getting tighter as my body tenses beneath his tight grip spread open before him. He slips his fingers from me, leaving me gasping for release.

Smack.

His hand comes down on my clit again, the sweet stinging pushing me just to the edge.

He pulls me up and flips me over, my legs hanging over the side of the table, and my ass on the edge.

"Count Gemma," he commands tightly.

Smack!

His hand lands hard on my flesh and burns me with his handprint.

"ONE," I grit out.

Smack!

"TWO," the other cheek just as hard.

The onslaught goes on until I rasp out, "Twenty!" my eyes are squeezed tightly shut with tears brimming in them.

He grips my sex and I tremble.

YES!

"You're dripping, Gemma," he whispers seductively at my ear with his hand holding my cunt possessively. "You need to come, but you're not. Not until we're home, and I make you beg for it."

I moan with hungry need.

"You're mine, all of you. Your body doesn't lie."

He pulls me up by my hair, straightens my skirt, locks me in an embrace, and kisses me. It's hard and demanding, making me yield to him yet again.

"This is so far from a game, Gemma. You know it and I know it, there's no denying it."

"I know, Alex, it scares me."

Don't, Gemma, don't show him how vulnerable you are.

He cups my cheek gently, his palm hot from spanking me.

"I know."

I see sincerity in his ice blue eyes.

Do you, Alex? Do you really know that I'm afraid you're going to break my heart?

CHAPTER 18

Alexander

Harden to her? That's a fucking joke. The only thing that gets hard is my dick, and that I have no control over. A game? Do I look like I'm laughing?

Jesús is waiting for me in the Hummer in front of the Black Building when I throw the front door open. In the car, Carlos is sitting in the front passenger seat and Patrick Stewart is waiting in the back for me. He is a retired Army major specializing in intelligence.

Carlos turns to me.

"This is Major Stewart. I told you he was my commanding officer in the Army. Major," he turns to the large man beside me, "This is Alexander Black."

"Major, thank you so much for meeting with me on such short notice. I'll assume that Carlos has gone over the details of the situation?"

The major is an imposing figure, the picture perfect image of a military issued soldier who commands confident authority. His credentials were impeccable listing successful missions throughout his extensive military career.

"Mr. Black, it is a pleasure to meet you. Yes, Carlos has given me a thorough explanation of all the known players, possible threats, and the casualties so far. I must say, Black, I knew who you were, but I had no idea what your real dealings are. I am thoroughly impressed. That is why I accepted the position. I am honored to be a part of this."

Receiving praise from a man that has been responsible for so many lifesaving important missions leaves me a little humbled, a feat not easily accomplished.

"Thank you Major, but it's not about me."

"I know, Black, that's why I'm here. Tell me what else I need to know."

"I'll begin with some of my unusual affiliations. You are fully aware of my desired results, what you have to understand is I will use whatever means I have to in order to achieve them."

"Understandable, the government does it too. They've been in bed with so many criminals in order to burn the house down, it's impossible to count," the Major nods his agreement.

I continue. "I'm glad we understand each other. My closest men, such as Carlos, are members of a Latin gang. As you know, once a member, always a member. The gang allows me certain liberties as I have opened up very profitable business opportunities for them. In return, some members are part of my team under my employ. I also have business dealings with the Italian mob. That is how I learned about the Russian connection, which Carlos has told you about. The name of the man that was responsible for the hit on Frank Trudeau and his wife is Anatoly Bykov. I believe he was with the Odessa group." I look intently at Major Stewart. "I'm not concerned about any of these mafia groups, Major. What I need you and your team for is to find out who is pulling their strings. There is a much larger, more important powerhouse behind this."

He returns my gaze, processing my meaning.

"Do you have any idea who it might be, and why?" he asks.

"Who it might be, no. Why, absolutely. My business dealings are global with the primary focus in the countries where I've established the underground situations. As you know, these countries are the most dangerous and corrupt. Therefore, it could be anyone, or any organization, even the government. Many of my contacts in these locations are government officials as well."

"Well, Mr. Black, it looks like we've got quite a few networks to zero in on. When can me and my men get started?" Major Stewart grins at me.

He's getting a hard-on for this. That's beautiful.

I return his smirk, knowing he's looking forward to the situation.

"Jesús," I speak to my driver, "take us to the house. Let's show Major Stewart the location they'll be working out of."

"You got it," he replies slyly, grinning from ear to ear.

"It's going to be good working with you again, Major," Carlos adds.

He's got a shit eating grin on his face as well.

"I'm looking forward to it, Ramirez," Major Stewart replies. Turning back to me, he says, "Let's get these bastards."

I lean back in the seat.

"That's all I need to hear, Major."

When we pull into the driveway at my home at seven east ninety-sixth street, Major Stewart asks, "This is where we'll be stationed out of?"

"Yes, this is my home. The lower level is being outfitted for your purposes. You can see what we've got in place so far, then you'll have carte blanche to obtain whatever you'll need. Don't be concerned that I won't be able to obtain the necessary equipment, just let Carlos know exactly what that is and it will be here."

He laughs.

"I don't doubt it, Mr. Black."

"When can you have your team here?" I ask.

"When do you want them?"

"Yesterday."

"They'll be here today."

"Have you supplied Carlos with the list of their names and information?"

I don't trust anyone. Even your guys get checked out.

"Yes, the Major gave them to me when we first met and I've gone through all of them. They're all clean, most I've worked with in the service," Carlos informs me.

"They're all battle trained as well?" I ask.

"We were all stationed in Fallujah together. Each of them could take out a single city block alone, Mr. Black," Major Stewart assures me.

"Excellent. How many men?"

"Ten to begin with, I can have more if necessary, and they are prepared to work remotely if the situation calls for it."

I nod.

Jesús leads us into the house, Carlos is at the rear, Major Stewart and I in the center. When we enter, I step to the side to let Major Stewart study his new headquarters.

The room so far has been outfitted with a large screen almost entirely encompassing a wall that the computers can feed information to display on. There are rows of computers all with their homepages illuminated, and a board for notations. Every piece of equipment is of the highest caliber, all at military and intelligence level, even the seemingly inconsequential.

Major Stewart paces through the rows of monitors.

"Are there any systems installed already?" he asks, bending to click open available links.

"Each one has Data Mining Technology, Data Agregation Technology, Pattern Recognition Systems, and Hypothesis Generation Technology," I answer.

He nods his approval.

"Those are excellent places to start. Is there a satellite already in place?" he asks, hitting the keys on the computer's keyboard.

"Yes," I answer simply.

The large screen on the wall lights up.

"Welcome to Data Mining Technology," a phantom male voice surrounds us. "Please input your information to get started."

The Major turns and grins at me.

I smirk.

"If you'd prefer a female, that can be arranged," I comment.

"No, this will suffice," he responds smugly, then straightens. "I'll call the team, then get started." He walks over to me and extends his hand. "Mr. Black," I take it with a firm shake, "Operation Black has officially begun."

"Excellent, Major Stewart, then I'll leave you to do what you do. Carlos has phones for you and your team, they're all programmed with the necessary contact numbers. He'll give you yours, it is the only one with my personal cell phone number. Call me at any time with anything. Welcome, and thank you."

I allow myself a slight momentary sense of relief, grateful for a positive move in the right direction.

This has to be a success, there are too many people in danger, especially Gemma.

"I'm honored to be a part of your team and what it stands for. Don't worry, we'll find the source, and extinguish it, you have my word."

"I know, Major. That is precisely why you're here. There is a mission in China, my representative is heading out in two days." I reach into my pocket and withdraw a sheet of folded paper. "Here is the guise it will be hooded under along with the parties involved in the mission. Focus on that to begin with. I need to head back to the office, but I'll be back later. You'll have keys to come and go as you please. My house manager has been notified of your arrival, you can reach her by the phone on the wall. She's Jesús and Carlos' mother."

"I'll have an update ready for you."

"Very good." I turn to Jesús, "Let's go."

We head out the door to deal with the next order of business.

In the car, my mind is calculating the upcoming sequence of events. The transaction in China is first, Russia has been coordinated and scheduled, with Africa following.

I need to contact my old friend to see what he's got on Malcolm and Gemma and let him know about Bykov.

I dial his number.

"I was just going to call you, old man."

I instinctively smile.

"Old man? Last I knew we are the same age."

"Yes, but I'm not a stuffed shirt with a two-by-four stuck up my ass like you. Age is a state of mind."

"Hah! Is that it? It must be the cop thing; it gives you a God complex."

"Bullshit, quite the opposite. Listen, I got info," he shifts to serious.

"Talk."

"Stevens had quite the active secret life."

"I'm listening," I retort.

"He's taken several trips to Georgia and San Francisco, none of them related to his day job."

"That confirms his affiliation with the Russians."

"Considering the Odessa group is most prominent in Georgia, those were the people he was seen with there. But how did you find out?" he asks.

"Gemma Trudeau's parents were killed by Anatoly Bykov, now deceased thanks to the Italians. He was a member of the Odessa group. Her father was a cop in Jersey."

"I know. I also know they classified the deaths as an accident, something some of the force strongly disagreed with."

"Interesting, wouldn't you say?" I ask sarcastically.

"Very."

"Stevens' trips to San Francisco make sense too."

"How so?"

"His online communications show a lot of traffic through Asian networks."

"The Chinese mob, people he was seen with there."

"Exactly, they're very big in San Francisco."

"Listen, Black, I've taken some time off. Each avenue I've gone down has led to bigger doors and only more questions. I'm coming up so don't send the paperwork, I'll get it when I arrive."

"I think that's a good idea. There's a lot more to this than I've told you."

"I'm seeing that, Black."

"When you arrive, I'll give you all the information, and you'll meet the latest team we've put together. I think you're going to like them. I have a very strong feeling this is going to be huge."

"Like I said, nothing is ever simple with you, Black."

You'll see this isn't about just me, Rico.

"I'll send the jet, what airport are you out of?"

"Damn, homes, I rank the Black private jet?"

"Shut up asshole, I would have sent it anytime you wanted to come home. What hick town in North Carolina do I send it to?"

"Wilmington. I'm ready to go, let me know when to expect it."

"Jesús will coordinate the flight plan and give you a call. It will be today."

"How is the little shit?" His voice is now strained with emotion.

"He's got a huge smile on his face. What's that Jesús? You're going to give him the ass kicking he needs? Just don't kill him until he's finished the job."

"Suck my dick, Black. Let me know when to be at the airport," Rico laughs into the phone.

I know you're looking forward to coming home, Rico. Everyone's got to face their demons eventually.

"I can't wait to see you, brother," I say quietly.

We've got so much history, so many things between us that no one else knows.

"Me too, but this is business," he replies trying to hide what he's feeling.

"It is. And I appreciate you coming. I'll see you soon. Bye."

The line goes dead.

Rico's got so much pain in his heart, he's hidden from it for years, and I only hope I can bring him back before bitterness takes him completely.

We've got a lot of history, some good, some grotesque. He was the one who found me when I was thirteen hiding in the abandoned building where we hung out. Hell, I was in the spot he and I always ran to, probably waiting for him. I was a crumpled ball of agony, bloody and broken. The moment he saw me he knew. I didn't have to tell him I'd been raped by the sixteen-year-old boy in my foster home. The blood and bruises covering me from head to toe had come from his friends that had held me down, beating me to stop me from fighting back.

Come on, negro, let's fuck them up.

I can still see his face when he said that, soft as a fucking peach, not even old enough to shave. He was filled with rage and not afraid of anyone or anything, and very dangerous, lack of fear will make you that way, but he had to be.

We took care of the friends, hiding around the corner of a set of stairs, emerging from behind dumpsters, they never saw us coming, but we made damn sure not one of them would live a long and happy life. I arranged for the scumbag who'd raped to befall a life changing accident. He's still alive because some things are worse than death.

Three years later when we were sixteen, Rico had fallen in love. Her name was Isabelle; she was Hilda's daughter. She was beautiful, and as tough as her brothers, but she had a huge heart like her mother. We were cutting through an alley, the three of us, me, Rico, and Isabelle, when we were surrounded by a rival gang. We shouldn't have been out in the streets, it was the middle of the day and we were supposed to be in school. We thought we had better things to do.

They had wanted revenge. Our boys had gone on their turf and they wanted to show us a lesson. Two of their gang members grabbed Isabelle while the others started to kick mine and Rico's asses. When Rico saw one of them punch Isabelle in the face, he lost it. She knew how to fight and was giving it all she had, at times getting the better of the two guys. The blow made her fall to her knees. Rico turned savage and pulled out his knife, slashing anything and everyone in front of him. The guys who had been holding Isabelle ran to jump Rico to get him to the ground. I was fighting off two of my own. They couldn't hold him down, the blood was flying everywhere, and screams were echoing off the walls all around us. Isabelle ran to pull the guys off Rico. That's when the gun went off. Everything stopped. I remember it, every long, drawn-out second. Isabelle collapsed to the ground. A second later the guys ran off. She was dead. Rico's gut wrenching wail tore my soul from my body, and from that moment, I never felt another emotion.

Rico left shortly after that, and for a long time no one knew where he was. Me, I decided I was going to get revenge, but my way. I went to school, got a scholarship, then I graduated from college. When I got out, and Carlos and Jesús had finished their term in the service, I finally took it. That gang was destroyed; their bodies still haven't been found.

Aside from revenge, that retaliation began a very long and successful relationship with the Latinos.

"He's coming home," I hear Jesús mutter.

"Yes, let me know when you've arranged it. Send someone with the plane, I don't want to take any chances. I have some paperwork they need to pick up so Rico has it to review on the flight. Have them get it at the office before departure."

"Got it. And for the record, I *am* going to kick his ass, payback for all the shit he gave me growing up," he adds with a smirk in the rearview mirror.

I smile remembering those days' years ago. Jesús was the runt of our pack of boys, Rico was the one everyone looked up to. Nothing could keep Jesús from shadowing Rico, his hero. Rico had a soft spot for the annoying brat, much like me. I wasn't family, and I was a white boy, but they called me *negro*, Spanish for black. Rico was the one who gave him all the hard lessons, many of them a beating to toughen him up. Jesús took every single one like a champ, and went back for more.

The day Rico's life was destroyed when Isabelle was killed and he left, he took a piece of all of us with him. He still blames himself for what happened, although there was nothing he, or me, could have done to prevent it.

It's obvious he's still punishing himself.

I hope this trip will bring him the healing he so desperately needs. All of us.

Own

CHAPTER 19

Gemma

He spanked me!

I involuntarily wiggle in my seat...without underwear.

He rips off my underwear, acts and looks like a man possessed, (and God, was it incredible), gets me to the point of exploding, spanks me!, then leaves me in agony, dying for release.

The way I felt, how my mind and body had reacted with each contact of his hand on my bottom, was intoxicating, a freeing I'd only experienced when Alex used the crop on me. It's extremely unsettling to admit it, to recognize those erotic sensations of pain is something I want.

The man who was with me in the conference room, he was the man I first met, the dark man who told me to use seduction as a weapon, the man who takes what he wants, relentless, seething with a need to conquer, vanquish, and destroy if necessary. Just like the tattoo he has under his arm, Veni, Vidi, Vici, We Came, We Saw, We Conquered. No matter the means, no matter the price.

Almost criminal.

That is what I'd thought about him when I first met him.

I am almost certain it's true.

He is the quintessential of forbidden, dark, and taboo. All things I've secretly craved, all things I tried to stay away from.

I crave him, hunger for him, yearn and ache for him.

He can destroy me, but only if I let him. Yet he is my salvation. In so many ways. He is the only one who can keep me safe, from what, I'm not sure of, but my instincts are certain of it.

The realities I'm surrounded with are surreal.

I have a stalker. Me, Gemma Trudeau, mergers and acquisitions attorney. I couldn't be any more boring if I tried, but someone is watching me.

The company I work for has a spy. The very company who is owned by the immensely powerful Alexander Black.

Was it Miles? He was acting very strange before.

My husband stole three million dollars from that same man.

I am living in Black's house. Sleeping in his bed next to him. And I fuck him every opportunity I get.

What about Tony Salvatore? He's dangerous, and he has connections. Could he have used Malcolm to get to Black? What about his obvious hatred for Alex? What better way than try to weaken his business?

The only common link between it all is Malcolm Stevens, my husband.

He's got to have a major role in all of this, I'm sure of it. But how? He didn't have the means, nor the connections. How was it possible for him to plant someone in Black's office?

I can't figure out how Malcolm would be able to pull this off. I was closest to him. Although our relationship had been strained for years, I knew him best. There is no possible way Malcolm could have fooled me that much.

That's because he didn't, he wasn't responsible.

This is obvious.

Someone else did, the same person Malcolm was working for.

The realization dawns on me slowly but with so much clarity.

Alex said it, but I hadn't believed him. I finally understand it.

"Gemma Trudeau," I absently answer the phone.

"Mrs. Stevens," the same anonymous man purrs.

My skin prickles and my hair stands on end.

"Malcolm was working for you, wasn't he?"

I'm done being clueless.

"Ah, I see the timid little wife is finally waking up. Are those nights being Black's whore doing you some good?"

His words are a slap to the face, but I refuse to back down.

"What do you want with me?"

"It's simple really. Information. I need to know what you know, and I need to know if you've told Black."

"I have no idea what you're talking about. I don't know anything."

"It's a shame really. Malcolm was so stupid. You, on the other hand, we would have done so much better with you."

"You're disgusting. I would never have worked for you. For the last time, Malcolm never told me anything."

"I wish I could believe you, Mrs. Stevens, truly I do, but I can't. And even if Stevens didn't tell you, you have something I want. You can make this simple, or we can do it the way I'd prefer, it's so much more exciting."

Malcolm left information!

"Tell me what you want and I'll find it for you if the Feds didn't take it."

"When I get a hold of you, I'm going to make you pay for thinking I'm stupid. You honestly don't think I'm stupid, do you Mrs. Stevens?"

His voice makes me want to vomit.

"Stop calling me that, I haven't been Mrs. Stevens in years. We stopped being married a long time ago. We never talked. I have no information; I don't have anything you want except the clothes on my back. But let me say this, I wish I did so Black could find you and kill you himself."

"That is precisely what I believe you would do, and why I need to know what you know, and retrieve what you have. Mark my words, *Mrs. Stevens,* Black can't keep you under lock and key forever, and when you're alone, I *will* be there."

He's gone.

A torrential wave of emotions overwhelms me; anger, fear, fury, confusion, rage...and a tiny slither of hopelessness. For the first time since my life began its downward fall a year ago, a crack begins to form in the walls of self-preservation I'd erected. Nothing had broken me, I knew beyond a shadow of a doubt I could overcome everything I'd been thrust into. This was beginning to shake that resolve. My body starts to tremble so hard, my teeth bang together. Suddenly needing to find some place I could escape to, I run to the bathroom.

I don't know how long I sat locked in a stall sitting on a commode with my hands covering my face trying to calm myself, I hear the door open.

"Gemma, are you okay?"

It's Natasha, the receptionist who is as stunning as a young Nubian princess. I cringe, not wanting to see anyone.

Good God, Gemma, get a grip!

"Yes, I'm fine. I must have eaten something that didn't agree with me."

"Was it that phone call I transferred to you? Did he say something that upset you?"

She received the call first!

My head darts up and my mind clears.

"No, no, not at all. Just a second I'll be right out."

After straightening my disheveled clothes, I leave the privacy of the stall as intact as I can possibly get.

"Don't ever eat anything from a restaurant that makes your stomach churn before you even unwrap it."

I make a lame attempt at a plausible story for hiding out in the bathroom. Checking myself in the mirror, I see my reflection would definitely support it because my complexion is pale and my eyes look haunted.

"That sounds like really good advice." She stares at me in the glass while I clean-up what's left of my makeup. She scrunches her nose on her perfectly made up face. "Would you like me to go get your handbag so you can, um, freshen up?"

"No, that's fine, I'll get it in a minute. But, I was a little out of it speaking with that client you mentioned, you know, feeling sick and all. Did you happen to get his name? I neglected to ask as my mind was a bit preoccupied."

Any information I can get, even though it's probably false, is better than nothing.

"Yes, he said his name was Bykov, Mr. Anatoly Bykov. Did he give you a hard time?" Her expression is sincere.

He gave her a name.

Appreciating her kindness and loving the fact I got some information, I reply, "No, he was fine. I like to keep notes on everyone I speak with, just in case something comes up in the future, I might need to reference back to it. Thank you Natasha, you're a lifesaver."

"Sure, no problem. Gemma," she pauses and shuffles her feet, suddenly looking shy. "I wanted to ask how you and that guy who sent you all those flowers are doing? He seemed like he was perfect and all."

She's beaming with curiosity.

I laugh.

The mysterious Faceless Man, even she was affected by him.

"I'm not seeing him anymore. He was…let's just say unusual."

"Oh, no! What happened?"

I sigh remembering him. "I guess I wanted more, and he couldn't give it to me. Believe me Natasha, it definitely wouldn't have worked out."

That's a major understatement.

"Aw, that's too bad. All those flowers, he seemed really thoughtful."

"I guess he was, in his way. We got what we needed from each other and parted ways."

That really is the truth.

"Oh well, but I'm sure it was good while it lasted." she sighs. "Are you sure you don't want me to get your bag? I don't mind."

"No, I've got it but thanks for asking."

"Okay, I've got to get back to the front. The girls get so touchy if I take too long, but I have to get up and walk around every once in a while. See you later."

"Bye Natasha," I say as she leaves.

After stealing one more glance at myself in the mirror, I rush back to my desk.

I have to tell Alex about the phone call.

"Is something wrong?" Alex answers the phone, his voice full of concern.

"That man called again," I reply tightly.

"I'll be right there."

Half an hour later, he's locking the door behind me to his office, and he's fuming.

"Jesus Christ! What the hell did he say to you? Sit down, can I get you anything?"

"I'm fine," I snap.

I know I look like shit, you don't have to throw it in my face.

"I'm sorry, Gemma, I didn't mean…shit! You just look like you're pretty upset."

"I was, Alex, I'm fine now. Sit down so I can tell you about the conversation."

So I can hurry and get out of here.

He leans against his desk in front of me and the closeness makes me even more uncomfortable. I get up and start to pace with my back to him so he can't look at me as I dive into recalling the conversation.

"He basically confirmed Malcolm was working for him. He said Malcolm was stupid and that they would have done much better with me. Also, he wanted to know what I know and if I told you anything. I kept telling him I don't know anything. He also mentioned that I have something. My guess is it's something that holds information."

"He said Malcolm was working for him."

"Yes."

"And he specifically asked if you relayed information to me."

"Yes."

"Interesting. He also mentioned something about an item?"

"Yes."

"Do you have any idea what it might be?" he asks, his expression hard.

"No. Even if I did, the Feds confiscated all of Malcolm's things from both the condo and his office. If it was around, it's highly likely it's in the police evidence room."

"It seems like he doesn't think so."

"Why?"

"Because he hasn't been arrested. If that item had been retrieved by the cops, it's sure to have been reviewed by now and an arrest would have been made. The guy's still out on the streets. I think it's safe to say they don't have it."

His voice is low.

I turn to face him.

"What does that mean?"

"That means, Gemma," he steps slowly toward me and takes my hands, "it's in your possession. Somewhere."

"Oh God…," I whisper.

The residual feelings that had consumed me after the call threaten to take hold of me again.

"Baby, don't worry."

He wraps his arms around me and pulls me close.

"He said," I choke out, "that you weren't going to have me under lock and key all the time, and when that happened he was going to be there."

"I'm not leaving you alone, Gemma. You're safe, I promise you."

His body feels so good against mine, and his strength ebbs into me and soothes me.

"He knows I'm staying with you, Alex."

"What did he say?" His hands are rubbing my back tenderly, comforting me.

"He called me your whore."

I cringe repeating those words. They're right, he was right. I agreed to stay with Alex, was relieved at the invitation, because I'd tried to tell myself I was only there for the sex. Decadent, dark, taboo sex. And lots of it.

He goes still, his body is rigid against mine.

"When I find him, I'm going to make him suffer."

Everything about Alex screams menacing and a part of me I'd always refused to allow in the light of day wants to suck him off right now because of that.

"Natasha said he told her his name was Anatoly Bykov."

His grip tightens around me.

"He did, did he? Interesting, but not true."

It's my turn to freeze.

"How do you know that?"

He hesitates as he takes a deep breath.

He knows something.

I pull away from him, my rational side needs all the facts, and needs them right now.

"What are you not telling me, Alex?"

"Gemma…"

"Don't fucking Gemma me, Alexander Black. What do you know that you're not telling me?"

I stand my ground; I refuse to be controlled by anything or anyone anymore. Not that man on the phone, not Malcolm, not even Alexander Black.

"Gemma, please trust me on this."

He steps closer and tries to pull me to him again. I press my outstretched hand to the middle of his broad chest, keeping him at arm's length. He could easily swat it away like a fly, but he doesn't. He knows I'm right, he knows me, and he knows I need this.

"NO. Tell me Alex, I have a right to know. I'M the one getting the phone calls, I'M the one whose life was destroyed, I'M the one he said has the information. Tell me now or so help me God…"

"Goddammit, Gemma!"

"If you don't tell me, I'm calling Gina and I'm walking out."

I glare at him, daring him to try me.

"Fuck! Alright, I'll tell you." He runs his hands through his hair roughly, "Anatoly Bykov is dead. Salvatore's people killed him."

"Why, and how do you know that?"

"Because I fucking asked them, that's how!"

He's glaring at me, his anger swirling around in his glacial eyes piercing me, his gorgeous face set in stone.

"Why did they kill him Alex?" The question is barely a whisper.

"For Christ's sake, Gemma, ENOUGH." He bellows at me, but it doesn't stop me from pushing him.

"No, Mr. Black, I'll call Salvatore myself if you don't tell me."

My voice is calm and even, I'm going to get this last piece of information one way or another. It has the power to completely crack my veneer of self-preservation, there's no doubt, but I have to know.

"Gemma, please, leave it alone," his voice is filled with frustration.

"Tell me, Alex. I need to know."

My heart is pounding and my vision is blurring. I know this is going to be bad.

"Alright." He hangs his head and inhales deeply. "Bykov is dead because he killed your parents."

I can hear the boom as the crack shatters and my walls crumble. My knees buckle as I let out a scream and my world goes black.

I awaken on Alex's couch with my head pounding and a cold towel over my face.

"Gemma…"

He's kneeling beside me on the floor, my hand clasped in his.

"I'm fine."

I am fine. I was shattered, but it's done, and I'm unbelievably calm. I try to sit up but everything starts spinning.

"Lay still, Gemma, go slow." He sounds worried as his eyes search mine.

"Alex, really I'm fine."

I don't feel anything. Maybe it's because I'm in shock, or emotionally dead, I'm not sure, but either way, does it really matter?

"I'm so sorry Gemma, I didn't want to hurt you again."

I push myself up and place my feet on the floor.

"It was a shock, that's all. Today has been quite a full day."

"I'm sorry about earlier, if I'd had known…"

I laugh thinking how ironic it is.

"Don't be, that's been the best part."

Relief washes over his face. I cup his cheek tenderly and love the feel of his soft facial hair under my palm. This man is so many things, ruthless and powerful, but also kind and thoughtful.

"You couldn't have, and you didn't want to tell me because you were trying to protect me. You're not as bad as you try to make yourself out to be, Alexander Black."

Surprise and confusion war in his expression. I can tell this is unfamiliar territory for him, but he doesn't back away.

"Tell me everything, Alex. I have to know," my words are calm, reflecting my state of mind.

"I know."

He sits on the couch next to me and pulls me onto his lap, cradling me close to him. I let him, I need this, he needs this. He knows I'm hurting somewhere deep inside, the residual pain had burst through me from the time I buried my parents and made me pass-out. The explosion had been building for a long time.

He takes a lungful of air then begins. "This is what I believe. I think Malcolm was hired by someone, an individual who is very powerful, to lure me into something that would begin to weaken my companies. Once that was established, I believe they intend to destroy the dealings that I have underground. That would cause my foreign connections to be severed, therefore, collapsing those enterprises as well. Everything would fall like a deck of cards, exposing my covert operations and ending everything I've spent a lifetime putting into place." He kisses the top of my head softly. "Your part in this, I believe, happened by sheer bad luck. Malcolm got you sucked in by leaving that information in your possession. Maybe using you like a safety deposit box, or by accident. That I'm not sure of." He pauses. "That's it in a nutshell."

"Why would anyone want to destroy what you're doing?"

He takes another deep a breath.

"Because the covert operations affect international governments and businesses, a bit round about, but it would stop a steady stream of very large amounts of illegal money, *and* expose corrupt officials and corporations as well."

I have to ask.

"What is this underground thing you do, Alex?"

I brace myself for the worst.

I supply munitions to foreign countries to kill innocent people.

I deal in body parts.

I rob banks.

"I save little girls from being sold into prostitution."

What?!

"Excuse me?" I ask him, completely shocked.

"I break up child prostitution rings around the world."

"Dear God, Alex!"

This strikingly beautiful man who is in control of multi-million dollar companies, who employs and is responsible for the livelihood thousands of people, the one thing that he holds dear to his heart is to save the world by saving our babies one at a time.

He looks so raw, so vulnerable, a place inside him that he keeps locked up from the world is open and looking at me in his eyes. A deeply buried hidden anguish glimmers in their depths searching for redemption.

I throw my arms around him and kiss him like it's going to save my life…and his as well.

Own

CHAPTER 20

Alexander

I had never felt so vulnerable, so exposed before in my life than when I told Gemma about what my real purpose is, saving children from a living hell. The only people that know are those who do the actual abduction of the children, and Jesús, Carlos, and Hilda. Now Major Stewart and his men know. And Gemma. Rico's going to know as well.

In all honesty, it's a relief.

"Gemma, get your things, we're going home," I state.

The situation has been accelerated. Whomever it was on the phone specified that Gemma is a target for information and he was going to obtain it, preferably in a way he chose. Which I am sure would be the most excruciating way possible.

She has been named next.

Over my dead fucking body!

"Mr. Black, I appreciate that, but I'm not about to let some sick man control my life. I've got work to do, I'm not going anywhere."

Stubborn. She is stubborn, mule headed, and ridiculously impossible.

"You are leaving. With me. This isn't a discussion."

"No I am NOT. You've just confirmed that my parents were murdered. You've informed me that you break-up international child prostitution rings. My whole world has just been thrown upside down, and it wasn't very stable to begin with. I need familiarity, I need to get my feet firmly planted again and get my head cleared. Work is the only way I can do that, it's the one place that doesn't change. You can send your Black Mobile for me later on, but I'm finishing out my day, just like a do every other day." Her chin is lifted in defiance, her hands are on her hips, everything about her is screaming at me to force her.

A pang of guilt spears my heart. I feel responsible for the mess she's in. I feel responsible for her. She's mine now, regardless of how she got here. I have to do whatever it takes to protect her, and make her happy.

She needs familiarity? I'll give her familiarity.

"Well, Ms. Trudeau, if you disobey me that would be an infraction, and you had an example of the repercussions of that a short while ago," my tone is very low and laced with promise.

"*Mr. Black*, you seem to think that frightens me." The defiant tone in her voice has dropped and I'm sure her body is reacting to the reminder of her spanking earlier, the one she admittedly enjoyed. "As I recall, someone once told me, 'Never assume, it makes you weak.' I never pegged you for weak." The memory of her earlier arousal is clear in her tone, and her face.

She still has the audacity to be cocky.

"Pet, you enjoyed it," I stroke her cheek with a knuckle, a smile lifting my lips.

"Sir," she purrs, "I have no doubt we will both find out all that I do enjoy." Stepping away to put some distance between our bodies, the act does little to extinguish the electricity between us. "But too much of my day has been used for selfishness." I quirk an eyebrow at her. She smirks at me. "I have to get back to work."

She turns to leave but I grab her elbow and pull her back to me.

"You'll go when I say you can go."

Wrapping one arm around her waist, I grip her jaw firmly and capture her mouth in a deliciously slow kiss. She molds into me, moaning into my mouth, as her hands feed into my hair.

"You can go now," I whisper against her lips.

She steps away wordlessly with a flush to her face. Standing in the open doorway, one hand on the doorknob, she says over her shoulder, "I'm still not leaving with you," and she shuts the door quickly behind her.

That woman is begging to be spanked, and I am more than happy to oblige.

I pick up my cell phone and call Rashad.

"Gemma got another call," I bark, not bothering with formalities.

"I know, I've already traced it. This one came from a trackable phone. We were able to get a location for it," he answers hesitantly.

"Well, where the fuck was the caller?!" I practically shout.

"In the coffee shop around the corner from Black Building."

He's fucking with me.

"And an ID?" I'm seething.

"It doesn't make sense, Mr. Black. The phone is identified as belonging to an NYU college student, a nineteen-year-old male who lives in Queens with his parents."

"He stole the phone."

"Major Stewart has already sent a man out to investigate it further," Rashad informs me in a rush.

"Good, keep me posted."

I hang up and call Jesús.

"Is the flight plan coordinated?" I snap as I look through the tremendous amount of messages left for me because I was out all afternoon. I'm barely containing my rage from the news about the caller.

"Yeah, the jet's picking up Rico at seven. He'll be here by eleven."

"Who's going with the plane?" I ask.

Sifting through the hundred things I have to catch up on, the one from Yun Lee goes to the top of the list.

Fuck, I hope this isn't bad news.

"Hector's going, I'm bringing him to the office to pick up the package you mentioned."

"Very good. You can take me back to the house when you do."

"Got it."

Despite all the shit that's going down, I'm looking forward to seeing Rico. Jesús and Carlos are like my family, but Rico is more than that. We have a bond that goes deeper than blood no matter how far each of us have tried to run, and regardless of how many years have passed.

I exchange my cell phone for the office phone, and take a few breaths to calm myself, then dial Mr. Yun Lee.

"Yes," the reserved Asian man answers his private line.

"Mr. Lee, I received your message."

"Mr. Black, we might have run into a possible complication," his voice is smooth.

I brace myself.

"That would be unfortunate, Mr. Lee. I can assure you that it can be dealt with easily, whatever it may be."

"I'm not quite certain, Mr. Black. I received word from my office in China that the paperwork has been held up in customs. It has been my experience that situations such as this can take months to rectify.

By that time, all merchandise disappears without any trace."

That's not going to happen.

"Don't be concerned. I'll call my official contacts to assist."

"I've already tried. They've refused to discuss it, Mr. Black. There's nothing they can do."

"Mr. Lee, with all due respect, I'll call them as well."

"Mr. Black, they informed me the only way they might consider looking into it is if you went to China and handled the situation yourself, not your representative," he smoothly delivers the news of the first sign of betrayal.

So, it's begun, has it? They want me to go to them and deal with them on their territory. They're forcing me to leave.

"Thank you for relaying the information. I will keep you informed as to the solution," I reply coldly.

"The shipment is ready, Mr. Black. You have forty-eight hours to advise me of your decision. If it can't be remedied, I will look elsewhere for an associate. Good day, Mr. Black."

"I will be in touch. Good day, Mr. Lee."

I replace the headset and sit back silently, pondering Mr. Lee's information, and consider my options. The seconds are filled with the unheard sounds of muffled voices throughout the office outside my closed door and the city beyond my window.

There aren't any options.

I have to go to China.

I have to leave.

In the past I would have welcomed the trip, been invigorated by the idea of the danger and excitement. It had always fueled me and pushed me. The possibility of a fight, no matter the form, had always been my way to success. I didn't get my reputation of being a ruthless prick for nothing.

This time I hate it.

"Simon, tell me what's pressing within a week's time," I say after pressing the intercom.

"Mr. Black," he immediately responds, "we're closing on a South African business in three days, and you have a luncheon meeting with the Dubai ambassadors at the Waldorf Astoria to discuss a merger. Those are the two most important items, sir."

And absolutely crucial! This couldn't have come at a worse time.

"Fuck!"

Can this day get any worse?!

"Excuse me, sir?" Simon asks casually.

He's used to my outbursts.

"Nothing, thank you."

"Mr. Black, there's a Mr. Hector here to pick up a package," he stops me before I hang up.

"Send him in. Also, I have to leave the office with Hector. I've returned Mr. Lee's message. Continue to connect me with the remaining ones on my cell phone when I tell you."

"Very good, Mr. Black."

Hector saunters in as I'm putting on my jacket.

"What did Jesús tell you?" I ask him as I shut down my computer and gather my things.

"I'm flying to North Carolina to pick up Rico with a package, then we're coming right back."

"Right. Keep an eye on the pilot, let me know if he makes any calls or talks to anyone. Don't let anybody near the plane, and watch to see if you're being followed."

"Jesús told me the pilot doesn't even know where he's going, he called a friend to get the flight plan approved. No one knows about it."

"Good man. Here's the package," I hand him the manila envelope. "Let's go."

Passing Simon, I inform him, "I'm leaving, I'll let you know when to start the calls."

"Very good, Mr. Black," Simon responds, standing to trail behind us.

He'll accompany me until I get in the elevator, just in case I need to speak with him regarding anything else, and to make himself available. He's an excellent assistant. It would be a shame if he were the spy. I hate to think of what I'd have to do to him because I genuinely like the guy.

I walk to Gemma's desk with Hector right behind me.

"Time to leave Ms. Trudeau."

It's not a request.

"I'll leave at five. If your car can't pick me up, I'll take a cab."

"Dammit Gemma," I lean in close to her ear. "Don't make me carry you out over my shoulder, because I will. This isn't a game. Someone wants you, and they're going to do whatever they need to get you. When they're finished with you, most likely painfully, they're going to kill you. Time. To. Go."

Especially with the sick bastard just around the corner.

I hate being so hard on her, but I need to make her understand how bad things are.

There's no way I'm leaving her here alone.

I stand and hold out my hand to her. Our eyes battle each other, hers filled with apprehension and fear, mine cold and hard.

"Fine," she states flatly.

I realize she doesn't want to believe the reality of the situation. She's in denial because she's completely unfamiliar with people like this, and it's helping her cope. I know them only too well, and am fully aware of everything they're capable of, and none of it's good.

After she shuts down her computer and gathers her things, Hector leads us to the elevators. He has no thought as to how much he stands out in my office, and couldn't give two shits.

Gemma

The three of us are alone in the mirrored elevator as it makes its descent, the nondescript music filling the strained atmosphere.

Understandably, Alex is tense. I can see it in the way his muscle flexes on his jaw and the intermittent tightening of his lips.

I feel like I'm going to snap.

It's been a hell of a day for both of us.

I can't stand the loud silence any longer, I'm so on edge, so I introduce myself to the Latin man accompanying us that I don't know.

"Hi, I'm Gemma Trudeau," I blurt out, extending my hand to him.

"Hector Ramirez." He takes my hand and shakes it firmly, matching my grip.

I consider a good, firm handshake a way to show I'm serious and strong. Working in a law practice and dealing with different clients for so long, many of them not very happy, the initial handshake was my way of establishing our working relationship.

"Are you related to Jesús and Carlos?" I ask him, attempting to make small talk.

"Yes," he replies simply.

Alex's eyes dart back and forth between Hector Ramirez and me before his eyebrows rise.

"What?" I snap.

"What are you doing?"

"I'm just being friendly," I retort, cocking my head to the side with a look that says, *Is that a problem?*

"He's not here to be your friend, Gemma."

"I can still talk to him. It doesn't hurt, you know, to be friendly for a change, Mr. Black."

"You're asking questions."

"I'm a lawyer, that's what we do, gather information. Or have you forgotten?" I ask tersely.

"No, Ms. Trudeau, I don't forget anything. If you want to know something, ask me. You'll get a more thorough response. Or have *you* forgotten?"

His reply is loaded with double meaning.

"Fine," I reply curtly again.

The rest of the elevator ride is done in silence, me a tight ball of nerves, Black surrounded by his authoritarian power, and Hector Ramirez an indifferent thug. Alex leads me quickly out of the building with his hand on my back and straight to his waiting car. I stare out the window of the ostentatious Hummer as we travel uptown to his even more ostentatious mansion. Hector is sitting next to Jesús up front, his attention fixed on whatever the hell guys like that focus on; street guys, gangbangers, guys that have had to fight for everything their whole lives, then defend it every day even more fiercely. I have a newfound sense of respect for these gang members, I'm certain that's what they are. It's plain to see these men are ultimate survivors, born from the streets and overcoming everything that life has thrown at them, winning when everything was against them where a lesser man would have failed. They are champions.

Black is one of them

Alex is beside me doing business simultaneously on the phone and his tablet. Tonight, he seems to be more tense than normal, and it's rubbing off on me.

Two fuses side by side, it's only a matter of time before one blows.

When we arrive, Alex turns to Hector.

"I'll see you and Rico here when you get back. Don't forget to give him the envelope when you land in North Carolina, he's expecting it."

"No problem, we'll probably be getting back here around eleven."

Hector gets back in the car without a sideways glance at me and he and Jesús leave.

Alex looks down at me with a slightly more relaxed smile.

"I told you he wasn't here to be your friend."

I roll my eyes at him.

"Come on, there's something I want you to see," he takes my hand and leads me to the garage.

Whatever it is, I can tell it gives him some relief.

"Hhmmmph," I snort anyway and follow him through the garage to an entrance at the back of the house.

When we walk into the dimly lit space, I feel as if I've entered into a military surveillance room.

"What is this, Alex?" I ask, scanning the space from one end to the other.

"This, Gemma, is going to find out who is responsible for your phone calls, for Malcolm, and for the threat to my business."

I small ray of hope penetrates my nervous fog.

"Who are these men?" I ask, quietly amazed.

The dark room is buzzing with everyone talking at once, into headsets, to each other, on the phones. Expensive high-tech equipment is glowing with photographs, information, and maps. Even the screen on the wall is talking, spitting out geographic confirmations, as a tall older man is scribbling various latitude and longitude coordinates on another board. Their uniform is all black.

"They're former military personnel. And they're working for me."

I stare up at him in awe. The depth of the situation slams into me as a tremor of fear slips through me.

Military personnel? Soldiers? He has the power to call them and build his own United States army? I am so far in over my head, I haven't the slightest inkling of the danger I'm involved in.

"Your power truly knows no bounds, does it Alex?"

"No, Gemma. Not when you deal in innocent human lives."

His tone is not condescending or cocky, there is no sarcasm or flippancy. Its matter of fact and sure, and full of sincerity.

My heart swells with deep emotion for this very caring, very kind man.

"Thank God," I whisper.

His face lowers slowly to mine as he touches his lips gently to mine, it's an act of tenderness and appreciation. It's one of the most beautiful kisses he's given me.

"Who's Rico, Alex?" I finally ask.

He breathes deeply.

"Rico is an old friend of ours. He's a cop who's now living in North Carolina. You've been compiling the employee list for him. He's going to check everyone out."

"Doesn't Black Inc. do a check on new hires?" I ask, confused.

"Yes, but Rico has a special process he uses, one that's a bit more unconventional," the corner of his mouth lifts in a half smirk.

I roll my eyes again.

"Of course."

He laughs at me. One of the few relaxed, unguarded moments that Alexander Black has allowed himself recently, and it helps to ease my unease.

"Let me introduce you to the man in charge in here."

He leads me across the room to the man feverishly writing on the board.

"Major Stewart," Alex says, the tone of authority is back in his voice.

The high ranking title does not go unnoticed with me.

He turns to us. "Mr. Black."

"This is Gemma Trudeau. As you know, she received another phone call this afternoon. The man identified himself as Anatoly Bykov. He confirmed Stevens was working for him. He also mentioned that she has something in her possession that has some information he wants, and he'd use any means to get it."

Alex and the Major share a long look and I'm sure an unspoken message passes between them

"Do you know about this item the deceased Bykov talked about?" the Major asks me, noting the caller used a dead man's name.

"No, I have no idea what he was referring to. I've never seen anything that would fit that description that Malcolm might have had."

"Not to worry, I'll have one of my men go through your things with you to see if we can identify it. Sometimes items like that are hidden in the most unsuspecting things," Major Stewart responds confidently.

"It appears I had a situation arise today as well," Alex adds, looking hesitantly down at me.

My stomach does a flip, but not in a good way.

That's why he's been extra tense.

"Oh?" the Major replies.

"One of my Chinese American contacts, a major player, informed me that the paperwork for some merchandise we've been working on has been tied up in Chinese customs. I have a representative scheduled to leave for China in two days to handle things. The contacts with the Chinese government state the only way they'll agree to review the situation is if I go to China myself and handle it."

"Is that so?" Major Stewart asks with a slow nod to his head.

"You're going to China? Now?" my shock and nervousness are now skyrocketing.

I'm devastated and suddenly scared to death.

Alex's arm tightens around my waist and he peers into my eyes with a hint of an apology.

"I'm going to do everything in my power not to Gemma. Even if I do have to go, I promised you I'm going to keep you safe. Besides my men," he lifts his eyes to look around the room, "each one of these men are battle trained. Nothing is going to happen to you."

He looks at me again, asking me to understand.

"But you have to go, Alex," I say, now knowing the full weight of what his trip is about. It's not only business, it's a lifesaving mission. "It seems there's no other way."

"I've got almost two days to make the final decision, Gemma. A lot can happen between now and then." He turns to Major Stewart. "Isn't that right, Major?"

"Affirmative. Let me tell you what we've found so far. This way, Mr. Black," Major Stewart answers, moving to the side of the large screen.

Own

CHAPTER 21

Alexander

I let myself breathe a silent sigh of relief,

They've found something. Anything is much better than nothing at all.

"Your man Rashad gave us the information he had regarding the communications between Stevens and his associates."

I glance at Rashad sitting at his new work station that was set-up for him here. He looks like he's jacked up on Monster energy drinks and porn shows, his excitement with being surrounded by technology of this caliber has his eyes bulging.

Major Stewart continues. "We've inputted the information, and this," he turns to the screen as two separate city maps pop us side by side, "is where we've pinpointed the locations they are as being. This one," he highlights the one on the left, "is Moscow. The one on the right," the picture next to it expands momentarily, "is Thailand."

"Interesting," I mumble tightly.

"We know that the location in Moscow is home to the Bratva, the Russian mob, and their holdings are indicated on the map with red numbers."

A smaller map of Moscow pops up on the screen with a listing beside it.

"This identifies numerically what each holding is on the map," Major Stewart explains. "Right here in the center is where the communications with Malcolm Stevens came from," he finishes as he points to the center of the aerial picture.

"And Thailand?" I ask.

The image immediately changes to an aerial view of Thailand.

"The Bratva is prominent in Thailand as well. Illegal arms distribution is rapidly rising to be their biggest, most profitable business, after human trafficking."

"Go on," I say deathly quiet.

"We believe they're working a deal with the Chinese mob, the Triads, for importation and exportation of both sets of merchandise."

Human beings are NOT merchandise.

"Continue," I say nodding my head in understanding.

"Our sources tell us that the locations on this map indicate facilities used by the Bratva. We don't know yet what each holding is used for. What we do know is that Malcolm Stevens' contact was, again, right in the center." His pointer hits the red X in the center.

"What about China, do you have anything on that yet?"

"Yes, Mr. Black, I do."

The screen changes to Hong Kong and the city is covered in red X's.

"When I was told about the upcoming meeting with Yun Lee's people there, we ran background on his representatives." He turns to the screen as it zooms in on a building. "This facility here," he touches it with his pointer, "is owned by the family of his right-hand man in China. We know that some of the building is used to detain human cargo, females specifically. One representative of that family has travelled to Thailand," the aerial of Thailand comes up alongside the aerial image of Hong Kong, "and he was seen entering this building several times during his stay," he indicates one of the Bratva's holdings.

"They're in bed together," I growl.

"That's not all, Mr. Black. A member of that same family is a prominent official of the Chinese government. That means…," Major Stewart turns to me.

"That means they can do whatever the fuck they want," I finish for him.

"Yes."

"It also appears they know what I'm doing. They're trying to cut off my head so my legs and arms can't operate," I say as the rage begins to rise in me again.

"It appears that way. I won't be surprised to hear that your other holdings abroad start to run into unforeseen difficulties as well."

"It's only a matter of time," I sneer. "I only hope it's only in paperwork and not bloodshed."

Gemma's nails dig into my hand, dragging my attention back to her.

Dammit! She shouldn't have heard all of that.

"Go upstairs, Gemma," I order her.

"No," her answer is flat.

"Go. Upstairs. Now," I repeat.

"I am not going anywhere, Black. I'm in this and if they're making you go there, throwing you smack in the middle of that trap, I need to know," she glares at me.

That's precisely what I don't want you to know, how much danger there'll be when I go to China.

But bullying her is not going to get her out of here, and I need her gone, she's heard too much already.

She doesn't need to hear that the caller before was right around the corner, and someone can slip with that information.

"Gemma, please go upstairs," I say with all the patience I can gather. "You've heard the worst of it. I need to fix it now. I can't do that worrying about you."

We stare intently at each other. I can tell she's on the verge of information overload, but she's stubborn. So much has been thrust on her today, and it appears she's strung tight. I hope she sees how much I need to protect her as her gaze goes back and forth across my face for what seems like forever. Finally, there's a glimmer of understanding in their clear depths.

"Fine, I'll go. You need to be aware that I'll know if you're lying to me when I ask you about this later. Rest assured, I *am* going to ask," she vows, her expression tight.

I crush her against me, and capture her mouth, needing to give her some of my strength, promising her that everything's going to work out.

"I'll be up in a little while, I promise. We have unfinished business, let me remind you." I tell her quietly, trying to ease her worry.

Her eyes get that haze of desire. I know she's back on that conference table.

"You'd better, or I'm coming after you."

"That won't be necessary. I have plans for you, Ms. Trudeau," I say quietly so no one else can hear me. "You're going to be tied up this evening."

Her sharp intake of breath makes me smile and my loins stir.

"Now go so I can finish here."

"Yes, Mr. Black," she gives me a forced smile then turns slowly to walk away to disappear through the door.

Turning back to Major Stewart, my expression hardens.

"Now Major, give me all of it."

"Mr. Black, the Russians have a huge business in arms dealings. The money they make from human trafficking is enough to fund the government, which it does. Xi Jinping and Vladimir Putin are known to have collaborated in international interests economically, and in the interference throughout the Syrian crisis. The muscle behind the scenes with each respective organized crime counterpart reinforces this union." He looks sternly at me. "Anything that interferes with their goal, they will try to eliminate."

"We're not going to let that happen, Major Stewart."

"No, Mr. Black, we are not. Especially now they're playing with us. That caller was pretty cocky calling from so close. My man reported the owner of the phone was in class when the call was placed and realized his phone was stolen after. The phone was called in as stolen when he got out. We found the device in a trash can on the corner where your building is, no prints were lifted, of course, and no other calls were made after the one to Ms. Trudeau."

He continues, "This is what I think we need to do. I have contacts throughout Europe, Russia, China, Thailand, the Middle East. I can have remote networks put together and operate them all from here."

He walks past his men who are barely on the right side mercenary. All these men are physically lethal, but even more so, highly intelligent. Their skills, both intellectually and tactically, make them the most dangerous human beings on the planet. This is who they are, programmed as war machines to use everything they have, mind and body. And they're mine for now.

The Major enters another room as I follow him.

"We can begin...," he starts as I close the door behind me, then take a seat to listen to what Major Stewart, the military strategist, has in mind while I contemplate the other players in this game.

Gemma

I'm numb. My mind has reached its limit for now, and it's shutting down to process it all.

Black has a military counter intelligence team working in his house.

The knowledge is mind boggling, beyond everyday comprehension, and is completely out of my league.

What am I doing here? Me, a girl from New Jersey! Alex stops human trafficking, some maniac thinks I have some information about it, and wants to kill me for it, and on top of that I find out my parents were murdered!

Everything that has happened to me, I've been able to overcome so far.

Everything except my parents being murdered. That is the one thing that has the power to break me.

I know it has something to do with Malcolm, I'm sure of it.

The guilt for not divorcing him and getting him out of my life, our lives, years ago is almost too much. They would still be alive if I had.

My father told me Malcolm was into something, he tried to warn me, but I didn't listen. I was so wrapped up in my career and keeping my head in the sand, I just kept going as if nothing was wrong, not wanting to make any trouble or changes. I had been miserable but I still stayed married to him.

I know I can't succumb to the guilt now, there are too many threats I have to focus on, too many puzzles I need to figure out. I have to keep my head clear. I have to face the fact that I *am* involved and there is too much at risk.

Lives are in danger.

The truly scary part is I just may possess the piece that could end all of this.

Or could kill me.

My brain feels like it's going to explode thinking about all that surrounds me.

I have no idea when I sank into Alex's huge Jacuzzi tub, it could be fifteen minutes or an hour ago, I have no idea, but this is where he finds me, eyes closed and the whirring sounds of the jets my only focus.

He gently coaxes me to sit up so he can step in and seat himself behind me to cradle me between his long muscular legs. He pulls my back to his front and wraps me tightly in his arms.

"Are you okay, Gemma," he asks, his voice tender.

"Mmmmhhmmm," I automatically reply.

The steady rise and fall of his chest from his breathing penetrates me. It moves through my body and ignites my flesh where our bodies touch. He must feel me melting into him because he begins to knead my tense muscles with strong, slow, steady movements. His arousal is largely evident pressed against my back. Finally, he guides me from him so he can stand and leave the tub. After drying himself, he reaches for my hand and leads me out. He looks almost deliciously illegal in the towel draped low around his hips, the strong V and his golden skin are a stark contrast to the white cotton.

No more words have been spoken, he's giving me space and time to process my chaotic emotions.

After he dries my body and wraps me in a towel, he takes my hand and we walk to his den of darkness. My darkness. With my King of Darkness.

The lights are dim, there's a heart wrenching opera playing softly in the background, and all I smell is leather and Black. In the center of the room, he steps behind me and pulls my hair to the side with one hand, and clasps my throat firmly with the other.

My breathing is now ragged and my heartbeat is speeding up.

"Do you trust me?" he whispers against my neck, his lips fluttering against my heated skin.

My head dips back as the word falls automatically from my lips, "Yes."

"Do you trust me to give you what you need, Gemma?" he asks before his teeth grip the tendon at the curve of my throat.

I suck in a deep breath, "Yes."

"Anything?" his voice is rough as his hands pull the towel from my body.

My back arches.

"Yes."

He steps back and the separation leaves me longing for him.

"Raise your arms, pet."

I do so slowly and without question.

The first sensation of something sliding over my skin makes me tremble. Then the white rope comes into view over my shoulder and down my chest.

....*You're going to be tied up tonight*...

My skin is humming where the rope glides over it. He moves it down between my breasts, around my body, over my shoulder, twists and crisscrosses it between my now captive breasts, then wraps it above them. My tits are now pulsing, squeezed and pushed out in their tied captivity. It was pure decadent pleasure watching Alex's face as he bound me, fixed intently on me as he masterfully wove the rope around my body.

He's still in his towel as he lifts both his hands to palm my captured breasts. With the nipples peeking out of his grip, he lowers his mouth to suck each one hard into his mouth, squeezing the globes into fleshy points. My body tenses as molten heat shoots straight to my core.

"On your knees," he commands huskily, pinching my nipples between his thumb and finger.

I slide down the front of his body as he lets go, answering him instantly as another erotic tremor slithers through me.

"Face down, pet, hands at your ankles."

As I lower my face and my ass and sex open for him, my tits throb and my loins ache for his touch.

He tenderly takes a wrist in his hand and places a soft kiss on the inside of it. Then I feel the now familiar touch of the rope there. He kisses the other wrist the same way before he proceeds to tie them to my ankles.

My heart is pounding wildly now, vibrating in my ears. All my attention is pinpointed to where the rope is tied around me. Feeling is escalated, sensations are heightened, and my body is thrumming with each beat of my heart.

When he's done, he runs his hands firmly up and down my body, over every inch of my curves, before cupping my now drenched mound. He slides his thumb inside my sheath and makes circles inside me. I can't help but moan loudly with pleasure.

He pulls himself from inside me and I can hear his quiet footsteps, then the sound of a drawer open and close. The sound of his footsteps again, then a clicking sound.

I can't see him from this position, but I can feel the closeness of his body. Anticipation of what he's going to do only feeds my desire. I can only imagine.

His hand is on me again, moving from my slit up to my tight, back hole, and it's covered in lube. A heavy breath silently carries the word, *Yes.*

I'm going to fuck your pussy and your ass with my fingers, and feel you come all over them.

The memory of his words inject me with a hot dose of that erotic drug that is going to fill me until I explode.

"I just might fuck your ass tonight, Gemma."

"Oh God," I quietly mutter, half here, half drunk.

With the first penetration of his finger into my ass, I start to soar. Oh so slowly, in and out, he works his way deep inside me, stretching me, fucking me, but not nearly enough. I grip him, pull him in further, taking as much as he will give me. But I want more.

He removes his finger, leaving me empty, only to feel him pressing something else at my entrance. Then he slips two fingers into my wetness, and begins the same wonderfully torturous movements, twisting them, bending them, curving them, thrusting them slowly in and out. I feel what I now know is the plug penetrating my ass, filling my ass up exquisitely.

"Alex," I mumble in my sexual drunkenness.

"Not yet, Gemma, you need to let it all go first," he whispers hoarsely.

"Please," I moan.

"Trust me."

I do.

He removes his fingers and I instinctively grasp at him trying to hold him inside me.

"Count," he states, before his palm lands on my ass.

SWAT.

Heat morphs through me with the sweet sting.

"One!" I grit out.

SWAT, on the other cheek.

"Two!"

SWAT, over my vulva.

"Oh GOD, three!"

YES.

On and on, until I'm almost delirious at twenty. I'm in an hypnotic space, no reality, just feeling and sensation.

He thrusts his two fingers back into me, hard and deep.

"Now, Gemma, come!"

"Oh, God, YES, YES, YES!"

He plunges them in and out of me as I crash around him.

The release is intense, pulling everything out from inside me, making it all shatter into fragments, the tension, the fear, the anger, it all explodes and is blown to bits.

When my waves start to slow, he stills his movements, but doesn't remove his fingers from me as he slowly takes the plug out.

"I'm going to slide my cock in your ass now, pet," he growls quietly.

"Alex," I whisper, already hungry for more of him.

"Such a beautiful, tight ass, Gemma," he whispers as he gently pushes the head of his cock in.

I greedily grip him, capturing him with my tightness.

"Fuck, pet, she's pulling me in," he grits out tightly.

"Give it to me, Alex," I gasp out hungrily.

My breasts are throbbing, my nipples rubbing against the carpet shoot desire through me, my pussy is still spasming from that explosive orgasm, and every nerve ending is coming alive as he fills me up.

Inch by incredible inch, he pushes deeper, until I feel his pelvis resting against me.

"Gemma, you took all of me," he whispers breathlessly.

I'm so full, so deliciously full, the pain is pushed away by the pleasure I know is coming.

Very slowly he begins to move. It hurts, it's wonderful, it's sending me out again higher than I was before. Alex sets a rhythm, three thrusts barely in and out, then he buries himself so deep inside me, and holds it there. It's incredible.

He reaches down and unties my ankles and wrists, holding himself deep inside me. He gives me time to get my limbs moving as he reaches down and rubs my clit. When I start to move back into him, asking him for more, he raises up.

"Touch your clit, pet, I want you to touch yourself."

Yes, Alex, and then you're going to fuck me.

My clit is swollen and hard, and so fucking sensitive.

He continues his pace, three gentle strokes in and out, then deep inside me. My fingers are rubbing harder and more demanding. My hips move back and forth now, pulling away farther when he pulls back, pushing into him harder when he pushes in. Our bodies begin to move faster, hungrier, thrusting deeper, needing more.

"Alex," I moan loudly.

"Give me that fucking clit, pet," he growls, bending over my body and pushing my hand away.

He grips it tightly between his fingers and pinches it.

"Fucking come for me, Gemma. Now!"

I slam into him as the climax crashes into me, pulsating throughout my body, as I scream out his name in ecstasy.

One last thrust as his moan bursts from his body, and he blows his cum and fills me up with it.

He lowers himself onto my back, completely spent. I fall to the floor, breathing hard, and my limbs sore.

"I'm going to get a towel, baby, then I'm carrying you to bed," he whispers tenderly.

When he returns, I'm almost already asleep.

Own

CHAPTER 22

Alexander

I slip quietly from the bed. Gemma is sound asleep…after I worked her anxiety out of her.

She'd been ready snap. I took her there, but my way, the way she needed.

Ah, pet, if I could save you from all this pain, I would.

I risk a light kiss to the top of her head and hope I don't wake her before pulling on a pair of sweatpants and a t-shirt. Shoving my bare feet in sneakers, I walk as noiselessly as I can to the door and head down to the basement.

Rico's here.

When the elevator doors open, I can hear the raised voices of the three of them, Carlos, Rico, and Jesús. It's a reunion.

Even though it's a shitty situation, it's good to have him home.

I enter the surveillance room, my eyes adjusting to the sudden darkness after the glaring lights of the outer room, and almost bump right into them.

"The fucking Russians, bro," Jesús is obviously filling him.

Most likely Rico's hearing it for the second time as I'm sure Rico was already introduced to Major Stewart and each man was given a quick summary of who each of them are.

Rico looks to me when I enter.

"Look who decided to get his sorry ass out of bed," he grins at me.

"Look who decided to get his ass back here and do some real work for a change," I reply, busting his balls right back.

"Fuck you, Black," his grin is a full blown smile, cutting his face in half.

We embrace, pounding each other's back like men do, the harder, the stronger the bond. We're pounding the fuck out of each other.

"It's good to see you, man, you look really good. North Carolina must really agree with you," I say to him with all sincerity, keeping my arm around his shoulders.

"Yeah, I really like it there, the people are good." He gives me one of his signature devilish chuckles. "It was crazy at first, I had to act like I was some douchebag and I pissed a lot of people off. But it was worth it, I got the bad guys and made some good friends."

"Act?" My grin matches Rico's, along with Carlos and Jesús'. "You *are* a douchebag; you always have been."

"Hey, I'm not the one they call 'prick'. Look at this," Rico turns and extends a hand toward the room, "you even had to put together your own army. Now that is some serious shit."

I run a hand through my hair, drop my arm from his shoulders, and take a step back. Rico shoves his hands in his pockets.

It's time to talk business.

"It's big, Rico," I say as I look evenly at him.

"It sounds that way, from the bits and pieces of information I've gotten so far," he is now the police professional.

"Let me try to put those pieces together for you," I move toward a table in the back of the room with Rico, Carlos, and Jesús following me. We each find a seat and I continue. "Gemma Trudeau, the new employee, wife of Malcom Stevens…"

"The woman you're living with," Rico adds.

I glare at him for a second. I don't know why, but that bothers me.

"Sorry, man, I was only confirming," he defends himself as he puts his hands up in front of him, palms facing me.

"No, you're right, the woman living with me. Her parents were murdered by Anatoly Bykov, a member of the Odessa group. Bykov was killed by the Italian mob."

"In retaliation of the murders?" Rico asks, somewhat surprised.

Nothing phases Rico, but I'm sure it will soon.

"Yes, Frank Trudeau, Gemma's father, was a good friend of John Salvatore. They did it for him," I answer him.

"Did the Russians order the hit?" Rico asks.

"That's the thing, it looks like it came from somewhere else, some place higher," I glance to the aerial picture of Moscow illuminated on the screen, "probably somewhere in there." My gaze returns to Rico, "You've met Major Stewart?"

"Yes," he replies.

"Carlos and Stewart will fill you in on how Stevens and the Russians fit in. It goes to Hong Kong and Thailand as well." I lean in closer, "What's not fitting is Frank Trudeau and why he was killed. Gemma says her father tried to warn her a couple of years ago that her husband was into something bad. Maybe he stuck his nose in and started snooping around and found something. He was a Jersey cop; you remember?"

"Yes, and I also know that some of his fellow officers didn't believe it was an accident. Apparently they were right, but it was hushed up, or covered up. I need to find out which, and if anyone knows what he found to get him and his wife killed. Gemma has no idea?"

I shake my head, "None at all, I just told her it was murder.

Rico pauses for minute, studying me.

"What is all this really about, Black?" he asks, his voice dropping.

"I believe this is all to stop me."

"Stop you from what?" he persists.

I take a deep breath. "Stop me from interfering with their child prostitution. Which means cutting off a large stream of income for a lot of important people."

"What do you mean, Alex?" he leans in closer, eyes squinting at me, making sure he heard me correctly.

"I go into these countries and rescue little girls from child prostitution. And it obviously pissed some people off," I state flatly.

Rico leans back in his chair, lowers his head and shakes it slowly. Carlos and Jesús are looking back and forth between Rico and I, like we're two tennis players hitting a ball.

"Holy shit, dude, that is fucking huge," he comments on a heavy exhale.

"Yes, it is. Here's the kicker: I have to leave for China in a day and a half. I had an envoy set-up to go handle a deal I've got. The paperwork got lost, or some bullshit, and they refuse to even look into it, or deal with anyone else, except me. In China."

"And you've got one of these underground missions going on at the same time, don't you?" he asks.

"Yes. That's why this particular trip is so crucial.

"They're forcing me to leave."

"Damn, negro, I knew nothing was ever simple with you, but this? This is so fucking complicated, no wonder you need a military intelligence team," Rico has his lady-killer grin back in place.

"That's why I called you."

"You never could do anything without me," he comments, busting my hump.

The incredible truth of that simple statement takes us both somewhat off-guard.

"You're right, and I'll always love you for it, man," I tell him honestly.

I even surprise myself with this new sentimentality.

The reserved mask drops down over his expression.

"Go back upstairs to your woman, Black. I've got to get caught up to speed, it's a good thing you've got people working around the clock." He stands, apparently uncomfortable with the sensitive area we've stumbled upon.

I'll let you go tonight, Rico, but you're not leaving New York until we've exorcised some of your demons. It's way past time.

I step around the table and pull him back in for another hug.

"I'm glad you're here, thanks for coming."

"I would have been pissed off at you if you hadn't called me. No matter what, we're brothers, and always will be," he returns the heartfelt embrace.

"See you tomorrow then," I turn to leave.

As the elevators door close, the sound of my three brothers together again adds a little more flame to the growing fire of my once dead heart.

Gemma

Consciousness slowly penetrates into my sleep hazed mind, bringing light into the comfortable warmth, along with memories of my unreal reality.

"Ugh," I moan as I roll over and bury my head in Alex's pillow and I'm instantly soothed by his intoxicating scent.

I breathe deeply and hug his pillow tighter, burrowing myself into the safety of his bed.

No, I don't want to get up yet. Maybe I can stay right here. The hell with life and responsibilities, it's all bullshit anyway.

I allow myself a few glorious moments of self-indulgence as the tiny aches in my body remind me of last night. The tenderness around my wrists and ankles bring back the memory of the rope, my bottom and sex tingle and clench from the memory of his palm, my breasts throb exquisitely after being bound.

But my mind keeps going to before that, down the tunnel of recollection, into the surveillance room downstairs. And just as my mind has been programmed to do, it picks apart situations, analyzes the most miniscule details, and gathers all the information to find a way to piece together the puzzle of a desired result. It's going a mile a minute and driving me bat-shit crazy.

"Fine, I'll get up," I mumble as I throw off the covers and stomp out of bed, "but I'm not happy about it."

I make my way to Alex's palatial bathroom, I'm still amazed at the grandeur of his home, *Who the in the world has an authentic suit of armor in their bedroom?* I turn on all the crazy jets and lift my shift from my body, then deposit it in the dirty clothes bin. When the water's just right, I step in and give myself over to the pulsating decadence of this magic machine.

He thought I didn't notice when he got out of bed last night. I know he went to meet this Rico who arrived from North Carolina. Then only a few hours later, he woke up to continue his pursuit in saving the world. He must be exhausted.

My heart squeezes with concern for this enigmatic man. At the same time, I'm looking forward to meeting the mysterious Rico, the one with particular ways to find out about people. An old friend of Black's with probably as many secrets.

Spurred into high gear now, I quickly finish and dress in record time. Giving my reflection a last look, it passes approval. I chose my outfit with care because I wanted professional with just a hint of sex kitten. A little femininity always opens more doors than an uptight ass.

As I enter the elevator and the doors slide closed, I pull on my lawyer persona. Personally, I know I'm still in emotional turmoil from all that's going on. I need all the arsenals I have to keep going and fight, and my lawyer personality is my greatest weapon. She has served me well professionally; I know she's exactly what I need now.

When I exit on the main level of Black's mansion, my steps slow. I can hear murmured voices coming from the kitchen area, one is Hilda and the other I don't recognize, a male, and even from this distance I can tell the conversation is heated and passionate. My curiosity pushes me forward and even though I feel like I'm intruding on a very personal moment, I can't stop myself. When I reach a point where I feel if I move any further I would be noticed, I wait.

"Nene, stop blaming yourself, it wasn't your fault. You're breaking my heart by staying away," Hilda's voice is full of pain.

"I can't help it. I should have saved her. I should have known better than to go down an empty alley, I was stupid Hilda, I'm so sorry," comes the man's anguished reply.

That must be Rico, and they're talking about something horrible that happened.

"Come with me," Jesús whispers behind me from out of nowhere, his hand wrapped tightly around my arm.

I jump, mortified I've been caught eavesdropping. Either from shame or fear, I'm not sure which, probably both, I follow him obediently. He leads me to the other side of the house and into the reception room, (I'm awed this house has a room specifically designated for receiving people), he turns and faces me. I cringe a little inside from the hard look on his face. I don't let it intimidate me, though, as we stare each other down.

He nods, so minimally, it's barely noticeable, as his expression relaxes.

"They were talking about my sister, Isabelle. She was killed when she was sixteen. Rico loved her, and she him. They were together skipping school, it happened in a fight between two gangs. She was shot in front of Rico...and Alex."

With each word of his very short story, my heart breaks until the pain radiates throughout my body. He didn't need to tell me anymore of this tragic event, he'd chosen his words wisely. I knew everything that had happened and why the people and things are the way they are.

"I'm so sorry," I whisper knowing my words don't make a difference to the pain this whole family has endured.

Jesús shrugs his shoulder.

"It's life, Trudeau, even you've experienced it."

His cold, hard, truth hits me in the gut and instantly evaporates any misconceptions that me and 'them' are different. All the false walls of differentiation come crashing down replaced by a bond I've never felt before.

"Yeah, that it is, as fucked up as it is, there's still beauty in it though," I reply.

He laughs softly, but still cynically.

"Come on, Rico wants to meet you," he walks quickly through the door, cutting our moment short, and back toward the kitchen.

I follow behind him trying to keep up. I don't know what I'm feeling now as residual emotions are colliding with new ones. I do know I'm looking forward to meeting Rico. When we enter the kitchen, all eyes turn to us. Rico's dark eyes are fixed on me. He's studying me, reading me, gauging whether or not I can be trusted.

It's Hilda who greets me.

"Gemma, come, have your breakfast. Rico has been waiting for you."

I can tell whatever transpired between Hilda and Rico was long overdue and has left them both where they needed to be: content.

I take my usual seat and Rico comes to sit next me. Jesús is again sitting at the other end of the breakfast bar, silent and taking everything in.

"Ms. Trudeau, I've heard a lot about you, I'm Rico, I'm also a police officer but I live in North Carolina, as I'm sure you know. You're an attorney, is that correct?"

Oh, he's good, smooth as silk. I bet the women give him whatever he wants, with the hints of sensuality in his demeanor and the danger just lurking below the surface, he can't hide that bad boy in him.

"I am, my father was a cop, he would have liked you, you're good," I glance sideways at him, telling him I know what he's up to.

He tilts his head back and laughs.

"I told you," Hilda cuts in, "she wasn't going to fall for your usual bullshit. You need to talk to her straight. She'll cut your balls off and shove them down your throat if you try and play her."

My face jerks to Hilda, mouth open, shocked at how she just cut straight through all the crap.

"Tell them, Mama," Jesús chuckles.

Rico puts his hands up in defense.

"Okay, okay," he laughs.

I extend my right hand as I hold a cup of coffee with my left.

"Hi, I'm Gemma, it's nice to finally meet you Rico," I offer with a friendly grin.

To be fair, I was going to do the same thing, with my professional and six kitten attire. His weapons of destruction were not quite as obvious.

"Pleasure to finally meet you, too, Gemma," his smile is warm and genuine.

"Thank you."

"Black and Stewart got me up to speed on the situation, but I wanted to speak with you too," he begins his somewhat of an interrogation.

"Sure, ask away," I reply as I eat my breakfast.

"Tell me everything your father told you."

He delivers the first blow.

I know he's referring to anything that might relate to why my parents were murdered.

I place my fork on my plate and move it away so I can rest my forearms on the counter.

"A couple of years ago was really the only time he said anything at all. It was during dinner, it was just the three of us, me, my mom, and dad. He told me that he knew Malcolm was into something bad, he didn't know what, and he was sure it was going affect me." I turn to look into his big dark eyes in his handsomely sculpted face. "That's it. He must have felt very strongly about it because that night he also asked me to set up a trust account for them and put all their assets in it."

"Gemma," his expression softens and becomes sincere, "I'm going to find out all that I can, that's why I'm here. Yes, things are happening very fast right now, but Alex is a good man, and he's smart as hell. Everything happens for a reason, that's why *you're* here, exactly where you need to be."

I can feel the knot form in my throat, everything I've held back, the torrent of emotions I've kept tightly checked threatens to explode in this room full of people I barely know.

I've got to get out of here.

I sit up straight and take a deep breath.

"If there's nothing else, I need to get to the office." I take another deep breath trying to keep it together. "Thank you, Rico, I sincerely appreciate any justice you can bring to my parents. I mean that."

"I know. I'll keep you posted in what I find, regardless," he stands to escort me out.

"Damn, it's a good thing I'm a fast eater," Jesús pushes his chair back and walks toward the garage.

His comment breaks the tension that has started tighten around me.

I grab my purse.

"Thank you Hilda."

"De nada, nena," she smiles affectionately at me.

All this kindness is wearing down my stoic resolve. If I don't get out of here now, I'm going to break.

I walk quickly to the front entrance with Rico by my side.

"I know it's tough when you've been on your own for so long," he states softly.

I turn to look at him. Knowing what I know about him now, he's being very open and honest.

"Yeah, it's going to take some getting used to," I mumble.

"Black can be very persuasive," he grins.

I roll my eyes and smile.

"You're not kidding." We both laugh.

Jesús is waiting for me outside, along with Carlos and one of Major Stewart's men.

The reality of the situation grips me again.

Rico leads me to the car and opens the door for me. He leans his head in when I get in the back and Carlos gets in the front passenger seat.

"Hey, ignore them. Just keep on keeping on, okay?" he winks naughtily at me.

That takes the edge off.

"Got it. See you later," I smile gratefully at him.

In the car on the way to the Black Building, I receive a text from Gina.

Ugh! I've been dreading this!

Where the hell are you?!

I cringe a little.

I'm a big girl, stop shouting at me.

I'm staying at Black's.

WTF!! You don't even know that guy! Granted, he's hot and can probably fuck like a madman, but I know what he did to Tony.

What HE did to Tony? He SAVED me from Tony!

Do you know what Tony did to me?!

Yes, I do, and I hate it. But we're family, you should be with us, you belong with us.

Are you out of your mind?!

A slow seeping of thoughts I can't believe I'm even considering about Gina floods my brain.

She's one of them, she'll always be one of them. They're family, and I'm just the kid she hung out with when we were younger. Her loyalties are to them and always will be, no matter the cost.

With this clear realization comes a melancholy from the loss of someone I thought would be there for me all my life.

I'm right where I need to be Gina. Family wouldn't do that. Thank you for your concern.

G, don't do this, I'M your family. I'm here when you need me. I got you a court date for the twentieth of next month for your divorce, you'll get the paperwork in the mail.

I don't reply, I can't right now. My heart is breaking.

When I get to the office, Carlos escorts me up. I go directly Alex's office. On my way I notice there's a man I don't recognize who's professionally dressed and is seated at a desk in front of a computer and he appears to be working.

I enter Alex's throne room, I can't deny how happy I am to see him, his presence is instantly soothing, especially after Gina's text.

"Good morning Alex. Thank you for making me feel...so much better last night," I purr as I approach him.

He turns to me.

"Good morning, Gemma. You're most welcome."

His cold, detached demeanor stops me in my tracks, and hits me like a freezing gale force wind.

This is the cold, heartless prick I saw staring at me through the glass wall when I first stepped foot into his empire.

Own

CHAPTER 23

Gemma

What a cold slap of reality.

"Well, Mr. Black, it seems I must be intruding."

The shock from Alex's frigid greeting catches me completely off-guard, and the hurt from Gina's text is still squeezing my heart. All I can think of is retreat. Immediately.

I spin on my heel and walk out of his office, then slam the door shut behind me, noting he's made no comment or attempt to stop me.

Fuck him!

I walk stiffly to my desk and throw everything down before storming off to the bathroom.

I don't need his Mr. Big-and-Bad-Ass shit on top of everything else.

I check my face in the mirror and touch-up my makeup from sheer habit, the ride to Black

Building from his ninety-sixth street mansion isn't long enough for the pollution of Manhattan to make a dent in my carefully applied mask. It appears I'm going to need it.

This day already sucks ass.

Back at my desk, I boot up my computer, seething with growing rage, my hurt only fueling it. I refuse to even glance at his office. Inside I can't help wonder if he's watching me. I pull my chair roughly to my desk and sit, preparing to dive into the proposal Alex has asked me to review for the upcoming meeting with the Dubai representatives at the Waldorf Astoria.

Being totally pissed-off will put me in the right frame of mind for the aggressiveness this project calls for.

Completely absorbed in what I'm doing, I barely notice the desks filling up around me as time passes by. When the IM pings on my phone with a message, my finger hits a key on the keyboard and a line of 's's' quickly runs across the page on the computer screen.

"Shit!" I mutter under my breath and undo the mistake, hoping there aren't any more lost somewhere in the pages of the document.

"Now I'm going to have to go through the whole thing again with a fine tooth comb," I grumble, mad at myself for such a careless mistake.

I apologize if I was curt with you this morning. I have a tremendous day scheduled.

"Fuck off, Black," I mumble.

Gemma.

"How the hell does he know I'm cursing?"

I know everything.

I'm completely fuming now. Somewhere in the back of my mind I realize some of the most unwise choices are made in this frame of mind. I really don't give a shit.

Then know this, we're all under a great deal of pressure.

I hit send then power off my phone, which is completely ludicrous because I'm well aware that I've just antagonized the shit out of the Great And Powerful Black, and am mighty pleased with myself for having done so.

Minutes pass as I attempt to make a concerted effort to check for any more mistakes. It's futile because all my attention is on listening for Alex's approaching footsteps. The minutes turn into a half hour, I know this because I've been watching the time pass by agonizingly slow on my screen, and still they don't come.

My anger has made a nose dive straight to sadness.

What happened between last night and this morning? Did I do something? Did I say something in my sleep that would have made him angry at me? I needed him this morning, and just like everyone else, he was worse than not there for me. He kicked me in the ass.

I turn to take my first glimpse of him since I left his office hours ago. He's got his back to me with the phone to his ear, but still an impeccable and imposing figure of a man. My heart constricts with emotion and pain.

You stupid little fool! You were supposed to be in this only for the sex. He's tired of you already, you and all your fucked-up baggage.

The self-reprimanding thoughts flare up and threaten to push me further into despair, a situation I cannot afford right now.

No. That's not it, not after last night, and these past couple of weeks. It's something else.

Refusing to succumb to the pity-party, I shake the thoughts away and try to ignore everything else but the proposal in front of me.

A couple of hours later, I notice Alex walking toward the elevator buttoning his tailor-made jacket with Simon following behind as usual. I glance at the time.

He must be heading to lunch...and he didn't say anything to me. Fine!

Gritting my teeth, I plow through the contract, make any final thoughts and recommendation's, and decide to call it a shit-ass day.

Alex hasn't returned by three. I shut down my system and pack up my things.

I'm leaving.

As I walk with my head high, the new 'employee', Major Stewart's man who was placed here a couple of days ago, meets me at the elevator.

"Where are you going, Ms. Trudeau?" he asks with a formal and professional tone.

"I forgot to send out the memo that I'm leaving now," I snap.

"I'll accompany you then."

My anger rages again. I'm furious that I have no privacy, no say to my own comings and goings, irate that I have to piss and eat with someone else's approval.

"I would prefer you didn't."

I don't bother to look away from my sudden interest in watching the numbers blink above the elevator doors.

"Ms. Trudeau," he begins.

"Don't." I jerk my attention to him, my eyes glaring.

"I understand how you feel," he tries to placate me.

"You have no fucking clue how I feel."

I know I'm attacking him, but I can't help it.

He shrugs a shoulder.

"You're right, I don't, but I have a job to do. You're an intelligent woman, you know what's going on. I'm coming whether you like it or not."

"Fine," I huff out.

I'm angry at him for being so damn precise, I'm angry at myself for being so damn angry, and I'm furious at Black for being such a bastard.

When the doors open in front of us, I step in with him right behind me.

Stop being such a bitch, he is *just doing his job.*

Still fixated on the blinking red numbers, I casually say, "We're going shopping," and smile smugly.

He laughs.

Shopping therapy is always good for whatever ails you.

When we arrive at Black's fortress hours later, I'm ready to take him on again, or ignore him as much as he ignored me. It's totally his call.

I never bothered to turn my phone on again. Occasionally as I was trying on outfits, I saw GI Williams on the phone glancing my way. I knew he was reporting in as to my whereabouts, and I hadn't cared. I was enjoying myself and I wasn't about to cut it short because His Highness was being pissy.

"Hey, thank you," I tell my chaperone once we get inside the house.

"No problem, to be honest, I enjoyed it. It was better than sitting at that desk."

For the first time today, the guy's being normal and not a soldier. I almost feel bad for putting him in a position that had nothing to do with him. Almost. The clothes I bought take away any guilt.

"I'm sure you've got a report you need to give on my escapades," I chuckle.

He smiles. "I think the worst is over, Ms. Trudeau."

I doubt it.

"Thanks again," I say as I get in the elevator.

The smugness I felt is beginning to ebb with each ascending floor.

He's going to be angry...I think. Unless he doesn't care.

I'm almost in full-blown panic mode when the doors open on the fifth floor.

Not because I'm afraid of his anger. That I can handle. What I won't be able to stand is if he's not, because that means he truly doesn't care.

Alexander

What the hell was she thinking taking off like that? If Williams hadn't been there, God only knows what could have happened to her!

From my desk I hear the elevator open.

"Gemma!"

I'm so furious, I want to spank that ass of hers until she screams.

When I finally see her and I know she's alright, I start to relax.

"What were you thinking?!"

Her lips tighten into a straight line.

She's mad at me.

She has every right to be, you've been a total dick.

"I finished the proposal so I took off early. Considering I come in every day at eight, I've also worked numerous hours at night, I didn't think I needed permission. Do I have to send a request to PR, Mr. Black?"

I step out from behind my desk balling my fists. I don't trust myself not to throw her over my lap and bare her ass.

"You don't mean that, Gemma. You know you don't have to ask permission from anyone at the company...except me. Why didn't you tell me what your plans were?"

Because you were an ass, Black.

I can see the anger flash in her eyes. It stirs me, I love her fire and her strength, even her defiance. It all makes her the beautiful woman she is.

"Mr. Black, *if* I'd like to go shopping, or get my hair done, or meet someone for lunch, those are all personal situations, and have nothing to do with business. I didn't realize I needed to report back to you regarding all aspects of my life."

She juts her chin up and glares down her nose at me.

That's it, pet, don't take my shit.

I inhale deeply trying to calm myself.

Everything about you is my business.

"Gemma, if it's about this morning...," I begin, a bit formally because I have to.

"Alex, please, it's not necessary." Her tone is clipped and cold, and rightfully so. "You are a very busy man. I shouldn't come barging into your office unannounced. My apologies. But as I had agreed to be completely honest with you, I have to tell you Gina, Tony Salvatore's sister, messaged me this morning. You don't have to ask what she said,

I'm going to tell you," she hurries before I can interject. "She asked where I was, she said I should be with them because they're family. That's about it." She clamps her mouth tightly shut and refuses to say anything else.

Her coldness hurts, but knowing that I caused it hurts worse. I can see a glimmer of it in her eyes and it stabs my heart.

"No, Gemma, you know it's not like that. Thank you again for your honesty," *and I'm so sorry I am such a prick*. "The situation we're finding ourselves in," I turn from her hating I have to be this way, "demands that we stay focused on it."

I hear her breathe deeply.

"Understood," is all she says.

I continue in the same business tone as I turn to face her again, "With that being said, yes, you do need to report to me about everything. I need to know where you're going, when you're going, and with whom. I may have to approve it, depending on the safety of the location, and if the people are questionable. I'm sorry if it's inconvenient for you, but your well-being is my primary concern."

Prick!

Her nostrils flare as she composes herself.

"As I said, understood. One other thing."

"What is it?"

I want this farce to be done with.

"I'm going home. Immediately," her words drop between us heavily and echo out in pounding waves.

I tense. "No you're not," my tone is low and steely, hinting at what's going on inside me.

"I am. Now, if there's nothing else…," she turns to leave.

I slam my fist down on the desk and effectively stop her in her tracks as the sound vibrates throughout our bodies and off the walls.

She's stunned. Before she has a chance to recover, I grab her from behind by her waist with my left arm, and grip her throat tightly with my right hand. Immobilized and silenced, I have complete control of her.

I watch her eyes dart back and forth from the door to my eyes as I peer at her from over her shoulder.

As if reading her mind, I sneer at her and push her feet far apart, throwing her body off-balance.

"Do I have your attention now, pet?" I whisper with mock affection at her ear.

I've left just enough air for her to breathe, not easily, but she still can. I can see the hint of panic in her eyes, she knows if I tightened my hand even minimally, I'd choke her.

The sick, twisted demon inside me is writhing with pleasure. It loves this shit, the fear, the danger, the holding a life in its hands. My cock hardens with every breath Gemma takes and with her rigid body pressed flushed against mine like a ragdoll.

"Now you will listen to me." My arm tightens around her abdomen, "You are not going anywhere. Do I make myself perfectly clear? If I even think you're planning it, I *will* lock you up in my dungeon, and if I have to restrain you, Gemma, I will. Now, be a good girl, and don't do anything else stupid."

The instant I begin to loosen my grip on her, she spins around and swings her arm to slap me.

In a flurry of motions, I clasp her wrist and restrain her arm at her back.

"You are an overbearing prick, Black!" she yells at me, practically spitting with rage.

My façade is gone, ripped away by the passionate fury of emotions exploding between us.

I chuckle, the sound only enrages Gemma further and she lashes in my grip. The hold I have on her arm shoots pain through her body and she screams but stops her fight.

"That I am, Gemma, but you're being ridiculous. Do you honestly think I'm going to let you leave? I thought I'd already proven this isn't a game between us, must I give you that lesson again," I can feel her resist the desire to fight me. "Yes, I think I do."

"Let me go!" she grits out.

Guiding her easily to lean her over my desk, I push everything out of the way to crash on the floor and bend her over.

"Consider this a reminder." I cover her body with mine until my cheek is pressed against hers. "There are people out there looking for you, very bad people. If you do anything to put yourself in jeopardy, you will not have the opportunity to do so again. I'll ask you one more time; do I make myself perfectly fucking clear?"

"Yessss," she hisses.

"Good." I stand, and yank her dress up to bare her ass. "I'm going to let go of your arm. If you move, things will not be as pleasant for you." I don't wait for her reply as I release her.

Her in those stockings and lace panties that don't even cover the cheeks of her ass always makes my dick throb. I yank them over her hips and down her legs to pull them off her feet.

Kicking her feet apart, I say, "This is for making me fucking crazy with worry all afternoon. Count!"

SMACK.

"Alex!"

"That's not counting!"

SMACK.

"One!" she yelps.

I know it's hard and it stings. That's the point.

SMACK.

"Two!"

At ten, I tell her quietly, again at her ear, "This is to remind you that your body doesn't lie, pet."

In five rapid successions, my palm slaps that succulent pussy of hers.

"Ooooh, God, Alex," it comes out as a long, loud moan.

I yank open my pants and pull out my throbbing cock.

"I'm going to fuck you because you're mine, and you need to be reminded of that. How you forgot is a mistake that won't happen again."

With one hand gripping her hip, I position my shaft at her sex, and before I penetrate her, I slide it over her mound, then rub her clit with the head as I cover it with her wetness.

I enter her slowly, just the head, and thrust in slowly, in and out, until finally I press fully inside her, so deep I'm hitting her cervix.

As I begin to move, I tell her again, "Mine, Gemma."

"Alex…," she moans.

"Say it," I growl as I bury myself again, so deep, it almost hurts her.

"Yours," she murmurs roughly.

The declaration drives me harder, faster, wilder. I pull her hips to me as I fuck her without abandon. As the white hot fire shoots through me, my balls tighten and my cock swells, ready to blow, I reach around to rub her clit firmly and slowly, pushing her over the edge with me.

We crash together panting, moaning, and screaming out.

I pull her up and hold her to me as I turn her face to mine to kiss her. This time I let her feel how much I care for her, let her taste the depth of emotion I have for her.

I murmur quietly, "Trust me, Gemma, no matter what."

I feel her tense slightly against me as she whispers, "I do."

I retrieve her underwear and wipe our passion from her with them. This time she takes them from me, and I let her.

"I have to go downstairs now and go over some things with Stewart, if you need to find me." The stoic mask has slipped back in place.

"I'll be fine."

Fine, a woman's famous last word.

She turns and leaves and it takes everything in me not to follow her to make love to her. Not fuck her, not tie her up and make her scream, but to make long and passionate love to her.

It's very late when I come back upstairs. Gemma's in bed sleeping. I'm grateful for that. At least I don't have to pretend to be the cold, unfeeling Alexander Black again, the only real piece she saw of me earlier was when I kissed her.

When I get out of the shower and slide into bed next to her, I pull her close, breathe deeply of her unique scent, and tell her silently how much she means to me.

Own

CHAPTER 24

Alexander

I've got to go to china, I have no choice.

I've put off the final decision until the absolute last possible moment, there are only hours left before I have to confirm with Mr. Yun Lee. After trying every available contact, I was forced to admit he's right, no one will even speak with me regarding the stalled paperwork.

I've been set up.

Deep down I knew this was going to be the final result even though I'd refused to admit it until now. I've spent the last twenty-four hours coordinating additional protective measures for Gemma to be in place while I'm gone. If I could, I would lock her in my home the entire time and face her wrath when I returned. But I have too much respect for her. And that would border kidnapping, not that I give a fuck.

Choosing not to was the hardest decision I have ever made.

I'm certain they're planning an attempt on her while I'm gone, I'm sure this is part of the reason they want me gone. So does Major Stewart. He also believes my absence will allow the enemy to show himself, and with his men and my men, he is confident we'll get him before he gets Gemma.

That's much too risky as far as I'm concerned.

But I can't help agreeing with him.

I've been standing staring out the window of my office looking out at Manhattan but not seeing anything. The sun came up unnoticed as I tried to figure out some other way this whole situation could be handled. I kept coming back to the same conclusion.

There's no other way.

Gemma and I have skirted the subject, although it's been looming over us like a ticking time bomb. Both of us are fully aware an attempt on her is highly likely, and we know it's only a matter of time before it happens, but neither of us want to address it yet. My frustration coupled with her worries have dug a chasm between us and each hour added to the distance.

The past twenty-four hours have royally sucked.

She took off and thankfully Williams followed her. When she got home, the fucking I gave her allowed me to feel down deep inside she was safe, and she was well.

We've barely spoken since she walked into my office yesterday morning, not that I made her feel welcome. On the contrary, I don't think it was possible for me to have been any colder and distant other than packing her bags and putting her out on the street. The only time I've allowed myself to let down my guards was when I was inside her, and late at night in bed, holding her warm body against mine. Those few stolen hours I let everything I feel for her come to the surface and I refused to let her go. When the morning came, I clothed myself with aloofness and detachment like the suit of armor by my bed. I had to separate myself, it's the only way I know.

I have never been faced with such a difficult decision as the one to allow Gemma to intentionally be put in danger. That is what Major Stewart suggested.

He presented a plan to have Gemma as bait knowing the Russian mob, and most likely the Chinese as well, know that I'll be in China. He's already organized a team for me overseas, along with someone shadowing me on the plane and en route to my hotel. Security measures are set-up for me in China as well. He's ensuring I'll be well guarded.

He also wants to focus on luring the enemy out here, using Gemma, and the possible information device they say she has.

In the past, this kind of shit would have gotten me off, like some sort of mercenary vigilante. This type of conflict used to fuel me, push me harder, my need to conquer and destroy would have been fed, and nothing would have stood in my way.

The five-foot, three-inch dark haired beauty is the only thing I'm concerned about. Her safety is my only focus. It's killing me to think I have to leave her and make her the focal point of danger here.

She knows it. She's angry at herself for it, I know she blames herself for everything that's happened, regardless of how many times I've told her she's only a pawn in this game, someone who was sucked in and is now a potential casualty of war.

That is what pisses me off. She has nothing to do with this, and yet she has, and is, suffering the most. I won't allow myself to think of the things they'd do to her if they get their hands on her, death would be better than what she'd endure.

The thought of Gemma being raped, tortured, burned, dismembered, all things that would happen, and do happen, if they got their hands on her because of Malcolm Stevens is my hell, and I live it in my mind every second of every day.

The door to my office slowly opens

"Alex," she says quietly behind me.

My gut twists with that perpetual burning knife that's been lodged in me since I heard I have to leave.

"Yes," my tone is cold.

I can hear her step closer.

"We need to talk," the statement is quiet but firm.

She's braced herself for a confrontation.

Fuck, Gemma!

"What would you like to discuss?" I turn to face her.

I know my features are a stone mask and it throws her off, I can see it in her expression.

She takes a deep inhale of breath before she begins.

"My part in this, and don't try to bullshit me, Black. I know what's going on."

A flash of angry frustration shoots through me and I know Gemma saw it before I could squelch it.

"It's true and very unfortunate," I reply, attempting to regain my façade of cold detachment.

She takes another step closer, her posture rigid, ready for a fight.

You're strong, Gemma, there's no question about that, but not strong enough for those sick fucks. I can't let them get you.

"Unfortunate as it may be, it's a fact, and I know I have a part to play. I've accepted it, as much as I hate it, but there's nothing you or I can do to change that. So stop being this cold bastard and talk to me about it. I'd rather hear it from you than Major Stewart."

I can't face her so I give her my back. I can't let her see how much it hurts to drag her into this. Isabelle's death was an accident, but it was quick and that in itself was merciful. What could possibly be waiting for Gemma is worse than a living hell.

I can't agree to put her in a position with any possibility of her living that.

"Gemma, I don't want you to have any part of this."

She lays her hand gently on my shoulder. It's the most painful, and beautiful, thing I've felt in a long time.

"Alex, I already have a part in this, it started the day Malcolm left whatever he did in my possession. We need to accept it; you need to talk to me. This silent treatment is killing me. Alex, I need you to help me...please." Her voice is filled with anguish.

It tears me apart.

"Goddammit, Gemma!" I turn and pull her tightly to me.

I can't get her close enough, I can't feel enough of her, I need to breathe her so deep inside me, she'll always be a part of me.

"This isn't your fight. You shouldn't have anything to do with this."

With her hands wrapped around me and her cheek pressed against my chest, I feel her relax into me.

"I already am. Carlos and Jesús will take care of me while you're gone, along with Stewart's men, I'll be fine."

"I should be the one here protecting you. I dragged you into this."

She pulls back and looks up into my face, her eyes filled with understanding.

"Is that what you think? No, no, don't you see? If it wasn't for you, I'd be out there alone and this would still be happening to me. You've given me more than I could have had on my own. If it weren't for my position with your company, I would never have found out about the stalker. I have no doubt that I'd already be…"

She chokes up and her eyes fill with tears. She can't bring herself say she might be dead. I can't either, not out loud.

I pull her to me again and stroke her hair soothingly, wanting to blot out all her pain and make her forget all her fear.

"Sssshhhh, pet, I know, you're right. I can't help it though. You belong to me, I should protect you, not some stranger. It will be alright, we're going to get them, nothing is going to happen to you, I swear."

"Alex, strangers or not, you've got a damn army at your fingertips. Nothing or no one is going to get through that. And Carlos and Jesús are like your brothers, Rico too, they'll do anything for you, along with their associates."

Gang members, and you're right, once again. But it won't be me, these bastards are making sure of it.

"Gemma, you have to know I wouldn't go if it was just business, that shipment doesn't mean anything to me…"

"Alex," she cuts me off and looks directly into my eyes. "I know that, you have to go for those poor kids. Somebody needs to save them. That's what you were put on this earth for, why you have everything you have; the power, the money, the connections. Everything you've worked for was for this. Don't let this, don't let *me*, get in the way of that. You're much bigger than they are, and they know it. That's why they're doing this. You've got this, Mr. Black. Go and kick their asses, then come back to me. I'll be right here waiting."

I clasp her face in my hands and kiss her. I pour all the devotion, all the admiration, everything I feel for her in that kiss, my pride and adoration, everything inside me. Her arms wrap around my neck, her hands feed into my hair and pull me closer, grinding her mouth into mine, giving and taking, feasting and devouring, consuming me with her will, and filling herself with my strength.

When we finally part, both of us breathless, I rest my forehead on hers, neither of us letting the other go, she tells me, "I've got to go to my house today, I'm sure you know. The car's waiting downstairs. One of Stewart's men named Williams is coming with Carlos and me."

I smile.

"I know, I picked him to accompany you. Get used to him, he's going to be your best friend while I'm gone. But not too much, understand, Ms. Trudeau?"

"Mr. Black," that snarky tone is back in her voice, the one that calls my shit, and I'm so happy to hear it, it's been gone too long. "There isn't a man on this earth that could ever take your place."

"Remember that, Ms. Trudeau, or you will be reminded when I get back. You won't be able to sit for a week."

"That I could never forget, but…maybe I should have some kind of infraction. You know, just to keep you on your game," she remarks with a naughty gleam in her eye.

"Is that right? Well, I might just have to leave you with a little reminder of what that infraction would get you," I smile broadly at her.

This woman has me wrapped around her finger.

"Promises, promises, Mr. Black. Put your money where your mouth is. But do it when I get back. Carlos is waiting for me outside your door, and Williams is in the lobby. They want to leave for Jersey City now so we can get back before you have to go."

Our intimate moment has been pushed aside by the somberness of our situation.

There's work to do, and it won't wait or be ignored.

"It's a date then," I comment as casually as I can while I lead her out, pulling the door closed behind me.

Our steps are slow and heavy, reflecting the weight we both carry.

"Everyone is aware of the plan?" I ask Carlos brusquely when we reach him.

"Yes, everything's in place. We got this," he answers me tightly.

Even Carlos is on edge. We both knew something was coming, we felt it that night I sat down with the five families of the Italian mob. He's primed and ready for whatever is coming, I can see it in the fire in his eyes.

"Alright, keep me posted, I want updates constantly."

"Got it, ten four," he snaps.

Carlos is now the military soldier, the image

of the perfectly manufactured military war machine. He's lethal, a deadly combination of street warrior and army issued killer. He is the only man I trust with Gemma's life, the only man other than me.

"Did you bring it?" I ask him.

"Yeah, I've got it right here."

He holds up a plain brown paper shopping bag.

I take it from him, set it down on Simon's desk, and proceed to pull out the contents. Gemma is looking intently at what I'm doing until she figures out what's in the bag.

She bolts upright.

"Who's that for?" she asks surprised.

"You...and me. Carlos and the men all have theirs already," I reply casually.

"Bullet proof vests?"

"Yep, hold your arms out to the sides," I instruct her.

"You're going to put *that* on over my clothes?" she takes a step back with her eyes wide.

"Yes, unless you'd like to strip, let me put it on you, and wear it all day? I've got something to cover it up. Give me *some* credit, pet," I smile crookedly at her and wiggle my eyebrows.

"You are completely impossible, Alexander Black," she glares at me with a grin as she raises her arms out to the sides.

"Yes I am, but you love me for it, pet," the words slip naturally from my mouth.

The world comes to a screeching halt with those few casually uttered words. Gemma's look crashes into mine and her lips part. Everything swirls and sucks into an unseen black hole between us, pulling us front and center.

What the fuck did I say that for?!

Five seconds seem to pass in an invisible tunnel of echoes and magnification with just she and I.

Finally, she says softly as her expression shows the depth of everything inside her, "Yes, Mr. Black, I do love you for it."

Never has Gemma looked more beautiful, more vulnerable, more intoxicating than she does at this moment.

"Me too," I whisper.

I can feel the flush cover my cheeks as a silly grin lifts my lips.

I'm reacting like a boy and his first crush.

She smiles happily at me, a genuine one that sparks in her eyes, one that shows the love and devotion she has for me, just like I have for her.

"Dress me, Black, I'm yours to do what you will."

"Gladly, Ms. Trudeau, but I have better things in mind," I smirk as I begin to fit the vest over her lush body.

When it's in place, I remove the Burberry trench coat from the paper bag.

"You have thought of everything," she chuckles, taking it from me and pulling it on.

"Don't I always?" I wink at her.

"Completely impossible," she mumbles, rolling her eyes.

I laugh as I slip off my jacket, and reveal a holster with a Glock 19. I watch Gemma, her eyes are transfixed on me, as I undo the leather straps, fit my vest on my torso, and replace the holster and gun. I leave my jacket on Simon's desk, then put on the trench coat meant for me.

"You guys ready?" Carlos asks.

"You're coming with us?" Gemma comments to me, snapping out of her daze.

"Of course. Let's go."

Carlos leads us through the office to the elevator, Stewart's silent man is sitting at his desk and blending in like a piece of furniture. I direct Gemma in front of me as I follow.

The mood has instantly shifted to heavy, each of us alert and wary. We ride down in silence and when we hit the lobby, we move quickly to the Hummer and Jesús. Through the crowd of early morning people hustling past us on the sidewalk, I can see even he's more cautious than usual with his hand ready to pull out the gun he's got hidden if necessary. Williams is at his side, and although he's in plain clothes, there's mercenary written all over him.

In the car, I automatically take Gemma's hand in mine. We drive to her house in silence, all of us on alert and lost in our own thoughts. I glance at Gemma, amazed at her strength and perseverance. It humbles me.

Jesús slowly pulls up onto her street as his eyes dart all around, surveying our surroundings.

"I'm going to go around the block, just to see who's around," he comments casually.

"Good idea," I reply tightly.

The hair's prickling on the back of my neck.

Something's not right.

Most of the cars are gone from in front of the houses in the neighborhood, people have left for work. There's an eerie stillness in the air, one filled with foreboding and danger. We make our way around the block with no noises except for an occasional dog barking somewhere nearby.

"See anything different?" I ask tightly.

"Nope," Jesús answers in his signature indifferent way.

I know his demeanor is practiced, he's on guard just like the rest of us, primed for anything.

"That's a good thing," Gemma states nervously.

I turn my attention to her and try to soften my expression. "He's just taking precautions," I try to comfort her.

She looks at me like I'm full of shit.

I lean to kiss her softly as we pull up in front of her house.

Williams gets out first and we wait for him to give us the 'All Clear' before we exit the car.

"Something's not right," she whispers, verbalizing my thoughts, her hand clutching tightly to mine.

"I know, Gemma. If it's not safe, Williams and Carlos will tell us. This car was upfitted for situations such as this, nothing's getting in here," I try to reassure her as I stroke the top of her hand.

"We're good," Carlos announces before he gets out and opens my door.

Gemma takes a deep breath and looks into my eyes and gathers all her strength.

"Are you sure you want to go in?" I ask her.

I'm ready to take her back to ninety-sixth street and lock her away where she'll be safe and no one can get to her, all she has to do is say the word.

"Yes, I'm sure. This is my parents' house, nothing is going to take it from me, it's all I have left of them," her words crack on the end.

I pull her close and kiss her forehead. I know how much it hurts to lose someone you love. I just don't want to lose her.

"Alright, I'll go first, then you follow. Are you ready?" I ask, trying to give her a smile.

She tries to laugh but it's a nervous sound.

"Don't try to be relaxed, it doesn't suit you. Let's get this over with."

I lift myself from the car and position my body to cover hers as I guide her out by her hand. Carlos is on the other side of her, both of us blocking any access to her small frame, with Williams behind me. We ascend the stairs to the front door. Jesús is staying outside to watch. Every instinct inside me is screaming at me. She slips the key in the lock, then turns the knob. Carlos moves in front of her to enter first as Williams takes Carlos' place at her side. When he pushes the door, it won't open, something is blocking it.

"What the fuck?" he curses as he gives it a shove.

When the door finally opens, he steps in.

"It looks like you've had some company," Carlos states as he looks around.

We all move inside, Carlos and Williams already have their guns drawn.

"Oh my God," I hear Gemma whisper as she takes in the destruction that is her parents' home.

Every piece of furniture is turned over, the cushions all have been cut open and their stuffing's pulled out, the pictures on the walls taken down and smashed. It looks like the house vomited all its belongings and spewed them out in a heaving, massive heap.

Thank God Gemma wasn't here! It would be blood all over the floor, not furniture. Her blood. Then I'd make sure they all died.

The only other time I've felt fury like I do now was the day in that alley when Isabelle was killed.

"Why?" Gemma chokes out as tears spill down her cheeks.

"They were looking for that information, Ms. Trudeau," Williams answers her in his official tone.

I curse myself.

Fuck! I should have been watching! I have camera's in place, I could have seen this happening and caught these son-of-a-bitches. I'm so stupid! At least I've got the recording.

Gemma turns to me. Her eyes are filled with so much pain, so much agony, and it rips my heart out.

"It's real, isn't Alex? They want to kill me, don't they?" her words are so quiet and so anguished, everything within me wants to take her far away and forget everything else.

But I know I can't.

"It's very real, Gemma."

Mine

Part III

"Tell me every terrible thing you did,

And let me love you anyway..."

Sade Andria Zabala

Mine

CHAPTER 26

Alexander

"Stewart, let me hear your plan."

I pause as I sit at the head of the conference table.

"Then I'll tell you mine," I add.

Seated at the large table with me are:

Major Patrick Stewart, retired military counter-intelligence strategist.

Captain Cornelius James, retired army skills and combat instructor, specializing in explosives.

Lieutenant Steven Williams, retired Army, sharpshooter, and a ghost in the dark.

Retired Special Forces, a man known only as Hawk.

Deadly weapons in human flesh. In each man's eyes, their own beast swirls in the depths. Intimidating and dangerous, hard, cold, deadly, the savage within scaring the shit right out of you. But I know that beast, have lived intimately with mine my entire life. I used to hate mine. As a boy, it used to control me, beat me, shredded me, whipped me. Then it taught me, carved me, and molded me until I was the master and the beast the grateful slave.

It has served me very well.

Carlos, Jesús and Rico are here as well because it's imperative to keep all facets of the operation in tune with the others. Carlos is a former military man, he served under Stewart. Rico is a police officer and is investigating the deaths of Gemma's parents, and any links with law enforcement and the Italian, Russian, and Chinese mobs. Carlos will act as platoon leader for the gang members if the shit hits the fan. Which it will.

"Mr. Black, as you already know, I have a man shadowing you on your flight to China, and another team set-up there once you arrive. You are going to be well protected.

"As for here and Ms. Trudeau, I recommend having her more visible in public areas, commuting for instance, with a man at her side every minute, you've chosen Lieutenant Williams to accompany her. Several others will be strategically located nearby and within eye distance."

My gut twists.

Not if I can fucking help it, especially after what happened at her house, and the man who made the call from around the corner of the Black Building.

I lift my hand to stop him.

I've got to leave for China in an hour, I don't have time to pussy foot around.

"This is what I want, Major."

I move to the board on the wall and draw two circles. One with an R and the other with a C.

Pointing to the circle with the R, I say, "This is Russia." Then to the one with the C, "China."

Saying directly to Stewart, "I want teams at each location immediately. Today. When we find out who ordered this fucking mess, I want him taken out. We don't know where he's at," I slap each circle with the marker. "So we've got to be ready at both. Put a bullet in his fucking head. We'll be doing everybody a favor."

The major starts to slowly shake his head.

I slam my hands on the table.

"If you've got a moral problem with this, tell me now. This filthy piece of shit killed Gemma's parents. He buys his thousand dollar suits with five-year old girls getting raped and beaten by old fucking pigs!"

Major Stewart's chair hits the wall behind him when he jumps to his feet.

"I've got no problem with that, Black! I'd skin that pig myself and let him fry after I cut off every fucking available body part. What I DO have a problem with is making more problems...FOR YOU."

I straighten.

"I'm listening."

He comes to meet me at the board.

"Depending on who and what he is, we'll find out soon, I promise you that, will determine how he'll be handled. If he is a political figure, we'll need to deal with him a little more tactfully. Especially if he is Chinese, those fuckers are so sensitive, nothing is only business. If he's mob affiliated, a loud statement will bring the message home."

I grit my teeth. I have to agree with him.

"Fair enough." Then add, "You've got the best talent available, I'm sure you'll use whatever means you feel the situation calls for. Now," I turn back to the board, "I have a rescue mission happening while I'm in China, Carlos will give you the details." I return my gaze to Stewart, "I believe the mission is going to be compromised. Therefore, I want a rescue team and combat soldiers ready for the operation. I'm handling the mission myself while I'm there."

There's surprise on all the men's faces. Except Carlos. And Rico.

"Are you fucking CRAZY, Black?!" Carlos shouts from the other side of the room.

"Listen, they won't be expecting me. I need to see for myself that the internal integrity of what we've got set-up is not compromised as well." I will not be dissuaded. If there's any affiliation whatsoever with the Yun Lee deal and the mission, I'll know.

"It's practically suicide, Alex!" He's on his feet, his body ready for a fight.

"They want this whole fucking trip to be a suicide mission," I shout back at him. "But if they're putting me there, I'm going to do it my way."

I've been set-up, my businesses are all threatened. I've pissed-off some very powerful people because I'm taking away the disgusting means by which they pay for the silk they cover their shriveled up dicks with. The same dicks they use to rape five-year old little girls.

Good.

The darkness in me wants the chance to cut their pricks off instead. And smile as I shove it down their filthy fucking throats. Listening to their screams ringing in my ears, the soul deep satisfaction of their torture before I killed them burning through my veins as I cut them open and see the terror in their eyes, the beast inside feasting on their blood and pain. But the man will get justice for Gemma.

The threat to my legitimate enterprises doesn't bother me, nothing can touch me that way. They will suffer, it can't be avoided, because the link that lines pockets reaches deep. Some hands are going to get cut off.

What's making me go to China, not the paperwork that somehow mysteriously got lost in customs, is the mission I've got scheduled to take place at the same time.

It took me a year to organize a talented team I can trust there, to establish underground routes, gather trained militia men who are honorable, and to get all the fake documentation together, in order to infiltrate a human trafficking circle and rescue the kids that are being sold into prostitution. My sources have confirmed the ages range from five through sixteen.

Those girls are the only reason I'm going. I couldn't give two fucks about the merchandise being held for export.

Under normal circumstances I would look forward to going to China and dealing with this myself, the thrill of the hunt, the lure of finding my enemies, then the sweet taste of revenge. But these are not normal circumstances.

They're dragging Gemma into this.

These same people, whoever they are, used her husband Malcolm to extort three million dollars from me in a bullshit Ponzi scheme. The fraud came out and now he's in prison, but he left something in her possession. Something that's so important and so damning to them, whoever is behind all of this wants it back, and they said they're taking Gemma with it. They've already had the Russian mob murder her parents.

I'm furious they're controlling me and forcing me to leave. I have no doubt they plan not only to try and kill me, but attempt to kidnap Gemma, find this thing they're looking for, torture her to uncover anything she knows, then kill her.

No one is touching her! I'll make damn sure of that!

The greatest advantage I've got is the element of surprise. I plan on using it to the fullest extent. This army is my way.

"If you know they're setting you up as a moving target, then why the fuck are you gonna do the mission?" Carlos yells at me again, spit flying out of his mouth.

"Because he has to," Rico states calmly, sitting back in his chair as he studies me. "He's sending a message, bro, telling them they can't stop him. And he's going to rub their faces in it as he fucks them in the ass right in their own house."

Rico and I share a knowing look filled with our history of times we did the exact thing side by side. A lifetime of dark secrets explodes in the room around us, ghosts from heinous moments when we extracted revenge, the blood is still on our hands and will never leave.

"Son-of-a-bitch!" Carlos growls as he throws his chair across the room before he storms out.

"He's upset he's going to miss the party," Rico comments as he watches his blood brother's retreating figure through the glass.

"He's got his own party to attend," I grit out.

"Still, it doesn't change the fact he's not going to be there, you are, and he fucking hates it," Rico replies casually, but couldn't be any more accurate.

He's right. I know Carlos is beating himself up because he won't be there to get my back.

"Rico, any ID's on the men who broke into Gemma's house?"

The day Gemma started working for me I planted camera's all over her house. It was ransacked…and I've got them recorded.

"Yes, two men, both Russian mob, both soldiers," his response is cool.

Of course they were.

My jaw clenches.

What is the link with the Russian mob and who's responsible for all of this? The question is driving me mad.

"Have the police confirmed how they got in?" I ask Rico.

He smirks. "Through the basement."

Just like I did the day I broke in to plant the cameras.

"I've already taken care of any further access into the home," Rico informs me smoothly.

"Perfect."

That right there is exactly why blood, even if it's not through birth, is always stronger.

Shaking myself from the heated exchange between Carlos and I, I address Major Stewart. "I want to make one thing perfectly clear: Ms. Trudeau is not to be used in any way, shape, or form as bait. She is to be kept out of any situation that could endanger her. If she'll stay locked right here in this house, that would be best, although I'm sure she'll be going to the office. This is not to change unless I approve it. I don't care what she says. Is this understood?" My tone is even and low, the underlying warning clear.

"I understand," Stewart responds hesitantly, "but consider the plans I've laid out for you."

"I will, but that will only be done when and if I feel she will not be facing any imminent danger, AND I am absolutely certain we have complete control," my voice is cold and hard as steel.

"Alright."

Major Stewart doesn't like the fact I'm holding him back from luring out the enemy with Gemma, it's written all over him with his tight lips and furrowed brow. *I don't give two fucks.* They've contacted her and virtually promised they were going to take her the first opportunity they'd get. I wasn't going to hand it to them with a hand delivered invitation.

"I'm going upstairs to say good-bye to Gemma, I'll be available in an hour." Fixing my attention on my driver, assistant, and childhood friend, Jesús, "My luggage is already downstairs, I'll meet you out front then."

For the first time since we all sat down, I focus on the other men at the table. "Williams, thank you, I know you won't let Gemma do anything stupid. But watch her closely, she's smart, and can be sneaky."

"Roger that, Mr. Black." He's all military.

Lieutenant Steven Williams is the All-American jock type with the perfect smile, hair, and personality that would get him laid seven nights, and days, a week. He has one-hundred fifty official long rage kill-shots on record, and he's an MMA fighter. His big blue eyes dazzle, but there is a dark, bottomless pool in their depths, cold and unforgiving.

"Captain James," I nod at the perfect soldier sitting next to Williams. Then my gaze shifts to the silent, intimidating man whose breathing and body movements are almost non-existent, his large presence could go unnoticed, "Hawk." I address the other two imposing men. "Thank you for coming on board, your skills and expertise are second to none."

Hawk nods his reply, James gives me the formal, "Yes, sir."

Captain Cornelius James' back is ramrod military straight, everything about him screams precision. He has to be, he blows shit up. He is personable, professional, and dangerous as hell. He adores his wife and three children, and would kill anyone who looked at them wrong.

Hawk, on the other hand, should have been

named phantom, with the ability to hide in plain sight just before the kill. He is Army Special Forces, all of his missions in the past five years are highly classified with the only information released confirming over two hundred official kills...the ones on record. Hawk has no known family, which could be a major contributor to his mysterious whereabouts most of the time. The guy lives in a Winnebago and has a post office box in Texas. It's known the mail gets checked sporadically with no rhyme or reason to the schedule. He looks like a hybrid motorcycle club gang member and GQ cover model. His favorite weapon is a blade.

"Major Stewart," I turn toward the leader of my army. "Update me in an hour with the status of my requests."

Major Patrick Stewart, heavily decorated military professional. He left the army when his wife was diagnosed with stage four breast cancer. They had been high school sweethearts, and married after graduation. He joined the Army and made it a career, his wife had been his mistress when he could get home. That guilt still eats at him and keeps him awake at night, along with being overseas when his daughter was growing up. When he'd arrived state side for good, he was a stranger to the then young woman and his dying wife.

"Roger that, Black," he replies almost absently, his mind putting together the pieces of the units I requested.

Fucking soldiers.

Thank God.

"Gentlemen," I nod to all off them as I leave

406

the intelligence/surveillance room in the lower level of my private home on Seven East Ninety-Sixth Street, Manhattan, the headquarters to my private army.

Rico eyes me silently as I pass him. He knows this isn't a suicide mission. It's war, and it's personal.

Very fucking personal.

Gemma

I'm terrified.

As I pace the floor in the Penthouse of Alex's home, his private space perched atop his five story mansion, wringing my hands, it takes every ounce of self-control not to shatter.

He's leaving in one hour. They broke into my house and destroyed it!

My heart pounds and my mind plays the scene at my parent's house over and over again. The house hadn't been ransacked, the entire interior had been destroyed and violated. *I* had been *violated.* Every piece of furniture had been cut open and ripped to shreds, all the pictures that had been hanging on the walls were smashed on the floors and against opposite walls, lamps crushed, even the personal photo albums that had been lovingly lined-up and chronologically placed in the built-in bookshelves laid torn apart and disemboweled.

Just like my life.

For a fraction of a second I was paralyzed as I'd stood in the middle of the destruction and thought of what could have happened to me if I'd been home.

Now, I smirk with misplaced gratitude to

Tony Salvatore for barging into my house and choking me. If it hadn't been for that incident, Alex wouldn't have come in to save me, and he wouldn't have insisted I come here where he could protect me.

The nagging question I'd had that day surfaces again.

How did he know to come at that exact moment? The timing was too much to be coincidence.

Right now I have bigger problems to worry about.

They say I have the information they're looking for.

My pacing begins again as I wrack my brain trying to figure out where Malcolm could have hidden something like that. It would be a hell of a lot easier if I knew what I was looking for. That's what they were searching for at my house.

I could just ask him.

I could go see Malcolm and ask him, march into the prison and sit down with him face to face.

Yeah, bright idea, then they'll kidnap me as soon as I stepped outside.

Shit!

Major Stewart's men and I were supposed to go through my belongings to look for this mysterious object that holds the answers to this massive situation. But when we arrived at my parent's house, that plan was immediately extinguished when we walked into the destruction. I know Stewart's men are going back, but I'm not allowed anywhere near there.

Fuck that! That's my house, I'll be damned

if they're going to take my childhood home from me.

Anger is vying for first place over my fear. It's winning.

I'll go anytime I want, I know they'll come with me, but they can't stop me.

They can if they tie me up and lock me up here.

Alex wouldn't do that...would he?
Absolutely!

I immediately think that Gina might help me, my best friend, and Tony Salvatore's sister.

No she can't, she's one of them, she said so herself.

I miss her.

The only person I can trust is leaving me alone.

Alexander Black.

The one person who should hate me is the only person I trust implicitly with my life.

He's leaving, and I have no one else.

Another thought comes on a sob.

The Faceless Man.

The memory of the man who'd broken into my house seductively ripples through me. He blindfolded and consumed me, and the lingering images envelope me in soothing warmth. In some sick, twisted way I know without a doubt I can trust him.

If I only had some way to get in touch with him, just in case, like an emergency jump seat.

I don't know how I know, but I'm certain if I needed him, he would help me. He'd told me the reason he came to me, as perverse and crazy as it was, he was there to give me what I needed.

He'd come for me.

I'd never seen his face, never actually heard his voice, (his words were always a rough whisper), but he had given me exactly what I'd needed: confidence, comfort, fire, and passion. He'd made me feel alive. For that, I will always be grateful to him.

Alexander Black, ruthless, dangerous, powerful. My protector.

"You're leaving," I choke out, my face in my hands, as I fall to the couch in the parlor of the Penthouse.

They're setting him up!

I know about the rescue mission, I know he has to go, I wouldn't let him stay even if he'd insisted. I could never live with myself if I stopped him from saving those innocent kids. I won't let him see me like this.

But he's walking into a trap. He has no idea what he's facing, who he's facing. That leaves him completely vulnerable. And an open target.

All of this turmoil, the danger that's everywhere, for both me and Alex, is raging around and coming at me from all directions.

I shoot to my feet when I hear the elevator doors slide open and drop the mask of control over my features.

Alex is coming towards me as he rips his jacket from his body to throw it thoughtlessly on whatever piece of furniture he passes. With each step he undoes another button on his crisp white shirt, then the ones at his cuffs.

His steps are sure and determined as he approaches me, his expression hard, feral, raw, savage lust. My body ignites as it reacts to him, our connection so strong, I have no control. Heat sears through my veins like lava, swirling with the anger and fear that had been gripping me, creating a lethal concoction. He can see the pain I've been battling even though I try to hide it, it flashes back at me in his ice blue eyes fighting with his need. He's on me instantly, pulling me into his arms and wrapping me in his iron hold until all the air rushes from my body. His mouth captures mine hungrily, devouring me, and leaving me weak. He's a tsunami and I'm drowning. Scooping me up in his arms, he carries me to his dungeon of darkness, my darkness, and kicks the door shut behind him, so hard it makes the heavy paintings on the wall jump.

He is possession and control, power and fury. He is going to consume me.

Mine

CHAPTER 27

Alexander

She's killing me!

Every cell in my body is raging to possess Gemma. I needed to feel her, taste her, smell her, own her, and completely consume her, nothing could have stopped me from walking out of that meeting. I'm losing control, unraveling at the seams, I can't think, I can't breathe, all I want is to take her. Hard. Rough. Savagely.

She is the only thing that will satisfy my beast.

My mouth hasn't left hers, starved for her, needing more, needing everything. Sucking her lower lip deep in my mouth, I bite down, and the rusty taste of her blood explodes on my taste buds. The beast inside me growls, hungry for more. Her long fingernails in my hair dig into my scalp as she clutches my lip between her teeth and bites me back, grinding our mouths together.

The beast has tasted her blood, there's no holding him back, he's clawing, busting through my walls to devour her.

He won't be satisfied with anything less than complete and total ravagement.

Gripping her blouse, I rip it open, the buttons fly across the room. Next the skirt, I shred it from her body, the sound of tearing fabric blends with our panting. I stare into Gemma's eyes, mine wild and fierce, hers glazed and mad with passion. Her pretty lace bra that lifts her tits tauntingly at me, begging me to take them in my mouth, gone, useless, now a rag. Her matching panties are no longer an obstacle between me and where I need to bury my cock, tattered and ruined on the floor. Walking her backwards, forcing her to the St. Andrew's Cross, I leave a trail of her torn clothing until her back slams against the crisscrossed planks with only her thigh highs still in place.

Primal. Animal. Savage. We are mouths, teeth, nails, flesh, tearing, biting, taking, giving. Colliding in a tempestuous desperation. She digs her nails into my chest and scores them down my front, drawing blood, as my teeth sink into the soft skin of her shoulder. The room fills with the sounds of our curses, growls and moans of pure primitive hunger. The slapping of our flesh, our sweat melding as our bodies come together. My mouth claims her nipple, sucking it feverishly, my tongue tormenting the hard tip, my teeth clench it, starved for her moans the onslaught pulls from her. We're feasting on each other, ravenous to consume, our longing driving us beyond all control.

I grip her firmly around the back of her neck and pull her face down to the wounds she gave me, the dark red blood oozing from my flesh.

"Take it," my voice fierce. "Make me yours."

Her eyes flash to mine, wide and sultry, as a smile curves her kiss swollen lips. Slowly her mouth opens and her tongue reaches out to take my life force. With her eyes never leaving mine, her gaze penetrating me straight to my core, she licks the blood covered welts.

"I want to be the blood that flows in your veins, the very air you breathe," I feed my fist into her hair and grip it, pulling her face up to mine. "I will be the only thing you need to live, Gemma, and you will be mine, the only thing that gives me life," I whisper roughly.

"You owned me the minute I saw you, Alex."

Our mouths claim each other, tongues swirling, clashing, entwining, searching to go deeper. I grind her into me with the hand holding her hair, needing to get closer,

"Turn around," I grit out between clenched teeth.

Clasping her wrist, I turn her roughly and press her front so hard against the wall, her beautiful tits squeeze out from both sides. Instinctively, she raises her hands and grips the chains that hold the restraints. With my body pressed against the length of her lush nakedness, I pull her to me just enough to slip a hand to clasp one of her nipples. It hardens under my touch as I graze my thumb over it.

"Ah, pet," I growl.

Taking the hardened point between finger and thumb, I pull and pinch it, as a hiss escapes her.

"Don't let go." I whisper huskily into her ear as I kick her feet apart. With my other hand I penetrate her with a single finger, thrusting into her heat until my hand hits her mound. She's soaking and it makes my cock swell.

Gemma gasps a loud moan as she pushes her hips into me, scrunches her eyes, and grips me inside her. Her back arches as she clasps my finger tighter, pushing me to the point of no return.

"Goddammit, Gemma," I growl, thrusting into her as I work her captured nipple.

"Don't be gentle with me, Alex." Her demand is rough.

"I can't, pet, we're way beyond that."

Slipping a second finger into her, I plunge in and out of her as I lick a long swipe up her back and close my teeth on her neck. She moans as her head dips back.

I'm so fucking hungry for her.

Pulling from her, I drop to yank her hose down one at a time, leaving her completely naked.

Fuck!

I want to punish her, she's infuriating me, owning me, controlling me. I want her to. It scares the fuck out of me. If I give her control, then I'll lose it. I can't afford that.

I don't know if I'll be able to stop.

I'm on the brink of losing it. She'll be the one to pay the price.

I grab a handful of her hair and pull slowly. Her head falls back again as her lips part and her eyes close.

"You're asking for it, Gemma. You and your fucking body, I can't stop."

"Then don't," she taunts me quietly.

She's fucking pushing me, taunting my beast, teasing him, begging for more.

I grip her hair tighter as I cup her sex and press my throbbing shaft against her beautiful round ass, wanting to pound the fuck out of that tight hole.

"I won't, pet, and I'm going to leave myself all over you. Every time you move, every time you think, every fucking breath you take will be me. You're mine, and you're never going to forget it."

"Do it," she goads me.

I'm going to leave myself all over her.

"Fuck," I growl again as I tear off my shirt and throw it to the floor. Grabbing my tie, I tell her, "Lift your face, pet."

I wrap it around her head and blindfold her with it.

Gemma

He's consuming me, penetrating me, seeping into every cell of my body. Burning me, shredding me apart, and making me whole.

The darkness wraps around me and pulls me into its erotic spell. My body is humming, my heart pounding, as I reach out for Alex with all of my senses.

Silent footsteps across the floor.

What is he getting?

Coherent thought is almost impossible in the lust filled madness I'm in.

His breath is now on my skin caressing me, his body heat stroking me.

"Hold on, pet," his voice rough.

He's controlled fury, leashed passion, a beast contained.

"Take me Alex, don't hold back."

His fingers dig into my flesh as a rumble escapes from deep in his chest, the animal stirring inside him.

Something is gliding down my back petting me, soft yet firm, gentle yet titillating.

The flogger!

It's gone but I hear a swishing noise. My fists clench the chains tighter as my body tenses, waiting for the sting of the soft leather strands.

Flick! Against the backs of my thighs.

Flick! It lands across my buttocks.

Yes!

I push my hips out, arching my back, reaching for it.

"Fuck Gemma..." Alex's voice is tight.

Flick! The soft leather licks my back with its stinging kisses.

"More..." My demand is long and guttural.

I'm floating in a sea of oblivion, each contact of the decadent leather another shot of the sweet drug. It's complete possession, total rapture, a claiming I've never experienced before.

I *need* Alex to devour me, I want him to tear me apart and leave nothing left. I need him to take all that I am, own it, possess it, claim it. Then and only then, can I be free.

Nothing exists, only each lash against my

needy flesh. It's screaming for more.

The contacts are coming faster and more demanding.

"Harder…," I moan.

Somewhere in my lust fogged delirium I hear Alex growl.

The darkness inside him.

Smack!

The leather bites into my skin and my body goes rigid.

"Yes!" I scream.

My loins are screaming for release; the final ravagement I need to be set free.

"Gemma…" Alex's voice is raspy and deep. He's breathing heavily, maybe from the exerted energy from my delicious lashing, or maybe it's from his pent-up need. Either way, it makes my entire being pulse wildly with an ache that almost hurts.

I hear a muffled thump on the carpet and my heart pounds wildly with anticipation.

"Your bleeding…I'm sorry." His words are tight.

I glance at him over my shoulder, my hands still tightly wrapped around the chains of the restraints.

"Take it, make me yours completely," I throw his words back at him, my voice hoarse from the ledge I'm teetering on, waiting to be pushed over.

"All that you are, Gemma, is mine," he says with a rumble from deep inside him as he grips my hips.

Lowering his mouth to my back, his tongue makes contact and glides across my flesh, the touch stinging and wet...and intoxicating.

I suck in a sharp breath and push back against him.

He slips a hand between my parted legs to glide it over my sex and up the seam between my cheeks. Everything inside me tightens, grasping on emptiness, hungry to be filled.

"Please," I beg unashamed.

Using my wetness as lube, he presses his thumb against my back hole and pushes in.

Oh God, yes!

"Fucking you is not enough, pet," he grinds out as the sound of a zipper echoes in my ears.

He's right, the ache and longing is so intense, I'm afraid I'll never be satisfied.

Gripping my hips with both hands, he pulls me back, my hands slide down the wall until I'm bent at the waist, my greedy slit open and waiting for him. I start to quiver when he slides his hardness through my wetness, grazing my sensitive clit. My legs start to tremble and my head drops as a wave of the oncoming orgasm taunts me. My entire body is one giant sex organ.

"Hold on, baby," he says as he wraps an arm around my waist and palms my breast with his other hand.

Slowly he fills me, it's exquisite torture as inch by inch he penetrates me. I'm tight, my walls already squeezing him because I'm so close.

"Fuck, pet," his words are strained as his grip tightens around me.

He begins to move. His thrusts are drug filled ecstasy, each glide over my raw nerves shoot through me in a hot languid stupor. At first he takes his time, in and out, giving me just enough to push me higher and higher. It's spectacular. I'm soaring, gliding through super nova's in a state of pure bliss. Then he moves deeper, then pulls back almost all the way out, only to push so far inside me, each thrust sends explosive jolts through me. I'm careening now, spiraling wildly toward that cliff.

"Alex…"

"I know, pet, I know."

He pulls me up, grips my chin with a hand at my throat, and turns my face to his. His lips take mine with such fervor, so hungrily, it sucks all the air from my lungs. He pulls out and turns me around to face him. Again, he captures my face, his big hand at my throat clutching my jaw.

"Look at me, don't close your eyes. I want to watch you explode."

His eyes are wild, he's breathing so heavy, his nostrils are flaring. But he's peering straight into my soul.

He lifts one of my legs and wraps it around his waist. My mouth falls open. He positions me at the tip of his huge, hard erection. I bite my lip. He slides his hand down my body and lifts my other leg to close around him. I moan softly. As he pushes slowly into me again, he traces the seam of my lips with his tongue.

"Oh, God, Alex…"

Holding me by my ass, he buries himself deep within me, pulling me into him, making us one.

"I need you so bad, Gemma, it hurts," he whispers.

Those words, the depth of his vulnerability I see and hear shatters me. I grip his shoulders as I stare into his eyes, diving into him, wanting to fill him with me, needing to penetrate all of his cracked broken places inside him, like he's done to me. Our mouths consume each other as our eyes strip any remaining barriers between us away. We are raw and naked, our souls bared to each other, fusing in completeness.

It's so much, too much, each thrust, every lick of his tongue, each moment his ice blue eyes captivate mine.

I scream into his mouth as my orgasm crashes down. It's not physical, it's a transformation, it's a union searing us together. I see what I'm feeling in Alex's eyes, I feel his soul molding with mine, burning, exploding, joining, becoming one. His body is against mine, but he's melting into me, and it's the most spectacular experience I have ever felt, sacred and pure.

"I love you, Alex...," the words slip from my mouth, but it's not enough to say what I feel for him.

His mouth is worshipping me, his hands are adoring me, but the man has completely possessed me.

"Pet, to say I love you could never express it." His expression is both hard and soft, claiming and submitting, giving and taking.

He lowers my legs to the floor but they're shaking from the force of what we both just experienced. He scoops me up in his arms and carries me to his bedroom and sits me on the bed.

He pulls the covers down and says, "Lay on

your stomach, I'm going to get something for your back."

Before going to the bathroom, he holds my face gently in his hands and kisses me lightly. It's so tender, it makes my heart swell again.

Then reality sets in, breaking through my glorious haze.

He's leaving.

I bury my face in the bed as the fear washes over me again. I feel the bed dip at my side.

"Gemma, look at me," he tells me softly as he lifts my hair away to peer at me.

I turn my head to peek at him over my arm.

"Please don't worry, I'll be back in just a few days. Nothing is going to happen." He sounds so sure, so certain. "I've taken care of everything, there are people in place, nothing can get to me."

I know he has, I've listened to the conversations between him and Major Stewart, he's going to have his own army with him. But I can't help it.

His smile is warm and genuine, and it reassures me just a little.

"I know, Alex. Just don't go in there and be a damn cowboy, okay?" I mumble behind my arm.

He laughs, and it brightens his face and makes his eyes dance. I can't help but giggle lightly with him, it ebbs my anxiety.

"Got it, no John Wayne. Now, no more worrying."

"Fine," I lie.

He gently rubs the ointment he brought with him over my back, and it takes the sting away.

"Roll over, pet, I've got one more thing I want to do to you," his voice is husky again, the sound is filled with lust, my loins clench.

I roll over and notice he's also holding a black Sharpie.

The handprints, the notes on my body.

The Faceless Man.

No...

Alex removes the cap from the pen as I stare into his eyes. My arms are at my sides, my heart is beating so hard, I'm sure he can see the thumps between my breasts. His focus is laser sharp, I can feel it penetrating me. He places his left hand on my right breast as if holding it to the side, his palm spread with his thumb feeding down my sternum. He begins to write across my skin. My breathing is fast as I fist my hands into the sheet. My gaze doesn't leave his face, the intensity of it locks me to it as he's working. He doesn't say a word until he's finished.

The click of the cap seems loud when he replaces it once he's done.

"Something to remind you, pet," he smirks at me as his eyes return to mine.

I lower my eyes to see what he's branded me with.

The word Mine is etched across my heart in black ink.

"Alex...," I whisper as a smile flutters across my face.

"I'll be back before the word disappears," he tells me softly.

"My turn," I hold out my hand for the marker, staring into his eyes.

A smile erupts across his face as he hands me the pen. He straddles me and lowers his chest above mine. His perfection always makes my breath hitch, every inch of him is exquisite, I would be content just to explore his body with my hands, lips, and tongue over and over again. Electric shocks course up my arm when my palm touches his velvety skin. My eyes shoot to his and I know he felt it too. I return my focus to his magnificent chest and write my claim across his flesh.

Mine.

He takes the Sharpie from me before his mouth takes mine in an urgent kiss. All of our longing, everything that we feel, every single of one of our unspoken promises and declarations is exposed in this kiss.

"Come shower with me. I don't have long but I can't stand not touching until I have to go." His voice is tight as he stands and holds out his hand for me.

I can see in his eyes his walls starting to come up as the impending time for him to leave rapidly inches towards us. My heart is breaking.

I'm torn, one part of me wants to run far away from saying goodbye, the other wants to wring every single second I can get out of cruel time.

A flicker of pain flashes in Alex's eyes as he waits for me to go to him. I can't deny him, no matter if it hurts me. I take his hand and let him lead me to the bathroom.

Under the hot cascading water, his body is constantly wrapped around mine, his lips and tongue are always stroking and caressing me, but not another word is spoken. I can't get enough of him, desperation keeps me touching him, needing to make sure he's still here with me.

I help him dress, pulling his shirt up his muscled arms and closing it over his broad chest. My fingers linger over the word I've claimed him with, outlining the lines with my fingertip. When I get to the end of the last letter, he grips my wrist and pulls my hand to his mouth and kisses each fingertip before placing a lingering one in the middle of my palm. His desperation seeps into me from his mouth into my hand. It makes me tremble.

I have to be stronger, I can't let him leave worried about me, it could put him in danger.

I take a deep breath.

"Mr. Black, while you're gone, don't be surprised if all your employees mutiny against their tyrant boss and put me in charge. I can't be held responsible for their choice."

A half-smile graces me on his beautiful face.

"I wouldn't blame them one bit. You already own me. Why shouldn't you have the same effect on everyone else?"

I smile coyly at him and press my body against his.

"I suppose taking over the rest of the world is going to be easy for you. Bring me back your victory, Mr. Black, and we'll have a celebration when you return."

"You're all I want, Gemma."

He squeezes me tightly against him, his lips cover mine gently, sliding across them and lingering. I'm savoring this moment, imprinting every sensation, each breath, every second to my memory to take out whenever the loneliness and apprehension I'm sure is coming threatens to overwhelm me.

Alex's phone chimes with a message. We both take a sharp breath.

He stares into my eyes.

"Gemma, promise me you'll be careful. Stay with Williams, don't ever be alone. Anywhere. Except up here in these rooms."

Alex's words are stern and his eyes are hard.

"I promise," I smile at him.

"I'm not kidding, nowhere alone."

Now I see what's really going on inside him. He's not afraid of what's waiting for him, but what he's leaving behind.

"I know, I won't," I answer him as I gently stroke his cheek. "I'll be fine. You've made sure of it."

He appears to relax minimally.

"Okay, walk me downstairs," he replies, his voice losing some of its edge.

My feet won't move as my body goes rigid.

"You go ahead, I'm not dressed," I comment quickly. "Hilda probably wants to give you a kiss and a lecture."

I can't drag this out, I don't know how long I can keep this façade up.

I hope my expression belies the turbulence of emotions raging inside me.

His eyes flick back and forth across mine. He knows I'm struggling, he can see it no matter how hard I try to hide it.

"Alright. I'll keep in constant contact with

426

you, Gemma. Get some rest, you're going to need it when I get back."

He forces a smile but he doesn't argue with me. He knows what I'm feeling, and I'm grateful.

He kisses me one last time, it's urgent, punishing, and possessive. Dropping his arms from me, he snatches his phone and wallet. Then he turns to look at me one last time.

Before my eyes, he's transforming. His eyes turn fierce, his body becomes harder, broader, more rigid. His expression is now cold, as if carved from stone.

The man standing before me is that dangerous being I'd always sensed inside him, the one he kept bound and caged.

This is raw power.

This is rage in the flesh.

This is death and destruction.

Dangerous.

Lethal.

Alex isn't going for business.

He's going to war.

I'd seen a glimpse of this beast when he wanted to kill Tony.

A tremor of erotic fear ripples through me.

Then he's gone.

For a long moment I'm riveted to my spot as an ache creeps through me. It starts in my stomach, then seeps through my entire body until it grips my heart and crushes it until it explodes. I fall to the floor and let the agony out, sobbing with my face in my hands.

Mine

CHAPTER 28

Alexander

Hong Kong International Airport is a glimpse of the sleek, modern, and obscenely wealthy city it represents. It's a blend of the old and traditional with modern and upscale. After an almost sixteen-hour flight, plenty of time to become enraged all over again about the situation, and even more time to allow the stabbing pangs of guilt about leaving Gemma torment me, Stewart's man, Jacobs, and I enter the Meet And Greet area of the airport to find the team Stewart has arranged to meet me.

I can't wait to finish here and get home to her.

I don't like this city, never have. True intentions are hidden behind the glimmer and the sleek. Everything and everyone smiles in your fucking face waiting for you to turn around to stab you in the back.

"Shit," I murmur under my breath.

Jacobs steps in front of me to block the approaching Asian man dressed in a suit as expensive as my own. Jacobs' taller and built frame towers over him, but the suit acts like he's not even there.

"It's fine, he's Yun Lee's man," I grit out behind him.

Jacob takes a step to the side to give the man guarded access to me.

"Mr. Black, welcome to Hong Kong, my name is Fu Chen. I trust your flight was pleasant," he gives me the formal introduction, albeit emotionless, with a hint of condescension. His English is impeccable with only a trace of his primary language, Cantonese.

"Yes, thank you."

"Excellent, sir," he bows slightly. "We have a car curbside to take you to your hotel if you'd like before the meeting." He extends his hand toward the door while smiling broadly.

It's almost sunrise and I've barely slept. Not a perfect condition for a confrontation.

I should have anticipated this. It's custom to cater to the needs of your guest. How convenient to hijack me.

From my peripheral vision, I see two men approaching us, both intimidating, one Asian, the other Caucasian.

Stewart's men.

"Thank you Mr. Chen. This is Mr. Jacobs,

my assistant. He has arranged for a party to meet us here," I return his formality.

His eyebrows lift fractionally. I've just insulted him by refusing his professional kindness.

Jacobs bows halfway at the waist, following custom, and attempts to extinguish the slight to Chen.

"Mr. Jacobs can follow us with your party, Mr. Black."

Fuck. I'll play nice this time.

"Of course, Mr. Chen, the hotel then. After you."

Mr. Chen flicks his wrist and a very large, well-dressed man comes forward. Chen says something to him in Cantonese, the man grunts his response, and not a muscle flinches in the silent man's stern expression.

"He will take care of your baggage, Mr. Black." Then addressing Jacobs, "Mr. Jacobs, welcome to Hong Kong."

Chen turns lightly on his heels and walks softly toward the airports exit. The silent Chinese mountain moves to Jacob and retrieves my luggage from him, then files in behind me. Stewarts other two men take their place, one behind the mountain, the other to my left. I glimpse a man, also Caucasian, lift from a column he was leaning against a few feet away as he tucks the newspaper he's holding under his arm. To my other side, a dark skinned man turns from the monitors he'd been studying as he slides his sunglasses in place. Both move with the flow of traffic, blending seamlessly in our direction.

Four so far. A lot of good that does, they've just cut me off. I breathe deeply as the familiar rush floods me. *Fuck it.* A sneer curves my lips.

Finally, the time is here. I've been waiting for this, looking forward to what's going to happen, relishing it even. My beast wants war, messy, gruesome war. I vowed I wouldn't take another life…unless it was absolutely necessary. If I had any piece of my soul left, I'd hoped it would be enough. I'm probably fooling myself, but that's what faith is: blind. But the darkness inside me makes my body vibrate with anticipation. When I find out who's responsible for the mess here, I *will* have retribution.

It's been a long time since I've been in a position like this, forced to take revenge, a place that used to be home for me. This time there's a lot more at stake.

Outside is an organized swarm of taxis, buses, the buzz of people all around, some confused, others moving in a hurried dash. Jacob stays by my side as Chen leads me to a BMW 5 as Stewarts other two men move toward a Mercedes Sedan parked two cars up. Two more men exit the Mercedes as their mouths move, but whatever their saying is inaudible.

Six now. They're reporting updates, make and model of the car I'm leaving in, probably plate number as well.

At the BMW's open rear door, the big silent guy extends his hand for my briefcase.

"Thank you, no, I'll need it." To Jacobs, "Enjoy the tour to the hotel, it's a beautiful city, I'll meet you there." The door thuds shut immediately as I slide into the backseat.

Mr. Chen joins me in the rear of the car as the well-dressed Sumo wrestler stuffs his body into the front passenger seat.

This is going to be the first longest ride of this trip.

I slide my cell phone from the inside pocket of my jacket.

I've just arrived. My finger hovers over the screen, pausing. **I miss you. Don't do anything reckless. I'll call you later. Xoxo**

Fuck it.

I press 'send' and leave the message for Gemma.

She knows I'm crazy about her, she might as well find out I'm completely wound around her delicious little finger.

"Mr. Chen," I turn my attention to my host, "thank you for meeting me. I take it everything's arranged?"

He nods, "Yes, Mr. Black, the meeting has been confirmed. You are to meet with the customs magistrate. Our sources tell us that it's just a formality and all should move smoothly afterward."

I grit my teeth and my fists clench.

"A formality? They insisted I come half way around the world with no notice, and its's only a formality?"

"Mr. Black," he beams that ingratiating smile at me again, "You understand, these things must be handled delicately. What one might label a formality in the politest sense can be something else entirely."

Yes, I understand exactly what it means.

"Mr. Chen, I'm fully aware of the nature of the situation."

His true maliciousness momentarily flashes

at me as his eyes shoot daggers, then it disappears.

"Then all will be taken care of," his Cheshire grin mocks me.

"Yes, it will," I return the look. "I will be returning to New York in a couple of days with the understanding that today's meeting and submitting final documentation tomorrow are the only obligations that require my *personal* attention."

He nods again. "That is correct. Although we were hoping to persuade you to tour other possible *ventures* while you are here in beautiful Hong Kong."

Something about his 'ventures' makes my skin crawl.

"I'm sorry, I cannot stay. I postponed a meeting with another associate to come to Hong Kong. They were able to wait for my return and meet at the end of the week."

"That's truly unfortunate," he states slowly.

I pause. There's an underlying dark message in his words.

"Send me an outline with the specifics and I'll review it. If it seems suitable for Black Inc., I'll send my representative, the man who was supposed to be here, and he'll notify me if we should proceed."

"You trust your associates."

I quirk an eyebrow at him.

"I don't trust anyone."

His smile morphs into a sly grin.

"That's very wise, Mr. Black. The only difference between the Americans and the Chinese is, we know that."

"Indeed," I smile tightly at him.

After a long tense moment, Mr. Chen fills the ride to my hotel with an audio tour of Hong Kong. I'm not listening, my mind is reviewing the files Major Stewart had prepared for me again. I spent the flight reading dossiers of three prominent figures.

The first was Vladimir Polchenko, a Russian oligarch, whose riches, and from whence it all came from, was disputed, worth over fifteen billion dollars. He is one of the most powerful and richest men in Russia, and the most dangerous.

The next was Li Xiu Ying, the head of one of the largest apparel manufacturers throughout mainland China. China Labor Watch has fined his companies repeatedly for such poor work conditions, he could run a whole other company with what he's paid out. It wasn't the poor conditions that was highlighted in the report, but the employees, more so, where they'd come from. All were young women from poor families. The numbers were phenomenal.

But the wildcard I'm holding in my pocket might just open Pandora's Box.

Finally, was Andre' Ryordan. A member of the South African Congress, also a member of the countries strategic planning board, who also has his hands in so many businesses, he makes money from every single citizen in the country.

All this is intriguing, but what is most important is what's not being said. The private business that fuels the public business, the puppet masters and the puppets, the game and the prize.

I have no doubt the reason I'm here is I'm now one of the players. They put me in the game and it's my turn to move.

Let's play, motherfuckers, let's play.

Forty-five minutes later, the BMW is pulling up in front of my hotel. The doorman is efficient, opening my door as soon as the car stops. The Chinese mountain and Mr. Chen are at my side on the curb immediately.

"Shall we pick you up in an hour for our preliminary meeting?" Mr. Chen dutifully asks with his faux subservient demeanor.

Two Mercedes arrive with my men. Jacobs looks pissed-off.

"No, my assistant and the rest of my team will handle things for me during my stay. Thank you for hospitality, Mr. Chen," *you piece of shit.*

There's a momentary glimmer of frustration on his perfectly schooled expression, but he's a practiced bullshit artist. It's gone.

"Are you sure, Mr. Black?" Meaning, *'Do you really want to play that hand?'*

I smile, it's the sweet taste of 'Fuck you!'

"Yes, I'm most certain."

"Very well, Mr. Black, my associates will find that most *interesting*," he dips his head in a slight bow.

"I'm counting on it, Mr. Chen. Good morning, I shall see you at the meeting." I know the flesh mountain is standing behind me with my luggage. "Jacobs, could you get the bags, please?"

"Love to, Mr. Black."

I've slammed the door on false propriety.

I'm mad as fucking hell they pulled some bullshit move to get me over here, attempting to set me up, make me vulnerable, put me in a position to be weak.

I. Don't. Do. Weak.

"Excuse, me," I tilt my head in mock respect, then enter the lobby as the sun is breaking over the skyscrapers with six men who kill efficiently and with absolutely no remorse behind me.

My own deadly, immaculately polished killing machines.

Jacobs and I are tired, but jacked-up on testosterone and caffeine. I decide to go to the hotel's gym to beat out my anxiety. When I return to my Penthouse Executive Suite, there's a message from Gemma.

Mr. Black, bossy even from across an ocean. Maybe I want to misbehave? I rather enjoyed my punishment in your conference room. Xoxo

A fist squeezes my heart until I almost can't breathe as my dick hardens. It would beat me over the head if it could for taking him away from her. I strip off the sweat soaked clothes and throw them on the chair in the corner and call her.

"Alex," her voice instantly soothes me.

"When I get back, Ms. Trudeau, I'm going to do much more than spank that luscious ass of yours." My heart aches and my hard cock is throbbing now.

"Promises, promises, Mr. Black. You'll have to do better than that." I can hear the smile in her voice, it shoots hot sunshine straight through me.

"Pet, I'm going to put a clamp on that greedy clit of yours and make you come so many fucking times, you'll be insane. Then I'll tease that tight little ass of yours until you beg me to fuck you."

Precum oozes from the tip of my swollen

shaft as I remember how it felt to be buried up to my balls in her.

"Alex...," her voice is low and sultry.

I inhale sharply.

"I can't wait to hear your sexy little whimpers and moans. You're my fucking drug, Gemma." *I need you.*

She sucks in a breath. "Hurry up and come home, Mr. Black."

She guts me. Her words are the knife, her love is the wound. And every time, it makes me feel more and more alive.

"I'll be home in a few days, Gemma. It's not long, but it feels like forever. Just promise me you won't go anywhere alone." I can't stress it enough.

She chuckles a little, "You'll be happy to hear that Williams is being a royal pain in my ass. I'm lucky he lets me go to the bathroom alone."

That makes me feel better. "If he even thinks of taking it that far, I'll kill him," I smile.

She laughs. I don't know how, but it makes me miss her more.

"How's it going there?" she asks me, her voice now full of concern.

I can't tell her about Chen's comment about this being all a 'formality', I know it's not. They want me here on their turf. They're going to introduce me to the game, maybe subtly, maybe they're going to lay everything out in black and white. A business negotiation. They're going to make me an offer. Their intentions are to corner me and give me no choice.

What I'm not sure of yet, is it going to be in

the boardroom or on the mission?

They didn't expect me to bring company.

"It's fine. I'm leaving in an hour to meet with Yun Lee's people and the magistrate. I'm interested to hear what bullshit they've got to say."

I had to come, I know it and Gemma knows it. It's not what's said, but the body language, the innuendos, the unspoken messages that tell the story. I need to know if they know about the missions and what, if anything, they've got planned.

"Promise me you'll be careful, Alex," her voice is tight.

"Baby, I've got seven men here with me. No one's getting close, I promise."

She breathes a sigh of relief. "Okay. Call me when you get time?"

"Nothing can stop me." I'm so pussy-whipped.

"Good. And Alex?"

"Yeah, baby?"

"I miss you. Come home soon. And remember, no John Wayne."

My heart swells as I laugh. "Got it, no blazing in. And I miss you more than you know."

"Bye Alex."

"Bye Gemma."

In five minutes, she's branded another scorching X on my heart.

After I pound out an unsatisfying orgasm in the shower, get dressed, have breakfast, then head to the meeting in the very swank business district of Hong Kong, I once again review the file on Li Xiu Ying for any connection between him and his companies to Yun Lee. My business with Yun Lee is technology and developing advanced, more efficient capabilities. Garment manufacturing is worlds apart.

It's something else.

"Stewart," I get him on the phone.

"Mr. Black, everything going according to plan?" He's short and to the point.

"Yes, the team is with me and I'm heading to the meeting now. I reviewed the dossiers you sent and I wanted to confirm the information on Yun Lee and Li Xiu Ying."

"Confirmed, and we have something else I think you're going to find quite interesting, I was just going to send it to you."

"Really? Excellent, I'll be knee-deep in the middle of their bullshit soon."

"Ten four, Mr. Black."

The remainder of the ride I research as many of Li Xiu Ying's business and labor offenses as I can cram into the ride. The gross negligence is disgusting, and he was allowed to repeat them again and again with just a slap on the wrist in the big scheme of things.

This guy is so dirty, he must wreak. Who is he paying off to get away with this all the time? Who's in his pocket? And where are these girls coming from? And going?

My mind is racing trying to find a link, any incriminating evidence, that would put me in control.

My phone pings, alerting me to the message from Stewart. I open the attachment.

"Son-of-a-bitch!"

It's a photograph of Russian mob members entering a building in Hong Kong, a very interesting building.

The ride is stifling in the close quarters of the spacious Mercedes, and the traffic is congested. It's organized mayhem, but I don't mind. We have two cars, me and Jacobs with two men in one, the other four men in the other. I go with Jacobs and the men to park the cars in the basement garage. Jacobs accompanies me to the floor where the meeting's being held. We're tense and guarded. Jacobs follows me into the boardroom that's surrounded by windows, accompanied by Mr. Chen's continuous refusals about Jacobs attendance. Seated at the table are two men, I know Li Ming-húa, but not the second man. I assume he's the Customs Magistrate. Under his professional aloofness, I can see he's shitting his pants.

After a few minutes of introductions and polite pleasantries, I drop the first bomb.

"As Mr. Chen informed me on the way from the airport, this is a formality. Please tell me why my presence was so vehemently requested?"

Li Ming-húa is the Chief Operations Officer of Yun Lee's Hong Kong branch. He is a regal man who speaks softly with a deadly hint of authority. No one looks him in the eye, or even moves, until he gives the signal.

He sits back in his chair and regards me with a bored expression.

I want to tell him to shove his merchandise up his ass and leave.

I want to find out how he and the scumbag Li

Xiu Ying are affiliated more.

"Mr. Black, I appreciate that you are American and things are done with a bit more finesse here in Hong Kong, but I assure you this is a bit more than a formality." His emperor has spoken.

I'm going to listen, hear how he's going to weave the situation with, as he says, finesse.

"We have had many successful years with Black Inc.," he begins. "Now it seems certain *complications* have arisen." His fingers are steepled in front of his chest with his elbows resting casually on his chair's armrests.

"Our business dealings have not changed. Apparently it's something else," my voice is cool and even.

"Perhaps not on the surface, but things have certainly...*changed*," Li Ming-húa replies with a slow confident tilt to his head.

I smile.

His eyes widen in question.

"What a coincidence this change happens to coincide with Li Xiu Ying's acquisition of one of your buildings." My tone is deathly calm.

The only outward sign of Li Ming-húa's shock is the slight flaring of his nostrils, other than that, he still holds his poised and confident demeanor.

"Well, Mr. Black, it's apparent why you are as successful as you are." He stares at me and tries to read me.

I smile. And I wait.

"This knowledge, I suppose, will allow us to do away with frivolous pleasantries. We can get right to all the business in front of us," he smirks, attempting to get the upper hand.

I nod slightly, the false smile never leaves my face. "Then please do proceed."

He separates his hands in front of him in a sweeping gesture. "All business is related in one way or another. Li Xiu Ying's business is directly affected by some anonymous...interloper."

I snort in contempt.

"And what particular business of his is affected? The girls?"

His jaw clenches.

After a long moment, he replies, "Yes." I'm forcing him to be blatant.

Good.

"Which part, the stealing or the selling...or the slaves?" I push.

"Mr. Black..."

"Which fucking part?" my voice is ice cold.

"It's more complex than that. More complicated transactions require additional...payments and gifts."

I'm furious. They pulled me and my business into their filth. They're trying to threaten me into becoming a part of their disgusting world of human trafficking.

"Li Xiu Ying would like to make you an offer...," he begins smugly.

I raise a hand to stop him.

"Would this also have something to do with the Russian mob being in that building as well?"

He contemplates before he answers, glaring at me, probably weighing how much he should tell me, wondering how much I already know.

"Business is business, Black, it crosses all boundaries with many associates," he grits out.

I rest my hand on the glass table, then strum my fingers on the sparkling surface.

"Then I suppose I have no choice," I finally say.

Li Ming-húa is visibly relieved. "Excellent." He turns to the man who's sat silently through our exchange, his eyes fixed looking to his lap the entire time. "The customs paperwork will be cleared immediately, now, and we can proceed."

I lift my hand again.

Li Ming-húa, Fu Chen, and the nervous man all look at me surprised. Jacobs hasn't moved a muscle and his expression has remained hard.

"Give me the paperwork," I say firmly.

Li Ming-húa looks at me wide eyed.

"Now." The single word is dangerously soft. I hold out my hand to the guy who hasn't said shit the entire meeting. He now looks like he wants to melt into the spotless carpet. Poor guy, wrong place, wrong time.

The quiet man shuffles through his folder, pulls out the documents, and quickly shoves them at me as if they were on fire.

Looking directly at Li Ming-húa, I tear the documents down the center.

"You didn't ask me what my choice was."

He stares, astonished, and watches the ripped pages fall to the floor.

"I refuse."

I stand, Jacobs follows, and leave.

The war has started.

Mine

CHAPTER 29

Alexander

It's been a veritable unlit keg of fucking dynamite, waiting for someone to drop that match or lit cigarette and blow this shit up. As soon as we left the meeting, I called Stewart. The past twenty-four hours since Jacobs and I walked out, Stewart's had surveillance on the men that have been tailing me. Initially, we knew that the first two men were with Li Ming-húa. Today, they have some new friends. White, Russian friends.

"Do you have a positive ID on them? Do they belong to Polchenko?"

The team here and I are finalizing our plans for tonight's rescue mission. It's *imperative* I get all the information I can.

"Any links that would lead to Polchenko don't exist. So far, I can't get anything on him anywhere," he replies. "It's common knowledge that everyone works for Polchenko in some way or another, illegally, politically, or shown as an expenditure on his fucking tax returns legitimately. He owns everyone and everything." Stewart continues, "The new men tailing you have been confirmed to be allied with the Russian Bratva."

"I wonder if Yun Lee knows he's connected to Polchenko now, too," I comment more to myself.

"Technically, Black, the connection is with the building that was owned by Li Ming-húa. On paper, Yun Lee had nothing to do with it. But Yun Lee is not a stupid man," he replies.

The building.

Of course.

"Stewart, what do you know about the building?" I ask him as I sit in the backseat of the Mercedes.

Hong Kong and China are the mecca of advanced technology. I have no doubt Li Ming-húa, and now the Russian mob, have planted surveillance devices in my rooms, the conference rooms in my hotel, and anywhere else I would hold discussions. The men have swept my hotel room - twice - and each time they've found them. One was planted on my damn suitcase, for fucks sake, probably when it was loaded into the BMW at the airport. Not willing to take any chances, when we have something to discuss, we do it in the car or with loud white noise crowding the background. It's too risky not to, and there's too much at stake.

"The building," he begins the rundown in his crisp, to-the-point, militarily brusque sentences, "is a luxury high-rise. As you saw from the photo, it is in an area completely void of any residential buildings. During the day, the area is teeming with business people. At night, it's a ghost town. All of the units are occupied."

I pull up the aerial view of the building Li Ming-húa sold to Li Xiu Ying, one of China's most unscrupulous and crooked business men on mainland China. As I study it, I notice the massive convergence of parked cars.

"Is there an underground level?" I ask him, reviewing the information I was sent on the building and occupants again.

"There is," he answers, "give me a minute to pull-up the plans. I assume it's used for the building's maintenance department." There's a minute of computer clicks over the phone line. Finally, "Yes, part of the space is being utilized as a maintenance office, a utility room, and there are two large rooms identified as storage."

"I bet I know what Ying's storing in there," it's almost a growl, my disgust and rage rising higher and higher.

"Ming-húa admitted to you that Ying deals in human trade, did he not?" Stewart confirms.

"That he did, and I'm sure the offer Ying was giving me was a slave to get me to back-off and roll-over. I should have taken her, then went directly to the American Consulate with her," I'm seething with fury.

He hints that he knows what I do and he wants to give me a fucking slave! The pig thinks anybody can be bought. It's time he had a little lesson.

"Mr. Black, the girl probably would have killed herself before she let you take her there," Stewart cuts into my visions of seeing Ying thrown in jail, as impossible as that would be. He's probably got every politician and police department on his payroll.

"I realize that, Major."

"She knows Ying would have killed her entire family. *That* is the hold these abductors have over these girls. They take them from their families. Some are fortunate, if you can call being sold into prostitution fortunate, if the girls are bought even if it is only a hundred dollars at the most, or worse, sold into slavery. The threats to their families keep them obedient and subservient."

"Fucking disgusting," I grit out.

"I agree. She would never have left willingly."

I grin. "Then she won't."

A long pause.

"Excellent, Mr. Black."

I'd bet a thousand dollars Major Stewart has a shit-eating-grin on his face. He knows what I'm thinking.

"Can you get another team here in five hours?" I ask as I motion for the driver to merge into traffic.

"Absolutely."

"Fill them in on the basics, I'll let them know

which location they'll be retrieving from when I meet with them."

"I'll send you the confirmation and when to expect the men."

"Might as well mix a little business with pleasure," I say before I hang up the phone.

I text the driver the address of Ying's swank office building we're going to pay a little visit to tonight.

They want to play? I've got a little message for them.

My phone rings. My heart actually fucking flutters.

"Hi gorgeous, how was your day?"

The image of Gemma's face, her body lying back in my bed, the sparkle in her eyes when she's thinking of all the things I might do to her, push every other thought from my mind.

"It was okay." She sounds anxious.

"What's wrong, baby?" My guilt for leaving her makes me feel like shit again.

It's first thing in the morning for me, but because Hong Kong is twelve hours ahead, she's still in yesterday. She's probably gone all day worrying, and it crushes me.

"Nothing," she tries to blow me off.

"Gemma, come on, tell me what's on your mind. Your imagination is worse than anything else."

I hear her sigh and can almost feel her breath on my skin.

"You're right, Alex. I just wish you were home, I know you're not telling me everything, and that's probably a good thing, because I'm sure *that* would make me crazier than I already am."

"Everything's fine, I promise. I have one last thing to take care of tonight and tomorrow, then I'm on my way back to you. I would suggest one thing though," my voice drops with innuendo.

"Oh, please do tell me what that is," I can hear her smile returning.

"Request a few days off from work. All the things I want to do to you to make up for the time apart is going to require more than just a few hours. If that tyrant you work for gives you any trouble, quit."

"Oh, and what did you have in mind? It would have to be worth it. My boss is almost as sexy as you. You'd have to make it worth my while," she teases me.

"If I was alone, I would tell you explicitly." Next to me, I can see Jacobs jaw tense as he looks out the car's window.

"Alex, why do you do that to me? They must think I'm some kind of nympho," she squeals into the phone, embarrassed.

I laugh, she sounds perfect. "Because you are, but only for me. And I love you for it."

Where the hell did my balls go?

"I love you more now that you've admitted it in front your bodyguards."

"I doubt that, baby." *God, I can't believe how much I miss her.* "Call me when you're getting ready for bed. I'm heading to an appointment."

"I will, tuck me in?" she asks coquettishly.

"I can't wait to do it in person...bye

Gemma." My heart constricts.

"Bye Alex, stay safe."

As I tuck my phone into my inside jacket pocket, we're pulling up to the building.

Knowing Gemma is in danger fuels my need to take this cocksucker down. There have been too many coincidences, Malcolm and the Ponzi scheme, her parents dead by a Russian, then breaking into her house, Russian's following me, and this fucking building. It's all connected, and I'm the one linking them all.

Thank God she's safe and well protected.

With what's going to go down tonight, things are going to get a lot more dangerous.

I tell the driver to circle the block a few times while Jacobs and I get out of the car to assess the area. We need to make a plan. We're going in tonight and hitting this bastard right where he lives.

At three in the morning, that's precisely what we're doing.

I'm with the team at Ying's building while Jacobs is at the original location across the city leading the other team. I met with the man I have here in Hong Kong, an everyday 'Joe' that no one would suspect helps coordinate infiltrations of prostitution rings. He drives a cab, can't weigh a hundred pounds soaking wet, who is the perfect invisible man that hears everything on the streets. He's got a personal vendetta, alike and different from myself. His family sold his sister when they were children. When she ran away, both his parents were killed and he was left homeless and forced to live on the streets, and between beatings, he begged.

He hates these bastards as much as I do.

Stewart was right. This place is the most glamorous fucking ghost town at night. Except for the vans that had pulled up an hour ago that had brought the girls back they're obviously holding in the basement, no one's been around. I would have loved to have blown each of the guys heads off, but the girls were traumatized enough. Some of them looked horror stricken, others were sobbing inconsolably, (which only got them a slap in the face, a kick to the ground, or a punch in the stomach), while a few of them, (the older ones), still had some fight left in them.

When we get inside, we're going to have to be quiet when we take out the guards.

Normally, bloodshed on these trips is to be used only if absolutely necessary.

This one is personal.

It's a fucking message.

Some people only understand one kind.

What I've got to say is going to be heard loudandfuckingclear.

Alexander Black, ruler of a business empire doesn't exist. That façade is gone. The hunger for violence, for destruction, for blood and pain surges in my veins, all the things that made me who I am, the very things that created me, all the things I've learned to use and control, I set free. My beast is pacing restlessly clawing me inside. He's going to feed.

We had exited our vans a block over and slipped into the dark, commercial alley that runs alongside the sleek shiny prison. It's not an elegant high-rise, it's hell, it's agony, and the worst nightmare of these girls' lives. A buffet for the perverse and the disgustingly deranged. Tonight, the pigs had had their last meal, the only thing that will be left will be the rotting carcasses of their captors with our seal carved into them.

There are no lights, that had already been taken care of once Ying's people had gotten the girls inside. We all can smell the adrenaline heavy in the air, feel the need for blood flooding our veins, taste the sweet flavor of revenge on our tongues. We are here for only one purpose, save the girls, and kill those fucks, gruesomely, and with intense pleasure. We move silently, death and salvation, and we aren't leaving without payment in full.

One of Stewart's men, I don't know which, picks the lock as if it weren't even there and we slip into the darkened bowels of the building. We move forward with no hesitation, like ghosts, like fucking black Hell Hounds, snarling, teeth bared, ready to shred, coming to drag them to hell.

The soldier up front motions for us to move into a formation to surround the entrances of the two large storage rooms on the other side. We hear men's voices, laughing, they sound drunk, then a scream, a girl.

Their raping her!

My beast roars demanding to attack. I pull him back…until it's time.

The men move, like a flock of beautiful fucking birds, in an inverted V, just as quietly, and just as efficiently.

Another agonized female wail cuts through

the air, followed by the sound of a fist hitting flesh and bone. I grit my teeth as my fists ball painfully at my sides, dying to pound into the cocksuckers.

They're right in front of us. I can smell blood, and sweat, and semen.

The man who led us in looks to me for the cue to move forward, his eyes bright with rage.

My fury is an inferno inside me.

It fuels me.

Burns me.

Rages into the form of my beast and possess me.

I move into the light and into their space. They're both Russian. It makes me grin with sick satisfaction. I have just about all that I need for my answer as to who is truly responsible for this.

The doors to the two storage rooms are closed behind them, but at this distance we can hear the whimpering of all the girls on the other side of the large metal doors.

We're coming.

"You two dickless pieces of shit, does that make you feel like a man?"

My voice is icy calm, but my body is tense as I fight the overwhelming need to gut them open, rip their organs out, and plaster their fucking pieces all over the walls.

"Что ебать Что ебать?!" (What the fuck?!)

The one with his dick in the poor little girl drops her to reach for his gun, but his pants tangled around his legs makes him fumble. The other pig with his puny cock in his hand jumps for his. A knife comes flying through the air from behind me and lands in his forearm and stops him. He falls to his knees, screaming, and yanks it out, gripping his useless arm to his chest.

"Grab the one who's raping the girl, he's mine."

One of my team is on him in two strides, with one arm around in his neck in a chokehold, and the other has the scums arms locked behind his back. He screams like a little fucking pussy.

Two soldiers have the other Russian on the floor. Any time he says anything or tries to fight, they slam his face into the cement floor to shut him the fuck up as they wait for my instructions. The other two soldiers wait behind me.

It's almost too bad there's only two of them.

Pulling my blade from its sheath, I approach the rapist slowly.

"You like fucking little girls?" I ask him coolly.

He yells something at me in Russian, but I don't give a fuck what he's saying. It doesn't matter.

"You know what my punishment is for rape?" I'm in his face.

The scumbag spits at me, the filth drips down my cheek. I laugh at him.

"Get his tongue, he's not going to need it."

I smile sadistically at him as two soldiers pry his vile mouth open and pull his tongue from it with a pair of pliers.

"It really is a shame this isn't dull, you don't deserve it quick," I sneer at him while he screams in my face as I slice off the thick, pink muscle.

The sound of the young girl whimpering,

cowering on the floor behind me, drags my attention to her. Guilt flashes through my haze of red fury as I look down at her. She's no more than ten or twelve, one side of her face is swollen, red, and purple, and that side of her mouth is dripping blood. She's filthy and her clothes are rags, and two sizes too big.

Then she shocks me. What she does shouldn't have, but it does.

She holds out her hand, her eyes fixed on the scumbag. They're filled with hate and rage.

I hold one hand out to her, offering her help, as I extend the other with the bloody knife toward her. She slowly gets to her feet, her jaw clenched and her mouth set tightly.

"Get him locked down." I give the instruction but my eyes don't leave the little girls. I want her to take what she needs from me, whatever it is, strength, anger, determination, it's hers.

I've been where she is, I know what it feels like to need revenge for something like this, a need so insanely powerful, you'd do anything.

She tentatively takes the large knife from my hand and turns her attention to her last tormentor. I point to his cock. She nods her head once.

"Hold him."

The Russian is thrashing violently and screaming through gurgling noises as blood pours from his mouth. The men hold him down and pull his limp dick in the air with the pair of pliers so it won't slip. The sounds coming from him are becoming strangled and less and less coherent as the stump of his tongue swells in his mouth.

The girl gets down on her knees and puts the

edge of the blade to his shaft and begins to slice. Her movements become faster and more determined, building up to savage force as she pours everything inside her into cutting off his dick. But try as she might, she's as ferocious as any warrior I have ever seen, she can't get it all the way through. I crouch behind her and place my hands over hers and help. It takes only two more cuts until she's got her prize. She looks over her shoulder at me as tears fall from her eyes. The thirteen-year-old angry, scared, and broken boy inside me stares back at her, feeling her rage, her fury, her agony and pain. And senses the beast growing within her.

She's beautiful.

The other girls locked behind the doors are pounding on the metal. The little warrior looks at me expectantly with a question in her eyes.

"Open the doors."

I stand to face whatever is behind those gates of hell. The doors slide open, at least twenty-five of the most scared, damaged, and horrified girls I have ever seen in my life are hovering together in a tight mass. They range from five or six to no more than sixteen or seventeen, all in the same condition, filthy, used, beaten, and some are almost completely broken. The little girl runs to them and says something to them in Cantonese. All eyes turn to us. They're filled with something they haven't felt in a very long time.

Hope.

One brave girl steps away from her sisters and holds out her hand.

"Give her a knife."

They'll all get a turn, if that's what they want. If that's what they need.

One of my men hands it to her.

She walks to the one we haven't gotten to yet and shoves the knife as far as she can into his stomach without hesitation. He's screaming, cursing, spitting, still trying to fight.

One by one, the girls form a half circle around the two men, each of them have their hands out.

By the time they're finished getting their retribution and we take them out of there, what's left are only chunks of meat, flesh, bones, and blood.

Payment in full.

Mine

CHAPTER 30

Alexander

Hostile takeover. Call me sick, call me twisted, call me whatever the fuck you want.

That shit gets me off.

Things have just gotten real. I've upped the ante by hitting them right where they live. There's no way they're going to sit back and take it.

Neither was I, that's precisely why I hit them in their own fucking house.

They want to fuck with me? Bring it, it's not about me, and I'll hit you with everything I've got.

They wanted to bring me into the game? Fine. They think they can manipulate me? No fucking way. The rules have been changed. I'm in charge. They want to play? Let's play. But my way.

Stewart's been informed, so has Carlos and Rico. This isn't just politics and business, it's street and the gutters, the penthouses, boardrooms, and basements. It's every dirty, illegal, conspiratorial, crooked person on the planet. Everyone and everything is part of the game.

Fuck with me and mine, and Gemma is mine!,
and now so are these girls, mercy will be the only
fucking thing you'll be screaming for.

The drive to the safe-house is almost three
hours out of the city and into the countryside of
mainland China. It was a clusterfuck trying to get the
girls into the vehicles without being physical.
They'd been emotionally all over the place, crying,
laughing, screaming, fighting, spitting, and just out
of their fucking minds. It was frustrating as hell, but
I loved every damn minute of it.

This isn't about business, it's about human
lives, innocent children. I would do whatever I
needed to in order to save them. The glimmer of
hope I'd seen in their eyes, their beaten, used, and
broken bodies, had unleashed a rage from inside me
I'd hadn't felt since I was living on the streets.

During the drive, sometimes one would start
giggling, then another joined in, until they all were
laughing so hard, they started snorting, then they
would all laugh even harder. Like kids. Like what
they're supposed to be. Then after a lull of silence,
sniffling could be heard, and the whole group would
start sobbing in one wave, their wail would rise in
chorus, start and stop together, then fall, as if they
were one entity. Because of what they'd been made
to become and endure.

In fact, they are one being, they'd been
through an experience together that no one should
ever have to go through, and they'd survived. It had
bonded them to each other, they got and gave their
strength to and from their sisters. As much as they

may never want to be reminded of this horrendous experience, they will never forget the souls that had comforted them during their stay in hell.

My mind wandered through so many places during the drive. I remembered Rico and how he'd been there for me, my strength and guardian, after I'd been raped. He'd refused to let that boy become a broken victim. He made me a survivor, took my hand and led me to conquer and vanquish, to become stronger, and finally invincible.

And I had.

I learned how to use my anger and violence, made it work for me. My beast, my darkness, is still as much a vital part of me as my body. But I felt I could only be strong in the dark, I existed on the peripherals of right, I owned the dark and seduced the light, like a fucking demon. I walked between them on a fine line. Darkness was my empire, light my lover who loved to indulge in the dark.

Until Gemma.

She stripped me of all my preconceived false realities. She awakened a part of myself I hadn't allowed to exist. She single-handedly destroyed all my barriers and filled me with her brightness, burnt me with her sun. She reduced me to ashes only to resurrect me with her love and strength. I was....more. I am whole. Because she loves me.

Seeing what those people did to these innocent girls, and knowing they want Gemma, unleashed my darkness. With its fury, I will destroy them to save her at all costs.

It's early morning when we arrive at the thatched-roof little village in the middle of nowhere.

It's a collection of five or six little huts in a clearing in the middle of dense trees at the end of a one-lane, narrow dirt road that's really only a path. Just one small structure has its door open, the rest of them are closed up. A lone woman shuffles out toward the big black vans, her steps are hurried and certain. When the car doors open, she starts barking orders at us in an authoritarian tone, rattling them off so fast, even if I did understand a little of the language, I'd have no clue as to what she's saying. The girls move together in formation, apparently following the old lady's orders.

I watch the girls walk away as they leave hell behind them. It hurts, good hurt and bad hurt, a thrashing contradiction of emotions. Regret for all that they'd gone through, and joy for the freedom they have once again.

But there isn't time to dwell in silent celebration. The old lady with the deeply wrinkled face is wagging a finger at me, obviously cursing me out. I look at my men searching for something to tell me what the old woman is talking about.

I run a billion-dollar company, organize international mergers and deals, foreign delegates come to me for favors, and one old woman who looks like she's pushing a hundred is uninhibitedly busting my balls.

The man to my right shrugs his shoulders, apparently as confused as I am. Her voice rises to almost a shout, and her eyes get wider as more gibberish, (as far as I'm concerned), falls from her mouth.

She must think we're deaf and dumb.

The sound of engines float toward us on the warm air. The woman stops her rambling mid-sentence and ogles the dirt road through squinted eyes, mouth open.

I guess she doesn't know we've got two groups coming in.

"Thank God," I murmur and roll my eyes, relieved that she's stopped the barrage of whatever the hell she was saying.

The other team rolls into the clearing in the center of the huts. Five more black vans line up with ours, leaving a swirl of dust behind them.

The front doors open and Jacobs steps out first, followed by six more team members from the other vehicles, all of us dressed in black with varying degrees of blood and human flesh stuck to our clothes. The men open the doors and an identical bunch of girls slowly emerge one by one, all with the same stricken look of horror, confusion, deathly fear, and a hint of hope.

The woman snaps to attention again and barks the identical commands she had the first group. This bunch, just like the first, immediately moves forward as if she were the Pied Piper.

The single mass of girls goes to the same hut as the first did, the large one in the back of the compound, then disappear inside.

And just like before, she turns to me and picks up her rant right where she'd left off.

I hold up my hand, palm to her.

"Stop." She does with a stunned expression. I turn to the new bunch of soldiers. "Can anyone *please* tell me *what the fuck she's saying?!*

"Mistah Brack," my man in China, Chang, the cab driver, slips between two of the large soldiers, like he's winding his way through very thick trees in a forest.

"Thank God you're here, Chang!" I haven't been as happy to see anyone as I am him at that moment.

"So good to see you," he says smiling hugely.

I think the little guy might get off on this more than any of us do.

Might.

"Chang, if you will, please tell me what the old woman is yelling at me about."

Chang turns to the matriarch and rattles of something quickly as he bows respectfully to her.

She immediately begins her very animated tirade again, her eyes bouncing back and forth between Chang and me. I'm starting to get a little pissed-off.

What in the fuck did I do? We always bring the girls here before sending them out to homes and acclimating them slowly back into society.

The girls are never returned to their homes because that's the first place the abductors would look for them when they discover they've been taken. Ignorance is bliss, and keeping the family in the dark could quite possibly save their lives.

Chang bobs up and down, nodding his head, his eyes downcast, still fucking smiling.

My jaw clenches tightly.

Then they both look to me. And laugh.

What the fuck?!

"Chang." It's a warning.

"One minute," to the woman he says, "Mistah Brack," then gives her his full attention again, saying something at length as he extends his arm in my direction.

She glares at me. For a long time. I feel like her eyes are burning into my soul. I don't break the look, I stand stock still, taking whatever shit she's got.

Finally, she moves to stand in front of me, a head and a half shorter than I am.

The only other person that has made me feel this off-balance is Hilda. They're the kind of women you can't hide anything from.

She turns on her heels and begins to walk toward another hut. She stops halfway, looks over her shoulder at me and smiles a big, toothless grin. My eyebrows shoot to my hairline. She laughs once, loud and deep, then jerks her head motioning me to follow.

Chang and the others have been silently watching the exchange.

"What the hell was she saying, Chang?"

"She said you rooked rike a heathen jack-ass, arr of you, and that you better not have scared the girrs," he replies, not batting an eye, still smiling.

"She did, did she? And what did you tell her?" I ask, cocking an eyebrow as a smile of admiration for the old woman tugs the corners of my mouth.

"I tord her you are the man who is responsiber for their freedom. If it weren't for you, they'd stirr be herd hostage," he dips his head on the last word, his accent heavy as shit.

"Then what did she say?"

"She said you were stirr a heathen but very, very good one."

I tilt my head back and laugh.

"She's right," I comment. "She requests our presence; we mustn't keep her waiting."

We walk to the hut she'd disappeared into and enter. Immediately the smell of incense envelopes us along with vibrant colors. It's a complete awakening of the senses.

"You must take off your shoes and sit cross-regged on the froor. She is bringing arr of you tea."

We all do as instructed and find our places on the floor at the low table. Another petite woman, younger than the matriarch, dressed in plain traditional clothing, comes in and whispers something in Chang's ear. He follows her out.

The old woman serves us in superior silence in a methodical routine I'm sure is centuries old. First the tea is poured for each of us, then the old woman takes a small brass incense holder and circles us around the table, mumbling something incoherently. I can only guess this is a kind of homage to life and peace, a celebration of the death of the past and a birth to the future. The girl's future. A ritual of negative cleansing and purification.

This is traditional China, the beliefs, practices, and customs. The heart and soul of it.

It is a humbling experience.

Chang returns, moves to the side of the door, and waits. A minute later, a train of girls and young women file into our hut. They're absolutely beautiful. They're dressed in traditional garb, their faces have the white powder and partially done red lips, their hair twisted up in old Chinese style. This must represent their 'coming out' party. They flow toward the back of the room and stand in a perfect line, eyes downcast, hands together and tucked into their sleeves. The last young girl walks in and stops at the door as her eyes scan the room. They stop on me.

Little Warrior?

I'm so fucking proud of her, I can't contain it. My heart swells with her reaction, the grin she gives me knocks me on my ass. I nod my head, and give her a look that screams, "Well done!"

Gemma would be so proud of them too.

She's across the room with her hands around my neck. I squeeze her tightly, overwhelmed by her raw and unguarded show of affection, untarnished by age, time, life, and the hell she just lived through.

She straightens, gives me a kiss on the cheek, then goes to join her sisters.

I am so goddam in love with this little girl!

Once they're all together, they bow to us.

This isn't right.

I stand and return the bow. They are the heroes, the warriors, the fierce and the brave. We should be honoring them.

All the men stand and follow suit, showing their admiration and respect for these incredibly amazing young women. And in typical American custom, we give them a round of applause that would bring the house down.

The joy on their faces is worth more than any price.

But now what? Where do they go? What if they need help again? How will they take care of themselves?

I'm not doing enough. They need so much more.

Yes, a doctor comes to see every girl before they move on to a home. But that's it.

I have to know what happens next, if they're okay, do they need assistance. There has to be more for them than, 'Okay, you're free, now go out there and fend for yourself.'

I'll have a complete outline for Chang and the old woman before I get back to my hotel of all the things that need to be put into place.

I'm not losing a single one of these girls. Ever.

The ride to the safe-house was the easy part.

What was virtually impossible was saying goodbye to my Little Warrior.

Mine

CHAPTER 31

Gemma

Three days. Alex has only been gone three days and I miss him so bad, my entire body aches, the emptiness is deep and resounding. I crave his presence, his body, his voice, his laugh, his everything. I need him. The only saving grace is the word 'Mine' he printed across my heart. I find myself so often unconsciously with my hand pressed against it, as if I can feel him close, imprinted on my soul. His calls and messages soothe my frayed nerves, but I still can't sleep, can barely eat, until he lets me know he's safe.

I can feel him, his worry, his anger, and his longing, we are so entwined, and that is the greatest comfort to me.

He'll be back in two days, get it together.

Although it's hard at both the house and the office, there's nothing to distract me at East Ninety-Sixth street, so I spend as much time as I can at work.

It, too, is only a shell without the king in residence. At least here I can attempt to keep myself busy in the never ending legal jargon of all Black Incs. holdings and proposals.

"Gemma Trudeau," I answer the phone apprehensively, hoping it's not the anonymous caller.

That's all I need.

"Gemma!" Natasha, the receptionist, squeals. "You've got f l o w e r s!" She drags out the word in a lilting sing-song voice.

The Faceless Man!

My heart thumps.

"You're kidding," I manage to croak out of my suddenly dry mouth.

"Nope," she squeals again.

Thank God Alex isn't here. He'd be furious.

My eyes dart to Williams, my shadow, watchdog, sometimes pain-in-the-ass, and other times my only reprieve from falling off the edge into hysteria.

What the hell does he do here all day?

"I'll be right out," I answer and hang up quickly.

Chewing on a nail, I take a few deep breaths to steady myself. I can't let Williams know about the flowers.

With apprehension, I start the trek toward him and reception. Just as I'd thought, he glances at me as I walk by.

"Half a day? It's only three o'clock," he asks with a smirk.

"No, smart ass, HR called, they need my

signature on something." I make up the lie and hope he believes it.

I don't need him following me to the lobby, which I'm sure he would. He'd probably take the damn flowers, dust them for fingerprints, interrogate the flower shop owner, every employee would be run through their top secret double clearance procedure, (whatever the hell that is), and I'd have to answer a million and one questions about who this person is sending me flowers. I can just hear that conversation.

Oh, he's just some guy I had sex with a couple of times. He broke into my house, tied me up, blindfolded me, and blew my mind. No one you'd know. I never saw his face or got his name.

Hah!

Then Alex would find out.

Fat chance!

The elevators are in the reception area where, according to Alex, I can either, a) escape, or b) get kidnapped, which is exactly why that area is off-limits to me. I have to pass reception to get to Human Resources so the story is believable.

"Touchy, touchy," he laughs at me. "Maybe you're getting fired."

I give him an icy glare.

"Or getting another promotion. Now, if you don't mind...."

I'm hoping my expression is annoyed and haughty. Inside I'm practically having a heart attack, I'm so nervous.

"Well, if that is the case, Ms. Trudeau, don't keep them waiting," he smirks.

"Thank you for your permission, *Mr. Williams*."

I turn with my back straight and continue, forcing my steps to remain slightly slower than normal to hear if he's following me or not. My heart is pounding as the seconds slowly tick by, the corridor seeming too short for me to fool him.

Please don't follow, please don't follow, PLEASE don't follow.

I slow at reception's door and glance at my phone stalling for time and to steal a glance at Williams. His cell phone must have caught his attention because he's turned the other way picking it up.

Holy shit, how did I get so lucky?!

I take this small window of opportunity and walk quickly through the smoked glass doors with the elegantly masculine Black Inc. logo emblazoned on them.

My pulse quickens when I see the most incredible arrangement of white orchids sitting on Natasha's desk.

"Aren't they gorgeous?" she coos.

"Yes they are, and extremely unexpected," I mumble, my brows furrowing.

I tread slowly toward her and reach to pluck the card from the holder that has the name of the same florist the others were from, La Vie En Rose. With hesitant fingers, I tear it open and read it.

I have to see you. I'm downstairs around the corner, if you don't come down, I'm coming up. xoxo

What?! No!!!

I shove the card back in the small envelope

and cram it in its slot, hoping that will stop any possibility of the impending catastrophe it promises.

There's NO way he can come up here. Wide-eyed, I scan the reception area and look at the door I just came through. *I need to go down. I don't have much time before Williams comes out.*

"What did he say this time?" Natasha's looking at me expectantly.

"Nothing. I have to run downstairs for just a minute," I mutter, rushing to repeatedly jab my finger onto the down arrow button of the elevator. "Come on, come on…"

"Is something wrong?" she asks me.

"Not yet," I sigh as one of the elevator doors finally slides open.

Wringing my hands as the doors close and the elevator begins its descent, I let out a huff of breath, grateful I made it out without Williams catching me.

I'll deal with the flowers when I get back. First things first.

My mind is racing. A thin sheen of sweat covers my body as fear begins to prick at me.

I can't believe he'd just threaten to show up, at least he gave me the choice. What an overbearing man!

But I already knew that about him.

As the red numbers blink, so does my apprehension, each tick another notch higher.

How am I supposed to find him? I don't even know what he looks like?

He'll find me, and I have no doubt I'll be able to sense him as the memories of our nights together flash through my mind.

My breathing is ragged as the doors open at the lobby. I walk slowly through the people rushing in and out of the cavernous room with its massive front window wall, sleek black obsidian stone floors, and sparkling chrome, while my eyes search through the crowd.

He said he was around the corner.

My heart is slamming against my ribcage. My mind is yelling at me to go back.

I can't let him go up.

I force my feet to move against every instinct demanding me to turn around and run...fast. But I don't. I push open the front doors and walk outside. Slowly I reach the corner and turn down the side-street. It's narrow, and lined with mostly service entrances receiving freight, a shoe repair shop, the coffee shop, an office supply store, and other small businesses.

The sound of my blood whooshing through my veins as my heart thuds echoes in my head.

Where are you?

My steps are slow, everything seems like it's in slow motion. The sound of traffic is a distant noise against my breath rasping in and out of my nose. My eyes are darting everywhere searching every corner, every face, every door, looking for The Faceless Man.

No one pays me any attention, not even the man cursing to himself who's fumbling in the open door of a van as I pass.

"Fucking piece of shit," he says.

"Come on, asshole," his partner pokes his head out from behind the van and shouts at him in a heavy accent.

Where in God's name are you? I don't have long.

Terror is gripping me trying to immobilize me.

The man from the back of the van steps out in front of me and almost bangs into me and makes me stumble backwards.

"I'm so sorry miss," he apologizes as he reaches out and grips my elbows at an attempt to steady me.

I'm panting as every nerve ending in my body surges at his touch.

"I'm fine, thank you."

He takes a step a closer, forcing me to take another step back.

"Are you sure miss?" he asks, still holding me.

"Yes, rea…," I begin to reply.

The words are cut short as a foul smelling rag is shoved over my face and mouth as arms come from behind me and hold me so tightly, it hurts. Shock instantly escalates to terror. Deathly terror. The arms around me pull me back as the man in front pushes me. My head is swimming, my eyes are blurring, and bile climbs up my throat and fills my mouth.

I think I hear him say as my head starts to fog, "Your fucking boyfriend is going to pay."

Please be careful, don't go anywhere alone. Alex's words resound in my brain.

OH GOD, Alex, I'm SO SORRY!

I'm kicking as hard as the limited space will

allow, my heels flying from my feet, before the man in front of me folds my rapidly depleting body into the van door. My limbs are heavy, tingling, until they're finally useless. The screams spewing from my lungs are only muffled little whimpers no one can hear as the door to the van is slammed shut once I'm inside, the heavy bang like a punch to my heart. I can't see, I can't breathe, and the world is swimming in a pool of blackness.

Blackness.

Black.

Oh, God...!!!

Nothing.

Lieutenant Williams had every intention of following behind Gemma, making up some lame excuse of why he was there. It's not that he didn't trust her, maybe he didn't entirely, (nobody likes to be followed every second of every day), but something didn't feel right. The message had delayed him.

I know who the spy is. Rico

Are they still on premise? Williams

Yes. Lock down the office until I get there. Rico

Williams was halfway down the hallway, already on his way to HR, as he issued the command to the buildings maintenance department to lock down all entrances and exits to all Black Inc. levels. He needed to get his eyes on Gemma. When he walked into HR, instantly he knew she hadn't been there.

"Where's   Trudeau?"   he   barks

unceremoniously to the five women at their desks.

They all shake their heads.

"We haven't seen her," the pretty young one closest to him answers as a blush creeps up her cheeks and a shy smile curves her lips.

Gritting his teeth, he turns and storms back the way he'd come. He hesitates a fraction of a second at the door to reception before he barges through it. Immediately he spies the flowers, knowing they hadn't been there this morning. His gaze darts to the pretty African American receptionist, Natasha. She's staring at her cell phone in her hand but jerks her arms down the instant she hears him as he pins her with his glare.

"The flowers," is all Williams says.

She stays mute, her eyes wide.

In two strides he's in front of her ripping the card from the arrangement and reads it.

"Trudeau," he asks, his voice dark and sinister.

If Williams hadn't seen thousands of people with secrets during his time deployed, he wouldn't have noticed the tell sign Natasha just gave with the slight flare of her nostrils.

"Downstairs," she replies quietly.

"Fuck!" he growls. Punching the numbers to maintenance on his phone, "Give me elevator number one. Don't allow access to it for anyone else except those on the list." He dials another number, "Trudeau's downstairs," he barks. "I'm going down now." His body tenses. "Ten four." He shoves his phone back in his pocket as elevator number one opens, then yanks Natasha out from behind the desk.

"You're coming with me."

Natasha snatches her phone.

"I'll take that," he grabs it with one hand and grips her with an iron hold with his other, dragging her into the elevator.

"What the hell do you think you're doing?!" she yells, trying to pull her arm free.

He doesn't bother to answer as his fingers dig into her arm. When the doors start to separate on the ground level, he's got both of them out and halfway through the lobby before they're fully open. He doesn't give two fucks that he has to drag her behind him, he doesn't care she's shouting obscenities at him in the midst of the minimal elegance, and he sure as shit doesn't bother with the people giving him dirty looks. The only thing he wants to see is one woman. Safe. A thorough scan of the bystanders tells him Gemma is not inside the building. As he and Natasha approach the front door and the security guard, Williams grabs the man's hand and clamps it onto Natasha's arm.

"Put the cuffs on her and chain her to something. Don't let her go until I come back for her," Williams commands.

He doesn't wait for an answer, hadn't even broken his stride out of the building. When he turns the corner, he knows Gemma's gone. Moving forward, that's when he sees the black patent leather stilettos with the red bottoms lying in the street at the curb along with a crushed cell phone.

"MOTHER FUCKER," rage engulfs him as he turns and slams his fist into the side of the cinder block building.

He doesn't feel the pain radiate through his hand and up his arm, he doesn't notice the shredded knuckles and the blood pouring from his fist. The only thing he knows is he fucking failed.

He picks up the shoes and mangled piece of metal and glass, then takes out his phone.

"Major Stewart, Trudeau has been abducted. She was taken from around the corner of Black Building, the same street the call was placed from." He glances up at the camera at the intersection. "She received flowers, there's no name. I believe they were from a man and the card said he would come up if she didn't come down." He listens. "I've got her. I'll take her back upstairs and await further instruction." Shoving the phone into his pocket, he walks back to Black Building to begin interrogating the spy until Rico arrives.

Then it's time to start hunting.

Alexander

After being awake for two straight days because of the rescue, I've only been asleep an hour when my phone rings. My eyes burn as I grab it.

Instinctually I'm on high alert.

"Black."

"Mr. Black," it's Major Stewart. My heart twists even without a word from him as the world drops out from underneath me. "Ms. Trudeau was abducted a half hour ago."

Nuclear destruction. Annihilation. The fucking Four Horsemen are thundering through me, tearing me to fucking shreds.

NO! She was supposed to be safe, I had a

guard for her. I was supposed to protect her!

I'm out of bed before he's finished the sentence. My heart blows up, there's no air, I can't breathe, my brain is exploding inside my skull, and my guts are an excruciating bloody massacre.

"How the fuck could this have happened!!" I bellow.

I'm half way around the fucking world and I need to be there now!!

I storm through the room and shove everything into my suitcases, holding my breath, waiting to hear how hell has just consumed me.

"She received flowers at the office with a note, we believe they were from a man…"

Dear God, no!

"They weren't."

My gut twists as horror grips me knowing they used the one thing that makes Gemma vulnerable, and I created it. The Faceless Man. They used me to get to her. I handed them the only thing that she'd want to hide from me, from my people, at almost any cost.

"How do you know?" he asks.

Because I'm fucking him!

"They used that man to get to her, I created him. He is me. There is no man," the words fight their way through the scorching sickness running through my entire body.

"The note said, 'I need to see you. I'm downstairs around the corner, if you don't come down, I'm coming up.' She left the office immediately."

"Where the fuck was Williams? How did she

sneak by him?" I yell.

I can't think because of the roaring in my head, I can't breathe because of the crippling pain in my chest, and my body doesn't want to work, it's paralyzed with fucking fear. Fear of what they could be doing to her right now.

It was perfect, they knew exactly what to say to get her to leave.

"She said she was heading to HR. When Williams glanced down for a moment to read the text from Rico stating he knows who the spy is, that's when she exited the main office areas."

A small sliver of hope pierces my agony.

"Who's the spy?" I ask, shoving my feet into my shoes.

"Your receptionist, Natasha Folami." He delivers the news we've all been waiting for, the identity of the spy.

That information literally knocks me on my ass.

"What?"

"Yes, I'm assuming you're packed and ready to leave. Call me when you're in transit and I'll give you the details, and any updates. The team there has been informed and by now everyone is ready to depart. Jacobs is outside your door. There's a plane organized to get you in the air as soon as you arrive at the airport. You will not be delayed; I've personally seen to that myself. And Black, don't worry, we're going to find her."

Dear God...

I can't bring myself to finish the silent plea.

"I'm on my way."

Rage and fury are my sustenance, I have only two purposes now: find Gemma, and destroy everyfuckingone involved with taking her, touching her, threatening her.

Shoving the phone in my pocket, I take a quick look around to make sure I haven't left my passport, anything else I don't give a fuck.

I hope it's not too late.

Unbidden horrific images force themselves into my mind, mutilated and dismembered limbs, gore, burnt charred flesh, rape, torture, all with Gemma's beautiful face distorted in agony. Fury blasts through me and blazes in my veins. The beast claws beneath my skin demanding to be unleashed and extract revenge in the most gruesome ways. Hunt, destroy, kill, obliterate. Catching a glimpse of myself in the mirror, I may look like a polished business man, I'm anything but. Death, pain, horror, oblivion, that's what I am now.

I'm a killer. A deadly sadistic predator that's coming for them.

Hold on Gemma, I'm coming. Be strong, baby, don't let those monsters break you!

Now in my mind, what I see is blood, lots and lots of blood. Theirs.

I'm the worst monster of them all.

Soon...

Mine

CHAPTER 32

Gemma

Splash!

I awaken gasping for breath, completely confused as water is thrown in my face.

"Ah, she finally stirs. Ms. Trudeau, so nice of you to join us."

Through the fog in my brain, the male voice sounds vaguely familiar. With it, it brings feelings of fear, dread, and anger. Recollection floods me at lightning speed, images tumble in an avalanche on top of each other in my head.

The Anonymous Man's voice.

I was shoved into a van and drugged.

I've been kidnapped.

They want to kill me.

I force myself not to panic as terror threatens to suck me in.

Stay calm!

I wipe the water from my face. Immediately

I recognize the man holding the dripping bucket as one of my abductors, the one from the back of the van. He's standing next to a very large, middle-age man who's seated in a chair across from me, extremely well dressed, his posture is relaxed and confident, and at a quick glance he would appear handsome. With a closer look, he's cold and emotionless, and he radiates nothing but danger. The power and confidence that's rolling off him is just as intimidating as his expression. He's casually looking at me.

The Anonymous Man.

"The water really wasn't necessary, I'm sure I would have woken eventually," my voice is raspy from whatever they knocked me out with.

Smack!

The man from the van on the street hits me across the face, snapping my head to the side and sending water droplets flying as jolts of pain surge through my eyes and skull.

"Шлюха, (whore), the next one won't be so gentle," Van Boy sneers at me.

Russian, and whatever he called me wasn't a compliment.

I slowly turn my head toward him and glare into his hard eyes.

"You are going to pay for that," I whisper coldly.

He bends so his face is an inch from mine. "So are you, пизда, (cunt)." Another blow lands on my abdomen, igniting an explosion through me. Pain like I've never felt before cripples me and sends the contents of my stomach to my mouth and all the air from my gasping lungs.

"As I was saying, Ms. Trudeau," the man who's voice I've unwillingly come to know continues smoothly. "Welcome, I've been looking forward to speaking with you. We have a lot to discuss."

Forcing my head clear and my mind not to succumb to the rising terror, I breathe deeply and ride out the pain and nausea. I draw myself within.

I am not going to let them destroy me. Alex is coming, I have to survive until he gets here!

I close my eyes and listen. Each sound becomes isolated.

Footsteps on metal stairs.

Shouts in Russian.

The unmistakable sound of a boat horn.

I slowly open my eyes and look at my surroundings. The walls are metal, there are no windows, and the door...bone shattering panic seizes me.

They've got me on a ship!

"Where am I?" I wheeze out.

"Don't ask me stupid questions, I hate stupidity."

I turn to face the seated man again, the one who's been watching me, the man responsible for destroying my home. The one who singlehandedly ruined my life. The memory of my parent's violated house flashes in my mind and gives me a surge of hatred that fills me with powerful determination. The intensity of my anger pushes my terror aside.

I want to take in every detail about him, study him, pick him apart in my mind and find his weaknesses.

A deep cutting shiver penetrates to my bones when our eyes lock. There's only one thing I see about him. He's a demon, a soulless beast who feeds on death and torture. His lips curve in a diabolical grin on his cold handsome face. He knows I see him for what he is and it whets his appetite. He's starving and he's going to feast on my agony.

"My apologies." The civility burns my tongue.

"Now, Ms. Trudeau, I thought we would have an intelligent conversation. I do admire you. But there's one thing you must tell me, the curiosity has been driving me mad," Demon Man asks as if we were pals.

"Of course, I'll do my best," I respond, mustering all the false propriety I can.

He leans in with his elbows on his knees in the chair across from mine. "This thing you have with Black. Is it for purely selfish reasons? Getting the position with his company was ingenious, the perfect way to get your credibility back, well done I must say. Are you fucking him for the same reason?"

The blow from his words is worse than Van Boys, and it tears my heart apart. Insinuating what I have with Alex is pure filth is sacrilegious on so many levels. He is the only person who has ever truly cared for me. But I'll be damned if I'll let this scum know the sanctity of what Alex and I share.

"I'm not a whore, sir." My reply is cold and hard.

He sits back and smiles at me. "Interesting. And really quite a good fortune for us. Your death will be like the icing on the cake, an added bonus with Black."

His threat has the effect on me he desired, it scares the living hell right out of me. My only saving grace that keeps me from collapsing into hysterics is latching on and hiding behind my hard lawyer persona. As long as I can be that person, not Gemma from Jersey, I pray I can bluff myself through this.

"I wouldn't know about that. Alexander Black is a cold and ruthless man. Everything is just business with him. I don't know if he has a heart." I hope the lie is good enough to be believable.

He shrugs his shoulders indifferently, "That is what I believed...until you. I suppose we'll find out, won't we?" He strokes his chin as he considers my words. "I guess time will tell. It will be fun either way."

You're a sick, disgusting human being!

"Using me as leverage with Black is a waste of time, he considers me an inconvenience. My husband stole three million dollars from him, he probably only hired me to find out if I had something to do with it," I counter, attempting to give credibility to my argument.

The truth of the argument I pulled out of thin air falls on me like a huge boulder, threatening to crash on top of me and destroy any hope I have of surviving this.

Oh my God, that's exactly why he hired me!

I begin to sweat with heart wrenching fear and isolation, terrified that the possibility of Alex's interest in me is so insignificant, I might truly only be a liability to him.

Don't panic Gemma! He told you he loves you, he got you a military bodyguard, formed his own army, for Christ's sake! He'll come. Treat this man like a witness, manipulate him, get him to trust you. But stay fucking calm!

I take a deep cleansing breath and shrug my shoulders as if my life wasn't at stake.

Demon Man's body language is casual but his eyes are penetrating.

"That may be true, but I doubt it. Black has never had a woman for longer than it took him to satisfy his sadistic appetite," he sneers at me.

My shock at this revelation is clear in the flash that sears through my body. Demon Man smiles broadly at my reaction, it's sinister and sends another wave of fear over me.

"Oh, yes, my dear, I know about Alexander Black's particular tastes. I must admit they're mild compared to my own. I'm looking forward to playing with you...to breaking you. I might even consider sending you back to him when I'm finished with you, all wrapped up in a nice ribbon. I can promise you, though, the best part will be killing you."

I steel myself against his heinous promises, forcing them to bounce off me and refusing to let their impact show.

"You are obviously a business man, as is Black..." I continue, attempting to reason with him.

"This is business, Ms. Trudeau, completely," he cuts me off. "Black has recently interfered with a very large...shipment of merchandise of mine. Aside from everything else, he owes me for that." He leans back in his chair. "But let's start with you. Tell me what you know of Mr. Stevens' dealings with us."

The rescue mission was his girls, and Alex got them. And he's fucking pissed.

My hands clench, I hope it's the only outward sign of the terror looming and ready to consume me.

"As I've told you on the phone, Malcolm never spoke to me about any of his business transactions. I knew nothing of the negotiations he had with Black Inc.. The first I heard of anything was when the police raided our home and took Malcolm to prison for embezzlement. As a matter of fact, the only things I *do* know is that he stole money from Black and he's in prison for it."

He cocks his head at me.

"Tsk, tsk, Ms. Trudeau, I thought because you are an intelligent woman, you'd be more forthcoming." Pinning me with his hate filled glare, he directs Van Boy, "Help her to jar her memory."

I grip the edge of the seat and hold on for dear life.

"This really isn't necessary...," I try again to speak sensibly with him.

Van Boy leans into me with his stinking mouth at me ear, "I'm going to enjoy this, шлюха, (whore)."

He raises his hand across his chest and brings it back to hit me across my face with a bone shattering blow, it throws me from my chair and across the room.

I don't scream, the pain is too great and too incapacitating, I can't do anything. It's everything, blotting out time, annihilating space, and destroying hope.

He grips my shirt and pulls me up, then shoves me in the chair again, before he rips it open. A deep nagging need penetrates the screams of pain resonating in my skull and forces me to protect something sacred. My hands fly to my chest to cover myself…and the word that has been my intimate secret since Alex left, the one thing that has kept him close to me. The word, 'Mine' he wrote across my heart.

"What is this?" Demon Man chuckles as he moves to stand in front of me, the sound of his words making me sick. Gripping my wrists, he tears them away from my front and pins them down. "How delightful! It seems you *are* more than just a plaything for our enigmatic Alexander Black."

Even through the excruciating pounding in my head, I know things have just escalated from bad to horrendous torture.

"Give me your blade, Vasily, I believe Alexander Black would love to have his mark on her permanently."

Automatic reaction kicks in as the terror crashes over me in multitudes. I shoot my stocking clad foot up and kick Demon Man in the balls with everything I have, the impact radiating painfully up my leg.

"DON'T FUCKING TOUCH ME!"

He lets out a wail as his eyes roll back in his head and he doubles over, gripping his crotch, while he falls to the floor on his knees.

Thrashing like a wild animal in the chair, I

can't comprehend rational thought, I'm running on pure fight or flight instinct. It's in overdrive and making me a maniac trying to hurt and get the fuck out of there.

My arms are still slippery from the water Van Boy'd thrown in my face. His grip slips and it gives me the perfect opportunity to yank my arms free and shoot out of the chair. My head is throbbing, my vision is still filled with stars from the blow I'd just gotten, and my ears are ringing like the bells of St. Mary's. None of it is stopping me from bolting toward the door.

I barely get out of the chair before a large hand grabs my ankle and stops me in midair. I crash to the floor with a heavy thud. Another jolt of pain rocks through my head from the impact.

"You filthy bitch!!"

Van Boy yanks me back by my leg, I'm flailing the other trying to kick him too. He easily takes hold of that ankle as well.

"I should break both of your fucking legs right now," he roars.

His first kick lands on my hip and instantly immobilizes me. Instinctually my body freezes and tries to bend-in on itself for protection. The second kick hits my ribs with such a piercing force, I'm sure he broke a couple of them. I let out a scream from the agonizing pain. The third kick lands on my crotch. Excruciating explosions shoot through me before I black out from a kick to my head.

As I begin to come to, I'm back in the chair. I don't know how much time has passed. My body is a throbbing mass of pain.

"Wake her up," I hear Demon Man's snarl through my haze.

Splash!

Another drowning of freezing water hits my face and shockingly clears my head, jolting me upright. I try to lift my hand to wipe the water from my eyes, but it doesn't move. I yank both my arms and legs, first slowly, then frantically as new panic surges inside me. My arms are bound behind me to the back of the chair, opening my bare front to the disgusting pigs, and my legs are spread open with my ankles tied to the chair legs, pushing my pencil skirt high up my thighs. The idea of my most intimate part wide open to them is hideously revolting. I have never felt so humiliated, so vulnerable, so utterly degraded in my entire life, it makes me nauseas. My pounding heart shoots spasms of pain through my body, and every panting breath is agony.

"Again, Ms. Trudeau, what do you know about Malcolm's dealings with us?" Demon Man's voice has lost all sense of fake civility.

He's furious with me, and I have no doubt he'd rather have killed me just now, but he's forced to leave me in a somewhat state of coherency. He thinks I have information he wants, and he'll bide his time to get it. It's more important than his desire for horror, my horror…for the time being.

I glare at him but I can only see him with one eye, the other is swollen shut.

God, give me strength!

I search for something, *anything,* to latch onto to be strong enough in order to get through this.

Alex…he's coming, hold on!

Thinking of Alex, remembering his intensity, his army, and hearing his voice in my mind telling me he loves me gives it to me.

I take another deep, steadying breath, as deep as the stabbing pain in my lung and side will allow.

"I've told you everything I know. Nothing," I state as evenly as I can.

He sneers at me and lifts his hand in front of his face. He's holding a knife. Touching the tip of it with a finger of the other hand, he examines the blade. He turns it slightly so the fluorescent lights dance off it, just to make sure I can see it through the slit of my bad eye.

"You are making this much too appealing for me," Demon Man's voice drips sweetly.

I force myself not to succumb to the rising hysteria that's threatening to overwhelm me.

Think, think, think!! Stall him somehow!

"I understand your concern, I do. Why don't we try this another way?" I ask, attempting to take control of the situation, as ridiculous as that may be.

"Oh?" he stops, then leans back in his chair, resting the knife on his lap. Tilting his head at me, a small smile lifts his lips. It makes me want to scream. "I knew you'd be a breath of fresh air, Ms. Trudeau. Please, go on."

Never before in my life have I ever been as happy to be a lawyer as I am now. The art of finding answers, looking at different angles, manipulating clever interrogations, all these things begin to roll through my brain.

"You said Malcolm may have left something," I begin to lead him.

"That is correct," he replies, nodding his head once.

"And you think that it is in my possession, is that right?" I ask, forcing myself to remain calm and my mind as clear is possible.

"It is," he answers confidently.

"How can you be so sure? As I mentioned, and it was all over the news, the Feds confiscated everything. The only things they left were some of my clothes, even some of those they took. They must have taken what you're looking for with Malcolm's things."

"They didn't."

"How do you know? You can't be certain of that." I try to be as firm as I can be, considering I'm bound and beaten, with my clothes torn open.

"Because, my dear, the president of South Africa, the Supreme Leader of Iran, and the richest men in Russia and China haven't been called to appear in front of the World Tribunal Courts. If the Feds had that little piece of insurance, as your husband called it, the world's financial systems would have collapsed by now, and quite possibly started a new war. The Feds don't have it." He smiles smugly at me. "You do."

My heart drops to my stomach as dread and desperation close in on me.

This is all too much…it can't be? How did I get sucked into this? This is global conspiracy. I'm just a girl from New Jersey!

"I think I'm going to be sick."

Mine

CHAPTER 33

Alexander

The Hong Kong streets are virtually empty at this hour of the morning. It's still pitch black outside and I can't make out the buildings as we head to the airport, there's only a blur of lights streaking by. We're doing almost a hundred miles an hour. Each minute that passes is another gut wrenching stab.

"Give me the updates on Gemma," I grip the phone tightly.

I feel so fucking helpless!

Everything inside me is raging to hunt, clawing at me with an overwhelming need to destroy. Rip them fucking apart.

Not being able to do *one fucking* thing is destroying me.

It's been an hour since she was taken. The more time that passes, the odds of finding her alive diminish. I know that after twenty-four hours, in most cases, it's almost hopeless.

This is not most cases.

I hear Major Stewart take a breath as he begins.

"We've reviewed the city traffic cams footage and have identified the two assailants who abducted her. We've confirmed their identities as Russian mob. They forced her into a van. It was just found empty, which tells us they switched vehicles. Williams retrieved Ms. Trudeau's purse and searched it. He discovered a high-tech USB drive hidden inside the lining, it's back here and we're reviewing it now. Black," he pauses as his tone drops.

"What is it?" I grit out tightly.

"It appears this is the item they were looking for." He sounds sure.

"Tell me what the fuck it is!" I bellow.

"I think it's safe to say it outlines a worldwide network including some of the most powerful people on the globe, political and illegal. And what connects them. There are hundreds of files, the ones we're concentrating on immediately are those we believe will lead us to Ms. Trudeau."

"Which ones are those?" I ask, almost caving to the dread clawing at me.

"Yours and Vladimir Polchenko."

Fuck, fuck, FUCK!

Polchenko, the notorious and obscure Russian billionaire with very questionable affiliations. The man the two guards were probably working for.

I force myself to stay focused. "Is there any indication as to who's at the top of all this so far?"

"At this point, it's still speculative. The information in that drive is apparently a 'Who's Who' in the operation though, we're not sure if it is only one entity in the end."

"Your best guess, Stewart," it takes massive amounts of my willpower to stay calm and in control.

"Regarding Trudeau? Polchenko."

That's good and bad, I try to remain optimistic and keep my head clear while my beast roars for revenge. On one hand, the Russian footsteps can be traced here in the states. With the manpower available to us, and the technology, we can move fast without most of the obstacles that would normally deter us. There's military intelligence and street intel at our fingertips, we can find these son-of-a-bitches. On the other hand, the vicious savages get off on torture. If there is a personal vendetta against me, and if there wasn't, there is now after the rescue, that will multiply Gemma's danger because of her link to me. That's aside from the information that was found in her possession that her scumbag husband left.

FUCK, FUCK, FUCK!

Malcolm. He's lucky he's in prison. There's nothing I'd like more than to kill him slowly and painfully. He did this to her. How could he? He was her husband, for fuck's sake! How could he throw her to the Russians knowing what they'd do to her?

The fact that this information was available to me while Gemma had it, regardless of whether she knew it or not, raises the stakes immensely. Me and my company having access to it has just made me the major player in the game holding all the fucking cards. From the little Stewart's told me so far, me and Gemma are immediately a much larger threat, apparently both politically and privately. On the other side, the value of our deaths has just multiplied by millions.

But I've got the winning card. Their winning card.

Those motherfuckers have got mine.

They're going to extract revenge on me on her perfect, innocent body!

My insides are shredded, screams of fury echo in my brain while on the outside I'm trying to appear rational.

I'll do anything to get her back.

"I need to know who's in charge. We can bargain for her with that information."

Just get her fucking back!

In one piece.

Alive!

"Or you can sign her death warrant if they know you've got it," Stewart fires back.

"This is business, Major," for the scum responsible for this.

"Big business, Black. One woman doesn't make a difference to them."

She's MY fucking woman, the only goddam thing that matters to me!

"It does if I'm holding it. I was a threat to their operation before Gemma and this information, I'm even more powerful now," my voice remains even, my meaning clear. My business connections have no limit, I line the pockets of governments and corporations around the world.

What fucking good is any of that if it can't help get Gemma back?

I just stumbled upon the pot of gold, unfortunately it's in the middle of a worldwide minefield.

Blowing up my fucking world.

Stewart takes another breath before he continues. "I'll get a feel on Polchenko. We're not even sure he's responsible. If he's not, and we approach him with a trade, the information for Trudeau, then we'll end up losing the only leverage we've got."

It's my turn to take a frustrated breath.

Goddam it!

"Okay," I hesitantly agree. "Is there anything that might tell us where they've taken her?" I'm absolutely desperate.

"Not that we've found in those files so far, but we're already reaching out to all our contacts. Every single one. My men, Rico, and Carlos have been very busy."

Both officially and on the street. Someone's GOT to find something!

"Good," is all I can say. It gives me a small sense of hope. A very small one.

"Tell me everything about Natasha." My voice is level belying the insane rage that's consuming me.

I'm watching this fucking city whiz by the car window dying an excruciating, painful death inside.

"I'm going to let you speak to Rico about that. I have the specifics, but there might be other things you two need to go over."

"Alright."

I grit my teeth as we pull into the airport. We bypass the commercial airlines exit and go directly to freight. I don't care how many dicks had to be sucked, or how much money it cost to get me out of this country fast, nothing was too much.

Not for Gemma.

"Alex."

Rico's voice cuts me. To anyone else he sounds in control and cold. To me, he knows my torment. I can hear it. He sounds exactly the way I did when Isabelle was killed. I grip the phone tighter, resisting the overwhelming urge to smash the fucking thing with all my pent-up fear and fury.

"Talk." The word feels like a choke, my throat is closing forcing back all my emotions.

"Natasha's father is affiliated with Boko Haram," the unbelievable news is delivered point blank.

"What the fuck?! The same group responsible for the kidnapping of those two hundred and seventy-six school girls in Africa?"

I'm totally fucking stunned.

"Yes. He's a South African so-called business man who has allegedly brokered deals that left any adversary compliant or dead. It's common for him use a bribe, slaves are the currency of choice, to coerce a situation in his favor. Something that he, and his associates, partake in regularly. Many of them have a collection of slaves in all nationalities and ethnicities. American slaves are more precious to them than their fucking diamonds."

There's the link to my underground

operations.

"She passed my security checks," I murmur.

"If you've got enough money and the right connections, you can get into the fucking White House, Black," Rico laughs sarcastically.

"That's how she knew about the flowers and the other man." It's so clear now, so damn obvious. Natasha spoke to Gemma about him; I have no doubt. Natasha probably pumped Gemma for information the way a dreamy eyed girl would.

"Exactly, handed it to her on a gold platter. When we got her here, she was like the Exorcist, bro, all she needed was the cross and the pea soup."

The car comes to a screeching halt in front of the building. I storm out and through the terminal doors before Jacobs has gotten my luggage.

As I approach security, I ask Rico, "Do you have enough on her for an indictment?"

The guards raise their eyes to mine.

Fuck them, they don't need to talk to me, all they have to worry about is weapons and contraband.

"There's enough to put her away for life on her phone, but because she's not an American citizen, we're looking at extradition. She'll probably walk because of her father's position when she's returned to South Africa. I hate it," he replies.

"Does she know where Gemma is?!"

He inhales deeply.

My whole body tenses.

"She keeps denying it, saying she was only asked to coordinate a plan to get Gemma out of the building for the Russians. After she spit in my face, she repeatedly insisted that's all she knows."

Fucking Boko Haram and the Russians working together!

"GODDAM IT!" I yell, not giving two shits that I'm standing in front of armed police officers in Hong Kong International Airport.

Jacobs and the other man from Stewart's team have caught up to me. Thank God, because I've just realized I have no fucking idea where we're going. They take the lead and I follow, Jacobs at my side.

I hate feeling so fucking USELESS!

The high polish from the rest of the airport has been extended to this area as well, it's sleek and appears brand new. Even though we're flying out of the freight area, we still have to go through clearance. Every minute of delay escalates my anxiety.

"Alex, stay confident. There's a file on that drive on Natasha's father and they're going through it with a fine tooth comb, looking for any U.S. information that would identify locations and accomplices. Especially with Polchenko. We've got a lot of contacts to lead us quickly to Gemma. We'll find her."

He knows what I'm feeling, he watched the one woman he loved get gunned down in front of him. He'd move heaven and hell to keep that from happening to me.

"Okay," I breathe out.

I feel like a caged animal who's being tortured, writhing in agony, desperate for retaliation and revenge. I know the team is the best of the best. But I'm not there, I'm stuck sixteen fucking hours away, and it's fucking killing me!

The government officials wave us by after they've gone through our documentation and confirmed our flight.

One step closer.

"Rico, do you think they're going to sell her as a slave?"

The horrible thought cripples me, I almost fall to my knees.

"Alex, don't fucking do that! Stay focused, we're going to get her before that can happen, goddammit!"

We go through a door that leads outside and walk across the brightly lit tarmac. Sunrise will be in about an hour here. I'm not thinking about that, my mind is already in New York, hoping Gemma is still there, praying with every damn breath I take. My mind is scanning the streets and wondering where she is, and if she's hurt. The thought wrenches my heart. I can't think about that, I can't allow the images to force themselves through my mind, pictures of her beaten and tortured, a fucking slave. I choke back a groan as the thoughts break past the barricades I've tried to put up against them.

"Just get home safe, negro. We'll let you know the updates when you approach New York."

"Tell Stewart to have the men send me all their info as they feed it to him, I want to go through everything myself even before he's had a chance to condense it. I might find something that may seem insignificant to someone else."

There are things that only I know. They can be used against me or against them. And with

Gemma and the files, I'm sure anything's invaluable.

"Will do," I can visualize him nodding in agreement.

"I'm glad you're there, Rico," this time the sentiment does come out choked.

"Me too. I'll see you when you get back."

As I approach the metal stairs to the plane that's taking me home, to Gemma, the rest of Stewart's team is already waiting for me. The cabin is large but empty, except for us, there isn't even a stewardess.

Good thinking, Stewart.

By the time we all get strapped in and the plane is taxiing for take-off, files are uploading to my laptop.

I've got sixteen fucking hours to find something.

I scan each file to decide where to start. But I can't ignore the feelings of helplessness, utter despair, rage, all of them pulling me apart, shredding me into a million tormented pieces. Now that the adrenaline rush has run its course, my demons are devouring me.

Jesus Christ, I failed her! I was supposed to keep her safe, I told her I would protect her! Forgive me, Gemma, I'm coming. I swear to God I'm going to find you.

Silent agony rages inside me. Images of my mother's dead body flash through my mind, Isabelle's scream pierces in my ears, and the look of complete fear on Gemma's face when we walked into her parent's house all take turns torturing me.

I will NOT fail her, I CAN'T!!

I haven't taken my eyes from my computer screen, I can't get through all the information fast enough. My head is pounding and my eyes are on fire. I don't deserve to even think about that fucking shit, not while they've got Gemma. I would put a knife in my own heart, then set it on fire, if that would get her back safe, I couldn't care less about myself. She has nothing to do with any of this, she shouldn't be made to pay.

As thoughts of her already being shipped off as a slave to some sick bastard filter through my already tormented mind, I have to practically shove a fist into my mouth to keep the wails from escaping me.

If I knew who was responsible for this, I'd call them myself and make a deal, whatever the fuck they wanted, it would be theirs. My company, gone. House, fucking take it. My missions...my rescue missions...fuck, I'd stop them too. For her. Only for her.

Chaos and madness is what I am on the flight. Desolation and fury. My beast is enraged to hunt, kill, and destroy. I exist on the hunger for death, and my memories with Gemma. I relive every single moment with her, the first time I tasted her as The Faceless Man, how she let go and gave herself to me, how she came into my office with fire in her eyes, then as I stared into their depths when I made her come on my desk, God how I'd wanted to feel her wrapped around me, but the most intense time was the last. She'd possessed my soul.

I can't survive without her.

She has brought me to life.

As we approach New York, and the buildings below come into view, the adrenaline rush floods me again and the sight gives me a new surge of hope.

Thank God!

Jacobs walks up to me and hands me another cup of that shit ass coffee.

"Thanks," I grumble and take it from him.

"Mr. Black, please come up to the cockpit, air traffic control tower needs to speak with you," the captain announces over the loudspeaker.

I shove the cup back to Jacobs as I push out of my seat. As I approach the door at the front of the plane, one of Stewart's men is backing out.

He turns to me. "All clear, Mr. Black." He nods his head once and steps to the side.

"Thank you," I mumble as I step into the cramped space.

"Mr. Black, there's a gentleman named Rico who'd like to speak with you," the pilot informs me.

Dread, hope, fear, and confusion all crash together inside me as I pick up the phone.

"Rico," my voice is hoarse.

"Black, you're going to Georgia," the words are clipped, I can tell he's in a hurry.

"Talk."

"The Salvatore's called me and I met with John and Tony," my gut twists, I don't trust those motherfuckers. Rico continues, "I know what you're thinking, I thought the same thing when they called and asked to meet. My contacts got word out to all the families about the situation. Tony, the fucking douchebag that he is, did a little snooping on his own after they heard what had happened. One of his guys had told him before that the Russian Bratva had been sending out shipments at the docks of, get this, windshield wiper fluid. The shit's actually grain alcohol they dye blue, take it back to Russia, remove the color, then sell it as vodka. Told him it's been a regular thing over the past few years. He wanted to find out for himself, so he went down to the West Side docks and hung around for a while. It didn't take long for him to hear that the Russki's took a 'broad on board'. They joked about how fucked up she was because they had to carry her. Her description fit Gemma's."

"Why the fuck aren't we on that goddamm ship?!"

My beast is maniacal now.

We know where she is but we don't fucking have her?!

"Because it's on its way to Georgia to pick up more merchandise," my outburst doesn't faze him.

"Son of a bitch! How long ago?"

"I was told ten hours ago."

Thank God! We've got some information and we have a goddam destination.

"And the flight plan?" I grip the headset so tightly, my muscles spasm, I can't stand being stuck in this goddamn plane another fucking minute. There's information on where Gemma is!

"It's all been approved. You're landing in New York to refuel, then flying to Jacksonville, Florida, it's closer to the Port of Brunswick, where the Russian Bratva are known to export from." His words are hurried.

I allow myself to embrace this as something

positive, one step closer to bringing Gemma home. Safe. Alive.

She has to be!

"Do we know if the ship's gotten there?"

We can't be too fucking late!

"It hasn't arrived there yet, and we've sent orders to detain them."

"Do whatever the fuck you've got to do to make sure NO ONE LEAVES THAT FUCKING SHIP!"

"We're on it, Black. Just get there, we're taking care of it."

I let out a heavy frustrated fucking breath.

"Are you going to Georgia?"

"I'm half way there, bro. We flew down last night. I'm in North Carolina, I'm getting a couple of my own boys, then we're heading down."

"Get me some clothes, if you can. Black, with a hood. And sneakers."

"You got it, and everything else you're going to need as well. The mother fuckers want to party? Let's show 'em how it's done, right negro?"

Time to fucking hunt.

"Just so we're clear, I get the scumbags who took her." The declaration is menacing and deadly.

"Without question, she's your woman." He knows. "We're gonna get her, bro. She's smart, and fucking strong as hell. Keep remembering that."

I can't speak, I can't breathe, I can't even fucking see. If I allowed even the slightest hairline fracture to whittle into my stone wall, I'd snap and lose the last tether of self-control I have, my tiny hold onto sanity. I know I'd wreak so much destruction in this fucking tin can if let myself for a moment slip even an inch.

What Rico had said is true, she is a tough woman, she had to be. She'd been thrown to the wolves, and had come out stronger.

But I am also very well aware of the Russians and how they liked to operate.

I slam down the phone.

Hang on, baby, I'm coming!

Mine

CHAPTER 34

Alexander

Rico is a cop, but before that he was a gang member, and I was right there beside him. He has no military training, hell, my only training is from being on the street. Because of Rico's early history, his skillset sometimes gives him an advantage. If this mission turns out to be what it promises to be, we're about to get thrown into the bloodiest battle of our lives.

The Russian mob deals in arms trading. Big weaponry, they have shit that will blow a hole in the side of a building. I'm sure the worst thing the bad guys had during the raids Rico participated in were machine guns, which is pretty damn bad. A cop on the street holding only a revolver facing off with a jacked-up gangbanger spewing endless rounds of bullets at you will change a man quickly.

He has no idea what he's walking into.

But neither do I.

I'm absolutely sure none of this is on his

mind though as he and Hawk pull into his driveway in Wilmington, North Carolina. The only thing, the one objective he's focused on is getting his brother's woman back, bringing Gemma home to me. Nothing else matters.

"Rico," he answers my call.

"Black, you're on the ground refueling?"

"Any minute now. Any updates?" I ask him.

I feel like a madman inside, caged in, chained, frustrated, hopeless and helpless. I just got off the phone with Stewart and he filled me in as to what point things are at, but I needed to speak with Rico. Our connection is personal.

"I'm getting your things, negro, just pulling up to my house. And I'm picking up my boys from here, Marines. I'll introduce you, so to speak, when they get in the car." He pauses. "Black?"

I clench my teeth. I don't reply, I know that tone of voice. I hear the car door slam and the sounds of birds in the distance.

"How you holding up, Alex?"

"I'm ready to do this," my voice is hoarse and tight.

"I know, very soon."

I fucking love Rico, there's nobody I'd rather have at my side right now.

"Call me back when you get in the car, I don't want to slow you down."

"Five minutes, bro."

I know Rico's with Hawk, Stewart told me. I'm sure the Special Ops man hasn't said a word to him since they left the airport, which is typical for him. Hawk learned a long time ago you can hear much more with your eyes. Stewart also informed me that Rico announced he was picking up two other members, the Marines he mentioned, on their way down to Georgia. Stewart didn't argue with him once Rico gave him their names and he checked them out.

John Wolfe and Brian Daniels. Both are technically retired Marines, although Wolfe still participates in the private sector on occasion. I've been assured each of them are an incredible asset to this mission.

Hawk is professionally a mirror image of Wolfe and Daniels on the Army side. He's Special Ops/Operations, the division known for unconventional warfare and combat skills in unconventional situations. Hawk's primary responsibility while enlisted was hostage rescue and manhunting.

And I fucking hate with every fiber of my being that I need him, but I thank God he's here.

I sit quiet and tense in my seat on the plane as I wait for Rico's call. I refuse to look at my watch. It's only a reminder of how long Gemma's been missing, and how much longer I have until I can get to her. We're landing in fucking Jacksonville Florida, then driving up the coast to the Port of Brunswick on the other side of the Georgia state line. More fucking precious time. A tremendously long minute later, my phone rings.

I'm in fucking hell!

"Yeah," it comes out clipped, reflecting my pent-up anxiety.

"We're heading back to the airport, I got your

things," I have a pretty good idea what he's referring to. "We'll be there in just a few minutes."

I can hear introductions in the background.

"How you doin'? I'm John Wolfe, that's Brian Daniels, Marines."

"Hawk, Special Ops."

"S'up," must be Brian Daniels.

"Not much," Hawk sounds almost civil.

"The rest of the teams' on the plane?" I ask, knowing they took my company jet.

Good.

"Yeah. Alex, John Wolfe and Brian Daniels, each of them Marine's, formally retired, very well decorated," but I already know that, Stewart had them checked out and was very impressed, "John still works in the private sector from time to time. They will be on our team. Stewart's identified us as the Rogue team, which I thought was fitting," Rico laughs dryly. "Hawk's going to fill the guys in, interject at any time, Black. It's good you're here should the guys have any questions."

I let out a silent breath. "Thanks, Rico. Go ahead, Hawk." I stand and begin pacing the aisle of the plane, listening with the phone at my ear. Feeling completely useless.

"It's a rescue mission, but...," Hawk begins.

Brian finishes for him, "It's not that simple."

Hawk replies, "Never is. Woman, Gemma Trudeau, taken in New York fifteen hours ago by the Russian mob, the Bratva."

"Son-of-a-bitch. Human trafficking you think?" John asks.

Hawk answers, "Not that simple. She's

Alexander Black's girlfriend."

"The successful business mogul. Blackmail?" John asks.

"Nope. Her husband stole three million from Black," Hawk replies.

"What the fuck, dude?" Brian comments.

I snort at the reaction. I can tell even with the few minutes of dialogue, these two men are good friends and work well together. The way they play off each other is comfortable and natural.

"It seems, with the information we've just found, the husband was working for someone else, we don't know who yet. It's not confirmed but we believe, as does Black, the husband, Malcolm Stevens, was the flunky in a much bigger global operation with one of its goals being to take Black down. The husband left files of information in her possession, assumedly without her knowledge, when he got arrested for embezzlement. The bad guys want it back, so they took her to find out what she knows. And unofficially, revenge to Black."

Fuck, fuck, FUUUUUUUUUUCK!

"Are we looking at only the Russians as being involved?" Brian questions.

"At this point, we believe they are the only ones holding her, she's on board a Russian ship headed to Georgia before it leaves for its homeland. That's where we're going for the rescue. But we feel strongly Boko Haram is involved somehow as well. One of their own helped coordinate the kidnapping."

My gut twists every time I think of how Natasha got clearance, how she pretended to be Gemma's friend, and how she handed her to them so easily knowing exactly what those goddam pigs would do to her.

"Mr. Black, I'm John Wolfe. I have to ask, who the hell would want to do this?"

I clench my fist. "Everyfuckingbody. From what we've seen in the file retrieved from Gemma's purse, there's information on government officials in China, Russia, South Africa, Iran, along with the Russian billionaire Polchenko, and a South African business man, the father of the spy who worked for me as a receptionist. She's been spying on me and Gemma, and she was the one who set-up the kidnapping. There are hundreds of people apparently involved. But the master mind behind it all, I believe, is Polchenko." I can't hide my rage.

"But why you?" the other man, Brian, asks, trying to put the pieces together.

I let out a long breath. "I have established covert, underground channels throughout the world that rescues children from prostitution rings, mostly girls. Obviously when we get in, we take everyone. We know how much money is made in prostitution and human trafficking. A lot of these girls are used as slaves for bribes. It's the people we've uncovered in the files these slaves are given to, and those transactions that are coerced, that are the biggest threat to me now. And to Gemma. That's what they don't want leaked. Because they knew Gemma was with me, and the information was left in her possession, technically it's in my possession. That's given me immense power over them." I pause. "And has put her in more danger."

"Damn!" Brian whispers.

"Yeah, the information is a clusterfuck pot of gold," Rico mutters.

I can't reply, there's a fucking vice grip around my throat, and around my heart. No one comments for a moment as the two men take in the small background of information they've just been given. My fury is bursting inside of me. I feel it, embrace it, and let it grow.

It's almost time to unleash it.

"Mr. Black," John Wolfe's voice cuts into my thoughts.

"Alex," I correct him. Our lives are about to depend on one another, we're all in this together.

"They took your woman. We're going to get her back. Those scumbags are going to pay," Wolfe's voice is menacing.

My throat closes around a huge knot that prevents my words from escaping.

I steel my emotions with a deep breath. "Call me when you get back on board the plane," then I hit end on the call.

I've got to get out of this plane or I'll start ripping it apart.

We're almost there, keep it fucking together!

I've had two hours of sleep in four days, I can't remember the last time I ate, and I'm sure my clothes look like shit. None of it fucking matters. Nothing matters, only getting to Gemma, holding her close, and letting her know she's safe. That is my sustenance, my fuel, the ONLY thing that matters.

Ten minutes later, Rico calls back. I've had enough time to focus again after stabbing a knife in my heart rehashing all the details of this fucked-up situation. I can't succumb to my pain, Gemma needs me.

"Yeah," I bark out.

"Stewart's going to do a preliminary rundown now. I'll send you the visuals so you can review everything. The leader of each team is going to sit with him when we get airborne so he can give each team their orders. We're going to meet you in Jacksonville and we're all going to ride up together."

My heart is pounding as new waves of adrenaline pulse through my system.

I hear Stewart's raised voice in the back. "Okay, listen up."

There's a sound of shuffling feet as all the voices stop. My heart is pounding, my palms are damp, but my mind is crystal clear.

"Our eyes in the sky tell us that the ship is here, approximately a hundred and fifty miles north of the Port of Brunswick. According to our estimations, we believe that she will be pulling into port approximately when we get there. We've ascertained that she'll be held up, we've guaranteed overnight with legitimate reasons, which will allow us time to get on board and retrieve Ms. Trudeau." A pause. "Yes, (Cornelius) James."

"Do we know how many men are on the ship?"

"The New York harbor recorded twenty men." Another pause. "Alright, this is how we're going to do this: Rogue team, Wolfe, Daniels, and Hawk will board the vessel coming from the water. Williams, you will be positioned in this dock master's tower, which will give you clear access to take anyone out that might be missed. Alpha team, once the deck is secured, you and Bravo team will move in. James, we will determine if explosives need to placed around the entire interior in order to take out the ship once Trudeau is removed, or just specific locations." Stewart doesn't say anything for a long moment. "Does anyone have any questions at this point?"

"Yes, sir, do we have any idea what kind of weapons they might have?"

Stewart's reply is immediate. "We are going to assume they've got everything, from Berretta's to rocket launchers. I'm sure I don't have to say it, but I will. We're taking every single one of these fuckers out, and getting the woman. That is our mission. Quick, quiet, and efficient. They're not going to see us, they're not going to hear us, they won't even have a chance to know we're there before they're dead."

There it was, out on the goddam table, spelled in black and fucking white.

We aren't men, they aren't soldiers. We are the fucking devil, we are death and annihilation, destruction and vengeance, and complete obliteration is our goal.

"They don't want prisoners, if they see us, we are merely a complication to them to be removed. We move first. We are going to leave a very clear message about how much they fucked up. Black?"

I'm envisioning the whole scenario. I've read everything I could on the port we're going to, I've studied the lay-out of Russian ships, I've devoured every bit of information I could find, not only to prepare myself, but to keep from losing my goddam mind.

"Yes, Stewart," I reply.

"You and I will be on the ground waiting for the men to come out with Trudeau. In the meantime,…"

"The fuck I will. I'm going on board. I'm carrying her out," I roar at him, the letters she wrote on my skin burning my flesh.

She's mine!

"Mr. Black, I can't allow that. Not only will you put yourself in danger, but the men will have to worry about protecting you and…"

"Then let's make this understood right now. Don't worry about me, you're only concern is clearing the way to Gemma. I can promise you this, it will be my hand that's going kill the cocksucker who kidnapped her."

"Mr. Black," he interjects.

"Major Stewart, gentlemen," Rico intervenes, "let me inform all of you, I've seen Black kill with his bare hands, with knives, and guns more fucking times than I count. Alex I hate to let out your sordid past, sorry bro. He's more than capable of taking care of himself."

I can almost hear Stewart gritting his teeth. Jacobs has been sitting quietly a few seats over from me. He, and the other men, are part of this meeting and listening as well. Out of the corner of my eye, I see a smirk on his face as he glances in my direction. He's obviously looking at me in a new light.

"Send me the visuals, I want to see what you've got planned. The plane is taxiing for take-off.

I'll see you when I land."

Gemma

I sob silently as I stare through my tears at the dried blood covering my chest and abdomen. I'm surprised I have any left, the wails and pleas shot through me every time they tortured me one way or another. I'm sure my throat is raw, but I can't feel it. I don't even feel the pain from where Demon Man carved the letters into my skin, MINE, over Alex's writing. I can barely make out the open skin through my swollen eyes. As my body shakes uncontrollably, the agony from my broken arm drowns out every other pain in my body, except when I breathe. Then my lung screams at me to stop. It's hard to cry and take short little breaths at the same time. I feel like I'm suffocating.

Demon Man had finally gotten tired of my questions, and silenced me with another backhand to my face. He sneered at me and said we were going to play a game. My heart lurched because I immediately heard the echoes of Alex's voice in my head telling me those exact words, and The Faceless Man. Never again will I feel sensuous tremors ripple through me when those words are spoken, my body and mind are now programmed to associate excruciating torture with those four words.

"Ms. Trudeau, I'm going to ask you a question. Each time I'm not happy with your reply, I'm going to etch a letter into your beautiful flesh. Do you understand?"

Horror exploded inside me. My mouth dried up and wouldn't work, it felt like my tongue was stuck to the roof of my mouth, and if I tried to speak, I'd rip the skin off.

"Sir, I know what you're going to ask me, but the answer's not going to change. With your help, maybe I can recall seeing the item you want, and then we can retrieve it. You can have what you want, then let me go," I'd tried one more desperate attempt to get him to work with me.

His sneer only grew more sadistic as he glared at me.

"What do you know?"

Cold dread seeped through me.

I knew the time had come.

"Nothing," I choked out.

His sneer widened to a sickening grin.

"Get her head," he'd said quietly to Van Boy as he leaned forward, the knife glinting in the light.

I heard Van Boy chuckle behind me as his hands wrapped around my head and held the back of it against his crotch. The pungent smells of body odor and urine wafting off the pig almost made me vomit. I tried to thrash and break free of his death grip on me, but the more I fought, the harder his dick got against the back of my head.

I don't know how long it went on, the slicing of my flesh, the pounding of their fists into my body. I vaguely remember one of them asking if he should cut my nipples off. The reply was, "Not yet, we don't need her to bleed out."

Terror seized me as I screamed for mercy when Van Boy picked up the bat and landed it across my lap.

"Does Black have the information?" Demon

Man asked me coldly.

I could barely understand what he was saying, the agony was too extreme.

"I don't know what you're talking about?" I choked the words out.

Then Van Boy swung the bat and it crashed down on my bound arm. I heard the bones break as a horrific scream exploded from my lungs.

Demon Man leaned in close as I sobbed incoherently.

"Did you give Black the information? Does he know?"

My words were barely audible. "I don't know what you're talking about," I'd repeated.

I would have told them everything if I knew, I would have done anything to make it stop, I was weak. I wanted to have the answers, God, how I wished I did. I cursed Malcolm, I cursed Alex, I fucking cursed God for letting this happen to me. I even thought Alex was never coming, he didn't care, that he never cared, he was safe and warm somewhere. And for a moment I hated him.

The questions stopped but Demon Man sat there glaring at me as Van Boy yanked my head back with a fistful of hair with one hand as his other fist flew to my face again. A fresh burst of blood exploded in my mouth, but I was barely conscious by then.

They'd untied me, my ankles and wrists bloody and raw from fighting against the ropes, and threw me in the corner, then left me half unconscious.

The excruciating pain was piercing through

the merciful fog that had enveloped me and was giving me a moment of unwanted clarity.

Agony.

Pain.

Terror.

Nothing.

This is all I am.

Alex, please know how much I love you...

I'm going to die before he gets here. The thought should torment me, but it doesn't. It calms me.

This is almost over.

I accept the reality with tranquil relief.

I feel guilty for my thoughts; I know he loves me. Knowing it and remembering our moments together give me some comfort in this fucking cell, the place I'm going to die.

I run the fingers that still work through the blood oozing from my broken body and begin to glide them across the floor. When I finish, I smile contentedly, then fold into a heap and let the darkness take me as memories of our last time together gives my solace.

What is dark within me,
Illumine.

Excerpt from Paradise Lost
By John Milton

Mine

CHAPTER 35

Alexander

The sky is black velvet when the teams silently slip into position as the stars mock us with sparkling enthusiasm. Wolfe, Daniels, and Hawk are somewhere beneath the surface of the water approaching the ship, Williams is positioned in the dock masters box hanging over us, rifle aimed and ready to send a bullet right in the middle of those fucker's skulls. Alpha and Bravo team are on opposite ends of the ship; Carlos is with them. Rico and I are crouched behind a forklift waiting for our cue to move, dressed in black pants and black hoodies, just like when I crept into Gemma's house in the dark.

The images of those nights fuel my rage and feeds my beast.

Hunt.

Torture.

Destroy.

It's time.

A savage calm settles over me.

Rico and I have been exactly like this before, when we waited behind the dumpster to take down the douchebags who helped raped me when I was thirteen. Rico was the only one who knew what had happened to me. I never told him, but he knew the instant he found me huddled in that abandoned building right after it happened.

I'd felt the same things then.

I trust Rico with my life. But more importantly, I also trust him with Gemma's life. There is no one I'd rather have beside me right now than him. He knows what I want, what I *need*. We're cut from the same sadistic mold, his is hidden behind a badge, mine beneath thousand dollar suits. But we're the same, he and I.

They think I'm civilized. They think I want power. They think I'm a man.

They're wrong.

I'm an animal. I want blood. I want revenge.

I'm going to kill them all.

I'm in control, all my senses are alert, even my beast is collared, ready to claim victims, waiting to be unleashed to destroy the men who took Gemma. Tonight my monster is going to feast on carnage and revenge, blood and flesh, but it's ultimate prize will be gruesome death.

Every God awful moment of my shitty life, every horrific second was for one purpose only. To prepare me. My life had beaten me and molded me to get me ready for this. My purpose and very existence was for only one thing; to save Gemma and do whatever the fuck was necessary.

"You got it, Black?" Rico asks me quietly, his voice steady.

"Yeah," I whisper.

Rico brought my blade, an exact copy of the one he's got strapped to his leg. These are our weapons, we stole them together as kids and carried them everywhere we went, they saved our lives too many times to count. When he left, I gave him mine and told him I didn't want to touch it until he came back. He kept them all these years, maybe he somehow knew that we'd need them again, together.

My fingers absently stroke the handle. Blades have always been my favorite weapon, the guns are heavy and bulky, but that's not why I like my knife. You've got to be up close and personal to kill someone with a knife, you have to plunge it into your victim, maybe have his warm blood splatter you in the face, or cover your hand when you twist it, or rip it to gut him open. You're close enough to look into his eyes and watch his terror as the life quietly slips from him.

I'm going to slice your fucking throat, then carve your heart out as I watch you die, knowing you can feel everygoddamthing I'm doing to you. Doing it a thousand times won't be enough.

It's been almost thirty-six hours since they took Gemma, and I died more and more with every fucking second.

I'm coming baby, hang on. PLEASE!

Reports kept coming in that things looked normal on board the Russian ship. There didn't appear to be any strange activity, or any unusual merchandise being moved. I knew they meant a dead body, Gemma's beautiful body. It fucking destroyed me each time I heard it.

Rashad and two of Stewarts men are back at headquarters, the location set up in the bottom floor of my home. They're monitoring satellite surveillance here, in New York, and Russia. Also, they're intercepting communications, many contacts taken from Natasha's phone, and the file found in Gemma's purse.

Glancing at my watch, I see it's about time John Wolfe said the three of them would be on board the ship and we should expect the signal. I jab Rico with my elbow and hold my arm up to him.

"Yeah, I know," he comments tightly.

Communications are restricted now, we're only using specifics noises, each one meant for a certain command. We can't risk the possibility of the Russians intercepting any of our radio messages and blowing the whole mission now that we're here.

From what Major Stewart got from his dialogue with Polchenko, the man has no idea what we're up to. The Russian billionaire hasn't given any outright declaration that he's behind this, but neither has he shut-down either. He's given us crumbs thinking he's baiting us, when really it's the other way around. Polchenko thinks he's been dealing with me. That's good. We've got a team on stand-by in Russia ready to take him out if we get the word he's the one behind this.

When we get the word.

I almost want to wait to give the order until I get Gemma out of here so I can go to Russia and kill him myself.

Maybe I will.

This isn't business any more, it couldn't get any more fucking personal.

Deep down in my gut I know Polchenko's in charge. Money is power, and he's got the most of both. No one really knows anything about him, where his money and prestige came from, who works for him, does he have any alliances, and who the fuck has he helped.

Finally, the signal comes through our ear pieces.

Blood surges through my veins and sets me on fire. All my muscles flex and tighten in my body, wanting to push me hard and fast into motion. I reign them in.

I'm coming for you.

Rico turns to me with a tight smile. His eyes are wild as he whispers, "Let's go."

He can't wait to kill those scumbags either.

We slip out from the cover of the forklift and move quickly toward the Russian ship, it's narrow gangplank looming in front of us. It's quiet on the dock in the middle of the night, tonight the air's heavy as each sound is magnified in my head, sharp and distinct. The noise from the metal plank beneath our feet that leads to the ship seems to echo all around.

Let them fucking hear us, Williams will put a slug in their heads. I can't wait to see their fucking corpses spread out at my feet. A bullet is too good for them. They deserve horrific torture.

The ship's deck is quiet, too quiet, when we

step on board. Rico's got his gun drawn one step in front of me, Alpha team came up before us, Bravo team is coming right behind us.

Everyone's been told the man responsible for this is mine. Stewart tried to argue with me, but the knife I put at his throat seemed to stop his argument.

If he'd have tried to stop me, I would have drawn blood.

The only voices I can hear are coming from the other side of the ship, they're Russian and slurred. I know Alpha team was going that way to remove any 'obstacles'. James is with them, strategically placing explosives throughout the boat, we're going to blow this fucker up and get rid of any evidence. As we step further on board, the feet sticking out from the around the corner show evidence that Hawk, Wolfe, and Daniel's Rogue team have been here, along with the puddles of water on the floor. They're headed below. Rico and I are right behind them.

That's where they're holding Gemma.

We know where the steps are that will lead us down. Rico's in front while I make sure no one comes up on us from behind.

The drunk Russian's voice stops mid-sentence. I grin as I step through the door leading below. A grunt followed by feet shuffling float toward us through the corridor.

The smell of blood, sweet blood, is almost hidden by the rank air down here.

As we go down the last set of steps, someone calls out, "Mikhail?!"

"Mikhail's not coming," comes the sadistic

whispered reply.

The sound of machine guns rings out as flashes of sparks ignite down the hallway.

From the map we studied, that is exactly where we're going.

A door opens behind Rico. My fist lands in the man's surprised face as I plunge my knife into his abdomen with my other hand, then pull it up to rip his intestines apart. He's dead before he realized we were there.

Moving quickly, we head to where the gunfire is coming from.

I'm coming Gemma!

Things have quickly escalated to a frenzied massacre, bullets shoot past my head, I tear open body after body in my path. Blood splatters me and coats my hand. I pass the knife to my other hand and rub my soaked palm on my leg to wipe it dry.

I have to feel them dying, *I* need to kill them, need *my* hand to do it, not a gun from a distance, their life has to be wretched from their bodies by my doing. My beast needs vengeance, craves mortal satisfaction, and he's just getting started. He won't be finished until every fucking body is dead, and Gemma is in my arms.

That's the fuck from the street!

A tall man with greased backed hair jumps out of a doorway in front of us, the same scum who shoved Gemma in the van, I recognize him instantly from the street cam. I plow into him and shove my blade into his wrist.

"AAAAAAHHHH!" he screams and drops his gun to pull the knife out.

I twist it and can feel the blade snapping the bones as I punch him in the face with my free hand. Immediately he doubles over trying to free his wrist from the torture. Gripping the useless limb with my empty hand, I extract the blade and pull his arm behind his back with my knife now at his throat.

I squeeze his mutilated wrist and ask, "Where is she?"

His eyes widen when he realizes who I am. Then he begins to laugh.

"Alexander Black, what a pleasure. Your whore was really fucking good," the scum taunts me.

The beast roars inside me, pushing me to gut him fucking open.

He lets out another scream when I twist his wrist. His body goes limp from the pain. Taking advantage of his moment of agony, I let his wrist loose to grip him tightly against me as I plunge my knife into his eyeball. He crumbles to his knees wailing.

I yank him back up by his throat.

"Where is she?" I ask again.

"She's fucking in there," he's screams, holding his good hand to his face as blood pours from beneath it.

My gaze follows the direction of his hand as he points to a door at the end of the hallway. Sliding the blade deeply across his throat, I let him slip from my hand as his gurgles push the blood out of the gaping wound on his neck as the life pours out of his body.

"ENOUUUUUUGH!!" the word bellows through the cramped space.

A lull momentarily falls over the massacre, the acrid smell of gunfire, and the metallic scent of blood.

Polchenko!!

The cocky motherfucker isn't even armed, he thinks he's untouchable.

"Where's Gemma," I step toward him.

Hawk moves out of nowhere to stand in front of me facing the Russian, the dangerous soldier's massive body stretched to its fullest height with his rifle at his side.

Gemma might be behind that door. I could go to her and get her out of here. Or mutilate him first.

The need to destroy this soulless man, kill him and prevent anyone else from becoming his victim is consuming me. The beast is ravenous for his blood. He deserves to die.

"Move," I quietly say, "he's mine."

Hawk steps to the side, his body rigid, primed to kill him instantly.

"Black," Polchenko spreads his arms, palms up. "This wasn't necessary. So much waste, you should have asked to meet." His pathetic attempt at informality enrages me.

Vladimir Polchenko thinks that everyone on the planet is here to serve him, his pompousness and disregard for human life is only surpassed by his greed. His greed built his kingdom, the foundation death and wasted human lives.

"Last time, Polchenko, where is she?" I sneer as I step closer.

"Black," he flicks his wrist as he steps over

the dead body of the man I just killed, his man, his blood still warm on my hand. "Apparently we have business to discuss."

"I warned you, that was your last chance."

I take the final step that separates us and clasp him by his neck, staring in his cold, dead eyes. A flicker of realization flashes across his face in a mass of confusion.

"Black," I hear someone say. "He'll go to prison for the rest of his life. We've got enough on him." It's Rico.

He's doing his job, he's a cop. Bring in the bad guys and let them face justice, the system will make them pay.

I push Polchenko to the side and open the door. Everything inside me is screaming at me to just kill him.

I choose Gemma.

The room wreaks of lingering death and human flesh. My heart stops in my chest as terror consumes me.

NO! I can't be too late!!

My feet feel like cement blocks as I run to the bloodied limp form huddled in the corner. I'm afraid to touch her because I don't want to hurt her any more than they already have. I scan her body to get a quick assessment of her injuries.

Fucking blood all over her! My jaw clenches, biting back a roar. *Smashed arm, the BASTARDS!*

I press two fingers to the side of her neck to check for a pulse. It's faint but it's there.

My eyes spy the words she wrote in her own

blood in this fucking cell, the place she thought she was going to die.

She knew I was coming for her. She never gave up!

Kill them all!

I stand and walk out.

Hawk has Polchenko by the neck talking to Rico when I step back through the door.

"Let him the fuck go," I growl, the sound savage and feral.

Rico turns to look at me. His expression hardens the minute he sees my face. Hawk drops his hand from Polchenko and steps back.

This isn't about justice.

This is about retribution.

This is about vengeance.

This is about fucking revenge!

"She told you she didn't fucking know anything, but you got off on torturing her, didn't you?" I grab his throat and slam him against the wall.

"It was business, Black," the words come out choked.

"Let's talk about business, Polchenko," I snarl in his face.

A look of satisfaction passes over his smug face.

"I knew you'd see reason, Alexander. You're a business man. You and I will do great things together," his confidence makes me sick.

Quickly pulling the knife from the sheath attached to my thigh, I shove it into his cheek and tear it across to his lips, extending his fucking disgusting mouth.

He's thrashing and kicking, trying to get free. I don't feel anything but insane fury.

"Talk, let's hear your fucking business."

I'm mad with rage, consumed with the need for revenge. My beast, the full fury of my monster, is going to extract every fucking drop from him before I grant him sweet death.

My fingers close around Polchenko's throat as blood pours from his now grotesque mouth, his screams an unrecognizable wail.

"I'm not going to cut your fucking eyes out. I want you to watch as I kill you."

Holding his throat, I put the knife just below his hairline, press it down, and cut around the outline of his face, then around his eye sockets, to finally cut open the other side of his mouth, his bloodcurdling screams music to my ears.

His hands are clawing at my arms trying to break free, slick with his own blood. He can't stop me. Nothing can stop me.

"You're not saying anything. What's the matter, cat got your tongue?"

I shove my thumb into his mouth and pull his jaw down.

"Nope."

I wedge the blade between his teeth and through his tongue then into his lower palate.

His dark red life force is pouring from him like a fucking river.

It's not enough.

"This is for Gemma," I whisper in his face as I plunge the dagger into his abdomen.

First I pull it up, just up to his heart. I don't

want to puncture it, dying quick is too good for him. I pull it out and push it back in, dragging it across his torso, then I release him and let him crumble to the ground at my feet.

I drop the knife to the floor.

I'm covered in his blood. It's my gift to Gemma, the blood of her enemies, spilled for her.

I go back and kneel down next to her. I cradle her gently in my arms, her head lolling uselessly side to side.

"Gemma...," it's a choked whisper.

Her face.

I hold back a sob.

Her beautiful face is unrecognizable.

They carved her chest. Her skin is gaping open and raw where I claimed her, Mine.

My God, I'm so sorry, so, so sorry!!!

Suddenly she screams as she tries to get away from me.

"Sssshhh, Gemma, don't scream," I say quietly at her ear, her terror ripping me apart.

Instantly she freezes.

Her good hand that's covered with the dried, crusted blood reaches up to my face and cups my cheek.

"It was you. It's always been you," her words are gritty and her voice is hoarse.

Relief floods me, the sound of her voice, her touch, the feel of Gemma against me sets the world right.

Then a nervous sliver inches up my spine.

She knows.

"I'm glad, I wanted it to be you, Alex."

"It was always me, baby, and always will be."

I stroke her hair and place soft kisses on the top of her head trying to reassure her and comfort her.

"Did you kill them, Alex?" she asks softly, the words forced and breathy.

My body tenses.

Do I tell her the truth? Does she really want to know what I did?

It only takes me a moment to decide.

"Yes, baby, every fucking one of them."

I *need her to know. She has to know there's nothing I wouldn't do for her. Nothing is too much or too forbidden. No price too great.*

Her arm falls to the side again as she dips back into unconsciousness.

Scooping her into my arms, I walk her out of this hellhole.

Finally.

"Ambulance is on its way," Rico informs me as I walk over all the corpses, not looking back.

"Make sure they bring the fucking fire trucks, James' is going to blow this fucking thing once we're all out," I say as I walk to the stairs.

I've got her, now we can send them all to hell.

"Me and Rico are coming up behind you. The rest of the men are doing a last check to make sure no one's left. They'll give me the all clear," Hawk says as I walk past him with Gemma in my arms.

He's savage and untamed, ruthlessness and death.

As I climb the three flights of metal steps to

the deck, my heart calms just a little now that I have her.

I've got her and I'm taking her home.

By the time I get to the deck, Hawk and Rico are right behind me and following me to the dock. The ambulance is waiting. Major Stewart is the only one around.

Good.

The paramedics rush to us with the gurney. I don't let anyone touch her until I place her gently on the thin, plastic mattress.

As they heave the stretcher into the back of the ambulance, the explosions begin to detonate on board that fucking torture chamber.

Too bad they're still not fucking alive.

Mine

CHAPTER 36

Alexander

Ten fucking hours. I've been pacing back and forth in the hospital waiting room for ten hours with no word on Gemma's condition.

"Alex, man, you've got to eat something. What the hell good are you going to be if you collapse when Gemma needs you?" Rico tries to shove a sandwich at me again. Carlos is sitting next to him throwing daggers at me from his eyes.

"Why in God's name hasn't anyone told us anything yet?!" I growl, raking a hand through my wild and dirty hair.

It's early in the morning, we've all been up – I have no idea for how long – but the entire team is here with us. We all look like shit, although fortunately we've changed into clothes that aren't covered in guts and chunks of flesh. The men are quiet and patient, some mumbling occasionally in quiet, tense tones amongst themselves, like Wolfe and Daniels, others a dark and deadly island unto themselves, like Hawk. Their unwavering support has left me humbled.

The mission, as far as the rescue team is concerned, is complete. The only things left to do are tie up the loose ends regarding the syndicate behind the threat to me and my company, and identify links to Gemma, if there are any more. I'll concentrate on that when I get back to New York, whenever that is.

The work for the men here is done.

Polchenko is dead.

I'm eternally grateful to each one of them. There is no way I can repay them all, every single one of them, for what they did for me and Gemma the past two days. This wasn't a job, not to me, and not to these men. It was an innocent woman being dragged into something that she had nothing to do with, and tortured.

My woman.

The woman I love.

But it wasn't just personal for me. It was personal, very personal, for every man here. For whatever their reason was, maybe it has something to do with someone they love, or someone they knew, or something they've been witness to. It doesn't matter. This wasn't just a job or a mission, this was, 'Fuck-with-me-mine-or-my-brothers-you're-going-to-fucking-pay.'

"Because," he answers me patiently for the hundredth time, "they're in there taking care of Gemma. Now shut the fuck up, sit down, and shove this down your throat."

I begrudgingly take the sandwich from him and choke it past my cardboard mouth and down my throat.

He's right.

As I empty the contents of a lukewarm bottle of water attempting to dislodge the dry bread and meat from my throat, I spy Williams slowly approaching me. His expression is tight and his body is tense. I watch as he crosses the room toward me. This is the first time we're going to talk since this all went down.

"Mr. Black," he's standing almost at attention in front of me.

"Williams," I dip my head in acknowledgement.

"I feel completely responsible for what happened to Ms. Trudeau. If I hadn't let her out of my sight...," his voice breaks.

"Williams," I stop him with my hand on his shoulder. "It wasn't your fault, don't blame yourself. It was a matter of circumstances all lining up at exactly the right time perfectly. It's as much my fault."

"How could you say that? You had to be in China, you weren't even there."

His comment makes me grimace, like a hot dagger searing into my skin. I know I wasn't there to take care of her. And I hate myself for it. I should have been there. I didn't have to go on that rescue mission, I could have left that day and let the team there take care of it like they've always done, I would have been home. But I insisted staying and going in there to play John Wayne, and making a fucking vendetta out of it, just like Gemma asked me not to. I should have been with her, I could have been. I wasn't, and I'll spend the rest of my sorry ass life making it up to her.

But the memory of my little warrior sheds a small light of forgiveness on my pain.

"Believe me, yes I was, for several reasons." I shake my head. "That's not the point. No matter if it was me or you watching her, if Gemma wanted to do something, that beautiful stubborn woman would have found a way to do it. No one could have stopped her. Not me or you."

He lowers his gaze and his shoulders hunch slightly. I know no matter what I say, he'll still blame himself. At least he knows I don't, and when he gets a chance to speak with Gemma, which I'm sure he will, she'll reassure him that she doesn't either.

"Williams, listen to me," his eyes meet mine. "You're a damn good soldier, and a good man. I'm lucky to have had you as a part of this. If it wasn't for you and the rest of the team," I turn my gaze and tilt my chin to the room full of men, "Gemma wouldn't be here." It's my turn to choke up.

"Thank you, sir. If you don't mind, I'd like to stay on for as long as is necessary. I'm trained in intelligence surveillance as well as my, um," his eyes flicker to the security guard approaching the vending machine, "my other skills."

I squeeze his shoulder, "We'd appreciate that."

This guy's got a huge cross he's carrying. But we still can use him.

A doctor in light green scrubs walks through the swinging doors as he pulls his face mask below his chin.

"Mr. Black?" He directs the question to the room.

My heart races as I approach him. "Yes, doctor."

It's about fucking time!

He scans the men. The fact that every single one of the occupants are big, dangerous looking men does not escape his scrutinizing glare.

"How is she?" My heart is pounding. I couldn't wait until he came out, but now that he's here in front of me, his expression so grim, I don't know if I can bear the news he's going to give me.

His eyes meet mine, his mouth a tight thin line. His head jerks slightly in the direction of the men.

"Are these men responsible for...," my gut twists, "getting her?"

Gemma was a fucking crime scene, her whole body evidence. His responsibility is to notify the authorities to report any suspicious activities.

This is so far beyond any category of suspicious. It's illegal as fucking hell.

"We all are," I don't flinch.

"I hope you made those son-of-a-bitches pay," he's serious as a damn heart attack.

"The ultimate price," my answer is deathly low.

It wasn't enough.

Carlos and Rico are now by my side, brothers but different, and still the same.

He extends his hand to me, "Good. Major Stewart called me when you were on your way in." The statement helps me relax a little as I take his hand. "We got her stable, but she's still in critical condition. You can go in now. I'm sure I don't have to tell you, don't do anything to upset her, or I'll throw you out myself." His piercing eyes tell me he'd do it.

"Of course," I nod in understanding.

That's the only free pass you'll have with me.

"I don't want her to have too much excitement for the first few days, so we're not going to let any other visitors in until I can assess her once she's coherent."

A knife twists in my heart.

"I'll be in, in a few minutes to talk to you."

"Alright, and thank you doctor," emotion overwhelms me and stops me from speaking. I'll break down if I try, I know I will.

"Go ahead," he clasps my shoulder as he moves past me. "I'm going to talk to your friends." He stops and his expression softens as he gives me a half smile. "You guys did good."

I fucking failed her.

My fists clench as I walk through the doors he came through, and I'm shaking. I steal myself as I walk past the nurse's station as they direct me to Gemma's room. I'm not sure what I'm going to find.

She's alive. She's strong, she'll get well, I try to convince myself.

The door is open and the room is dark except for a lamp glowing on a table across from her bed.

"Oh, God, Gemma," the quiet words are

tortured.

I crumble into a chair at the side of her bed, my head bowed and my hands clenching the side.

Her arm is in a cast and raised in traction, she's got stitches over one eye and on her lip, but her face is a swollen mess of red and purple, her eyes are only slits in the puffy skin. There's white gauze and tape poking out of the neck of her hospital gown.

Flashes of her smiling face as she laid beneath me the last time we were together when we branded each other, MINE.

Fuck, Gemma...

The sick motherfuckers.

I should have peeled the skin off of his fucking skull!

My throat hurts so bad from the vice grip closing it. I swipe at the strange sensation on my face and my hand comes back wet.

I haven't cried since my mother died.

I can't stop it, the overwhelming love I have for this woman, my heartache because of the torture she's been through, my enormous guilt for not being there for her, everything crashes through all my walls and brings me to my knees.

I have no idea how long I sit there quietly sobbing, wanting to hold her, needing to feel her, and swearing I'm never leaving her again.

"Mr. Black?" the doctor is beside me with his hand on my shoulder.

"How is she?" I ask him again. I have to know everything, every horrible, gory, and gruesome detail.

He inhales deeply. "She almost died. If you

hadn't gotten there when you had, she would have bled out from internal ruptures. They tortured her, beat her up pretty bad." He takes another breath. "She's got a couple of broken ribs that almost punctured her lung, her arm was virtually crushed, she needed facial reconstruction surgery, her spleen was ruptured, and the damage to her chest...well, that could have been worse." He's killing me, *this* is killing me, reliving her torment with the play-by-play description. I wince with every word, feeling Gemma's pain. But nothing can compare to what she endured. "But, Mr. Black," he looks to me, "she's one hell of a fighter. And so is the baby."

What the fuck?!

I'm stunned. I blink. Once. Twice.

He cocks his head. "I take it you didn't know."

I shake my head slowly side to side. I'm a fucking mute.

"And I'm assuming then neither did she."

If she'd have known, there's no way she would have put herself in danger.

I shake my head again.

He smiles. "I'm not surprised, she's not even a month along according to our calculations."

A baby...our baby. Holy shit!

A warm, glowing feeling seeps throughout my body.

It's love, incredible, undeniable, overwhelming love!

It's shoved fiercely aside by fear, knocking it on its ass, laughing in its face, sneering. *You think YOU can be a father? You're going to destroy that poor innocent creature just like everything else you poisoned just by existing.*

"Then let me be the first to congratulate you." His grin is broad as he shakes my hand.

"Thank you," I reply automatically.

Ever the master at deception, I hope I'm fooling the perceptive physician who is now examining me with his eyes.

"Now," he crosses his arms over his chest and spreads his legs, his stance confrontational. "Let's discuss what happened."

I'm immediately on guard for his interrogation.

"What do you know? You spoke with Stewart," I ask him coolly.

A muscle flexes in his jaw under my stare. "I know she was kidnapped by Russians. I know those men out there are former military. I know no one else came off that ship except your men."

I dip my head in agreement. "Correct."

I'm not telling him anything.

He continues after a moment's staring stand-off. "This is more than just a kidnapping."

I hesitate before I confirm, reading him to see if he figured that out on his own, or if the information was given to him.

"It is."

He leans in to me, invading my space.

"I don't give a fuck about business, politics, or any of that bullshit. What I do care about is laying in that bed," he points to Gemma. He glares at me, hovering an inch from my face. I don't budge. I've got to give it to him, the man's got balls.

"You know what I think?" he asks, his eyes narrowing at me.

"What?" I reply quietly, tense and rigid.

"I think you don't give a shit about any of that either. I think," he continues, "your whole world is in that bed, and you did whatever you had to do to get her, and would still." He leans back and stands to his full height. He's a fairly big guy, probably played ball in school, and has the attitude, I-don't-care-if-I-piss-you-off. "Take care of them, Mr. Black, the outside world can be a terrible place. But yours," he turns to look at Gemma, "can be everything you want it to be."

Another vice clamps around my throat. I take a deep breath through my nose to steady myself. "Thank you," is all I can say.

He grips my shoulder then walks out, leaving me alone with my family.

My fear gives me another pathetic laugh. I rip its fucking head off.

My family.

My whole reason for existence. Anything and everything.

I take my seat again next to Gemma's sleeping, beautiful, broken body.

"God," I whisper as I lower my forehead to the bed. I don't know if I've ever prayed, but I am now. "I don't fucking deserve it. It's not for me, it's for her, and the baby. Please..."

Gemma

It hurts. Dull throbbing, but it still hurts. Bad.

I pry my lips open, they're stuck together, and so dry I think some skin peels off when I pull them apart.

"Ugh!" I moan.

My mind is fuzzy and my vision is hampered when my eyes flutter open. My head, the entire thing, feels funny.

"Gemma."

Alex.

I turn my head, but a slow throb thuds inside it.

"You're here," I try to smile but my lips feel fluffy. And they hurt too.

Then everything comes back to me like a tidal wave. I jerk my head around, ignoring the jolt of pain from the sudden movement.

Where am I? Did they get him too? Where are they?

"Gemma," he takes my hand gently, the one not strung up. I jerk it back, the involuntary reaction to protect myself kicks in. "Baby," he continues softly, "it's okay, you're in a hospital." I look around the room, a television is hanging on the wall across from me, there's an IV in my arm, I'm on a bed, and I see what was making that annoying beeping I kept hearing in my sleep. And Alex. He's here.

He came.

I look at him, drink him in, and let his nearness soothe me. "Hi," I say, finally relaxing. "How long?"

"Two days. They gave you something to sleep to let your body heal before you woke up."

My heart settles and I relax into the bed.

Finally, I look at him, *really* look at him. He looks exhausted, his beautiful hair is a mess, his eyes are bloodshot, and his scruff is getting really long. But he's in one piece.

"You're okay," I whisper and reach for his hand, I can feel the tightening in my throat warning me that the dam is about to blow.

"Yeah, baby, I'm okay," he gives me a tortured smile. His eyes glisten over.

"Alex, I'm okay," I squeeze his hand as tears slip from my eyes.

"God, Gemma, I got to you as soon as I could, I swear," his words are choked.

"I know, Alex, I always knew you would come," it hurts to talk, my throat is so restricted.

He puts his head down and I hear him sniffle. It wrenches at my heart. I know he's beating himself over what happened to me, blaming himself.

It's not his fault. I know it, my heart knows it. Hopefully he will too, in time.

"Gemma, I have to tell you something," his expression gets serious.

Thoughts start speeding through my head, all things impending doom crash together bringing the worst of the worst with them.

Oh God, I'm going to die, Van Boy and Demon Man got away, and they're coming for me, Alex doesn't want me...what?! What the fuck is it?!

I stare at him wide eyed, as far as I feel as my eyes can go, yelling at him with my stare to spit it out already.

He takes a deep breath. Then smiles, it's so big, so happy, I've never seen him look that happy before.

"We're going to have a baby."

I must be high, they must have given me some strong pain medication that's making me hallucinate.

I shake my head slightly, but the pain rattling around in my skull stops me short.

"What?"

He laughs and stands, bends over the bed, his lips are a breath away from mine.

"Gemma, we, you and me, we're going to have a baby," he whispers.

His lips graze gently over mine, his eyes peer into mine tenderly.

"But...I'm not supposed to...I can't...it's not possible...," I mumble, kissing him back, my words tumbling in between.

"Yes, you are...yes, you can...yes, it is."

"Are you sure?" I pull back, afraid this is all a terrible joke, a horrible mistake, and I'm not really here with him, that I'm dreaming in that damp, dark cell in the ship.

"The doctor told me after he examined you when you were admitted. You're pregnant, pet, with our baby." A cloud passes over his face, covering his happiness. "Gemma, I understand if...,"

I grab him by the back of his neck and pull him back to me.

Now that he's here, I'm never letting him go again.

"Oh, no you don't Alexander Black. Don't you dare get all scared on me. This is so perfect. I'm having your baby! I would almost go through that hell a hundred times for that. I'm not going anywhere, and neither are you. Ever. Again. Got that?"

His hand slips behind my neck and holds me close.

"I got it. But there's one thing wrong," he smiles lasciviously at me.

If it wasn't for his grin, I'd be worried.

"What?" I ask quietly.

"We have to make an honest woman out of you."

My heart jumps.

"Oh?"

"Marry me, Gemma, make me the happiest man in the world. You're giving me a baby, but I want you too, I want you today, tomorrow, forever. I want to spend the rest of my life making you and our family happy."

His eyes search mine. He's afraid I'm going to say no, I can see it.

My heart pounds, my words falter, and fear seeps through me.

"There's one thing, Mr. Black," his nostrils flare.

"Anything, just name it."

I hesitate as I stare into his beautiful blue eyes.

I love this man. But will he still love me, can he still love me? I'm so broken, beyond repair.

The words choke in my throat. I can't answer as fear grips me and binds me in its grip.

I can't.

"We've both been through a lot. I think it's

best we don't rush into anything." He's shocked, I can see it. "We'll talk about it again when I'm better."

I'm paralyzed inside.

I'm damaged.

I'm nothing.

I can't look at him. I can't bear to see the painful honesty in his eyes.

You're right, I shouldn't have asked. It was just for the baby so it wouldn't be a bastard.

He doesn't say it, he doesn't say anything for a long time.

My anxiety rises with every beat of my heart until my mind is screaming and laughing at me, mocking me with contempt.

"Are you sure?" he finally asks as he inches away from me.

My heart breaks more and more the further he gets.

"Yes, Alex," this is one of the hardest things I've ever done. "We shouldn't make any emotional decisions right now," I know I'm too screwed up, I'll probably always will be, I know it. If I see his disgust and pity, I know that would be my complete destruction, it's better to push him away now. "Let's enjoy the news of the baby."

I'm shattered, totally shattered.

He's in his seat now, but he feels like he's as far away as China again. The worst part is, I don't think he's ever coming back to me.

I feel more alone now than I did in that cell.

Mine

EPILOGUE

Fifteen Months Later...
Gemma

Fear is crippling.

It is absolutely possible for one to be bodily whole and mobile, and still be paralyzed.

That was me. I had my arms and my legs, (my arm had healed but would always be damaged), my body was intact, but I was a fucking paraplegic. When fear got its claws into me, I was more than useless, I was annihilated.

Destroyed.

It wasn't fear of *something*. It was fear of life, of happiness, of contentment, and control. I had none of it. The worst part was, I thought I'd never again deserve it. So I didn't want it.

Couldn't want it.

I hated it.

I was broken.

Knowing gave me something to hold on to.

I'd found there was solace and comfort in my misery. It was safe there. Nothing could hurt me there. How could hurt be hurt? I was the posterchild of the perfect Les Miserables, and I wasn't ever going to make myself vulnerable again. I'd found a place where I could just *be.* Nothing was demanded of me. I couldn't let anyone down there.

And no one would let me down.

I'd wanted to go home to my parent's house and burrow myself in my solitude. I didn't have the courage. The last vision I'd had of my childhood home was buried in destruction and more fear. Fear that was too familiar. Fear that Demon Man and Van Boy would come back and finish what they'd started. I knew they were dead, but that didn't matter. That was a fear I couldn't embrace.

I couldn't handle that fear.

I withdrew into my new world. On the outside, I was aloof, distant, and cold. On the inside, I was scared, broken, and worthless. I was nothing. Nothing was safe. Nothing was the end. Nothing had nothing so nothing could be taken.

I was still a prisoner, but of my mind. It was my prison. I couldn't be touched there. When I'd been pulled out of one hell, I ran as fast as I could into another. And I was silently going insane. I'd wanted to die.

I had nothing, I had no one, everyone I'd ever trusted either betrayed me, or had been taken from me. Except Alex. He'd killed for me.

He'd *killed* for me. That fact bombarded me with so much guilt, I knew he must hate me for that. I'd gotten to the point where I couldn't even be in the same room as him.

We'd finally come home. I was quiet, Alex was very considerate, and constantly catering to my needs, making sure I was comfortable and okay.

I felt like a terrible burden. I wanted to run. I wanted to tell him he didn't have to pretend.

I wanted him to love me again.

God, there wasn't anything in the world I needed more. Or anyone. His very presence gave me strength. He was my lifeline. I was too much of a coward to cut it.

It wasn't just me anymore.

I was pregnant.

The reality of it didn't sink in for a long time.

Finally, I'd developed new routines to accommodate for the pregnancy. My fear was so powerful; it overrode everything else. I still possessed common sense, and mechanical practices ran my daily life, I relied on them to get me through every day. Without routine, I would have been up shit's-creek-without-a-paddle, (except it would have been Niagara Falls).

Until the day I had my first ultra-sound.

I was a high-risk pregnancy because of my age, and because of the ordeal I'd been through, so I was ordered to have an early test. Ordeal – as if I'd gotten a bad pedicure.

I shouldn't have gone to that appointment by myself. I was afraid to witness to the rejection I was sure Alex would give me if I'd had asked him to go with me. Williams was there, he was still my watchdog, but there was a barrier between us that was made-up of his guilt, and my new coping mechanism, fear. We didn't joke anymore, we didn't give each other a hard time anymore, he escorted me, and I was just…there.

When the doctor asked me if the father had accompanied me, the first fissure quietly trembled in my newly erected comfort zone of frozen ice.

When I saw the baby for the first time on the screen, and heard his heartbeat, the whole goddam world erupted in a violent earthquake, and I literally collapsed inside.

A cataclysm of emotions exploded inside me, rushing through me like a fucking tornado. I was Dorothy, and sorrow, anger, and rage rushed into my window and beat the living shit out of me. My fear had hauled ass and never came back.

I sat paralyzed on the table in the darkened room as she worked the probe inside me, as I gave her all the proper responses while I battled the storm within.

The door flew open and the doctor and I both jumped.

"Who the hell are you?" the doctor'd demanded.

"I'm so sorry, doctor, he stormed in asking for Ms. Trudeau…," the nurse was babbling behind a very pissed-off Alexander Black.

"I'm the father," he said quietly, staring directly at me. "And the husband."

Anyone who knows Alexander Black knows that was his don't-fuck-with-me-voice, it was calm and deadly.

I've always loved it.

Apparently the doctor'd gotten the gist of his

tone and turned to me, searching for my approval.

He was my salvation; he always had been, right from the beginning. I'd slipped further and further away from him, and that had been my destruction. The mere sight of him in the doorway instantly settled the raging storm of emotions rolling inside me.

...*the husband.*

"What are you doing here?!" I'd quietly said to him.

His voice rose only a little, "I'm here for you, and for the baby. And I'm not leaving." He answered as he stepped in and slammed the door in the nurses face.

He walked around the bed as my wide eyes followed him, and came to stand by my side to watch the monitor with me. The doctor looked from me to him. He reached down and took my hand in his, and squeezed it.

That had been the first time I'd let him touch me in months. I'd thought he hated me. But the look in his eyes when he stared into mine was complete adoration. It gutted me, and tore me open, and all the pain I'd been living with since the kidnapping came flooding out. His touch purged me of my agony as his assurance and strength eased into me. He was, had been, and would always be my salvation.

I started to silently cry.

The doctor immediately became on guard, "Sir...," she began.

"No, it's okay," I stopped her from kicking him out.

"Damn right, it's okay," he leaned down and

brushed his lips against mine. My body exploded with love for him and the baby, so much, I thought I might burst. "I love you, and I'm not going anywhere, no matter how long it takes."

The tears poured down my face as I smiled into his. My first genuine smile in months.

He'd come for me, he'd been waiting for me. He loved me. My king, my warrior, my dark angel. He didn't know, but he was slaying my demons, my fears and anguish, with only his presence.

God, I love him, I love everything about him, his indomitable power, his control, his broodiness, absolutely everything.

Today is Christmas Eve, and our son is almost six months old. He looks just like his father. I insisted on naming him after Alex. I don't know why my husband hesitated, (we'd eloped), maybe it's because of how his life had been before we came into it. He should be proud of it, it made him the amazing man he is.

That day at the doctor's office was my first step back to life. Alex came for me - twice - saved me, and in return, I've given him a family, and all the love that incredible man deserves.

I wanted to give him more. But what do you give a man who has enough money to buy a small country?

The only thing I could.

Me.

It's been a long road back, it hasn't been easy, there are still detours and roadblocks, but we always get around them.

One big thing that has helped me in my

journey to heal was receiving the files on all the girls that had been kidnapped and rescued, containing all their progress. It had been a major inspiration to me. It was heartbreaking at first, to read about them, and hear Alex tell me the story about that night of the rescue, and his little warrior, we call her Karma. But their triumphs overrode any and all sadness. They're all incredible survivors.

He's built a school and a compound for any of the girls who wish to live there. There are guards, and teachers, and a garden. The government has been forced to acknowledge the problem publicly, which has helped in keeping the community safe.

Karma has come to spend Christmas with us. When Alex told me about her, I immediately fell in love with her too. Little Alex has her wrapped around his tiny finger. We're working on having her live with us permanently. Hilda is totally over the moon with children in the house. Even Carlos and Jesús are cooing and playing. Rico will be here tomorrow; he's been working on a big case, but promised he'd come. Williams is a permanent fixture in our lives, and the illusive Hawk is making an appearance tomorrow as well.

The whole family is going to be together.

Tonight Gina and her family came for dinner. We talked about how Tony found the piece of information that had led to my rescue. She is my family, always had been, and always would be.

I've NEVER seen Alex so happy. I've never been so happy.

This is all I need, my family happy, together, and healthy.

Alex is the ultimate father and husband, he is protective, considerate, would do anything for us regardless of any danger to him, or what it cost, he has built an impenetrable fortress for his family. We are, without a doubt, his entire world.

Tonight is just the decadent icing on the cake…for me and Alex.

Finally. Again.

The entire Ramirez family is with Little Alex and Karma now, the kids won't even notice Alex and I aren't around.

I approach Alex as he gets out of the shower, holding a present for him. I'm wearing a black velvet sleeveless gown with a high neck, bare shoulders, and my new favorite, I'm-ready-for-you-to-fuck-me heels. He's in nothing but water droplets.

He is the sexiest man alive. Sin and desire, fulfillment and rapture, danger and promises, and he's mine!

Power, strength, control, sex enveloped in soft golden skin. Muscles ripple beneath the surface, the contours, dips, and crevices all demand my tongue to explore every hidden inch of him. He radiates sensuality and command – still – as easily as he breathes.

When he sees me, he smiles. It seduces me instantly.

"You. In that dress. Is all the present I need. Come here, Mrs. Black, let me touch you." That tone, the one that says want. The one that says need. The one that says I-want-to-devour-you-consume-you-fuck-you-until-you-scream-my-name.

My whole body vibrates with lust.

I walk slowly to him and shake my head twice. I notice his deliciously large shaft is already swelling.

"Present first, Mr. Black."

He cocks an eyebrow at me. "Now that you're Vice President of Black Inc. does not make you the boss, Mrs. Black."

"Tsk, tsk, tsk, you seem to forget that all things must have a majority vote, otherwise it's a stalemate. It would serve you well to take my suggestion," I purr at him.

He smirks wickedly. "That's what I get for marrying a lawyer."

I hold out the present and keep myself an arm's length away. If I don't, he'll grab me and then I'll give in to him, I can't resist. He takes it and begins to untie the ribbon, then slowly he opens the paper.

It's not large, about the size of a shirt box, and even before he opens it, his expression says it's the best present he's ever gotten.

I don't have much time.

I turn to leave.

"Wait. Aren't you going to wait for me to open it?"

A slow, seductive smile curves my lips. Lust flares in his ice blue eyes and stokes my already simmering fire. I turn my head side-to-side again, once.

"What are you up to, Mrs. Black?" he grins at me and slants his eyes, studying me.

I bring my finger to my lips and whisper, "Ssshhhh," then leave the room.

I walk quickly out of the master bath, trying to get to where I want to be before….

The lights go out.

My heart pounds faster.

My temperature rises.

My steps falter, then quicken.

I have to hurry.

The only sound I hear is my now heavy breathing and the clicks of my heels over the polished wood floors.

We've never discussed the fact that Alex was/is The Faceless Man. We both hid him from the other, we each have our own reasons for that. After everything that we've been through, and survived, together, there can be nothing left unexplored between us.

Tonight, I want him to know that I love – need – want - every single facet of him.

Dammit! Which door is it?

I'm stumbling around in the dark, feeling my way along the walls. I counted the doors earlier to make sure I would be able to find the one I want when the lights went out. Being in a hurry, the dark, and mostly Alex naked and wet, has left me disoriented.

My hand dips in at a doorframe. I slide it along the smooth surface until I hit the doorknob and turn it. When I push the door open, I breathe a small sigh of relief. This is it.

The dungeon.

There's a single candle burning on the far end of the room on the bureau.

We haven't been in here since the night Alex

left for China.

When we'd gotten home after the kidnapping, I was a fucking basket case, a total nut job. The road back was long, then I was huge with our baby, and finally, Little Alex came into the world.

This, what we are here, hasn't been discussed either.

I was afraid Alex thought I wouldn't want to come back. I wasn't sure I'd be able to either. But the more I thought about it, the stronger my desire became.

I'm breathing heavily now as I stand in the center of our haven of dark intimacy, the place where we are raw and primal, savage and abandoned, the place we became one.

A hand covers my mouth firmly as another grips me tightly and presses me against a hard body. Shock ignites every single one of my nerve endings.

I scream into the large palm on mouth.

"Sssshhh, don't scream," his voice whispers roughly at my ear, his warm breath caressing my skin.

Heat floods me as fear instinctually threads up my spine. My body is tense in his grasp. I can feel my nipples harden beneath the fabric of my dress, and my loins pulse with emptiness.

"The things I'm going to do to you, pet," his mouth is at my throat, his tongue stroking me between words.

I automatically thrash in his arms.

His palm splays out against my abdomen, and pulls me tightly to him. Jolts of electricity spread from his touch throughout my entire body.

"You're mine, Gemma. Do you want to run?" His words are quiet on my skin, each one stroking me.

He's giving me this opportunity to see if I've changed my mind.

I shake my head silently as my heart pounds harder beneath my chest.

"I'll never let you go, pet. Never." The declaration is a dark promise of possession as his lips, mouth, tongue, and teeth brand the flesh over my bare shoulder.

Erotic tremors pulse through me. I'm his, he owns me, completely. He feels my body tremble against his, I know because I feel his deep inhale at my back.

"Pull up your dress, Gemma, I want to feel how wet your cunt is," he commands me roughly.

He is so deliciously filthy.

Arousal seeps from inside me and escapes between my legs. His hard-on is pressed firmly against my ass. I have no underwear on, the thought of his shaft slipping between my legs against my bare mound makes me quiver with anticipation.

I slowly inch my dress up my legs until its gathered around my waist. My chest is rising and falling quickly with my heavy breathing.

"If I take my hand away, do you promise not to scream?" he whispers.

I nod my head twice, my breath hot on his hand.

"Good girl," he drags his tongue up my cheek with the term of endearment. The words still send butterflies flying in my stomach just like the first time as The Faceless Man.

He slides his hand down my body, over my breast, the touch on my hungry nipples sends shockwaves straight to my core. I'm sure I'm very wet, and if I wasn't already, I am now. He inches further down until his palm cups my sex tightly.

"Do you have any idea how much I love your pussy, Gemma?" he bites the tendon at my neck lightly.

"No," I pant out, as my head dips back against his chest.

"She's heaven, pet, so hot, so wet, so sweet. I can't wait to bury my cock in her. But first, *I* have a present for *her*," his finger presses down on my clit. Jolts shoot through me as I thrust my hips into Alex's touch.

"Alex…," I moan deeply.

"I know, baby, I need you so bad, it fucking hurts," he grits out between clenched teeth. He captures my mouth in a desperate kiss. His hunger and desire sear into me with his tongue as it clashes with mine. He lifts the dress from my body, only breaking the kiss to pull it over my head. "Take the heels off, pet, I'm not going to be gentle with you." My blood thunders through my veins as I kick off my shoes. "Now, I'm going to bend you over the horse, slip a clamp on that greedy clit, suck all that sweet juice from your dripping cunt, then I'm going to slide the plug in your tight ass. Then I'm going to fuck you, pet. Hard. Deep. And probably very fucking rough."

With the plug I gave him in the present, along

with my note telling him the presence of The Faceless Man was requested in the dungeon.

"Oh God…," it's a long deep moan as the hot drug of desire burns through me like scorching lava.

I had to let him know how much I love everything about him, every single part of him. The powerful business man, the thoughtful husband and caring father, the dangerous man who'd killed for me, and the man who'd seduced me in the dark, the man who'd begun my journey back to the living.

He guides me toward the horse with fingers of his one hand clasping my nipple, and two from his other gripping my clit, still holding me tightly.

At the tall bench, he lifts his body from mine, my body aches from the emptiness, then places a palm between my shoulders blades. "Bend over, pet, give me that ass."

I'm trembling, panting, and holding back moans, as I lower myself, my legs spread, open and ready for him.

I have missed this soooo much…

Alexander

Mine!

Possession. Desire. Need. Lust. Ravenous hunger. This is what I am. This is what Gemma makes me.

All this is what's going to take her.

I thought I was losing her. There was no fucking way I was going to let her go without the most important fight of my life. I would drag her back to life, kicking and screaming if I had to, but I wasn't losing her.

I knew if I had, she'd never come back.

She amazes me. Her strength and perseverance are my constant motivation.

She is the one who saved me that first day she walked into my office. Everything about her stood up to me and got in my face, daring me. 'Fuck you, give me all you've got!'

She owned me the moment she stepped off that elevator.

Her trust humbles me, her love strengthens me, her strength feeds my own.

Tonight she's trusting me to give her what she needs, what she yearns for. She's trusting me and telling me she's ready.

My body is strung tight, my dick is so hard, and my heart fucking hurts, I love her so much.

I'm going to ravish the fuck out of her.

Gemma

"I have two more presents for you, Alex," I whisper to him.

Sated, spent, and thoroughly well fucked, we lay in our bed.

His eyes search mine. They're full of love and devotion. How I ever thought he didn't love me, didn't want me, is completely unimaginable to me now.

"You, the baby, that's all I want, Gemma. You've given me everything I thought I could never have."

Perfect. He's so damn perfect.

"Alex, you brought me back to life when I was dead. You gave me everything: a home, a family, a reason to live." Tears are pooling in my eyes with the magnitude of everything I feel for him, of all that he is to me.

He is the blood that flows in my veins, and the very air that I breathe.

"Turn the light on, Alex. I want to show you your first present," I smile cheekily at him.

He looks at me with a question in his eyes before he reaches to the bedside table to switch on the lamp. When he turns back toward me, he freezes. His eyes are riveted to my chest.

Whenever I'd caught Alex stealing a glimpse at the scars on my flesh where the word MINE had been carved into it, where he'd written it, my heart broke with the intense pain I saw in his eyes. He never told me he blamed himself, but I knew he did.

I am his. And I want to remind him every chance I can.

Every time he looked at the raised, pink word on my skin, and cringed, Demon Man/Polchenko was still wining.

I'd be damned if I'd let that son-of-a-bitch have any control, even the smallest, over any part of our lives.

I'd gotten the word tattooed over the scars. They'd done a beautiful job of creating a masterpiece in Old English script using detail and flourishes. A worthy homage to that incredible experience Alex and I had shared that day. We'd stripped each other bare, ripped away any masks, and tore down any boundaries between us, like savages, like animals, like two people who *needed* to claim and possess the other.

That experience, the moment we became one, when our souls had merged and exploded together, that is what we need to always embrace. That is what got us through hell, and brought us home. That is what would always make us stronger.

Love.

"Gemma...," his voice is low as he raises a hand to trace the word across my heart he'd claimed me with almost a year and a half ago.

"I'm yours, Alex. No one, or nothing, could ever take that away from us." Cradling his face in my hands, I pull him to me.

"Always, Gemma. You are my life, my reason for living. You and our baby."

My eyes are blurry with unshed tears of joy as I stare into his.

I hold up two fingers. "Babies, Alex, I'm pregnant. Merry Christmas."

"Fuck, Gemma, I love you so much, a baby...," he growls. His lips claim mine as his arms envelope me and hold me tightly. "Thank you," he murmurs, his voice heavy with emotion.

"Don't think I've forgotten what I left you with those nights," his lips move against mine.

That flash of heat you get when you look up to the car in front you and realize it's suddenly stopped short and you're this close to kissing its ass? That all of a sudden 'Oh-Shit!'?

Yeah, that's me, that burst of electric jolts and heat that instantly brings a sheen of sweat over your body.

A slow smile spreads across his face. He turns back to his bedside table and opens the drawer.

He comes back with a black marker.

"Arms up, pet, and don't move." Gritty and low, every syllable like a nail scraping softly down my skin, making me tremble.

I lift my arms over my head as he pulls the covers from our bodies. The air licks my goosebumps, shooting a fresh burst of life into them.

Quietly focused, he uses my body as a canvas. Handprints clutching my breasts, then he catches the hardened nipples between his teeth and teases them with his tongue. I thrust myself into his mouth. His large hands outlined, holding my thighs open. He lowers his head and dips his tongue into me, then drags it up my folds, flicking my clit when he lifts from me. My hips buck up, desperate for more. Words drawn across my abdomen – Need – Want – Desire – Hunger – Love. Felt tip, lips, fingertips, teeth, tongue all take turns covering every inch of my flesh. I'm visibly panting when he finally returns the cap, and the click echoes in my ears.

Nothing else exists, except him, slipping into me, taking me again.

He is dark, he is dangerous, he is formidable, and compelling. He is goodness, and kindness, my sanctuary and deliverance.

He has an empire to rule, enemies to destroy. Threats surround him like air. But I am his queen, and he is my king. This is our kingdom, right here, right now, and every brush of his lips over mine, each glide of fingertip across my flesh, every word he whispers is a vow.

And the Black ink.
This. Is. Home.

The End

Keep going, there's more…

If you enjoyed BLACK INK, please take a moment to leave a review. Indie authors rely solely on your recommendations and reviews. A word or two is perfect ☺ Without your reviews we get lost in and buried. Without them, we can't survive. So, please click the link >>> http://amzn.to/2fZlH3O

A NOTE FROM ME

I hope you enjoyed BLACK INK as much as I LOVED writing it. To be honest, when the initial story began to come to life, it was originally intended to be written as a novella. Short, hot, sweet, heart pounding, but...it didn't work out that way. There were too many hidden secrets, innuendos, unspoken promises, well, you know, you've read the first part, (and all the rest, lol.) There might be more in the future, at this point, I'm not sure, but we'll see if Alexander and Gemma have to let us know about anything else happening ;).

When I wrote KINK, (and I've just reread it), I cried, choked up, my heart hurt, you name it, I felt it. It was about survival.

BLACK INK is also a story of survival, of conquest, of abandon, of letting go of all that holds you prisoner, and finally freedom.

It's a long road for so many. It's scary and painful, but SO worth it. Sometimes filled with depression, anger, and confusion. The battles each of us face are lonely, and sometimes overwhelming. But in the end, even if the victories are the small ones along the way, celebrate the hell out of them.

Love yourself first. I guarantee that love will touch everyone around you.

And if you did enjoy this story, PLEASE leave a review. Indie authors rely heavily on them, without them, we get lost in the great cyber abyss.

Those reviews, and when you tell your friends about us, are what bring us to life in the world.

I can't tell you how much I appreciate your taking the journeys with me through the worlds in my stories. My greatest wish is that I can bring some of the love I have for my characters to you in the pages.

Because, really, that's what makes the world a sacred place. Love.

With my love,

~ N.M. <3 xoxo

p.s. My plan is to finish Rico's story, HIDING, (wasn't he great in this one! I flippin' love him <3). This is also what's possibly in the works:

- HAWK (;))
- BOY TOY
- a paranormal/supernatural story that's been talking to me for a while, (yeah, I know, schizophrenia, lol). ...and a few other things I can't leak out yet.

...keep going...

ABOUT THE AUTHOR

N.M. Catalano is an Amazon best-selling, multi-published author. She spent many years in the corporate world, and owned several businesses. Having been fortunate to have such varied exposures, she had many opportunities to be exposed to different societies and cultures. After years of studying people and lifestyles, her fascination comes to life in the pages of her stories.

"I am just a woman, like many of you, who has lived through beauty and ugliness, happiness, (sometimes extreme), and sadness, (sometimes heart wrenching), and have grown to love life and myself even more. I write because I love the characters, I am madly and hopelessly in love with them and want to share them with the world. Life is beautiful and is meant to be enjoyed day by day, sometimes you have to pick out the good stuff with a magnifying glass like a needle in a haystack, but enjoyed none the less. The stories that I put on paper, I think, help us to find that enjoyment a little bit more.

I am just a woman who is in love with love............<3"

Connect with her at:

Blog: https://nmcatalanoauthor.wordpress.com/

Facebook:
https://www.facebook.com/nmcatalanowriter

Twitter: @nmcatalanowriter

Pinterest:
https://www.pinterest.com/catalanoauthor/

Newsletter, (to receive notices of giveaways, and chapters of upcoming releases nowhere else available): http://eepurl.com/bpEW9X

OTHER WORKS

<u>One Night With A Stranger</u>

I thought I was fine. My scars were healing, my dirty little secret was safely buried, and I was living an almost normal life. Then a stranger came along and blew the doors off the prison I had built around myself. After one night of erotic abandon, all I wanted to do was give myself to Marco in any way he wanted me, over and over again. I surrendered to him and it was more than I could have hoped for.

I should have known my past would rear its ugly head and annihilate my chance for happiness once again. I couldn't let my problems destroy the man I was coming to love more than life itself. The only way to save him was to give him up.

<u>Made To Switch</u>

Betrayal. Just like that everything I had built, my entire life, was falling apart. My world threatened to collapse beneath me, and it looked as if there wasn't a damn thing I could do to stop it. But the worst part was I was going to lose Elizabeth. She loved being dominated, and she was beautiful in her submission, passionate under my control. But she found my secrets. My past fell open at her feet. I'd do whatever it took to keep her, even give up control.

Kink

She's a damaged girl, hiding behind a tough façade and a razor sharp tongue, afraid to open up to him and trust him. Her wounds are deep, the scars are many, some are visible, and others cannot be seen.

He thinks he doesn't deserve her, that he doesn't deserve to be happy. The demons he fights are loud and strong, some are real, while others are not. But he wants her. And he'll have her.

He'll share her. They'll plunge her into the most erotic oblivion she's ever experienced.

**Warning, this book contains very strong sexual content, BDSM, menage, and a scene or two which could be a trigger containing sexual assault/rape. 18+

Perfect

Brian Daniels has life by the balls. He's gorgeous, so much so, it hurts so good to look at him. And his dominant sexual skills leave the women he's with in a state of complete erotic delirium for days, knowing exactly how to bring her the most pleasure. The dark and dangerous beast inside him, the one that was born in the Marines, is released in the cage when he fights, and in the bedroom when the women are tied and begging for more. He is absolutely perfect. But he's miserable, empty, and hollow, wondering if this is all there is to life.

Everything about Brooke stops traffic. Her perfect body and face have men following behind her like a trail of whimpering little puppy dogs. And she hates everything about herself, because it destroyed her. She lives with its curse every day, one that will never allow a man to get close to her heart. She's a brilliant Marine Biologist fighting against the clock amid brutal shark attacks, trying to find a way to stop the animal before it strikes again. But she's defenseless against the monster inside her.

When Brian and Brooke collide, it's an erotic war zone, one that Brian will not lose.

Can he save her from her demons? Can she finally submit and let Brian free her from her hell? Or will tragedy strike first and rip Brian from her, destroying any chance they have at love?

The Rooster Club, The Best Cocks In Town

We all have that first true love, the one we never forget, the one that makes our heart hurt, even today.

This is their story. It spans decades.

This is his story….

All wrapped up in the decadence of the '80's:

Sex (lots of it).

Drugs (almost as much).

Discos (where it all happened).

How it all crashed in the 90's.

And today, how it found her once again…

<u>Black Ink, Part I</u>, <u>Black Ink, Part II</u>, <u>Black Ink Part III</u>

The BLACK INK Trilogy
In Part I we met the man,
Alexander Black
Ruthless. Powerful. A prick.
Intoxicating, intriguing.
He took, he claimed, he possessed.
In Part II,
He owned.
I a world of seduction,
Danger,
Darkness.
In Part III,
The beast is unleashed.
In a deadly race against time,
The only thing he wants is
Blood,
Revenge,
Annihilation.

Coming Soon, <u>Hiding, Book 5 in the Stranger/Evolution Series (Rico's Story)</u>
….a sneak peek…

Maria Santos was rushing down the stairs to the DeKalb Avenue subway station in Brooklyn, NY, when her phone rang. Her mind was such a mess that she almost didn't hear it. Her body was wracked with grief, and her heart was being torn from her chest. She'd received a call earlier in the morning from her boyfriend's, Raphael "Rafi", mother. He had been shot and killed, the latest victim in the gang wars in her Spanish Harlem neighborhood.

Maria is blinded by fury and heartache, nothing will stop her. She had just left her friend's apartment she knew from school whose brother is a cop. She'd told him everything she knew about the drug wars in her neighborhood, and she demanded that he record her. She wanted those filthy scumbags to fry for what they'd done to Rafi, she would make sure of it.

"Mami, what is it?" Maria said tightly into her cellphone.

"Mi hija, DON'T COME HOME!" Her mother yelled.

Panic began to rise in Maria.

"What happened?" Maria asked worriedly as she gripped the metal handrail.

"Julio was just here with three other boys," her mother began, her voice trembling.

Fucking Gangbangers, not boys!

"And they had a gun, baby." Her mother's voice cracked.

"Mami, it's okay," Maria tried to soothe her.

"NO, IT'S NOT OKAY, THEY ARE LOOKING FOR YOU!!" She screamed.

OH GOD, MY FAMILY, WHAT HAVE I DONE?!

"Go to Port Authority, there will be a ticket waiting for you. You're going to North Carolina with your aunt and grandmother," her mother said hurriedly.

"No, Mama, I can't…" She tried to argue.

"You are going! A bus leaves in an hour. And Maria?" Her mother choked.

"Yes, Mama?" Maria started to sob.

"I love you, but don't use your phone again. Your aunt will take care of you. I'll talk to you when you get there."

"Ok," she sighed heavily.

"Bye, baby." Her mothered cried softly.

"Bye, Mama, and I am so sorry…"

The line went dead.

Maria swiped her subway pass for the last time. She was leaving her life, her family, everything she had ever known, but the greatest pain was that she wouldn't get to kiss her mother goodbye, and give her last respects to the only man she had ever loved.

She was going to a hick town in God only knows where.

With no clothes, no memories of the life she's leaving, to live with people she doesn't even know.

How did life get so fucked-up so fast?

Made in the USA
Lexington, KY
17 September 2018